Partition Majik

The Xun Ove Series: Book 2
Step Across The Barrier

James William Peercy

www.3FatesPress.com

PARTITION MAJIK
Copyright © 2014 James William Peercy

Published by 3 Fates Press, LLC, 2025 Bell Rd. Morgantown, IN 46160

ISBN 978-1-940938-27-1

ACKNOWLEDGMENTS

I wish to express sincere appreciation to family and friends. In particular: Claudette Peercy for putting up with me when I've said, "Come look at this..."; Clifford and Dianne Peercy who never set limitations on what I could become; Brian Miller and Darrell Miller with whom I used to swap stories and dreams as we rode to school on the bus; Elizabeth Mendoza whose excellence in photography is equal to her personality and friendship; Arash Mahboubi for reading and commenting (to the point of asking, 'When is the next one?'); Lana Bernardin for her enthusiasm in utilizing her promotional skills; and Jose Jimenez whose graphics were used in the artwork of the cover. Thanks to Amanda Rotach Huntley and the team at 3 Fates Press for all the hard work.

To all of you, highest commendations.

PROLOGUE

"Are you listening?" Väinämö reached forward with his crooked staff and smacked the arm of the chair.

Jonna jumped; there was a book with strange symbols staring at him. "Where am I?"

"Mage School, where else?" The mage scowled. "If you don't learn, how do you expect to do the magic?"

"The way I always have?"

"Come now, man, you can't rely on luck forever!"

He was right, but at this moment Jonna was thinking of other things, and his instant family was one of them. Then there was Stephanie becoming Elfleda, Elpis coming to live with them, Freya his new mother-in-law...

"Jonna McCambel!" Väinämö slapped the arm again.

Jonna jumped.

"This is useless," Väinämö shook his head. "You have to spend time—" He looked at his new wrist watch and held it up. "Built one like yours. Not a bad job if I say so myself, and smaller than my first try," he smiled amused but then sighed. "Oh well," the mage glanced toward Jonna, "when you find the time, call me. You know where I'll be." The teacher vanished.

1

Chapter 1

QUESTIONS WITHOUT ANSWERS

Elpis looked up with those big, round eyes twinkling in the sunlight. "Jonna, can I call you daddy?"

He knew it was coming; he and Elfleda had talked. Jonna had sensed the unspoken question since the first part of the week, ever since the duel with the giant. At that time, Elpis had come running up, thrown her arms around him, and his heart melted.

Stephanie, his wife, er, a.k.a. the Elf Princess Elfleda, had smiled warmly and not without amusement. Her only comment being, "Whom do we have here?"

Maybe it wasn't the best time to break the news, but Elfleda took it in stride, sincerely welcoming Elpis.

And why not? From the beginning of their vacation, their family had grown exponentially. Instead of Jonna and Stephanie, it was now: Jonna, Stephanie, er, Elfleda (his mind was still having a hard time with that), Sir Verity, Dorothy, Bob, Elpis, their personal servants, and their personal guards. Freya, the queen of the woodland elves, had graciously granted them private living quarters. It was a short walk across the suspended tree paths to the main citadel but far enough away to keep out intrusions—well, at least it was a good idea.

"Good morning!" Bob the pixie appeared and took his

usual stance on Jonna's shoulder. He changed and switched to Elpis. She giggled.

"Good morning," she echoed, but her eyes were still on Jonna.

Jonna smiled, "Of course," and bang, he was a dad—not that he had any idea how to be a dad. What does a dad do? For some strange reason, he was beginning to panic.

"Okay you two," the pixie leaned against Elpis' hair, "what's on the agenda today?"

"We're going for a walk," Jonna announced. This whole dad thing required a private talk with Elpis. "Alone."

"Good by me," Bob waved at the guards by the door. "Shoo, shoo!"

"That means you too, Bob."

Bob's face fell. "Me too? You can't do that!"

"I can. I have. We'll talk to you later." Jonna waved a hand in Bob's direction.

A mischievous look crossed the pixie's face. "Fine." He vanished, but his voice left in a final note, "I'll be back."

"I have no doubt," Jonna smiled down at Elpis. "Now, where do you want to walk?"

"How 'bout," she thought real hard, "the stream!"

"The stream it is," Jonna agreed, reaching up and taking hold of the amulet with his left hand. "Take my other hand and hold on."

As her tiny fingers reached up to grasp his, a shiver went through him. This small girl, who he barely knew, trusted him with her whole heart—trusted him so much that she held on to his every word. The panic grabbed him again; what parents must feel for their children! Jonna paused, the words sinking in; he had become a parent.

Feeling the amulet in his grasp, he thought of the stream and watched the room fade from view. Although Väinämö had told him he needed to learn the elvish traveling spell and not rely on the amulet, he couldn't seem to make the time.

After all, it had only been a week since he had defeated the giant in the tournament. Upon defeating the giant, he discovered he was now the protector of the queen's realm. The formal ceremony for this was to be next week. It was a job not to be taken lightly, but since he wasn't officially sworn in yet, surely they could give him a few days off.

"We're here!" Elpis let go of his hand and moved toward the stream. Tilting her head, she listened to what it said. At the same time, Jonna found a log and sat down to watch.

"Elpis, you do know what happens if I am your dad?"

Elpis looked up and grinned. "We get to do things together?"

"Well—" He spotted that mischievous look in her eyes. "You know what I'm talking about. That means Elfleda is your mom. Are you okay with that?"

She looked up at the sky and then at Jonna. "Mom approves."

Jonna laughed. "I'm glad. Tell her thank you."

"She says you're welcome." Elpis smiled and stared bright-eyed at the water.

Okay, that type of reaction might be fine for some, but it gave Jonna the willies. He had heard that some kids had imaginary friends, but knowing that Elpis had The Sight- the ability to know things others didn't- could he be sure it was imaginary? Maybe it was time to pay Väinämö a visit.

Elpis teased the stream's edge and tiny, white fingers started to creep toward her feet. The last time those fingers had grabbed hold of Jonna he had almost drowned, along with the leprechaun O'Connor McBear.

"No you don't," Jonna stared at the fingers. They immediately withdrew.

Elpis frowned. "Aw, they want to play."

"I know how they play," Jonna moved closer and picked her up, "and they get carried away."

She giggled, hugging his neck. "You mean, they carried you away."

"That too." A shiver hit his spine. From the corner of his eye, he spotted a mist moving in the shadows of the forest, but when he turned his head, it was gone.

"Well, I ssssee you havvvve a daughter now." The edge of the forest stirred almost where the mist had been, and a snake slipped out of the foliage. It had the same markings as the first that Jonna had seen along this stream.

"Hello snake. It is snake?"

"Call me Colubrid," the snake answered amiably. "I ssssee you found the gem." Colubrid slithered back and forth then formed a coil near the base of a tree.

"That I did." Jonna smiled and then frowned. He had first met Colubrid on his way to find the gem; it was now in the amulet around his neck. He suspected Colubrid might be more than a snake; he might be a cursed mage, but there was no proof of that.

Was Elpis shivering? "Are you okay?" He looked into her face; she was terrified. "It's okay. Colubrid tried to help me last time." The words did not calm her down, and he felt the tension grow.

"Yessss," the snake uncoiled. His tongue came out, testing the air. "It isssss okay. I won't bite you."

Colubrid moved further away, still within talking distance, and found a spot closer to the water. As his gaze eyed a small puddle, a tiny frog jumped. Colubrid caught it in the air and swallowed; it formed a lump in his throat and began its slow journey down. "You sssssee, I only eat small thingsssss."

"Daddy," Elpis had that faraway look which he knew to be The Sight, "mom says we need to go home."

"Colubrid really bothers you, doesn't he?" Jonna's brow wrinkled. He looked toward Colubrid. "I think we need go."

"Havvvve it your way," the snake smiled, "if you can." Was Colubrid laughing?

"Daddy!" Elpis voice reached a high note, deafening one of his ears.

Jonna turned and saw a greenish-yellow glow dropping in from above his head; he shifted so it struck the ground. It grew two arms and legs, formed feet and hands, and lastly a neck and head. Jonna reached to grab the amulet.

"Won't work friend." O'Conner McBear appeared beside him. "That glow is attuned to you. For you, the amulet is useless."

Jonna listened to the words and caught McBear's hint. He pulled the amulet from around his neck and placed it on Elpis. "Think of the palace."

Elpis nodded, eyes wide, reached up, and held it. She vanished from his arms.

"Okay McBear, what's going on?"

"Sorry about the intrusion, and please don't take this personally. They made me do it." O'Conner nodded to someone behind Jonna.

Jonna leaped forward, avoiding a blow. "What is going on?" Now there were three greenish-yellow glows, and they were multiplying by the moment. The small creatures were about a quarter of Jonna's size. Not only did they drop from the sky, but they also came up from the ground. "What are they?"

"Sidhist," McBear answered, not helping them to capture Jonna. However, he did not hinder the process either. "They have come to take you to the Otherworld."

"What and why?" Jonna picked up one, spun him around, and tossed him into his buddies. They fell over like bowling pins. While they were not fast, they did keep multiplying; now the count was up to six.

"Don't know, but someone let them take my pot of gold hostage. The only way I can get it back is to deliver you to them."

"McBear, you didn't!"

"Sorry laddie," McBear shook his head, "I didn't have a choice." He looked disgusted. "Aren't very good, are they?"

"Bob!"

"At your service," the pixie appeared though his smile quickly changed to a frown. "What did you do?"

"I knew you were around." Jonna tried to laugh, but it was taking all his attention to watch out for the sidhist. "As far as I know, I haven't done anything."

Two sidhist grabbed hold of Jonna's legs. A third climbed on top of their heads, trying to add extra weight and pin his left arm. He grabbed the sidhist' hand, put him in a wristlock, and flipped him over backwards.

"I can't confirm that," the pixie shook his head. "When the sidhists come, something guilty has been done."

"Who said that? Did you make that up?"

"It's a pixie story."

"You were here. You saw what happened."

"Well," Bob looked sheepish, "actually, I only had one ear listening. Crystilic and I—"

Jonna sighed. "Crystilic, are you here too?" Crystilic was the female shape-changer he and Bob had found trapped at the dark mage's fortress.

One of the trees changed to a woman's shape. "We didn't want to intrude—"

"Intruding might be nice." Jonna eyed the growing number of sidhist. Now there were twelve, and it was getting harder to keep them off.

"You seem to be doing fine," Bob admired.

"Oh, pooh!" Crystilic changed into a rhino, scratched the ground, and rushed forward, knocking sidhists in every direction. "Climb on top of me," she raised her chin. "I'll get you free."

Jonna grabbed hold and pulled himself up. "Thanks." The sidhist tried to do the same, but they had a hard time grabbing hold of the rhino.

"No problem. As for you," she glared at Bob, "I'll talk to you later."

Bob ducked his head. "But you don't understand, they're the sidhists!"

Crystilic turned a hoof in his direction. "Talk to the hoof; we have a friend in need."

"More trouble," Jonna noted, pointing out the growing number of sidhist. The twelve had changed to twenty-four with more rising from the ground. "Run!"

"You can't do that," McBear threw down his hat and stomped on it. "I want my pot of gold!"

"Sorry Charlie." Jonna turned to Crystilic. "We need Väinämö's hut."

Crystilic took off. "On my way."

She tore through the underbrush. Her rhino feet struck the ground, thundering warnings to the small animals standing in her path. Branches broke as she landed on them, leaves crunched, and small trees were bent to breaking.

Bursting from the side of a clearing, Väinämö's hut came into view. The debris of the old hut had been swept to one side, destroyed by the dark mages not so long ago. In its place was a new one, though it did not look that much better. You would think the mage would have at least used new wood.

Jonna pointed. "Quickly, over there!"

Crystilic ran toward the hut, shaking the ground. The closer she came the more the house jumped.

"Hold!" Väinämö appeared outside the door. "Who, by all the gods, is making that racket? Are you trying to shake down my house?" He glared at the approaching rhino and caught sight of Jonna on top. His expression changed. "Jonna?"

"Väinämö, am I glad to see you!" Jonna prepared to dismount.

Crystilic slowed, slid a few steps, kicked up dust clouds, and halted. As he slipped off her back, she stood catching her breath. After a brief pause, she changed into a woman.

"Ah, that explains it," the mage chuckled. "I thought it strange to see a rhino in these woods. That's more connected with the north west kingdom."

"Isn't that where Artemis was from?" Jonna glanced at Bob.

Väinämö looked at them all. "Who's Artemis?"

Artemis had been one of the companions Jonna had met on the way to save his wife. He had forgotten that the mage had never met her.

"Never mind," Jonna pushed it away. "We have other problems. There are sidhist—" He stopped and stared as a sidhist walked out of Väinämö's hut; he pointed.

"We were just talking about that," Väinämö motioned to the small greenish-yellow creature. "Jonna, I'd like you to meet Dagda, King of the Sidhist."

"But they—"

Väinämö shook his head. "Be polite."

"But they tried to capture Elpis and me!"

"Technically, no," Dagda answered quietly. "You were the target."

Jonna turned his gaze from Dagda to Väinämö. "But why?"

"First things first," the mage motioned toward the hut door. "Let's all go in and have a nice cup of hot chocolate."

"I don't want hot chocolate," Jonna boomed, "and I'm not sitting down with a sidhist, king or not. They tried to kidnap me!"

"Now, now," Dagda cautioned, "let's not make false accusations. This was not a kidnapping." He pulled out a piece of parchment and read:

"Be it known that Jonna McCambel, a.k.a. Xun Ove the Fast Blade, has blatantly entered, coerced, and invaded a section of the underworld, henceforth known as the Otherworld. Be it known that in order to make amends, Jonna McCambel, a.k.a. Xun Ove the Fast Blade, is required to serve a period of six years, four months, and two days in a location of the Sidhist's choice. Quote, unquote." The sidhist looked up and smiled. "It's all legal and binding."

Jonna straightened. "And when did I invade the Otherworld?"

"When you fought and defeated the Dark Mages." Dagda looked surprised, "There are rules, you know."

Jonna was a little ticked. "I saved your little green skins, along with everybody else's, and this is the thanks I get?"

"He is very rude," Dagda turned to look at Väinämö. "Are you sure he's the one that defeated the Dark Mages?"

"The one and only." Väinämö nodded and then spoke quietly, "You'll have to excuse his manners. He's not from around here."

Jonna's eyes widened. "I don't believe this!"

Glittering sparkles in all directions, Elfleda boomed as she appeared, "What is going on?" She wasn't alone. A troop of elves-in-arms followed at her heels. She turned to Jonna. "Are you okay?"

"I'm fine," Jonna simmered, "just mad as—"

"Tsk, tsk," the mage caught Jonna's eyes. "It's hard to take back words once you say them. They can be magic you know."

Dagda turned toward the princess and bowed. "Elfleda, it is good to see you are safe."

Elfleda nodded, but Jonna knew the look; she was not happy. "What is this?" She held up a parchment for all to see. "After Elpis came running to tell me what happened, this scroll arrived."

"You know what it is." Dagda frowned. "It is clearly written and filed with a sidhist clerk. Multiple copies have been sent to all the major species."

Elfleda became regal. "I will not allow this. It is preposterous!"

"It was correctly filed," Dagda nodded, "and with witnesses. There is nothing I can do."

"He is correct," Väinämö looked at them, catching all in the group. "Unless we can find something to countermand the order, they have every right to take Jonna away."

Jonna's eyes widened. "Does the definition of right and wrong have no meaning here?"

Crystilic whispered to Bob, "Do it!"

Bob raised a finger to his lips. "Shh."

"Jonna, you don't understand," Väinämö ignored the other two. "This is a formal complaint from one species to another. Someone has accused you of violating inter-specie law. That law is the only thing that keeps the peace between our cultures. The Dark Mages violated it, and they were stopped."

"By me," Jonna looked around. "Am I the only one who sees this?"

Crystilic happily chimed, "I see," and then poked Bob, adding in a whisper, "Do it!"

"I see, too," Elfleda's eyes narrowed. "I don't know what game you're playing, but I don't like it! Be warned, if this is a trick—"

"No trick," Dagda held up a hand, "and I will do everything I can to get Jonna's sentence reduced. But, in the meantime—"

Jonna fist tightened; Elfleda's eyes shot flames.

Väinämö watched them both. "Perhaps you should give us a moment." He turned toward Dagda, guiding him into the hut. As the door closed, all began to speak at once.

"One at a time," the mage boomed, "and no, he cannot hear us."

Glaring at Bob, Crystilic pushed him again.

"I know, I know," he mouthed without making a sound.

"What is going on?" Elfleda looked at Väinämö, ignoring both Crystilic and Bob. "You can't consider going along with this?"

Väinämö sighed. "I'm afraid so. If you don't believe me, ask your mother."

Freya faded in. Everyone kneeled.

"Daughter," Freya spoke, her voice drifting on the wind. She came through the trees to their right, her own elven guards beside her.

"Mother," Elfleda bowed in respect. "Mother they—"

Freya held up a hand. "It is unfortunate, and I suspect planned, but it is nonetheless binding." She turned toward Väinämö.

Väinämö gave a slight bow to the queen. "I will do all in my power to find the truth. We will find a way to get Jonna back."

"I still have to go?" An incredulous look crossed Jonna's face. "Don't they have probation or something? What if I choose not to?"

"Then you will be outlawed," Freya stated with finality. "Your refusal to cooperate means war to the Elves. We cannot be a part of it."

11

"Mother!"

Freya's eyes bore into her daughter's. "It must be so."

Although Jonna had never detected racism from the queen, he was starting to think it was buried there. Whatever happened to standing by family? None of this made sense!

He turned toward the queen. "You told me. You encouraged me—" Jonna glared, protocol gone. "If you had let me know the rules—"

"Would you really have left your wife there, knowing the consequences?" The queen's eyes now bore into Jonna.

Jonna's head dropped. "No." He looked up. "I would have done anything to rescue Stephanie."

Dagda stepped out of the hut. "Thus convicted by his own lips."

Jonna swung around and glared, "This is a personal conversation between family." His temper rose, and he turned to the mage. "I thought you said he couldn't hear!"

"Until a few moments ago, he couldn't." The mage turned to the queen. "You know this is necessary?"

A sorrowful look crossed her face, but she nodded. "I know." She turned to Jonna. "By the authority of the Elves, Jonna McCambel, I hereby place you in the custody of the Sidhist."

Elfleda went to him, despite the shake of Freya's head. "We'll find a way to get you out." She looked into his eyes. "Do not lose hope."

Until this moment, all Jonna saw was the word jail, but now it sounded like a prison. What type of place was he going to?

"Ah, er, Jonna?" Bob moved up, forcing a space between the couple. Elfleda glared, and the pixie's eyes widened, but he pushed between them anyway. He extended his hand wearing a tiny ring; Jonna had never known the pixie to wear jewelry. "*Hukerleiger.*" A smile appeared on Bob's face as he added, "Safe journey."

Caught off guard, Jonna reached up and shook the tiny hand. Was that pixie dust falling from between Bob's fingers or the play of light through the trees?

Dagda motioned for Jonna and Elfleda to part. "I came as a favor to the queen. However, my time is short. We need to go." The sidhist king stepped from his place beside Väinämö, moved to Jonna's side, and reached for Jonna's arm.

"You're brave," Jonna spoke without looking at him, fighting the urge to do something mean. However, Bob's actions had thrown him; the pixie had never shaken his hand or worn jewelry. What were he and Crystilic up to?

"Don't let my size fool you, human." Dagda glared. "I have ways of dealing with your kind. I can make your stay easy," an evil grin crossed his face, "or hard." He waved a hand, shooing Bob away. "Besides, it is not often we have a celebrity."

"Celebrity?"

"Of course." A gratuitous smile crossed Dagda's face. "You destroyed the gem of the Dark Mages." His vise-like grip clamped down on Jonna's wrist.

"Then why am I being treated like a criminal?"

Chapter 2

SIDHIST BLISS

The world changed; the last glimpse of sunlight gave way to a sky of overcast blue. Jonna stood on a bed of greenish-purple grass, set beside a purple lake.

Dagda turned toward him. "This is your place. There are only two basic rules: one, fighting is forbidden, to do so will be to your own peril; and two," he pointed to a cave opening, "that is for sidhists only. You see those letters above the opening?"

Jonna spotted the strange alphabet carved above the door. He could not read it, which was unusual.

"In human terms it means 'keep out'. If I catch you there," he smiled inviting Jonna to try, "you won't get a second chance."

"Second chance to do what?"

Dagda met his gaze, not quite sure if Jonna was toying with him. "To stay in Bliss, of course."

"Bliss as in," Jonna thought, "Paradise? A nice place?"

Dagda nodded. "We have far worse."

"I see." Jonna looked at him. "You do know this is bogus?"

Dagda wrinkled his brow as curiosity crossed his face. "What is bogus?"

Jonna sighed and looked around. "Never mind. So what do I do now?"

"That's entirely up to you." The king laughed, fading from sight.

Jonna watched as the wind blew through the leaves of the trees and listened as the forest sounds met his ears. He had to admit, it was a good reproduction; although, the creator was certainly off on color. The anger he had felt on the surface still simmered. "Why didn't I learn the traveling spell?"

Jonna tried to remember what Väinämö had said in class, but it was no good. He looked around and spotted a bench beneath a group of trees. With glum determination, he walked over, took a seat, and then had an idea. "*Unum-Clastor-Pratima.*"

There was a distant rumble, but nothing else. An approaching voice laughed behind him as he waited.

He spoke again, "*Unum-Clastor-Pratima.*" The distant rumble repeated, but nothing else happened. The laugh came again, this time much closer.

Jonna adjusted himself on the seat. How could he concentrate with that going on? He turned, trying to see where the sound came from. "Who's the comedian?"

"What's a comedian?" the same voice asked, now very near.

It was amazing how many words the people of this magic realm did not know. Then again, look at all the strange things he had learned from them. "A jokester, a—" No, that wasn't quite right. "Someone who laughs at something that isn't supposed to be funny."

"Oh, I see." In front of him, a one-horned man faded into view. "Well, I guess I am. Mind if I have a seat?"

Jonna shrugged. "Why not?"

The man sat down and leaned against a tree. "Bitter, bitter, I was laughing with you, not at you."

"But I wasn't laughing."

"A minor thing. Give it a few minutes and you will be." He smiled expectantly, saw Jonna was not going to join in, and skipped the idea. "It won't work, you know."

Jonna eyed him. "What won't work?"

"Your magic." He chuckled again. "You don't know how many times I've seen it. Some mage gets brought down here thinking he'll use a couple spells to escape, and wham—no magic."

"Magic doesn't work down here?" That piqued Jonna's curiosity.

The man shook his head. "Not *your* magic. This," he held up two fingers, "Mi Fsicut." A tiny flame leaped to life from his fingertips. As he moved his hand around, the flame stayed upright. When he separated the fingers, the flame went out. He looked at Jonna. "What do you think?"

"You're using a different language. Is it Sidhist?"

"Ha, ha, ha, no. You see, when magic comes down into the earth it separates. The heavier portion sinks deeper; the lighter portion goes up. That's why what works above doesn't work down here. Oops, company." He faded from view.

Dagda strolled toward him. "I see you found a starting point."

Jonna looked up to see the king coming in his direction. "Do you have a better suggestion?"

"Väinämö was right; you do have quite a tongue. Too bad we cannot do anything about that right now, but in the meantime, a nice, cozy bench may be just the thing. You haven't found any company yet?"

"And whom would you suggest I get Great King of the Sidhist?"

"I would have thought working with Väinämö would have taught you better manners. Can I assume you have tried to do magic?"

Jonna didn't answer.

Dagda chuckled. "I thought so. They all do, you know. Each and every one—dead and undead."

The last phrase caught Jonna's attention, despite his annoyance with the sidhist king. "Dead and undead?"

"Ah, I see a keen mind somewhere in that boorish exterior. Yes, dead and undead. You see, the Otherworld is a place of punishment and bliss for both those that die and those who do something of an extremely punishable nature, such as yourself." The sidhist leaned toward him. "We take great pride in our impartiality." He stood straight again. "Death brings the dead. You qualify as undead."

"I see," Jonna looked around. "I take it this is not part of the dead area?"

Dagda waved his hand. "Yes and no. When your mind adapts, when you accept the fact that you are here, you will see them. Just remember, you are currently in Bliss; we can always let you try another level." On his face, a maniacal smile broadened.

Jonna caught his eye. "As always, your kindness is noted."

Dagda laughed as he walked away and faded from sight.

"As I was saying," the one-horned man continued, making sure Dagda was gone, "that's why what works above doesn't work down here."

Jonna looked at him. "Okay, which are you, dead or undead?"

"What?"

"Dagda told me there are dead and undead. Which are you?"

"Why, I'm undead of course." He held up his hand and looked at both sides. Concern filled his face. "Do I look dead to you?"

There was a splash in the lake, and for the first time Jonna could make out different types of waterfowl. "I don't remember seeing those." He pointed at the water. "There was nothing in the lake."

The man nodded. "Dead, of course."

"They're birds?"

"Why not? Everything is something."

A lion walked past, ignoring them both.

"This is getting weird." Jonna closed his eyes and opened them again. "They're still here."

"You think?" The man stared at the ground. "Try spending a thousand years down here."

"You've been here that long?" His own sentence came to mind: six to seven years. Jonna leaned back. The more he thought about it, the more his determination grew. "Teach me your magic." He extended his hand. "I'm Jonna, and I want out of here."

A smile crossed the man's lips as he took Jonna's hand. "I'm Lokke," they shook, "and I would be delighted."

Chapter 3

SWANS IN A GAGGLE

"Stop!"

Jonna looked up and caught sight of a bird high above his head. "Stop what?"

"I saw you," the bird angled its head, "fraternizing with the enemy."

"Enemy?" Jonna looked to his left, but Lokke was gone. "What enemy?"

"Be warned, Jonna McCambel," the bird's voice was ominous, "wolves come in sheep's clothing, even in the Otherworld." The bird took flight and disappeared into the sky.

"Never mind him." Lokke adjusted himself to face Jonna. "He's jealous because he can't do magic. Now, there are two laws you have to remember: always keep your fingertips held close together, and never use more than two words. You got that?"

Jonna put his fingers into the proper shape and repeated the instructions.

"Good. Now, repeat the spell you heard me say."

Jonna thought, trying to recall the phrase. However, the words were so strange he could not remember.

"Mi," Lokke gave a hint.

"Mi."

Lokke watched closely as he gave Jonna the second word. "Fsicut."

"Fsicut. Mi Fsicut." Jonna stared at his fingertips. The flame appeared, moving over the tops. Surprisingly enough, it did not burn.

"Wonderful," Lokke watched with admiration. "You're on your way to becoming a great magician both here and there."

Jonna spread his fingertips, and the fire vanished. "Lokke, I—"

Lokke was gone. Somebody else sneezed.

"Bless you," Jonna looked to his right and caught sight of a hound dog sniffing the grass.

"It's too late for that," the hound dog spoke between sniffs. He traced the scent across the lawn, over Jonna's shoes, and up to the empty seat beside Jonna. "I see you've had some company."

"Who are you?" Jonna resisted the urge to reach out and pat him on the head.

"Sir Reginald Richard The Third, at your service," the hound dog looked Jonna in the eye, "worlds' best hunter."

"You're a hunter? Here?"

"Of course, who else is better equipped?" He touched a paw to his nose. "The nose knows."

Despite his present circumstance, Jonna's mood was starting to lighten. With characters like this, who could stay mad?

"It is good to meet you Sir Reginald Richard The Third. Might I ask whom you are looking for?"

"A sly one, he is," Reginald growled. "Been trying to catch him for close to fifty years."

"Who?"

"The trickster, the prankster, the one who might trip your legs one moment, or tie your tail in a knot the next." He growled again. "He always gets me when I'm sleeping."

Jonna tried to keep a straight face. "He should let sleeping dogs lie."

Reginald's brow wrinkled. "Exactly." He looked from one side to the other. "If you find a clue, please let me know."

"Of course."

Reginald brought his paws back from the bench and placed his nose to the ground. "Thanks." He walked off, still sniffing the grass.

"Dead."

Lokke appeared and nodded with raised eyebrows. "Undoubtedly."

"Say," Jonna looked in Lokke's direction, "why do you keep disappearing?"

A strange smile crept over Lokke's face. "Call it common courtesy." He waved at the world in general. "Actually, most don't even know I'm here."

That didn't make sense. "Why's that?"

"Being one of the few who know how to do magic makes a lot of people jealous."

"If knowing how to do magic—wait a minute. Why are you here to begin with? A thousand years?"

"It's true," Lokke's face dropped, "and undead."

"If you know magic, then why haven't you escaped?"

"That's the catch." Lokke sighed. "Magic here only works here. Magic in the surface world only works there."

"So what good is it to learn your magic?"

Lokke's eyes twinkled. "It will help you survive." He saw the doubt in Jonna's face and quickly added, "Until you reach the entrance to the Otherworld."

A light clicked on. "And beyond the entrance, I can use my own magic." He nodded. "I see your point."

"Do you?"

There was something hidden behind those eyes, and Jonna could see it. This wasn't a friend helping a friend; there was something else he wanted. Jonna would rather get to the point. "And what in return?"

"My freedom." Lokke's humorous tone vanished; he was deadly serious. "Will you help me?"

A tiny voice whispered into Jonna's ear, "Don't do it. He's not from our world."

Jonna looked to the right, but could not see what had to

be on his shoulder. The voice was familiar. The size and position was correct. "Bob?"

There was a startled look on Lokke's face. "Who?"

"Don't," it whispered again.

A million thoughts went through Jonna's mind, and none of them made any sense. "Bob, how did you—"

Eyes wide, Lokke made sure no one was to Jonna's right. "Who's Bob? Who are you talking to? The dead?"

This guy was really paranoid.

Bob growled. "Who's calling whom dead, bucko?"

"Bob, that's not very nice."

"Who's Bob?" Lokke jumped to his feet and peered around. Pushing through the plant growth, he came up on Jonna's other side. A big smile formed on his face. "I get it. You're trying to throw me off."

"Throw you off what?"

"I don't know," a puzzled look crossed Lokke's face, "but it must be something. Why else would you pretend to hear voices?"

"He's calling me a pretense?" Bob revved up. "Who does he think he is?"

The situation was getting out of control. "Bob!"

"Stop doing that," Lokke pleaded, "you're making me nervous." He put a finger to his chin. "Either you're trying to throw me off, or you really are crazy."

Jonna shook his head. "Just call it crazy. It's the easiest explanation."

Bob put his hands on his sides. "I am not Crazy. I am Bob."

"Not you Bob," Jonna exhaled. "The situation is crazy."

Lokke huffed and sat down on the seat. "That's better, at least I know where you stand."

That seemed a little strange to Jonna. "It's better to be crazy than to throw you off?"

"Of course." Lokke chuckled. "Everyone has to be a little crazy. How else would we get through the Otherworld?"

"He has a point," Bob finished, considering.

"So now you're agreeing with him?" Jonna couldn't believe his ears.

Lokke jumped again. "Agreeing with whom?" He looked around. "Oh, yeah, wacko."

Jonna scratched his neck, thinking, "You can sense when the dead approach, but you can't hear the voice on my shoulder?"

Straining, Lokke listened, but after a moment he shook his head. "Not a thing."

"It's not speaking now."

"Good," Bob was smug, "serves him right!"

More dead were appearing, fading in one by one; it was distracting Jonna. "Serves who right?"

Bob pointed at Lokke. "Him, your new *friend.*"

Lokke watched as Jonna seemed to be having a conversation with himself. Moving his face closer to Jonna, he studied him and spoke into his ear, "Jonna."

Jonna's head snapped toward him.

"Are you going to help me or not?"

Bob pleaded, "Don't!"

The whole situation was too much too quick. In his mind, Jonna had felt completely cut off from the surface world, and now he discovered he was not, so to speak. "Can I tell you tomorrow?"

"You don't trust me?" Lokke sounded shocked. "I've never broken my word."

How did he explain the voice of a pixie on his shoulder without the rest of the body? For that matter, did he want to? "I don't doubt that, it's just—"

Bob nudged him, "Go ahead, tell him I'm your conscience. You already told him you're crazy."

"You are not my conscience!"

Sitting back, Lokke shook his head. "Nutty as a fruitcake."

A laugh left Bob's lips. "See, problem solved."

An ensemble of distorted honks exploded from the direction of the lake, catching Jonna's and Lokke's attention. Out of the noise came a distinctive name, "Jonna!"

Since when did swans honk out names? Jonna listened and shook his head. Oh yeah, they were people who had died and had taken the form of swans. He searched for the source with his eyes. How did they know who he was? Did Dagda do this to annoy him?

"Careful," Bob's eyes widened, "they're a close relative to chickens."

From what Jonna could remember, the only thing close between a swan and a chicken was the idea they were birds. "I forgot you're afraid of chickens."

The look on Lokke's face changed to puzzlement. "I am not afraid of chickens." He glanced toward the lake and gave a small chuckle.

"Excuse me," Jonna nodded toward Lokke. He headed down the grassy knoll and moved toward the edge of the lake.

Bob began to narrate. "Take your time, easy stroll, don't get in a hurry."

Now that Lokke was out of hearing, Jonna could find out what was going on. "Bob, what are you doing? Not that I'm complaining, but how are you here?"

"Well," the pixie thought, "I'm not exactly sure so I'll explain it the way Väinämö did." He cleared his throat. "The magic I cast before you left lets me see, hear, and speak to you. In the same way, it lets you see, hear, and speak to me. Although, I seem to see more of your environment than you do of mine."

"But I can't see you."

Bob sounded smug. "That's because I'm invisible."

Jonna laughed. "A little better than the last time then?"

Though he couldn't see it, Jonna knew Bob was squinting at him. The last time Bob had tried to stay invisible, a mage in Chernobog had seen him. It had driven the pixie crazy trying to make his invisibility spell work better.

"It was a mage that saw me, thank you very much. They're almost impossible to fool."

Did Bob not realize Jonna qualified as a mage too? Maybe that was why he could see him without seeing. "Don't be so defensive; it was a joke." The ring on Bob's finger and the pixie dust sparkling, came to mind. "I thought it was strange, us shaking hands. No one else knows?"

"I don't know about that."

Jonna could tell Bob was smiling; so, Bob's invisibility was not so invisible after all. There was no sense in spoiling the pixie's mindset. Maybe it was part of the spell.

A swan swam up and struck the water, splashing at Jonna to get his attention. The drops rose but fell short, failing to get him wet.

Jonna turned toward the swan. "Can I help you?"

The swan spoke, its voice firm but high-pitched, "Someone wants to talk to you."

"Okay." He looked around, but the other swans had retreated to the reeds. "Why are they leaving?"

"Perhaps they don't like the presence of the undead." She turned her tail feathers in Jonna's direction. "Maybe they don't think you belong here."

"I concur."

"You do?" The swan turned its long neck around with a shocked expression on her face. She stuttered a moment, "But I—"

"I was forced here by Dagda."

"That cad." She shook her head as it dropped in sympathy. "We should have known." Glancing back, she honked out, "Okay girls, it's safe!" The other swans started swimming back as she looked up at him. "We'll let you in on a secret then."

"You will?"

Bob shifted position. "I'm all ears."

"Quiet Bob."

"Who's Bob?" The swan looked around. "Are there more undead with you?"

"No, no," Jonna assured, "there's only me."

Bob chimed in, "And me."

"No, there isn't." he said firmly.

The swan looked at him strangely. "Maybe the secret

should wait. This way." The swan swam out further from the shore.

He hesitated.

"What are you waiting for?" She looked back. "Change and jump in."

"What?"

"I said change—" She turned her head to look at Jonna better. "Dagda didn't give you shape-change magic?"

One of the other swans tapped her with its wings and leaned its head toward her to whisper, "Undead aren't given shape-change."

"They aren't?" The first swan looked startled and then sighed. "He'd make a good snuggle. Are you sure?"

"He'd never be yours anyway." The other tapped her gently on the back. "Remember?"

"True." The first let the second console her for a moment. "Oh, well."

Jonna made a funny face. "I think I was hit on by a bird."

The pixie chuckled.

Ducking her head in slight embarrassment, she turned and blinked her eyes at Jonna. "Are you coming?"

"I would like to," he agreed, "but I'm not sure I want to get wet."

"Well, if you're not sure," the swan wiggled as it turned to go and quickly looked back, "but you really should accept."

Bob jumped in. "Accept what?"

"Accept what?" Jonna mirrored and then shook his head. "Bob, stop it."

The swan shook her head. "I'm not called Bob. You and I don't merit a first name basis. Maybe after a couple of years—"

Jonna took a step back from the edge. "Yeah, this is strange."

The pixie volunteered, "They seem harmless. After all, they are swans."

"I thought you were afraid of swans?"

"Well," Bob mused, "they don't look as bad as chickens up close, and they do seem friendly."

The swan's head pulled back a little, confused at the one-sided conversation. "Why would I be afraid of myself?"

"Bob, whose side are you on?"

The swan shook its head. "I told you, my name is not Bob."

Listening to the swan's response, Jonna dropped his voice a notch and directed it toward Bob. "This water thing makes me nervous, not to mention, I have no desire to take a swim." He looked from the shore to the water, remembering all he had to wear were the clothes on his back.

More animals appeared walking on the shore. If he didn't want his only change of clothes getting wet, he would have to leave them at the edge. If he left his clothes and someone stole them—

"Oh, take a chance," Bob pushed. "What do you have to lose?"

"My clothes."

"But with only animals around—" Bob shrugged.

"These animals used to be people." Jonna turned as if to see Bob on his shoulder, but of course he wasn't there. "It makes me a little uncomfortable."

"So what are you going to do?"

Rather than answer, Jonna stepped into the water and felt the squishy part of the mud as he slid down the slippery bank. A moment later, he was swimming behind, following the swans into the reeds. It was not the best method of swimming; his clothes weighed him down. At least he knew they would be there, albeit sodden and dripping, when he returned to shore.

One of the other swans called, "Pooh, he did it!"

Another swan honked, "I can't believe it!"

They turned a corner and slipped between the thicker water plants.

"I win," a third flapped its feathers, rose briefly from the water, and sped to get next to the first swan.

"Stop it, all of you," the first swan scolded. She glanced back and fluttered her eyes at Jonna. "I think he's brave."

Bob whistled. "What an entourage!"

Jonna kept his voice at a whisper. "Bob, they're swans." This was embarrassing, and his little shoulder friend wasn't helping one bit.

"But they're swooning swans to boot!"

"How about we focus on what's ahead, shall we?"

Sixty feet in on the left side, hidden by tiny islands with trees, was a clearing. A series of logs had been combined to form a small hut on stilts. Jonna climbed the rough ladder as water poured from his soaked clothes and knocked on the door. No one answered.

"She'll be here in a moment." The first swan's eyes sparkled. "Make yourself at home, or," she winked, "you could always wait with me." The swan's eyes batted again. A chortle of swan honks went off as the rest of the bevy moved away.

"Thanks," he smiled, "but I need to get the water out." He stood there, his wet clothing draining all over the porch. "Uh, by the way, why am I here again?"

The swan moved closer and whispered, "Well, that's the secret, isn't it? Now, if you get tired of her, look me up. I know how to shape-change into a human too." She wiggled off into the water.

Bob's eyes lit up. "Wow, just like Crystilic!"

Jonna reached for the door handle and found it unlocked. That wasn't too surprising since this was supposedly Paradise, er, Bliss. Come to think about it, if this were Bliss, no one would have stolen his clothes had he left them, but did he want to run around without clothes? No, definitely not.

Turning the handle, the door swung open. To his surprise, the inside was much nicer than the outside with the inner decor rivaling that of the Elves. As a matter of fact, it was larger on the inside than the outside. He did a double take and tried to compare the exterior limitations with the interior expansiveness, but it did no good. It definitely smacked of magic.

"Bob, what's going on?"

"Why are you asking me?"

"Well, you're from here."

The little pixie huffed. "I'm not from around there!"

"You know what I mean."

Jonna stepped in, conscious of his still wet shoes, clothes, and hair. Lake water, either in his world or down here, hadn't changed much; it still smelt like lake water. In an effort not to mess up anything else in the house, he decided to stay where he was. The door closed behind him.

Bob shot back grudgingly, "I do not!"

"You do too."

"Are you calling me a liar?"

"Okay, little pixie, if you don't know what is going on, why did Väinämö arrange for us to communicate?"

Bob huffed. "To keep you out of trouble!"

"And to do that, you have to know what's going on."

The pixie paused. "Not—not really."

"It is exactly like when I went to save Stephanie. You knew all the time who Stephanie really was."

The door opened behind Jonna, and a woman's voice exclaimed, "Oh my!"

Jonna turned slowly. "I can explain." The soaked clothing stuck against his skin and was dripping to the floor, though not as bad as it had on the porch. He really should have waited outside.

"Look what they've done to you!"

"They?" Jonna noted the female behind him. Her kind, understanding eyes said the water did not matter.

"Yes, they." Her eyes narrowed. "All of them. They knew there was an entry from the land."

Jonna looked down at his clothes. "I could have walked?"

"Yes," the woman gave a small chuckle, "you certainly could have."

"The swans gave me directions."

"The females ones?" There was a knowing look on the woman's face. "Think nothing of it. It was a little jealousy."

Bob couldn't help himself. "And a little flirting."

"That's enough, Bob," Jonna spoke before thinking, stopped, and watched the woman's face. "I'm really not crazy."

"I know you're not," the woman laughed. "Please," she motioned to a chair, "sit down."

Wet and dripping, he uncomfortably took the seat. The idea that she did not think he was mental brought a million questions to his mind, but he had to start somewhere. "Why have you asked me to come?"

"We have a mutual acquaintance," the woman smiled, getting straight to the point. "I'm Cassandra, Elpis' mother."

Jonna's mouth dropped, and even the idea of speech seemed impossible. He swallowed, attempting to reclaim his voice, "You're—"

Bob stuttered, "W—Wow, I've got to check on this!" Something gave a small pop, and Jonna knew that Bob had disconnected.

Cassandra nodded. "You can say it," she smiled, her eyes laughing at his reaction, and then whispered, "and you can tell Bob, I know what's going on."

"I'm sorry," he swallowed again, trying not to stare, "now that you mention it, I know it's true. If I didn't know better, I'd think you were Elpis all grown up."

"They used to tell us that," her eyes sparkled. "She was my wonderful little girl." Her expression dropped, becoming forlorn. "I have missed her."

"Okay, back," Bob spoke in his ear again. "Yep, she's her mom."

Jonna grinned. "She said she knows you're here."

The pixie's eyes widened. "She can see me?"

He ignored Bob's last response, focusing on Cassandra. "She talks to you all the time. She tells me when you've approved of things."

Her smile returned and pushed the sadness away. "We do communicate, and yes, you do have my blessing to be her dad."

Wham, there was that word again. Remembering how far he was from Elfleda, his face dropped. Dagda was keeping him from his family.

Bob whined in his ear, "Ask her if she can see me."

"Don't worry," Cassandra's eyes were bright, "you'll make a great dad."

Jonna hesitated, trying to focus on the here and now. "You think so?"

"I know so. Why else would I let her go?"

Bob leaped up and down. "Can she see me?"

Jonna ignored him. "Elpis said that," he agreed. Although to him, the whole dead thing played a very big part. Once a person died, they had to let go, at least in his world. "Cassandra, truly, I don't know what to say. It is a privilege to meet you."

"And likewise, you." She pointed out the window at the swans beside the hut. "That's why they lead you through the water." She looked at Jonna with a stern eye. "Not every mom gets to pick the next parent. I'm very particular about who cares for my daughter."

Jonna sighed in relief, though still edgy about the 'dad' thing. "She's a wonderful child."

Bob attempted to pinch him though Jonna felt nothing. "Can she?"

Jonna had enough. "Can you see Bob?"

"Bob the pixie? Elpis' Bob?" Cassandra put a finger to her lips, looked slightly up, thought, and then changed direction, taking in the spot on Jonna's right shoulder. "No Bob, I can't see you standing there on Jonna's shoulder with your light green shirt and dark green pants. That little bag of pixie dust won't do you any good down here."

Bob squeaked and tried to hide. "She can see me!"

"She said she couldn't," Jonna reminded him. "You're not listening."

Cassandra pointed a finger at Bob. "And don't go hiding behind Jonna's neck."

Bob froze in midstride and swallowed. "But how?"

31

"Elpis can," she sat back smiling. "She can see what you're doing on the surface and tells me. She is listening to you speak right now and relaying the words."

Now she had Jonna's attention. "Uh, how does this work again?"

"The spell Väinämö had Bob cast allows him to keep connected to you, as long as he wears the ring. Elpis can see Bob and communicate what's going on to me."

"So she can see Bob even though he's invisible?"

Bob had a fit. "What? No, no, no! I'm invisible so only certain mages can—" He stopped and looked at something beyond Jonna's area. "That's right, she did see me when we first met in the city of Diggory."

For Jonna, knowing there was more than one way to communicate with the surface world relieved the stress of the separation a little bit more.

"That's a relief." The pixie wiped the sweat from his brow. "I was afraid for a moment I could be seen by anyone."

Jonna turned to look by instinct. "And what would it matter?"

Cassandra answered, "The undead in the Otherworld must be here by invitation. Caught uninvited, they could forfeit their life. Bob walks a dangerous line."

The pixie nodded. Jonna remembered something Elpis had told him. "Cassandra, when your husband was taken, where did he go? Is he here with you now?" Sadness formed in her eyes, and he regretted asking the question.

"I never saw him again." Her voice halted. "My Sight does not work where he is concerned."

That was easy to understand. When Jonna had searched for Stephanie, he had the same problem. Strong emotions tended to mess up the sensory perceptions of The Sight. It was sort of like detecting a radio signal. As long as you are not generating your own on the same frequency, you can pick up the signal without interference.

"Then that is why you are willing for Elpis to call me dad?"

"I don't know if he is living or dead, and Elpis needs a family. She needs to be held and loved."

"Unfortunately, there might be one small problem; I'm not here by my own will. I was given a sentence of six to seven years." His voice trailed off as his mind fought to find a way out of it. So far, he only had one candidate that had offered to help get him out early, and Jonna wasn't sure about accepting. He frowned. "That loving family may have to wait for a while."

Cassandra shook her head and met his gaze. "There are things involved here that you do not know. Things going on which you will discover in time. Suffice it to say, very soon you will be leaving. There is a child—" She stopped; a strange look crossed her face as she glimpsed the future. "When you do, you'll need me to be along." Her eyes met his. "I need you to bring me along."

"Okay," Jonna nodded slowly, though confused, "if that is what you wish. However, I got the impression that Dagda has a problem with people trying to escape."

Her head nodded. "The penalty can be severe."

"And you would risk losing Bliss?" Jonna looked into her eyes, seeing those of Elpis. He didn't have a clear idea of this Otherworld yet, but if it were anything like Hades in Greek mythology, it wouldn't be all nice.

She nodded again.

"Then, I'll do my best." He smiled, hiding the concern. "You are welcome to come wherever you think I'm going." He tried to sound confident, but the prospect bothered him. It was one thing to risk his own life, taking his own chances, but it was something else to risk another person's place in eternity.

"Thank you." Her face relaxed. "You don't know how much this means."

The pixie was unusually silent.

"Bob, do you know something?"

"Me?"

"What did you learn from Elpis?"

"Who says Elpis did anything?"

"That's my point. I didn't say she did anything, you did."

"Now, now." Cassandra rose and moved to the kitchen. "Maybe it's time to change the subject? How about some nice hot chocolate?"

Jonna shifted his arm, the dampness of his clothes coming vividly back; during the conversation he had forgotten that he was wet. "Cassandra, is there a place I might be able to get my clothes dried?" Ordinarily, he would throw them in a dryer, but since entering Elfleda's world—

There was a knock at the door right before it flew open.

"Where is he?" A fairly tall, stocky man stomped into the room. He went past Jonna and stared into the kitchen. "Where is he?"

Cassandra looked puzzled. "Where is who?"

"Your new boyfriend. It's all the talk with the swans!"

"Boyfriend?" Cassandra laughed. "Brutus, you're jealous!"

Brutus' face went red. "I am not!"

She scolded, though not too harshly. "You are too. Go sit down on the sofa and have a nice conversation with Elpis' dad."

"Dad?" Brutus turned, wide-eyed, and looked at Jonna. "I thought you said your husband—"

"He's not my husband, silly. He has accepted Elpis as his daughter." Cassandra walked out of the kitchen, giving him a look. "Although", she teased, "he is cute."

"Fine!" However, Brutus seemed to be in better spirits. He turned toward Jonna. "Brutus Augustus." He extended his hand.

Jonna shook it. "Jonna McCambel."

"I take it you're new around here? Don't fret, you'll find your place in the first thirty or so years."

"Uh, honey," Cassandra gently touched Brutus' arm, "Jonna's undead."

"Undead?" Brutus gave a wide smile. "Well, that's even better!"

Jonna's eyes narrowed. "Better how?"

Cassandra laughed. "Better as in you are not a threat to Brutus here. He's always so nervous I'll leave him."

Brutus began, "If you had the life I did—"

"She didn't deserve you." Cassandra patted him on the arm. Brutus blushed.

A question crossed Jonna's mind, but he decided it was better to wait, and since Cassandra and Brutus seemed to be settling in, "I think it's time I should go."

Cassandra looked up. "Are you sure? You're welcome to stay."

"I—" Jonna shook his head. "But thank you so much for letting me meet you." He stood up, looking one direction and then the other.

"This way," Cassandra led, showing him the door to the dry land. It swung out over a porch that then changed to a walkway forming a bridge; the bridge connected to the shore. She stepped onto the porch, closed the door, and walked to the middle. "Let me know when," she whispered in cryptic tones.

He nodded.

"Good." She moved forward and kissed him on the cheek. "Thank you, Jonna. You don't know what a godsend this is." She stepped back, disappearing into the hut. As the door closed, a twilight curtain dropped over the sky.

Bob could not help himself. "Boyfriend! What do you mean boyfriend? She doesn't even know what happened to her husband!"

"Don't judge Bob; we don't know her motives. Marriage in my world is till death do us part. Maybe it is not so different here."

"Do you really believe that?"

Jonna laughed. "Never judge a situation until you know all the facts. We don't know what's going on, and she is willing to chance losing her blissful afterlife in an effort to help us. That tells me there is more here than meets the eye."

Whatever qualified as a sun was now completely down.

Twilight vanished, and he stood staring up at a dark sky with twinkling lights. Whoever had set up this blissful place was quite good at the simulation.

"Now where?" Jonna's clothes had stopped dripping, though they were still wet. In the warm air, maybe the clamminess would go away too. He should have accepted Cassandra's hospitality and stayed, but somehow he felt three was a crowd. Besides, no matter how many times Cassandra assured Brutus about her intentions, Brutus seemed like the type that would always doubt.

His eyes dropped from the sky to the land, and he caught sight of a white mist moving through the trees. It looked like the one he had seen before the sidhists had attacked, and he was sure it was watching him.

"Psst."

Was that a rustling in the reeds? Jonna looked over the bridge and spotted a frog in the water.

Bob whispered. "Did you hear that?"

"Psst," the frog said again. It stuck its tongue out and caught a fly. "Yeah you," it spoke, seeing it had Jonna's attention.

The voice sounded like—he raised his eyebrows. "Lokke?"

"One and the same. So, what's it gonna be?"

"Don't," Bob's voice raised a little. "We don't need him; he's trouble."

"Be?" Jonna thought out loud; meeting Cassandra had made him forget. "Oh, yeah." He mulled it over.

Bob shook his head. "You can't be considering—"

"I can see you're still hesitant," Lokke announced. "How 'bout I show my good intentions by giving you another spell?" The frog smiled widely.

Jonna hesitated. "O—kay."

"Repeat after me," the frog croaked out, "Piqjimi Desfie"

"Piq—ji—mi Des—fi—e?"

Lokke strained to listen. "Close," a frown crossed his face, "but let's try it again. Piqjimi Desfie."

"Piqji—mi Desfi—e."

"You're getting better, but you forgot to hold your fingers together."

Jonna put his fingers together trying to focus on the words. *"Piqjimi Desfie."* He looked around, but nothing happened.

"Well," Lokke tapped a frog leg, "get on with it."

"I did," Jonna looked around again. "I held my fingers and said the words."

"Hmm," Lokke considered. With his eyes, he retraced the actions Jonna had taken, and then his face lit up. "I know, what did you think of when you said the word?"

"I was supposed to think of something?" He looked at his clothes, "Wow, my clothes are dry. Guess I was thinking of that."

Lokke gave him a scolding look. "You were supposed to think of being a frog." He frowned at Jonna. "That spell couldn't have possibly dried your clothes."

"A frog?" He looked at Lokke. "But I don't want to be a frog."

"You'll have to if you want to find the way out."

Jonna considered. Diving into the lake with all his clothes didn't seem like the smart thing to do, especially after they had dried, and yet—

"I don't have all night," Lokke wrinkled his frog nose. "If you want to go, fine. If not—" he raised one of his tiny frog arms as if to say, C'est la vie.

Bob huffed. "Jonna—"

"Piqjimi Desfie," Jonna decided and dropped toward the ground. As he touched the walkway, the clothes, now much too large, dropped over the top of his frog form, cutting off the light. Something stirred from above, and he saw Lokke, the frog, opening a path for him to get out. "Thanks."

"Don't mention it." Lokke looked in both directions. 'Ready?'

The last word was heard in Jonna's head without his frog ears. 'How did you do that?' He jumped. 'How did I do that?'

'Frogs do it naturally. It is for communication beneath

the water. You'll get the hang of it.'

The sound of Bob's voice came from Jonna's back. "Wow, we're almost the same height."

"I take it you are no longer on my shoulder?"

Lokke made a funny, frog face and slipped to the side, muttering, "Raving mad."

"Who could fit?" Bob continued. "But seriously, you don't think you can trust him?"

A chuckle escaped Jonna's lips. "So you didn't change into a frog too?"

Bob's eyes widened. "Did you try to change me into a frog?" He checked his arms and legs. "They still look pixie to me."

"Of course not," Jonna laughed, "that would be crazy."

Lokke came back and looked down at Jonna surrounded by clothes. "Whenever you are through talking to yourself, I'm ready to go."

Jonna gave a sheepish, frog smile. "Sorry about that." He climbed up and out of the pile of clothes. "I've got one last stop before we can leave."

Chapter 4

BON APPETIT

Lokke nodded. "I can oblige. I'll wait here."

"Thanks." Jonna hopped over to Cassandra's residence and bumped against the door.

Brutus grumbled, "Who is it?"

"Jonna," he croaked out in his best frog voice. "I need to speak with Cassandra."

"She's asleep." Brutus yawned. "Come back tomorrow."

"No, I'm not," Cassandra opened the door. "Jonna?" She didn't seem concerned that he was a frog.

"We're ready when you are," he stated, not bothering to explain.

"I'm ready now. Give me one second." She closed the door, but Jonna could hear them clearly, and Brutus was waking up fast.

"Ready for what?"

"You know what," she refused to explain. "We've already talked about this."

"You're going to help despite the warning? Despite what they will do when they catch you?"

"If," she threw back. "I'm betting they won't."

"When," he tried to overrule her. "No one ever goes back!"

"I don't want to go back," Cassandra reminded him. "I only want to help." Something slammed inside the house, and

Jonna hopped away from the door. Inside, footsteps came toward him. The door opened.

"I'm ready," Cassandra smiled as if none of the conversation had occurred.

Brutus shouted after her, "Cassandra!"

"Are you sure this is a good time?" Jonna glanced toward the inside of the house.

Cassandra closed the door. "Yes."

"Okay," he turned toward Lokke, "what is the spell to take my clothes with me?"

"Who are you talking to?" Cassandra looked from Jonna to the water.

Bob warned, "She's gonna think you're loony."

Lokke thought. "Teff Jilvus, but be sure and think of your clothes when you do it. To get them out, say and think it again."

"Got it." Jonna turned to Cassandra unable to miss the strange look on her face. "Oh, uh, yeah." He turned to Lokke. "Will you please let her see you?"

Lokke chuckled. "Certainly."

"I want you to meet Lokke." He pointed a frog leg at a log floating in the water.

Cassandra followed with her eyes but only saw the log. "You know a log named Lokke?" There was nothing in her words to say this was unusual. "Hello log."

"Lokke!"

"She can't see me," Lokke chuckled. "Not all the dead can. I am not a part of their world."

"What do you mean? The bird saw you, and the hound smelled you—"

"But I was a part of them," Lokke announced with pride, "like I'm a part of you. There was something within each of them that allowed me to be detected. I don't always know who can."

"So, she can never see you?" He looked toward his right shoulder. "Bob, can you get Elpis to confirm what's going on?"

"Elpis isn't here right now." Bob shrugged. "You'll have to do it yourself."

"Can you find her, please?"

"Elfleda said she needed to rest."

Cassandra listened to the one-sided conversation. "Elpis is taking a nap. She needs her rest."

Jonna caught the look on Cassandra's face. It wasn't disbelief, rather confusion. He understood how she felt. It had been the same way for him since entering this world. He turned to Lokke. "She never will see you?"

"I wouldn't say never." Lokke gave a mischievous look. "With what she is about to do, I'm sure it's a matter of time."

"I don't get it."

"You don't have to." Lokke gave a big, wide smile. "I'll handle the details."

"She can still come with us?"

"Of course," Lokke assured. "You'll have to relay my incredible wit."

"Right." Bob rolled his eyes. "He doesn't even know what wit is!"

One Bob was enough, but a Lokke and a Bob? "I see." Jonna turned to Cassandra again. "Uh—okay. Here's the deal. Apparently, the person who is helping me find the way out—" He frowned, not exactly sure if the word person described him, "—can't be seen by just anybody." It sounded lame, but then again, she knew he was talking to Bob. Surely she wouldn't think he was insane? Unfortunately, most people only saw things from their own point of view.

A skeptical frown formed on her face. "Really?"

Was it hesitancy or disbelief? "I—" It was time to change the subject. "Are you sure you want to go?"

"Now you're sounding like Brutus," she warned. "Are you saying you don't want me along?"

"No, no," he shook his head. Okay, maybe there were some things better left unexplained, at least until they could be proven. "Here's the deal, can you change into a frog?"

"A frog? What does a frog—"

"Cassandra, you trusted me with your daughter. Will you not trust me now?"

"Ah, I see," Lokke hit himself on the head, which wasn't easy being a frog, "you're taking care of her live daughter." He tapped himself on his frog head several times, this time not so hard. "Why didn't I see it before?"

Bob shook his head. "Boy, he's slow."

Jonna ignored them both, keeping his eyes on Cassandra. "I need to know you will listen to me and follow my instructions."

Cassandra nodded. "The last man I did that for was my husband, and now I don't know what happened to him." She sighed. "I trust you. Tell me what you want me to do."

"A smooth one, you are," Lokke congratulated. "Never seen it done better."

Clearing his throat, Bob called, "Flattery will get you nowhere."

How long could a sane man handle hearing two additional voices in his head? Jonna held his tongue and kept focused on Cassandra. "Can you change into a frog?"

Cassandra nodded.

"Go ahead. As soon as you're done, follow my lead."

Cassandra snapped her fingers and appeared on the walkway in frog form.

Jonna said his new spell, forcing his frog fingers together. "*Teff Jilvus.*" His clothes vanished.

'You're ready, Cassandra and Lokke?' He glanced toward them both, still surprised he could do this.

Bob huffed. "So, I get the silent treatment?"

"You get a dunking," Jonna laughed, speaking out loud.

"Thanks."

'She is cute,' Lokke chuckled. The chuckle sounded more like a cough than a chuckle, through his frog throat.

'Who is cute?' Cassandra looked around. She, too, was naturally picking up on the frog's communication channel.

'You can hear him?' Jonna asked. 'In frog form?'

Lokke laughed. 'She can hear me. We're off to a great start!'

'Hear who?' Cassandra glanced at Jonna. 'Who is the other frog?'

'Lokke,' Jonna tried to convince her. 'He's down there on the log, but you cannot see him.'

'And why not?'

Jonna thought a moment. 'I do not know how to answer that. However, he said after a while you might be able to.'

'I don't understand,' she said, but there was something in her voice that said she was getting the picture. 'What next?'

'Follow my lead.' Jonna leaped over the walkway into the lake and dropped below the surface. Spotting Lokke, he followed.

Lokke chuckled, 'But watch out for snakes.'

Cassandra looked into the water. 'Snakes? We don't have snakes in the lake of Bliss.'

'And giants.' Lokke snickered. 'You can always go back.'

'Fat chance.' She leaped and followed after Jonna. The last part of him dropped into a hole at the bottom of the lake. Without hesitation, she dived. A short time later, she popped out the other end and felt a chill in the water. 'This place,' she shook, 'there is something not right.'

'Not as nice as yours, is it?' Lokke teased. 'Now you see how the other side lives.'

'Other side?'

'Those that do not live in Bliss,' Lokke said pointedly and then changed the subject. 'In order to go up, we must first go down.'

It sounded like Lokke's voice contained jealousy to Jonna. 'Lokke, do I detect bitterness there?'

Lokke went silent.

'By the way, what got you sent to the bad place anyway?'

The silence continued.

Bob was trying to say something, but he could not make it work well underwater.

'Okay, have it your way.' Jonna spotted Cassandra floating not far from him. 'Cassandra, make toward the shore.

Everything seems quiet.' He looked above the water's surface and spotted a bush where he could change. 'This way.'

Bob burst out as they broke the water's surface, "Jonna!"

Jonna crawled out of the water and moved close to the bushes.

Cassandra followed behind and whispered, 'Why are we hiding behind a bush?'

'Because I have to get dressed.' Jonna looked toward the lake. 'Lokke?'

Still no answer.

"Jonna, Lokke's been—" Bob ducked as a branch swished toward him and then realized it would have no effect.

Jonna turned around and moved to the water's edge. 'What happened to Lokke?' He gazed over its still surface. 'We have to go back.'

'Okay.' Cassandra pushed out into the water and prepared to dive.

As Jonna slipped in beside her, Bob pointed. "There."

'What's that?' Jonna turned and spotted three objects coming in their direction. By the narrowness of the wake—

'Snakes!'

Both Jonna and Cassandra backed up. Two of the snakes stopped short, but the one in the middle kept coming. A foot from the shore, the middle one stuck his head above the water. It said gruffly, "You Jonna?"

Jonna blinked his frog eyes. "That's me."

"Hmm," the snake nodded, "you don't look like much."

"Look like much for what?" Was the snake hungry or something? Personally, he thought he appeared about right for a frog. He caught sight of more movements in the water; more snakes were coming to the surface.

"Bring him up, boys," the snake closest to them called. Behind the three in front, five additional snakes dragged up the body of a frog. "Is this one yours?"

"Mine?"

"For such a big hero, you sure ask a lot of questions." The middle snake frowned. "I'll have to keep that in mind. Is he yours or not?"

"Does he have a name?"

"Wake him up, boys." While four of the snakes held the legs, the fifth rammed him in the stomach.

"Plaa!" The frog spewed out water and went into a coughing fit.

"Hey you," the snake that hit him called, "what's your name?"

The frog's eyes opened and uncrossed. "Lokke," he croaked.

"That's him," Jonna nodded, cleaning his eyes with several blinks. "What happened to him?"

"Caught him trying to tie two snake tails together. The boys showed him what happens to meddling frogs."

"Lokke!" Jonna could not believe his ears. Here they were trying to find a way out, and he had to stop to play a practical joke?

Bob scratched his chin. "Actually, that's not a bad trick, if you can do it."

"I'm innocent." Lokke coughed.

"Yeah right." The lead snake sneered. "I know that expression; I've seen enough frogs in my day to know the difference." He turned to Jonna. "Tell you what, since you're a celebrity and all, I'm gonna cut you a break. You can have your friend in one piece."

Lokke's eyes lit up. The fifth snake hit him again, and he groaned.

Jonna thanked him. "That's nice of you."

"It is, isn't it?" The lead snake looked proud of himself. "If you're ever in this lake again, tell 'em my name, Snadrid, and the boys will leave you alone." The four snakes holding Lokke came forward and tossed him up on the shore.

Bob mouthed the name himself. "Snadrid, not bad for a snake."

"And if he ever tries to tie your tails together again," Jonna offered, "you have my blessing to keep him."

"Thanks," Snadrid accepted. "You're all right." The snakes disappeared below the surface.

45

"Thanks." Lokke looked irritate. "Why did you have to steal all my fun?"

Jonna glared. "It was fun getting the water beat out of you?"

"Well—"

The ground jumped.

"So this is Lokke?" Cassandra showed amusement. "You used Jonna's status to get yourself free?"

Lokke groaned. "Whatever works."

"You can see him?" Jonna looked surprised but then thought about what Lokke said. "I guess it was a matter of time."

"Yes," Cassandra's eyes narrowed, "I can see him, but I'm not so sure we need him."

The ground jumped again, but lighter this time.

"See," Bob stressed, "even she agrees!"

Jonna's voice sounded whimsical. "Do you want to throw him to the snakes?"

Bob grinned. "I do, I do!"

"You wouldn't," Lokke looked from Cassandra to Jonna. "You still need me."

"What do you think?" Jonna turned to Cassandra.

The rustle of leaves sounded behind them.

Cassandra looked at him, folding her frog arms. "Personally, I don't know him, but he acts like a lot of trouble." Her eyes narrowed.

Lokke swallowed. "You can't leave me. Please don't leave me!" What had been fun before turned serious.

Shaking his head, Jonna looked at him. "Lokke, are you okay?"

Lokke was beginning to sob. "You don't understand. I've been here for a thousand years, suffered every kind of torment you can imagine, and I can't take it anymore!"

"Lokke, it's okay. We're not going to leave you." Jonna moved closer, sniffing a strange smell in the air. He patted Lokke with a front frog leg.

"Gotcha!" Lokke began to laugh hysterically, hopping up and down. "Did pretty good, didn't I?"

46

"Tsk, tsk, tsk." Bob shook his head. "I told you he was no good. However, you have to admit, he played you on the 'gullible' part pretty well."

"Bob, are you saying you two are alike?"

Bob stopped and then scowled. "Now you're being nasty."

"Lokke," Cassandra growled, not liking the joke at all. She turned away and faced Jonna. "Don't you think it's about time we get out of these frog shapes, please? I'm starting to feel the need to jump into the lake."

"Of course," Jonna searched the area. "Let me hop over there to change—"

A giant hand reached down and scooped up Cassandra. "Frogs! I've got one. I've got one!"

"Let me go!"

The ground began to shake rapidly.

Pointing as more giants ran toward them, Bob's voice shook. "We'd better hurry."

Lokke panicked. "Hide!"

"We can't hide." Jonna still couldn't believe what had happened. "The giant has Cassandra!"

Lokke grabbed Jonna by the leg, dragging him further into the thicket. "You won't do her any good if you get trampled!" Two other giants stomped into view.

One of the two boomed, "Where is it?" Looking around on the ground, he glowered, "I don't see it."

"In my hand, buffoon." The first held out Cassandra. He licked his lips. "It's been a long time."

"Wonder why they're showing up now?"

"Who cares." The third tried to grab her, but the first jerked her away. "It looks delicious."

"No!" Jonna hopped forward, but Lokke caught him and pulled him back.

"Stop that," Lokke warned. "They're playing for keeps!"

"He's right." Bob nodded.

"I know they're playing for keeps." Jonna shook off Lokke's hold. "They're going to eat her. We have to stop them!"

"It doesn't matter," Lokke stated matter-of-factly. "She's dead anyway."

"They haven't eaten her yet!"

"Jonna," Lokke spun him around, "watch my frog lips. She's dead anyway. No matter how alive she seems down here, she is already dead. They can't hurt her by eating her."

The image of Cassandra being chewed, swallowed, passed through the stomach, and out the— "No."

"What do you mean, no?"

"I said, no. I won't let them do it."

"Jonna, they're giants, you can't—"

"*Piqjimi Desfie.*" Jonna changed to human form. Despite his size, the thicket still covered him. As he stepped forward, the branches hit his skin, and he remembered, "*Teff Jilvus.*" His clothes appeared in a pile at his feet.

"Fine." Lokke spoke the change-form spell and appeared beside Jonna. "Get dressed, hero."

Jonna finished with his shirt, pants, and shoes. "Much better." He looked from the thicket to the three giants. They were engaged in some sort of debate.

The first giant bared his teeth. "It's mine."

"Come on," the second begged, "surely you can share at least a third?"

"It's way too small. Find your own. There's at least one other."

"There is?" The third looked up. "There's another?"

The first nodded. "I found mine by the thicket when they scattered."

"Duck!" Lokke grabbed Jonna by the arm and pulled him toward the ground.

Jonna shook loose but kept his head down. "What are you doing? They can't see us."

"It's not the seeing." Lokke touched his nose. "It's the smelling." Both of the giants reached the thicket and began to sniff.

"I don't smell any frogs." The second shook his head. "Only a bunch of lake water, dirt, and—what's that?" He sniffed again, pushing a part of the thicket.

"I don't see anything," the third giant muttered. "I think he's pulling our leg."

Laying his club down, the second looked closer at the thicket. "No, I smell something."

Jonna volunteered, "You draw them. I'll hit them." As they stepped away from the club on the ground, he quietly moved behind them, reached out, and claimed the club. It was heavy, but he could manage.

Lokke didn't act convinced. "You want me to jump out and go boo?"

"You like playing jokes, right?"

"Yeah."

"Yeah," Bob echoed, and then realized he was only there by magic. "Oh man!"

"Think of this as a big prank with a big surprise at the end." Jonna shifted silently through the thicket.

"A prank." Lokke frowned, looked up, and took in the size of the giants. "Okay." He could see the second giant working his way back. "I'll prank him with a heart attack." A devious look crossed his face. "Let's see. Big prank, big prank, got it! He wants a frog, let's give him a frog!" Lokke closed his eyes. "*Laupiqjimi Desfie!*" The thicket swallowed him.

"Here froggy, froggy." The second giant moved closer. "I know you're in here somewhere." The giant froze. There was something green ahead, hiding. "Gotcha!" The giant parted the bushes right before a half-ton frog leaped in his direction.

"Holy Moly!" The giant fell backwards, hit his head on a rock, and knocked himself out.

The third giant looked up. "Kimur?" He pushed pieces of the thicket back. "Where did you go?"

Bob fell backwards, dying with laughter.

Lokke hid in another part of the thicket. "Hey you!"

The giant looked around. "Me?"

"Yeah you!" Lokke croaked. "You want a piece of me?"

The giant sniffed and gave a broad smile. "Frog," his eyes lit up. "Wait right there."

Lokke chuckled. "Okay."

Jonna jumped, moving out of the giant's path. The club slipped from his hands. Scrambling to find it, he came around the other side.

"I'm here froggy. Come out, come out, wherever you are."

Lokke snickered. "Right here, goof brain!"

The giant parted a thicket. Lokke blinked, a huge grin breaking out over his frog face. "Boo."

The giant screamed. Jonna knocked the giant out to get silence.

"What are you doing?" he whispered, though why he did not know. Both giants were out. "We needed to do this quietly!"

Bob couldn't stop laughing.

"You said prank," Lokke rolled with laughter as he changed back. "I'm following orders."

"I didn't want the whole army here!" He looked for the first giant. "At least the other one hasn't eaten—where'd he go?" His heart stopped.

Lokke spoke offhanded, "I saw him head to town."

"Lokke, now we have to go to town!"

A mischievous look crossed Lokke's face. "We do?"

"You planned this!"

Wiping tears from his eyes, Bob agreed. "Oh yes he did!"

"Did I?"

Jonna inhaled. "Come on." He started through the thicket. "If she gets eaten—"

"She'll come out the other end," Lokke chuckled.

"If she gets eaten, I'll throw you to the snakes!"

"You wouldn't," he smiled, "you said you wouldn't." His teeth gleamed.

"Then I'll find something else," Jonna warned, "and I promise, you won't like it!"

Moving up to match Jonna's speed, Lokke shook his head incredulously. "What would the fun be in taking a journey without a little adventure?"

Bob leaned toward Jonna's ear. "He's right, you know."

"Safer," Jonna threw a glare. "We're already on dangerous ground. Promise me you'll not do that again."

"Me?" Bob looked shocked. "I didn't do anything."

Lokke put his hand behind his back and crossed his fingers. "I promise." His teeth gleamed.

Jonna looked for the giant's tracks. If they weren't careful, they might trip in one.

"He went this way." Lokke followed a second pair of tracks.

"How do you know?"

"Well," he thought out loud, "if I were a giant about to eat a frog, though why I don't know since I don't eat frogs, I would take it to a more secluded spot. Maybe a cabin or cottage outside the city."

Jonna studied the tracks; he might be right. Most of the tracks headed toward the city, but one pair lead away.

"Uh oh." Bob's voice changed. "Gotta go!"

"Go where?"

A pop sounded as Bob removed the ring.

"Bob?"

Lokke shook his head. "We've discussed that, and I'm not Bob." He mumbled, "Crazed human."

They changed course. Over the next rise, there was an oversized cottage. They moved to the outside wall and listened under the front window. A giant was singing.

"I didn't know giants could sing." Lokke stuck his fingers in his ears. "Actually, I don't think this one can."

Jonna grimaced. "At least the noise should give us some cover. Come on."

Moving around the corner, Jonna spotted a wooden wheelbarrow rolled next to the cottage. It sat below an open, side window.

"Up here." He climbed, balanced on the edge, and grabbed the windowsill. Peeking over, he could see the giant moving. Where was Cassandra?

"Lokke, change into a frog."

Lokke came up beside him. "Why? I just changed into a person."

"We have to find Cassandra. You'll be able to talk to her."

He closed his eyes and then opened them. "Can I be the big frog?"

"Can you do it without drawing attention?" Did he have to spell it out every time?

Lokke grinned. "Probably not."

"Well," Jonna looked at him, "what do you think?"

"Oh, come on. I really want to be the big one!"

'Children!' Jonna thought and then realized Lokke should be his elder. He paused a moment to consider that. Nope. "Okay, but—"

"*Laupiqjimi Desfie.*" Lokke changed into an enlarged frog. The wheelbarrow groaned. Jonna leaped to safety. Lokke jumped because he could and then hurried to the front door.

"What was that?" A giant came to the window. It looked left, right, and down. "My wheelbarrow!" He dropped his dipping spoon and rushed to the front door. Throwing the door open, he stared at the huge, half-ton frog.

Lokke demanded, "Give her up."

The giant's eyes widened, and he fainted. As he struck backwards, the cottage shook. Lokke rolled over, doing nothing but laughing.

"Lokke." Jonna tried to get his attention, but a one ton frog laughing was a little hard to control. "Lokke." Jonna was losing patience. "Come here, now!"

Slowly, the one ton frog rolled over and landed on its feet.

"Did you contact Cassandra?"

Lokke snickered. "Didn't you laugh even a little?"

"No. Where is Cassandra?"

"Let me check." He paused. "Hmm, mmmm, hmm." Lokke looked at Jonna. "She doesn't know where she is."

"I know that. Is she in water? In a pot of some kind? Can she knock on the side?" Sheesh!

"Oh, that, let me see." Lokke consulted again. "A pot." He paused with his eyes still closed. "With a lid."

Jonna heard knocking from within the cottage. Stepping

over the legs of the giant, he entered the one-room cottage. It was a little awkward, but he made his way to the kitchen table. The sound was coming from the second pot on the stove.

Lokke blinked. "And she's knocking."

"I know." Jonna kept his voice down. "I heard her."

As he raised the heavy metal lid with two hands, Cassandra, still in frog form, leaped onto the table and jumped to the floor. She transformed into a human, turned around, and glared at Lokke through the open door.

"You—" Her face flamed red.

"Me?" Lokke croaked. He tried to make an innocent expression, thought better of it, and cringed. "What did I do?"

Cassandra turned to Jonna. "Leave him. Leave him now!"

Jonna turned from Cassandra to Lokke. "What did you do?"

"I helped him find you," Lokke offered as penance. "Doesn't that count for something?"

"You let him take me!" Her temper had reached its limit. "You stood there, and let him take me!"

Lokke cowered from her words. "I did help find you."

"I could have been eaten!"

"You would have passed through." He cringed again. "It wouldn't have hurt that much."

Cassandra picked up the nearest loose object and threw it at him.

"Hey!" Lokke ducked and looked offended. "There's no call for that!" He ducked another item and watched it bounce off the ground. That was not easy for a frog his size. "*Laupiqjimi Desfie!*"

As she reached for a set of knives, Lokke leaped for the side wall, and Jonna caught her hand. "Shh," he pointed down at the giant. Though still unconscious, the giant could wake up. "I think we ought to leave."

"Leave him!" She pointed at Lokke, dropping the volume of her voice only slightly. "I don't trust him!"

There was the sound of a pop in Jonna's ear. Bob had

returned. The pixie gazed around at the change in scenery and spotted the giant on the floor of the cottage. "What did I miss?"

Jonna took Cassandra by the hand, guided her out the door, and over the sleeping giant's body. "We can't."

Bob tried again, attempting to make some sense of the situation. "I hope nothing good?"

Her eyes shot daggers. "And why not?"

"He's the guide, and you know we need him, unless you have a better idea."

Cassandra turned and glared at Lokke.

Lokke gave a half-smile. "He's right. So you see, you have to forgive me."

"Do not." She turned away as they walked.

Bob huffed. "I knew I missed something!"

Lokke begged, "Aww, come on. I was having fun."

"Bob, shh!"

Lokke shook his head. "I told you, I'm not Bob."

It was obvious to Jonna this was going nowhere, and he had to do something to intervene. "Lokke, look at me."

He turned to look at Jonna.

"How long have you wanted to get out of here?"

Lokke kept rolling his eyes, but they finally stopped. "Well, I," his shoulders dropped, "at least a thousand years."

"I thought so." Jonna glanced at Cassandra, confirmed she was watching, and then turned back. "If you don't protect Cassandra with all your might, she and I will turn around and go back. Do you understand?"

Lokke looked at Cassandra. "But what about Jonna getting out?"

"She and I will find another way without your help," Jonna answered for her, and then turned to Cassandra. "I promise."

Her eyes shot darts at Lokke. "That's good enough for me."

Bob hit himself on the forehead. "So that's what I missed!"

"Oh, all right. No more jokes, at least not with our lives." That mischievous look crossed Lokke's face.

"Lokke."

He looked away whistling. "I know, I know."

"You mean it?" Cassandra turned to Jonna. "You'd really go back?" She faced him.

"If it means keeping you safe, I would. I'd rather you were not here now."

She smiled. "My husband used to be that way," she reminisced fondly, "but that was a long time ago."

Bob jumped in. "Elpis says he was taken away by the mages in the city of Diggory. He could have been in Chernobog."

No one spoke for a moment as they walked in silence.

The pixie growled in Jonna's ear, "You're not listening!"

Jonna whispered to Bob. "Based upon what I saw in Chernobog, there's a strong probability he wasn't." Jonna knew that Cassandra was familiar with some of the finer points of Chernobog. Elpis had gone with him when he was trying to find his wife.

"What's Chernobog?" Lokke caught the word from the whisper. He paused and then raised up a hand. "I know. It's a surface town."

"It was more like a prison. The Dark Mages would send people there who they wanted out of the way."

"Really?" Lokke's eyes brightened. "You think when we get out I can go and see it?"

"You want to go to a prison?"

"Well, no, but if it's a surface town, it can't be all bad." He looked from Jonna to Cassandra. "Can it?"

Jonna cleared his throat. "I think we're off the subject."

Bob jumped in. "We certainly are! I'm not going back, at least not on purpose."

"Bob, watch what you say."

Lokke spun around. "How many times does it take for you not to call me Bob?"

Jonna started to laugh. It took Cassandra by surprise, but after a moment she joined in.

"What's so funny?" Lokke looked from one to the other. He joined in despite the lack of understanding. He wiped the tears from his eyes. "Please, tell me why we are laughing?" He tried to catch his breath but started again.

"He's serious." Cassandra glanced at Jonna. "He really doesn't know?"

Jonna shook his head. "You would think he would have figured it out."

"Don't know what?" Lokke tried to stop again, fighting his own chuckles.

"Jonna's not calling you Bob. He's talking to his pixie friend."

Lokke's head snapped toward Jonna completely sober. "Where?" He spun around, extremely fidgety. "Where is he?"

"Right here, buffoon." Bob pointed a finger at Lokke. "And I've got your number!"

Lokke stopped and stared. A grin started across his face. "Oh, I get it. It's play a joke on Lokke time." He walked over to Cassandra and pointed a finger at her. "You know more than you let on." A smile crossed his face. "You know pixies and my kind don't get along. We're diametrically opposed forces."

Jonna was surprised. "You are?"

"Of course we are," Bob huffed. "Didn't Väinämö teach you that in mage class?"

A sheepish grin passed over Jonna's face. "If he did, I might not have been listening."

Turning toward him, Lokke stared. "There you go again. You might as well add the name Bob at the end!"

"That's because Bob is here." Cassandra pointed at him.

Folding his arms, Lokke stared at them both. "So you can see him, too?"

Cassandra shook her head. "No."

"Then how do you know?"

Bob pushed, "Tell him!"

Shaking his head, Jonna declined. "I thought you wanted it a secret?"

"I'd rather see the terror in his eyes." Bob glared,

interlacing his fingers and stretching them palms forward. "Maybe it will keep him in line."

The idea was intriguing. He turned toward Lokke. "Though magic I don't understand, Bob, the pixie on my shoulder, can hear, see, and interact with me while he's still on the surface."

Lokke's eyes widened. "No way!"

"Yes way." Cassandra pushed the point.

Bob gave a smug smile.

"And," Jonna added, "if you don't behave, he has your number."

Cassandra gave a mischievous chuckle of her own. "I rather like that."

"But he's not here." Lokke tested the waters. "So, he can't do anything." A grin hit his face. "This is great!" Looking one to the other, he pushed, "So where's he at? Come on, please tell me!"

"Oh," Bob threw up his hands, "go ahead. Tell him."

"He's on my right shoulder."

The look in Lokke's eyes was pure delight. He turned to face Jonna's right shoulder and stuck out his tongue. "Na-na, na-na, na-na. You're on the surface and can't do a thing about it." Kicking his feet, he danced around Jonna.

"Lokke?" Jonna tried to get his attention.

Bob fumed as Lokke continued to dance.

"Lokke."

Forced to pause for breath, Lokke stopped. "This is more fun than I've had in a long time!"

Jonna gave Lokke the same look Väinämö gave Jonna in class. "You do realize you are trying to get to the surface?"

"Yes." He danced back and forth, making pointing motions at the unseen pixie. "I know you're fuming now. Powerless, I say!" He jumped with glee.

"And you do realize you will probably meet the pixie you are teasing in the flesh?"

Lokke froze in mid-step. "I hadn't thought of that."

"You tell him," Bob growled, "I've a handful of pixie dust waiting for his little red skin!"

57

"Let's not be hasty," Jonna warned. "I'm sure Lokke will be a little more agreeable now."

"What did he say?" Lokke fidgeted, his fingers moving quickly.

"He says if you don't straighten up, he'll send you back."

Bob's eyes widened. "I did? But I can't do that!"

"He did?" Lokke bit his lip. "He can do that?"

Jonna shrugged. "Have you ever faced a pixie before?"

Lokke shook his head. "But my great grandfather did. He-er—" He looked at Jonna's face. "Maybe some other time."

Jonna nodded. "That might be better."

"Pixie on the shoulder." Lokke nodded. "Gotcha." He reached over, and attempted to pat Bob on the head. "Good little pixie. We need to be friends."

"Hey, back off bub!"

A laugh escaped Jonna's lips. "We need to go."

Lokke spun heel and took off.

"Where's he going?" Cassandra was impressed at his burst speed. "Isn't this toward the lake?"

Jonna nodded.

"That'll teach him." Bob resumed his smug expression.

"I hope so."

Jonna started after him with Cassandra by his side. They reached the hill and turned to the right, heading for a group of boulders. Lokke moved to one of the boulders and pushed it. As the boulder slid, a small cave appeared, slanting down into the earth.

Chapter 5

ANAXA

"From here, we crawl." Lokke motioned toward the hole. "I'll close the boulder." With the boulder removed, there was a slight sound from inside the cave.

Bob rolled his eyes. "Thinks he's something, doesn't he?"

"Quiet, Bob." Jonna listened but could not be sure what it was. Maybe the wind? He bent to all fours and moved into the darkness. The air smelled moist. As his eyes adjusted, he began to see.

Wow, Bob's spell still worked! When he had gone to rescue Stephanie, Bob had given him pixie sight, but he had not used it since. He had assumed it would wear off after a while.

The pixie's explanation about how it worked was simple. While the female pixies used an entourage of fireflies to see with, the male pixies used a form of magical x-ray vision. He stopped to listen for the others. Cassandra ran into him.

"Ouch!" Pulling her hand back, she felt the area in front of her and found Jonna's foot. "What happened?"

"I can see. The spell still works."

"Of course it still works," Bob stood proudly. "It's pixie magic. Not at all like Otherworld magic."

Lokke was all ears. "What spell?"

"The—" Jonna smiled. "Now I'm starting to understand."

59

If a spell were established on the surface, it would continue to stay in effect wherever a person went. At least that was his hypothesis.

"Understand what?" Lokke asked expectantly. It was a little too expectantly. Was Lokke simply curious because he wanted to learn surface magic, or was there something else? Bob kept preaching danger, but Lokke seemed sincere in wanting to get out. For the moment, Jonna let the debate slide.

"The way is straight so far," Jonna hurried along. The sound he had heard became clear enough to understand. It was dripping water. He stopped abruptly at a crossroads. "Lokke, which way?"

"It doesn't matter. All of them go down."

Jonna looked down the first tunnel, but could see nothing to distinguish it from the other. "Down is a relative term. How far down do we go before heading up?"

Lokke paused as if in debate. "Left."

Bob shook his head. "That took way too long."

Jonna started forward. The dripping echoed all around.

"But watch out for the—"

Jonna hit something wet and slick; he should have seen it coming. Turning around, he spun and grabbed for the sides.

"Jonna!" Cassandra reached out and tried to grab his hand in the darkness but missed and tumbled forward. Like slipping on a super slick water slide, she zipped down behind him. "Lokke!"

Lokke laughed and listened to them slide down the water drenched path. "I tried to tell you!" Sitting down, he put his feet forward and pushed off, speeding up to catch them. "Jer-ron-a-mo!"

Bob kept yelling in Jonna's ear. "I told you, I told you, I told you!"

"Bob, cut it out. I have to think!" Seeing on a slide with no way to stop was certainly better than not seeing at all. Unfortunately, all Cassandra could do was follow the sounds he made.

That brought up an interesting question. Why couldn't the dead see in the dark? Instead of pursuing it, he pushed the rabbit from his mind.

Turning onto his back, he pulled his legs together, kept his knees slightly bent, and placed his arms on his chest. He only hoped there were no unexpected obstacles.

What choice did they have? They were out of control in a situation where they did not know the way. They were led by a creature who would as well help as see you dead for a joke.

Bob closed his eyes. "I can't look!"

"Bob, now is not the time."

The stalactites and stalagmites whizzed by as shapes close up became a blur. Those far away showed glimpses of greenish light. Every once in a while, he saw a humanoid shape. Humanoids? Where were they heading now?

Lokke called out with glee, "To the left on the next slide!"

Cassandra shouted, her echoes sounding around them, "I don't think this a bit funny!"

"Don't be a sourpuss," Lokke shot back. "Enjoy the ride!"

Jonna saw it; there was a fork in the slide. "Hard left," he called back, seeing at a glance the other two behind him. He shifted his weight to the left, but it was not enough. At his present speed, he would ram into the middle of the fork.

A hand reached out tagging his shoulder. How Cassandra had reached him in the dark, unable to see, he did not know.

"Hold on!" She tried to use her momentum to push, but her efforts were no better than his.

Jonna called to all, "We've got to go right, or we'll never make it!"

"No," Lokke hollered from behind, "not right!"

Cassandra tried to look back. "We don't have a choice!"

Jonna shifted, the additional mass of Cassandra being enough to do the job. They slid away from the center and dropped down the right slide.

"Dog-gon-it!" Lokke growled. He rolled and bounced off the left side of the slide. It shifted his body to the right, but not enough; he was going to hit the middle.

61

"*Tmuw Fam!*" The words echoed down the cave. In slow motion he spread his arms, flew into the air, caught a pillar, swung around, and dropped onto the right slide.

"*Mitmuw Fam,*" he coughed between breaths as his speed picked up. A moment later, Lokke was matching speed behind them.

"Good save." Jonna noted the phrases as his brain worked on their meaning. "For a moment, I thought you were a goner."

"I never had a doubt," Lokke wiped the sweat from his forehead, blotting his horn, "but we're still on the wrong slide."

Jonna began as the echoes stopped, "So what happens—"

Cassandra shrieked, Jonna turned, and Bob shook his head as they flew into the open air. Down below was a steaming lake; bubbles exploded from its surface.

"Lokke, we need a spell!"

"I'm thinking, I'm thinking!"

Jonna watched the heat waves dance. Water sprayed into the air. "That's some hot lake."

Cassandra clung to Jonna's arm. "It's coming up fast!"

Lokke focused on the lake below. "*Jid Vusb!*" The entire surface of the lake froze into ice.

"Not enough." Jonna thought about what Lokke had said earlier. He held his fingers together and spoke, "*Tmuw Fam!*"

Their momentum slowed, and they floated toward the ice. The moment their feet touched, the ice began to crack, and he spoke "*Mitmuw Fam.*"

The ice cracked around them. All three jumped to separate sections.

"What spell can we use to speed ourselves up?"

Lokke closed his eyes. "You said it already, Mitmuw Fam."

So Mitmuw Fam meant speed up, and Tmuw Fam meant slow down; at first Jonna thought Mitmuw Fam meant return to normal. He said the spell. "*Mitmuw Fam.* Run!"

"Run," Lokke mimicked, terror in his voice. "The ice won't last long!"

All three raced for the shore.

"Why ice?" Jonna breathed quickly, never slowing a moment. "Couldn't you have come up with something else?"

"I didn't have much time to think," Lokke panted. "All I could think of was not getting boiled, and since the opposite of hot is cold, and ice is really cold—" He huffed. "I've never done this before!"

Jonna laughed. "Me neither."

The ice was melting on every side. The spell Lokke had cast was radial, rather than linear. As a result, as they neared the shore, the ice broke free, having melted on the outer edges.

"Jump!" Jonna grabbed Cassandra's hand, leaped over the steaming water, and landed on the edge of the bank. Their feet no sooner touched than Lokke hit them from behind, shoved them forward, and knocked all to the ground. Jonna and Cassandra gasped as they hit, the air knocked out of their lungs.

Lokke covered his head, afraid to open his eyes. "Did I make it?"

Taking in air, Jonna breathed, *Tmuw Fam,* bringing them to normal movement "Lokke, please get your elbow out of my back."

"And mine." Cassandra turned, pushing Lokke to the side.

He rolled over onto his back and looked up. His eyes moved slowly as he scanned the sky above them. "Shh," he whispered, "I think we're being watched."

"After our last display, I wouldn't be surprised," Jonna whispered. He spotted a large hut with several rooms attached. Directly in front, looking down at them, was a tall humanoid with light blue skin.

"Lokke," the humanoid glared at him, "how nice to have you visit."

Lokke swallowed, rolled over onto his stomach, and stood up. Placing himself between the humanoid and his group, he gave a slight bow. "Er, a—Master Anaxa." He looked rather sheepish. "I've brought visitors." He turned to wave a hand toward Jonna and Cassandra. At the same time, he mouthed the words 'play along', and then swung to face Anaxa, a half-grin on his face.

"I'm sure you did." Anaxa looked down at Jonna and Cassandra. "More guests? What did you tell them this time?"

"You've brought other people down here?" Cassandra's face snapped toward Lokke. "I thought you wanted to get out?"

Bob put a hand over his eyes. "I knew this was bad. I told you!"

"He does." Anaxa caught their attention. "He just can't seem to do it."

"What?" Jonna turned toward Lokke, not exactly sure who was playing whom. "I thought you knew how to get to the gates?"

Lokke slipped to the right and backed up to put distance between himself and Anaxa. "I do." He made a strange hand sign behind his back. It was something Anaxa could not see, but Jonna could. Unfortunately, Jonna had no idea of the meaning.

A strange smell erupted behind Lokke. Glancing back, he saw the lake water nipping at his heels. He took an abrupt step forward.

"I'm sorry," Jonna turned to Anaxa, "we did not mean to intrude."

Anaxa pointed to the area past the lake. "It's not me you have to worry about." Small, dark groups of beings moved in their direction. "The humanoids on this level don't like intruders. They're not fast, but they keep coming." Anaxa nodded his head. "I would suggest we retire to the hut."

As Anaxa turned to face them, Jonna caught sight of a white mist moving through the creatures' ranks. What was that? He could have sworn it was following him, but how? Rather than draw attention to it, he continued, "Thank you." He helped Cassandra to her feet. "We appreciate the hospitality."

"You might not later," Anaxa shook his head and turned to Lokke. "Move."

Lokke's eyes lit up. "Thank you, sir." He shot forward, passed them all, and disappeared into the hut. The door slammed closed before the other three could get there. Anaxa waved a hand for them to follow.

As the door opened, the furniture inside mirrored the barren landscape. The walls were not adorned, and the seats were carved from stone. Cassandra entered in front of him with Anaxa bringing up the rear.

Anaxa spoke pleasantly, "Please, be seated."

"I must confess," Jonna made a frown, glancing at Lokke. "This news about Lokke makes me doubt everything he's said."

Bob growled, "Maybe next time you'll listen to your old buddy Bob!"

Lokke tried to look sorrowful but didn't do a good job.

"What did he tell you?" Anaxa reached for a stone pitcher, pouring out a drink into stone cups already on the table. "Tea?"

Jonna and Cassandra accepted, sipping it.

"That he escaped from the worst part of the Otherworld."

Anaxa nodded. "True."

"See," Lokke made a smug face, "I was telling the truth!"

Bob laughed. "I give it a pinch of salt, but I'd like to use a pinch of pixie dust instead." He stared at Lokke, hand on his pixie dust bag as he measured what he would need. "Too bad he's not up here with me!"

"That he's lived here for at least a thousand years."

Anaxa nodded again. "True."

Closing his eyes, Bob thought. "That might be true, although, he does seem a little young."

"You should never have doubted me." Lokke folded his arms, still maintaining his smug face.

"That he knows the way out."

"True."

Jonna and Cassandra looked at each other, and both spoke, "He does?"

Bob couldn't believe it. "My thoughts exactly!"

Anaxa nodded his head. "Everyone knows the way out. It is not knowing the way out that is the problem. It is getting through the gates. The gates are guarded by three different obstacles. Not only that, if you do get there but do not get through the obstacles before they catch you," he threw a glance at Lokke, "you lose your present status and get sent to the bottom level."

"Torment, incredible torment!" Lokke screamed and sighed as if reliving it all again. "That's why I've attempted escape three hundred times!"

"Three hundred?" Jonna and Cassandra spoke at once. Anaxa laughed, Lokke looked embarrassed, and Bob groaned.

"How else do you think he's learned the way so well," Anaxa chuckled, "and he was not alone, were you Lokke?"

"Er—no," Lokke sighed. "Most of those that went with me never regained their beginning status."

"They couldn't," Anaxa agreed. "They were caught outside their area. Because of this, it became part of their punishment."

"I told you," Lokke stressed again, "Cassandra should not have come."

"Sir," Cassandra turned to Anaxa, "Jonna is not dead and has been brought to the Otherworld against his will."

Anaxa raised an eyebrow. "Is that so?" Lokke knew more than he was saying; it was in his eyes.

"Unfortunately, yes," Jonna admitted, but felt nervous about saying much more. "Cassandra is not to blame for leaving her own level." Jonna could feel Cassandra's eyes on him as he said it, but she remained silent.

"I see." Anaxa left the room and returned with some paper. "Obeying the law," he glanced at Lokke, "has earned me a few favors over the years. I was made magistrate of this level and hope to continue to work my way up. Perhaps I can help."

Cassandra accepted the paper, reading down the page, and then she looked up. "It's an application against wrongful placement. I don't understand."

"It can also be used to return a person to their level if taken against their will. Though, there may not be much I can do for Jonna, I may at least get you to your own level. We will have to verify that you were brought against your will."

Bob couldn't stay silent. "He's trying to separate the group."

Jonna cleared his throat. "So there is a way to work up levels?"

Anaxa paused only a second. "Yes, although, it doesn't happen often. Most try to sneak up." He glared at Lokke.

Cassandra did not like what the paper implied. "Is there not a way to help Jonna?"

"Possibly," Anaxa tugged at his beard, "but I'll have to do some asking, and won't be able to do it until the morning. I would suggest you both have a good night's sleep." He took the paperwork from Cassandra. "You can fill this out later."

Come to think about it, Jonna was getting sleepy, and that in itself was sort of strange. This was the first time he had even thought about sleep since he had entered the Otherworld. To his surprise, Cassandra was nodding off. Did the dead have to sleep too? Brutus had acted like he was sleepy when Jonna had first gone to get Cassandra.

Lokke yawned, pretending to be tired. "Can I go too?"

"You stay." Anaxa gave a thin-lined smile. "I want to talk to you."

Jonna and Cassandra stood. They moved toward the room Anaxa pointed out, almost zombie like. As they passed by Lokke, there was something in his eyes. Was Lokke trying to warn them of something?

The room Anaxa gave them was bare but clean. There was one stone bed with hay for a matress.

Cassandra dropped onto the bed glad to rest. "Jonna," she turned toward him, "I fear I've only made your peril worse."

Jonna sat down on the edge of the bed, thinking of all the things they had gone through so far. "Is that The Sight talking, or the result of talking with Anaxa?"

"I should never have let you leave Bliss." She fought against it but could not help the yawn. "You've put yourself in great danger. This is my world, not yours, not yet, and maybe never."

"What do you mean never? From what I understand, all those of the surface come here."

Cassandra shook her head. "We were born to this world of magic. You came from another. What happens when you die is determined by the Fates."

"You mean fate," he yawned. "Nobody knows until the time comes."

She shook her head again. "I mean Fates, plural. Only they can tell you what will happen when you die."

Then it hit him. "They are real here?" Despite the revelation, his eyes wanted to close. "What do I have to do? Go talk to them?"

Cassandra looked up as if seeing something. "If you want to find your place in this world, you will have to talk to the Fates."

"You've seen something else. Does that happen often?" It would make sense. If Jonna retained his pixie sight, other mages could certainly retain their gifts.

"There are some things which stay forever. This is good and bad."

"Why?"

"For instance," she looked toward one of the blank walls, "when I see that my daughter is heading into danger, that she will be hurt or scared, so often I am tempted to intervene, yet there are times I cannot without causing further harm."

Something clicked in Jonna's mind. "You see these things even better in the Otherworld. In Bliss you are relaxed, unhindered, yet you cannot find the fate your husband?" Could the thought of her husband's fate have such a reaction in her that even in Bliss she could not relax?

With eyes closed, Cassandra nodded. "The more at peace a person is with their surroundings, the more The Sight can communicate the future and present. It can even bring up the past."

Jonna chuckled sleepily. "That explains why I have seen nothing since I defeated the giant in the duel."

She studied him, waiting.

"Ever since I found out who Elfleda was—"

"And Elpis called you daddy." Cassandra smiled. Her eyes were extremely heavy, yet she continued to follow his thoughts.

"That too," he nodded, fighting another yawn. "Ever since then, I don't know what to do. Who am I? What is my purpose other than protecting the queen's realm?"

"All the more reason to talk to the Fates." Cassandra laid her head on a makeshift pillow and gave into a final yawn. "Wow, I've never been so sleepy."

"Come to think of it," Jonna had a hard time focusing his eyes, "me neither." He turned to Cassandra who had already fallen asleep, shook his head, and watched the bedroom wall fade from sight.

*   *   *

Lokke slapped Jonna again. "Wake up!"

Jonna's cheek stung as he half-opened his eyes; they were so heavy. On top of staring at Lokke, his ears picked up another sound. It was someone rubbing on paper. "Bob, what are you doing?"

"Writing my memoirs."

"Your what?"

"My memoirs. You know, all the details that are happening while you are in the Otherworld."

"But those aren't your memoirs, they're mine."

He shook his finger at Jonna. "Don't you be jealous. Just because I can pop in and out, doesn't mean I'm not there."

Lokke's hand went back as he prepared to strike again.

Jonna reached up and caught it. "Lokke, what are you doing?"

"You're awake!" Excitment danced in his eyes. "Good! Up! We've got to go." He tried to drag Jonna to his feet.

Jonna pulled back. "What's got into you?" His legs were not responding yet, and fog was in his brain. He looked down. "What's wrong with me? Why am I beside the bed?"

Lokke glared at him. "What do you think? You fell asleep before you laid on it. Come on, let's go!" His arms jerked at Jonna.

"Lokke!" Jonna pulled back again. The emotion helped clear his mind.

"Didn't you get the hint?" Lokke imitated the look he gave them as they walked out of the living room.

Jonna did remember something, but recalling the details was fuzzy. "What do you mean?"

"He drugged you. He's trying to keep you here until Dagda comes. Don't you get it?"

Still trying to clear his head, Jonna closed his eyes. "Why would he do that?"

"Why wouldn't he? How do you think he gets promoted to the next level? On his good looks? No." He grabbed Jonna's arm, and this time Jonna complied, opening his eyes wider.

"You're sure?" Jonna looked to the bed. Cassandra was still asleep.

"I'm sure. Let's go!" He tried to pull Jonna toward the door.

"Cassandra first." Moment by moment, he regained his bodily control and with it his mental facilities. Lokke was right. The more his mind cleared, the more he knew they had been drugged.

"There's no time. He'll be back soon!"

Jonna moved to Cassandra's side and tried to wake her up.

"There's no time!" Lokke attempted to get between them. "The drug is stronger on the dead than the undead. We will have to leave her."

Jonna raised up her head, trying to get a response. "No. If she won't wake up, we'll have to carry her."

Bob's writing speeded up and sounded like scratches on wood. Jonna's head throbbed. "Do you have to do that right now?"

Lokke looked from Cassandra to him.

Jonna sighed. "Not you. I'm talking to Bob."

The pixie looked up from his hands and knees, grinning. He was standing on all fours with the top part of a piece of paper showing. "Sorry about that; the ink ran low. I'll get another ink bottle."

"You do that."

A pop sounded in Jonna's ear.

Snapping his fingers, Lokke caught Jonna's attention. "Back to the subject, please." He tugged at Jonna, but when he wouldn't budge, he threw up his arms. "We'll never make it out if we carry her," he folded his arms stubbornly, "and you can't do it alone."

"If you don't help," Jonna countered, "I'm not going."

"You wouldn't."

"I would." The look in Jonna's eyes backed up the point.

"You would," Lokke growled. "Fine, we'll try it, but when we get caught—"

"If we get caught." Jonna lifted Cassandra up. Throwing one of her arms over his shoulder, he waited for Lokke to get the other.

Lokke jumped as a part of the hut creaked. "When."

Jonna ignored him. "Ready?"

"No!"

"Good."

They moved toward the door, looking out into the hall.

"You said he was out?"

"He'll be here at any moment!"

"Is there a back door?"

Lokke thought and shook his head. "Our only chance is the way we came in. We need to move faster!"

"That's it." Jonna thought about what Lokke had done on the slide down. "We'll make our own back door. *Mitmuw Fam.*" He pushed the door to the bedroom and watched it move slower.

"What are you doing?" Lokke fidgeted. "That's not faster."

"The faster we move, the slower the objects around us will appear."

"You can't do that."

"Whose side are you on?" Jonna dared him to answer in the wrong way.

"I only meant," Lokke back-stepped, though he could not go far holding Cassandra up, "I've never thought of using a spell in this manner." He cleared his throat.

"That's exactly what you did on the slide."

"But that was on a slide."

"And that's what we did on the ice."

"But that was the ice."

Jonna inhaled. "How do I make us move even faster?"

Lokke looked around. "I don't know."

"I want faster." Jonna thought of a few comic books he remembered. "If we go fast enough, we can walk through walls."

Interest sparkled in Lokke's eyes. "Really?"

Jonna stared at him. "Do you want to stand here or tell me how to say it?"

"I—" Lokke thought. "How about Wiseotmuw Fam?"

"*Wiseotmuw Fam.*" Jonna reached toward the door and pushed it. It moved slow, but not slow enough. "Nope, not fast enough."

"Not fast enough?" Lokke's eyes widened. "Do you realize if you pushed the door right now, it would take a day to fly closed?"

"Still not good enough." Jonna shook his head. "Give me another."

A pop sounded in Jonna's ear. "I'm back," Bob called. "I got a new one."

Lokke huffed and closed his eyes. "Okay, how about this? Fyusftmuw Fam?"

"*Fyusftmuw Fam.*" Jonna touched the door again. This time it warped inward, like pushing on jelly.

Bob stared at the swinging door. "What did I miss?"

"Wow," Lokke poked a wall, "That's fast—I mean slow. How does this work again?"

Jonna shook his head. "But not fast enough."

Lokke stared at him.

"I need something else." Jonna paused. When it did not come, he spoke, "I'm waiting."

"Hmm." Lokke thought, closing his eyes tight. "How about Tupytfyusf tmuw Fam?"

"You expect me to say that?"

Lokke grinned. "You asked."

"*Tupytfyusftmuw Fam.*" Jonna hoped he got the syllables correct.

Slapping his forehead, Bob almost lost what was in his hands. "Oh, I get it!"

The mischievous look in Lokke's eyes came back. He was starting to enjoy this. "Not bad."

Jonna reached forward. Instead of warping the door, his hand passed through. "That's it." They turned, heading toward the nearest wall.

"Did you see that?" Lokke glanced to Cassandra and then paused when there was no response. "Oh yeah, you're asleep." He looked to Jonna. "You saw that!"

Jonna chuckled. "I did. You said we needed to go, remember?"

"I didn't know this was possible!"

Eyes wide, Bob shook his head in awe. "Me neither!"

Jonna moved forward with a chuckle as Lokke kept in step. "Even after a thousand years? I am honored." The three, including Bob on Jonna's shoulder, passed through the wall of the hut and emerged on the other side. It was daylight. "Bob, you still there?"

"Yeah," he breathed heavily. The something out of sight made more rubbing sounds. Whatever method he was using to write did not seem easy.

"Honored?" Lokke narrowed his eyes at Jonna. "You were being sarcastic."

"Was I?" Jonna chuckled again. "Which way great guide?"

"To where?" Lokke looked around. "Up or down?"

"Neither. I want a place to hide until Cassandra wakes up."

"But, when Anaxa finds we're gone—"

"I know. This area will be swarming with something designed to hunt us down, but I don't want to move until Cassandra can give her thoughts."

"Why?"

"Cassandra can answer that." Jonna nodded toward the nearest rocks. "What about a cave?"

Lokke shivered. "Not safe. You remember those humanoids?"

Jonna nodded.

"Imagine more of them with sharp nails all trying to tear you apart."

"Okay, no place easily accessible." Jonna's eyes searched the distance. "But there has to be some place." He looked across the steaming lake and spotted a waterfall which dropped from above. The waterfall poured out of the cliff somewhere beneath where they first emerged. Jonna looked up to the right, and a thought crossed his mind. "Is there something behind the waterfall?"

"How should I know?" Lokke did a double-take. "You want to go across the boiling lake?"

"We can pass through walls, and the ground seems solid." He stomped it. "So why not?"

"Walls can't burn you." Lokke shook his head. "This water—"

"We should be moving fast enough to compensate." Jonna watched for motion in the lake. "It is as still as when the water was frozen. Ready?" He stepped out onto the lake and tested the surface with his feet.

"Sure," Lokke rolled his eyes. "Go for it." He sighed, mumbling to himself, "Boy, can I pick 'em."

Jonna watched the water. Whatever speed they were going, there was enough density to hold them up.

At any moment, Lokke expected his feet to heat up and burn off. "You do know this is bad stuff?"

Jonna snickered. "I guessed that. I noted how fast the ice melted."

Lokke switched subjects, trying not to think of the lake. "And now you know why I didn't want to see Anaxa."

"I do," Jonna smiled, "thanks for the warning. By the way, why did he want to speak with you privately?"

"He offered a bargain. If I helped him turn you two in, he would get me promoted."

"And you said?"

"What does it look like I said? I lied to him so he would leave me in the hut unrestricted, and then, when he left, came to get you. He practically watched me all night!"

Jonna gave him a look of disbelief.

Lokke cringed. "I'm here, aren't I?"

"But you did consider it?" Jonna asked evenly.

"Of course I did," Lokke exclaimed. "What being trapped in the Otherworld wouldn't? But I heard this little tiny voice in the back of my mind, and now I'm a renegade like you."

Could it be they could trust Lokke? Jonna was not sure. That little nagging at the back of Jonna's mind, as well as on his shoulder, came to the surface, though he had no evidence to doubt him. Perhaps it was the situation that had him on edge. Then again—

Bob cleared his throat. "I told you."

"Lokke," Jonna spoke calmly, "spill it. What really happened?"

Lokke swallowed. He would have adjusted his collar, but he had none. He looked away. "Nothing."

"Lokke."

"Oh, alright. I went along with it."

"Yes," Bob chimed in Jonna's ear. "I knew it!"

Jonna slowed, turning toward Lokke.

"Don't stop!" Lokke nodded toward the waterfall.

Jonna picked up the pace again.

Sweat was building on Lokke's forehead. "I—I planned to turn you both in, but," he looked around at the lake before him, "you changed the plan."

"So that was why you didn't want me to use the spell. You were trying to set us up."

Lokke turned toward him and half-grinned. "Yea, unfortunately."

"Lokke, after all the times we've trusted you."

Bob smashed a fist into his other hand. "Wait till I see you on the surface!"

"I couldn't help it," Lokke moaned. "I don't want to go back. I can't go back!"

"You get us to the gates, and you won't have to."

"But you don't understand." Lokke sighed. "They know we're trying to get to the gates. They'll be looking for us, waiting us out. We don't have a chance!"

"And yet, you haven't turned back to let Anaxa know where we are." Jonna looked at him. "Why?"

Lokke, forgetting the water beneath their feet, laughed. "If I have to go back, at least it was fun trying to get away."

"You have a twisted sense of humor." Jonna shook his head but chuckled anyway. What could he do, but work with what he had?

The frozen water drops held in place as they stepped up on dry land. There had to be a density difference between the waterfall and the water in the lake.

When he fell through the bridges at the dark mage's citadel, he had chased down the kidnappers who took his beloved Stephanie, this had been the case, too. He frowned feeling the separation; his family was very far away.

"Well, I'll be." Lokke grinned. "I had no idea." He turned to Jonna. "How did you know there was land here?"

The land they stood on held boulders and rocks up against the sheer cliff wall. At one time, there must have been a larger land mass, but the waterfall's pounding had eroded it away.

"Just a guess."

This time Lokke studied Jonna. "More than a guess, I think." He bit his lip. "Okay, spill it, what do you know about me?"

"What do you mean?"

Lokke let go of Cassandra. Jonna caught her and laid her down.

76

"You know what I mean." Lokke waved a finger suspiciously. "You always act like you know more."

"Me?" Jonna shook his head. "You're the one who acts like he knows more. There's that mischievous smile along with all the pranks you play. Surely being around a thousand years—"

Bob mumbled, "Go get him," with lots of scratching in the background. "Make him tell the truth." He grinned and glanced up at Jonna. "This is good stuff!"

Lokke refused to budge. "You're trying to confuse me. I want to know what you know about me." For the first time, Jonna saw Lokke get mad. His face turned redder than his normal red tint, and his eyes were set to bulging. "No matter what plans I lay, you keep interfering."

"You're serious?"

Chapter 6

FABIUS' DILEMMA

"You bet I'm serious," Lokke growled, "and if you don't start talking, I'm gonna march right across that water and leave!"

Cassandra's eyes fluttered. "Will you two stop that." She rubbed her eyes with both hands. "It's not him." She sat up on one elbow. "It's me."

"Me what?" Lokke and Jonna said at the same time.

"Me." Cassandra chuckled a little. "I'm the one who knows about Lokke."

Bob glanced up from his writing. "You do?"

Lokke narrowed his gaze. "You do? But how do—"

"Why do you think I wanted you out of the group?"

"Well," Lokke began, "I thought it was the whole giant eating thing." His voice dropped off. "It wasn't?"

Cassandra shook her head. "I know your nature. I know the harm your kind can bring."

Jonna looked at Lokke. "Harm?"

"Harm?" Lokke shifted between them. "What do you mean harm? I play jokes. I don't harm."

"You will," she assured, "though I don't know when."

"If you don't know when," Lokke shook his head, "then that's not saying very much!"

"You don't understand, I have The Sight. I see the future."

"Then your sight is marred," Lokke denied. "It can't be me!"

Jonna stepped between them. "Is it possible The Sight can be influenced by what we feel?" He saw the stubbornness in Cassandra's face. "Like how you cannot know your husband's fate? Until we know more, this discussion is futile." He looked at them both. "I suggest we deal with other matters, like," Jonna helped Cassandra up, "are you okay?"

"I'll be fine," she gave a nod, "though still a bit woozy. Where are we, and why?"

"Master Anaxa was going to turn us over to Dagda. Lokke let me know and helped us to escape. That's the why." Lokke's attempt at betrayal would only make things worse between him and Cassandra, so Jonna didn't say anything. "Lokke, you want to tell her where?"

"Behind a waterfall," his voice shook. "In the middle of the steaming lake!"

Cassandra's eyes followed the sparkling drops suspended in the air. "Wow." She looked out across the lake. Vapors hung like mist in the early morning. "How?"

Jonna shook his head. "It's Otherworld magic."

She stopped and looked up again, but this time The Sight took hold, and her voice sounded far away. "We need to get you to your family." She snapped out of it with a sad smile on her face. "You need to be with Elfleda." Cassandra stepped next to the waterfall as if trying to forget she had said those last words.

Jonna's heart skipped a beat. What did she mean that he needed to be with Elfleda? Of course he did, she was his wife.

Cassandra reached up and pushed slowly at a single water drop. It was difficult to move it, but it stayed right where she put it. "It's not falling."

"Oh, yes it is," Jonna moved one himself, "but at such a slow rate of speed it appears to hold still, thanks to a few spells Lokke knew."

"It was nothing," Lokke accepted. "Just a typical moment in the life of Lokke."

Bob gaged. "Oh please, strangle me now."

"Every dog has their day," Jonna remembered the line as he thought over the magic they used.

Cassandra stared at the water drops, her eyes saying what her words did not. "So how long can we stay this way?"

"That's right," Jonna turned to Lokke. "When you did it on the slide, you ended it quickly."

"That's because you don't want to do it too long. It—"

Jonna's brow wrinkled. "Why?" He could still hear Bob scratching. Was he recording every word?

"I'll finish if you give me a chance," Lokke growled. "As I was trying to say, it plays havoc on living creatures. Something about the subconscious equilibrium. At least, those are the words Fabius used."

"Who's Fabius?"

"My mentor." Lokke raised a hand. "About this tall with gray hair and a—"

A gray-haired man fitting Lokke's description faded into view. "Lokke, will you never learn? You're causing quite a stir you know!" He spotted Jonna and Cassandra. "And I see you've dragged in others as well!"

Lokke fidgeted.

"After a while, he inevitably gets tired of them and brings them down here." Fabius shook his finger. "Shame on you!"

"It wasn't like that this time," Lokke pleaded. "I told them not to go down the right slide, but they couldn't get to the left one."

"Really? I've never heard of anyone who couldn't choose the correct one." He eyed Jonna and Cassandra warily. "Are you sure they want to get out?"

Cassandra stood defiantly. "It was impossible to control which one we went down. No one could have done it."

"Hmm, this is a first." He looked at Lokke. "Are you sure you didn't help them down the wrong path?"

"Absolutely not." Lokke's head shook with eyes wide. "I would never want to come here again."

"Very well." Fabius adjusted spectacles so he could see better. "It isn't safe for anyone, especially the dead."

"That's what I tried to tell them." Lokke threw his hands in the air. "Why doesn't anyone listen to me?"

"No," Jonna shook his head, "you were more afraid of getting caught."

"That too," Lokke pointed a finger, "but the first is still important." His finger pointed three times: once at Cassandra, once at Jonna, and the last at Bob.

Fabius looked around the group. "Is there another I can't see?"

Jonna turned in Fabius direction. So the mage could not detect Bob? "Should there be more?"

"Witty too." Fabius clapped his hands and turned to Lokke. "They're not boring, I take it?"

"Definitely not boring." Lokke shook his head. "Had me glued to my seat most of the ride."

"How exciting." Fabius was giddy, which looked funny for his apparent age. Jonna couldn't figure out why 'not being boring' would matter.

Cassandra's eyes bounced one to the other. She touched Jonna on the arm. "Why are they talking as if we are not here?"

"I don't know." He waved his hand and caught the attention of Fabius. "Now that you're here, may I ask why?"

"Why? Oh, yes." Fabius chuckled. "It appears your arrival at Anaxa's has stirred things up. He told Dagda, and Dagda is sending his minions."

Cassandra stepped in. "That didn't answer his question."

"No," Jonna frowned, "it didn't. It only told us what is coming our way."

Fabius smiled at both of them with a gleam in his eye. "I'm here to help, of course."

Jonna was sure there had to be a catch. He had made a bargain with Lokke. Did he need one with this person too? "At what price?"

Bob looked up from his recording and spoke scholarly, "Remember Jonna, trust must be earned." A smile lit Bob's face. "I'll have to quote that." The rubbing resumed.

"Tisk, tisk, tisk." Fabius came near Jonna and placed an arm on his shoulder. "Don't sound so suspicious. Certainly nothing you cannot do, being alive and all."

Okay, so it could only be done by someone alive. Great. "And it is?"

"A little favor." Fabius waved it away. "We can talk when there is more time."

"From the spell we used to get here," Jonna motioned toward the water drops standing in the air, "we have plenty of time."

A howl sounded from the shore. Everyone looked up surprised.

"You see," Fabius nodded toward the sound, his voice almost a whisper, "if I could find you, Dagda's minions won't be far behind."

A small shiver went down Cassandra's spine at the words sank in. "His minions?"

Two large white wolves sniffed around on the shore, moving at the same speed they were.

"Hold very still," Fabius whispered lower. "They are good at catching noises."

The wolves moved closer, following something on the ground along the edge of the lake. They were looking for how the three had left the hut.

Bob whispered in Jonna's ear, looking up from the writing materials, "I can't see. Where are they?"

"What are they?" Jonna had never seen anything that could move at this speed. Of course, due to magic, he was moving at that speed now, but he had never experienced that before either.

"They are Zaman wolves, minions and servants of Dagda, used to find level jumpers."

"They're very efficient," Lokke whispered, stepping backwards and moving further from the two wolves. Turning his head, he caught sight of two more on the opposite shore. As Lokke shifted his body, he slipped.

"Lokke," Jonna whispered as he reached out, but he was

too far away. Cassandra leaned forward and caught him but could not hold on. Her hands slipped from Lokke's arm. Fabius closed his eyes and cringed.

Thud.

It wasn't that loud. Jonna could have sworn it was no noisier than their whispered voices. However, all four wolves brought their heads up and turned toward the waterfall.

Everyone froze. Three of the wolves dropped their heads down. The fourth kept watch.

Lokke swallowed. "We've been made." He used Cassandra's arm to get to his feet. The wolf started toward them.

Cassandra looked around. "Which way to run?"

The waterfall fell into the lake, equal distant from both sides. There was no way to leave without being seen.

"If you want to help," Jonna whispered to Fabius, "now would be the acceptable time." He moved to the wall behind them, searching for something, anything, they might be able to use. It was too steep to climb, but maybe some of the boulders—as Jonna went around a rather large rock, he spotted a small opening. A boulder sat to one side of the opening half-dislodged. "Over here!"

"What are you doing?" Lokke looked from the wolves to Jonna. "We don't have time to hide in there!"

"It's better than out here." Jonna allowed Cassandra to slip in first. "Coming?"

"If you'll give me a moment," Fabius sounded frustrated. He mumbled something under his breath and shook his head.

"We don't have a moment." Jonna pushed Lokke toward the hole. "Ready or not." He grabbed Fabius by the shoulder and thrust him toward the cave.

Fabius huffed but did as directed. "Be careful. It's not easy working out a spell like this."

"If we get caught," Jonna stressed, "it won't matter anyway."

Fabius chuckled, "No," and scooted more quickly into the hole.

To cover the tunnel entrance, Jonna tried to shift the half-dislodged boulder while he was inside the small cave. He had been right. Certain types of items, such as the ground, boulders, and the cliff rock, were different in density. The denser the object, the easier they could affect it. "Lokke, help me."

Lokke crawled over Fabius and came to the Jonna's side. "You called, oh master?" He rolled his eyes.

"Grab and pull," Jonna pointed to the edge of the boulder.

Fabius shook his head in the dim light. "It won't stop them." He returned to moving on all fours, mumbling over spells.

"But maybe it will slow them down."

Both pulled. The rock moved a few inches and then turned, falling down over the opening and sealing them in. The light went out.

"Hey," Bob growled, "if I can't see what's there, how can I write it down?"

"Bob, you have pixie sight. Remember?"

The pixie grinned. "Oh, yeah."

"That's a big help." Lokke felt around and changed the direction of one leg. "Now, we can't see at all."

Fabius groaned. "Stop kicking me."

Jonna dodged as Lokke shifted his leg. As Jonna's eyes adjusted to the darkness, he went around the two and came up beside Cassandra. "That's better."

Cassandra jumped.

"*Mi Fsicut.*" Fabius created a light that danced around him. "You see pretty well in the dark."

"Thank you," Lokke grinned, "but it's an erratic second sense. It sort of comes and goes."

"Not you," the mage shook his head, "Jonna."

"I've been told that." Jonna took the lead, searching the deeper part of the cave. "Anyone know where this thing goes?"

"Not me," Lokke felt the walls, "and I know most of the caves on this level."

Cassandra laughed, following behind Jonna. "I bet."

"Was that a snide remark?" Lokke watched as Jonna and Cassandra moved out of the illuminated area.

Jonna glanced behind. "Are you and Fabius coming?"

"If I could get the spell right," the mage continued to mumble, "we could all get out of this mess right now."

"When you do, great," Jonna moved deeper, "but until then, try to keep up."

"Humph." Fabius hurried after them.

Lokke began, "Maybe the wolves haven't found—" Something hit the rock behind them and jarred the entrance. He hurried to catch up, running into Fabius.

"Lokke!"

"They're coming." A second jar made small pebbles drop. "Faster!"

Jonna moved into a larger cavern. To one side, an incline gave a gradual rise. Small pools of water were scattered about the floor. Along the far wall, smoke hissed from vents. Something shook the ground and knocked Jonna off his feet. "What was that?"

Fabius caught up. The mages' light cast deep shadows around them, making it hard for Jonna to focus.

Lokke came scurrying from behind. "They're digging out the rock!"

"We need to go up." Jonna headed toward the incline, keeping an eye out for side passages. What they needed was something to slow their hunters.

The ground shook again. Some of the smaller stalactites dropped from the ceiling and crashed to the floor.

"They are working their way through!" Lokke dodged as another one dropped and splintered as it hit. "Fabius, the spell?"

"Patience," Fabius glared at Lokke. "You know how precise I have to be."

"Yeah, but," Lokke glanced the way they had come, "if they get in—"

"If they get in, and I'm not ready, all this running won't do any good. Let me concentrate!"

Lokke closed his mouth. His face contorted as another comment popped into his head.

Jonna found another tunnel. Through a crack in the wall, it moved to the right.

"Here." Based upon his estimated size of the wolves, it should give Fabius time to finish his spell.

"That's putting the old thinking cap on." The mage smiled and slipped into the side tunnel behind Cassandra. As Jonna turned to guard the opening, Lokke pushed past.

Bob huffed, the rubbing temporarily stopped, and he looked over at Jonna. "Is tunnel spelt with two n's or one?"

"Two," Jonna frowned, "at least in my language. I don't know about yours. Bob, I don't have time for this."

"It was just a question. Besides, what else are you going to do waiting around?"

The pixie had a point. Jonna glanced at the others behind him. "How's the space?" He turned to watch out the narrow crack.

"Not very good," Lokke croaked. "Pretty tight back here."

"Like a sandwich," Fabius added, "but at least I can focus."

As the ground shook, a breeze came into the cavern.

"Good," Jonna's frown deepened, "because they're in."

As the wolves moved out the entry tunnel, their growls became more distinct.

Bob looked up, thinking. "How would you spell the growl they make? G-a-r-r-r-r or more of a g-r-r-r-r?"

"Definitely a g-r-r-r-r," Jonna added tongue-in-cheek. He stepped back. "Bob, why are you recording this?"

"Väinämö said I should document my adventures for the Pixie Library of Congress."

"There's a Pixie Library of Congress? What do they do, keep documents and books?"

"Wow, how did you know?"

A single howl filled the cavern, echoing in all directions. "So what's all the rubbing when you make notes?"

"I'm using a recorder," Bob held up a hollow reed with a

86

cut on one side. "You know, a vertical pipe with eight finger holes. You blow in the end like this." He put it to his mouth and blew. Nothing sounded, but the rubbing started again. Bob stopped blowing. "See?"

Jonna frowned. "And this writes something?"

"The notes tell the magic stick what to do on the parchment."

"And that produces the rubbing? Wouldn't it be easier to use a quill to write on the parchment?"

The indignant voice of Bob sounded loud, "And where would be the fun in that?"

The growls came closer. Jonna backed up.

"Hey," Lokke howled in pain, "that's my foot."

A pair of glowing eyes looked in their direction. The wolf stepped nearer, followed by two others. They moved around the cavern floor, sniffing the water puddles, and shifted toward the incline.

"Count down," Jonna said to no one in particular. Three sets of wolf ears perked up. "Forget the count down. They found us."

A growl was so near Jonna jumped. He peered closer to the crack. One of the wolves stared at him with glowing eyes. In spite of the distance between them, its hot breath hit his face.

"Fabius?" Jonna's voice was strained. His gaze locked with the wolf. The wolf's jaw dropped; its teeth showed above and below.

"I think he likes you," Cassandra's voice was sarcastic. She shifted around the other two, coming up beside him.

"Yeah," Jonna spoke without looking away. "Now what?"

"They wait," Fabius predicted quietly, "until we come out."

Cassandra shook her head. "I don't think I like that idea."

"Maybe someone should go negotiate?" Lokke nudged Jonna.

Cassandra glanced at Lokke. "I take it you volunteer?"

"Me?" Lokke worked further into the back. "I don't do well with animals."

"As we saw with the snakes."

"Those were reptiles." He stopped and thought. "They were a little upset, weren't they?"

"Fabius?" Jonna kept his eyes on the wolf.

The mage huffed. "It's not easy you know. Organizing a new spell is dangerous."

"New?" Jonna shook his head. "I thought you knew magic?"

"Most definitely. However, unlike surface dwellers, the Otherworlders can only use two words. I've got to create an exit as well as bring us back to normal speed, all at the same time."

"Surely you have something?"

"Good point," Lokke smiled. Fabius glared at him, and Lokke's smile dropped.

The wolf, too large to get in, raised up one of his paws and held it in the air.

Cassandra tried to see. "What is he doing? Being friendly?"

"Raising his paw." Jonna watched, unable to see the other two wolves.

The paw stayed suspended, waiting for Jonna to do something. A strange feeling passed over him.

"I think you're right." He moved closer to the wolf. "He is being friendly."

"What are you doing?" Lokke was frantic. "Don't touch them!"

Jonna paused. "Why not?"

Lokke threw his hands up. "Humans! It's a trick, don't you know that? You'll play into their paws. They—" He made a tight fist. "They draw you in with a false sense of peace and gobble you up."

"I've got it!" Fabius leaped. "*Cerosyn Dettoyt.*" At the back of the cave, an archway appeared. "There, we can all go through that." He hurried toward it and then turned around. "What are you waiting for? Come on!"

"You heard him." Lokke grabbed hold of both and pulled them toward the archway. The wolf tilted its head, howled into the cavern, and started to dig.

The walls shook. Bits and pieces fell as all the wolves joined. The small entrance became larger, causing the ceiling to shake.

Lokke herded them toward the archway. Fabius helped guide them in. The cavern shook so badly no one could stay on their feet for long.

The tunnel entrance began to rip. Part of the wall fell in. As soon as it cleared, the first wolf leaped forward.

"Jump!" Fabius shoved them the final few steps. Jonna and Cassandra tumbled in. Lokke leaped into the air and passed through midjump. Fabius tripped, rolled to his feet, and dove in behind them. The arch vanished as his feet pulled through.

"That was close." Fabius exhaled and abruptly looked around. "I don't remember a draft in here."

Cassandra stood up, dusting herself off. "I think the draft is because of your clothes." She pointed to the back of his shirt. There were four tear marks matching a large paw.

"Hmm, a little closer than I thought." He turned to the others. "Make yourself at home. At least for the moment, we're safe from searching wolves and prying eyes." He headed toward a side door.

Jonna could hear Bob still rubbing, so he inspected the dusty room. "Where are we?"

"Prying eyes?" Cassandra looked around.

"Fabius' private lab," Lokke nodded. "Dagda has spies everywhere." Wide-eyed, he gazed slowly around.

The white mist, could it be a spy? Jonna laid his hand down and realized it was on a tabletop with glass jars and containers. "Then why didn't we see into them before?"

Lokke watched them explore the room. "Who says we didn't?"

"You're saying we've been watched all along?" Jonna's eyes caught Lokke's. Lokke diverted his to another area.

"Uh, m—maybe."

"Maybe?" Cassandra stomped her foot. "Why didn't you tell us?"

Bob shook a fist. "Yeah!" He grinned, "This is really good stuff."

Jonna held up a hand. "Because he was afraid I wouldn't go." He picked up one of the vials on the table. A greenish substance bubbled when he swirled the liquid within. "Isn't that right Lokke?"

"Maybe."

"No maybes about it." Cassandra's eyes narrowed. She turned to Jonna. "Leave him."

"Leave who?" Fabius walked in tying a cloth belt around his robe. "Pardon the appearance, but after that close call, I need to relax." He went to the far wall, opened a hidden door, and pulled out a wine bottle. "Drink? Anyone?"

Lokke licked his lips. "I will."

"We were talking about leaving Lokke behind," Jonna volunteered. "He continually leaves out important information."

"And that's the least of it." Bob's eyes narrowed as he focused on the wine bottle. "Can you read the bottle's label?"

Jonna glanced toward Bob. "Look who's calling the kettle black."

"See, see." Lokke pointed. "I'm not the only one. I don't even have to know what he said to know what he said." He paused. "Did that sound right?"

"Lokke always leaves out information." Fabius raised an eyebrow and laughed. "That's part of his trickster nature." He poured a portion for Lokke and handed him a glass. Turning to the others, he motioned toward the wine bottle. "Are you sure?"

Jonna nodded, "But thanks for the offer."

Cassandra shook her head. "No, thank you."

"Have it your way." Fabius poured his own, placed the bottle on the shelf, and closed the hidden door. It vanished into the wall. "And no sneaking," he pointed at Lokke.

"You were saying?" Jonna noticed that one corner of the room held a plush chair. Books lined the wall behind it.

"Oh," Fabius tried to remember, "yes, it is part of Lokke's nature. He is a demon you know."

"A demon?" Jonna looked closely. Lokke did remind him of Azazel in the city of Chernobog.

Bob smiled smugly. "I knew that."

Jonna glanced at Bob. "Then why didn't you say something?"

"Half-demon," Lokke glared. "Why is it no one ever gets it correct?"

Cassandra stared. "Maybe because the word demon overshadows everything else?"

Jonna turned to Lokke. "That explains a lot." He thought about their first meeting: the bird in the tree, the detective hound, and not wanting Dagda to see him. "So the magic you use—"

Lokke spoke with pride, "Is demon magic."

"So the two word bit and holding the fingers together—" He scratched his head. "I don't remember Azazel doing that."

"Holding fingers together?" Fabius raised both his eyebrows and turned toward Lokke.

The look on Fabius' face and the reaction on Lokke's gave Jonna understanding. "You don't hold your fingers together?"

Fabius tapped his temple. "It's the words and the way you think about it."

"Like magic on the surface?"

"Like magic on the surface."

Jonna chuckled. "I guess the joke's on me."

Lokke let go. "It was hard not to laugh."

Cassandra studied them all. "Are you sure it's wise to learn demon magic?" She faced Jonna. "Could there be repercussions?"

"You don't understand." Fabius held out his hands. "All magic is demon magic down here. It's a title, not the origin."

"It is?"

"I'm afraid so. That's why it takes training for a human to do spells. Anything they learned on the surface has to be learned in demonese."

Jonna's curiosity piqued. "So, there is a conversion process?"

"Oh yes, but it is not a conversion. It is a translation. Translation is understanding the abstract and finding a close meaning in another magic. Conversion is specific. It implies a tighter formula. That was my problem in the cave. The translation has to be correct. Otherwise, anything could have happened or nothing at all."

Jonna studied the mage. "I take it you're not from around here?"

"Do I look like I'm from around here?" He held his arms out, palms up. "But I bet I know your next question."

Jonna saw the laughter in Fabius' eyes. "Are you dead or undead?"

"Neither."

The knowledge made Jonna's mind swirl. He was undead, Lokke was undead, Cassandra was dead, but how could someone be neither?

"You're lying," Cassandra stepped forward and jabbed a finger. "There are only two types: undead or dead."

"You are partially right. I am held in a place between life and death. Because of that, I do not fall into either."

Jonna saw it. "Your body is alive, but you can't go back." He had read stories like that. "Like a deep sleep."

"Exactly," he pointed at Jonna, "and hence the favor." His hands dropped to his side. "I want you to wake me up."

Chapter 7

DANGEROUS NOTIONS

Lokke gasped. "I didn't know that, and all this time—"

"We all have our secrets." Fabius turned to Jonna. "Will you help?"

Cassandra stepped nervously closer to Jonna and whispered, "Why is he that way?"

Jonna leaned against the table and studied the older man. He considered Cassandra's question. It was important, and yet, what other choice did they have? "How do we find you?"

"All you have to do is locate a golden box, er, coffin, in a stone built room. If I remember right—" Fabius closed his eyes to think. "They placed the letters R.K.H on the outside door. It's sealed of course, so you'll have to break in."

"And the stone built room is where?"

The mage chuckled. "That's the part I don't know. A city I'm sure, and someplace it can be kept secret."

Cassandra would not let it slide. "Might we ask how you got into this predicament?"

"Ah, well," Fabius' cheeks turned red, "I made few creatures a little bit upset."

"A few?"

"A few thousand," Lokke snickered, unable to hold it in anymore; Fabius gave him an evil eye. "Oh, come on," Lokke shrugged it off. "I may not have known the whole story, but I certainly know some."

The mage smiled rather sheepishly. "He's right—to a degree at least."

Jonna nodded. "Should we ask what you did?"

Fabius' face darkened. "It involves another, and it's quite embarrassing. I'd rather not say."

Lokke burst out in hysterical laughter, and a few moments later he was rolling on the floor, unable to stop. The rest of the group watched. As the chuckles finally died away, he took a deep breath and slowly stood to his feet. "Er, sorry," he sobered up.

"And you called me crazy?" Jonna shook his head. "I'm not even going to ask." He turned to study Fabius. "Promise me you did nothing like kill or hurt innocent people?"

"Nothing like that," eyes wide, Fabius promised. "It was an accident really." He glanced at the floor. "I mean, sort of. It was interesting the way in that she, uh, they, trapped me." His voice resumed as he stopped the reminisce. "But that's a story for another time." He looked up. "Nothing malicious, I assure you."

Jonna caught the she, and it was obvious why Fabius wanted him: he was undead, held prisoner like Fabius, and he was trying to find a way out. Queen Freya's words came rolling back: 'Your refusal to cooperate means war to the Elves.'

Yet, he could not stay here; it was a trap, and he knew it. Relying on the powers that be to get him out would only serve Dagda's purpose. The longer he was away, the more in danger his family would be. "Fine, we'll help, but you'll have to give me a few more clues."

"I didn't know too much about where they took me. I woke up only briefly in the stone built room and then found myself down here."

"Jonna," Cassandra motioned for him to lean toward her, "are you certain you ought to do this?"

He whispered, "Honestly, I don't know, but if we want his help—" He caught her eye.

Cassandra inhaled. "I know. I just don't like it."

"There are others in the room you know." Lokke walked up and wormed his way between them. "And it is impolite to whisper."

Bob grunted, but kept on writing. "I'd tell him to butt out."

"Says who," Cassandra challenged.

"Says—" Lokke caught the expression on her face and changed directions, "him." He pointed to Fabius who was no longer paying any attention.

Cassandra looked to Jonna. "I still say leave him."

"Aw, come on," Lokke begged. "Maybe I do overstep the line once in a while," he made a sad face, "but you know you need me. Besides, who better to make the trip fun?" He gave a big, wide smile.

"Well," Fabius sat back in the comfy chair and sipped his wine, "what do you say?"

Jonna was getting tired of weighing all the possibilities. He wanted to get out of here and back to his family. "We will help."

"Jonna," Cassandra mumbled, "you're not listening."

"Never fear," Jonna looked into her eyes, "I'm sure it will be fine."

There was uncertainty in her face. It was a look that told Jonna The Sight had not confirmed or denied his words.

Fabius pulled a book from the shelf and began to read.

She turned so Lokke would not read her lips. "I don't want you here before your time. You have a daughter to take care of."

"I know."

As if on cue, Fabius looked up from his book. "Then it's settled." He jumped up, eyes sparkling. "Now that we're in agreement, we can focus on other problems."

"Problems?"

The mage looked from face to face. "Of course. We still have the wolf problem, the gate problem, and the three challenges problem."

"You make it sound pretty simple." Jonna shook his head. "Nothing is that easy."

"Of course not." Fabius reached underneath the table and sorted through a series of scrolls. "If it were, everyone would do it."

"I can imagine."

"Here." The mage unrolled a scroll and laid it over a space on the table. "This is the safest route to the gates."

Lokke's eyes widened. "You never told me."

Bob's eyes widened at the same time. The rubbing in the background became a furious rush.

"You never asked," the mage chuckled. "You kept running off to find a way up."

"You could have volunteered!"

"Boys, boys," Cassandra interrupted, just a little cross, "can we get to the point?"

"Of course." Fabius traced a line on the map. It was anything but straight. "Jonna, do you understand this?"

Actually, he did. It was amazing how similar this was to geological mappings of other caverns. He nodded.

"Good, that makes it easier."

"It does." Jonna looked from the map to Fabius. "Why don't you use magic?"

"Ah," Fabius smiled, "an excellent question. Actually, you can only use magic to gate to where you have actually been. If you've never been there, then odds are you will appear where you don't want to be."

Lokke gave a mischievous smile. "Like in a cave wall." He laughed. "I saw a mage do that once. It took time to dig him out." He leaned toward Cassandra. "Being dead, he was fine."

Fabius nodded. "It happens. People get so desperate they will try anything. Besides, what good would it do for me to go there? I can't get out."

"You can't?"

Fabius shook his head. "If I did, it would make things worse." He changed the subject and handed Jonna the rolled map. "Now, the three challenges."

"I thought we needed to deal with the wolves?"

"All in good time." Fabius slid open a shelf door under the same table and shuffled through the stacked parchments. "There they are." He pulled out three. Blowing on them, he dropped them onto the table. Dust flew, and clouds billowed.

Cassandra waved her hand and coughed. "I've never seen so much dust."

"If you like that," Lokke laughed, "you should look outside."

Suspicious, Cassandra asked, "Might I ask what level we're on?"

"You might," Fabius did not look up, "but I wouldn't."

Cassandra moved closer to Jonna.

Lokke didn't help. "He's right. It's better not to know."

"Thanks," Jonna smiled sarcastically, "that reassures us both. What about about the challenges?"

"Ah, yes," Fabius leaned closer to the notes, "the first challenge." He read down the page. "The first challenge is *What you don't know.*"

"What you don't know?" Jonna waited for an explanation. He glanced at Cassandra who shook her head. "Fabius?"

Bob mumbled, "Got it."

"Give me a moment," Fabius read down the page. "Old—single foot—pattern of—" He made a funny face and moved his head back. "Hmm."

Cassandra leaned forward. "That's it?"

Fabius waved them off. "Give me a moment. It seems somewhat cryptic." He looked up. "You'll have to pardon me. I was writing fast."

With a sneer, Lokke stuck in, "And running."

Fabius nodded. "And running."

"I thought you said you had never been to the gates?" It sounded to Jonna as if he had.

"No, no," Fabius shook his head, "you don't understand. I heard a rumor that some undead tried to sneak down before their demise. A group of them, I think, although I only found one—hmm." He shook his head. "Anyway, as I was trying to get the information recorded—"

Lokke yelled out, "White wolves! White wolves!"

Everyone jumped.

"Lokke," Fabius scolded, "don't do that!" He turned to Cassandra and Jonna. "But he's right. The white wolves found the person minutes after I did. Had I not been in the lead—" He shrugged.

"What you're saying, then," Jonna translated, "is that you don't have all the notes?"

"Of course I have all the notes." Fabius looked indignant. "The three challenges are *What you don't know*, *What you do know*, and *What you will know.*"

Bob tried to get a better view of what Fabius was reading.

"Huh?" Lokke looked at the others. "Am I the only one who thinks that is nonsense?" He moved closer to Fabius and tried to read over his shoulder. The mage politely moved the parchments.

"That's what it says," Fabius shrugged, "in spite of my hastily taken notes. Believe it or not. It is up to you."

Cassandra looked to Jonna. "But the path is safe?"

"Possibly," Fabius mused. "Though what I said was 'the safest route'. Safe is a relative term."

"Probably not," Jonna shook his head, "but at least there is a route." He tapped the rolled up map on the table edge. "Now, how about the wolves?"

"Ah yes." Fabius brightened. "A simple matter—"

Jonna's eyes narrowed. "You gave the impression they were difficult to beat."

"It all depends on your point of view." The mage moved back and looked through another stack of parchments. Finding the right one, he pulled it out, blew it off, and studied the writing. "Okay, I'm going to give you a spell."

"You're giving him a spell?" Lokke huffed. "You're just *giving* it to him?"

Jonna reminded Lokke, "You gave me a spell."

"That was different. Mine wasn't of real value." He stopped and looked at Jonna. "I mean—"

"I know what you mean." Jonna shifted his eyes from Lokke to Fabius. "Go on."

"No, no," Lokke waved his hands, "you don't understand."

"But we do." Cassandra's tone stopped him, and she too turned away. "Fabius, please continue."

Lokke dropped into a sullen silence.

"Very well, say the following phrases—" He turned toward Lokke, thinking.

"Aw, come on," Lokke rolled his eyes. "Don't send me out. I want to learn too." He gave a hurt puppy look, but it didn't have the right effect with the horn on his head and the red skin.

The mage reluctantly nodded and turned to Jonna. "Repeat the following phrases: Tu."

"Tu."

"En."

"En."

"Eup."

"Eup." Jonna remembered the way Väinämö had taught him and put it all together. "Tueneup."

"Very good." Fabius grinned. "Most mages get all the syllables out of whack."

"I've had a good teacher."

Lokke beamed. "Thank you."

Jonna laughed. "Not you."

Lokke's face dropped.

"Not that you don't have the potential."

Lokke's face brightened.

Cassandra sighed. Bob shook his head.

"And now, the final phrase." Fabius nodded. "Ae-neo."

"Tueneup Aeneo."

The whole room stopped. After about twenty seconds, Fabius began to move. He checked the others. "Good," he motioned Jonna to come closer. "There are a few things you should know before the others come around."

With a smug smile, Bob folded his arms. "I'm still awake. Take that, half-demon!"

As Fabius approached, Jonna frowned, "What do you mean?"

"This spell is dangerous, and not all creatures can cast it. I doubt Lokke will be able to remember it at all, even though he is half-demon."

Bob grinned, "But I've got it down."

Jonna threw the pixie a look. "That's why you let him stay?"

Fabius nodded. "Normally, only a true mage or a full demon can cast this spell. Depending upon the creatures it is cast upon, the duration may vary. Take for instance the wolves. They have some control over time, therefore, the duration will vary depending upon each wolf's ability to resist."

Bob's eyes widened. "That must mean I qualify. Ho, ho, wait till I tell the half-demon that!" The scratching and rubbing resumed.

"What you're implying is that I could cast the spell, and one by one certain wolves may come out of it before the others. As you did?"

Fabius nodded. "And it might not work at all."

"A last resort, then." Oh well, a weapon is at least a weapon even if you aren't sure of its effectiveness. "Thank you."

"You are welcome." Fabius watched Lokke and Cassandra. "I believe the others will wake up soon."

"What does it mean?"

A curious look crossed Fabius' face.

"The spell. If you translate it to the language I understand, what would its definition be?"

"Oh," Fabius smiled, "that's easy. Stop time."

"Stop time," Jonna repeated, remembering another spell in the magic of the surface dwellers that did the same thing. "Stop time is Stamato Zaman."

Fabius looked at him. "I don't understand."

"The phrases, they are close. Is there a way of translating surface magic to demon magic?"

"Sure, but remember, there is no direct method between the two. The rules that apply there do not apply here; it is the concept that is translated, not the actual words."

"And yet, there are common phrases for similar things."

Fabius closed his eyes to think and then nodded slowly. "Yes, but that does not change the fact that there is no direct correlation."

"But there is." It was all too clear to Jonna. As he had spoken the new spell, he could see the method forming in his mind. All he had to do was—he looked at a spot on the floor.

"Qisvo."

Lightning leaped from out of nowhere, scorching the spot to a burnish black. Thunder sounded in the distance.

"What have you done?" Fabius rushed to the area Jonna had hit and ran a hand over it. He jerked his hand back. "How did you do that?"

"How do you think?" Jonna's eyes twinkled. Somehow, someway he had figured out how to change surface magic to the language of this place, even if it only used one word.

Fabius looked around in terror. "Leave, leave now!"

"Fabius, what's wrong?"

Fabius spoke each word slowly, "You—must—leave!"

"I don't understand."

Fabius jumped up, moved to the door of his house, and pressed an ear to it.

"All I did was—"

"No, you did not," Fabius interrupted with harshness. He turned from the door and looked at Jonna. "But you think you did. What you have truly done is created a hybrid language. Do you understand?"

Jonna shook his head.

"It makes no difference. The fact the matter is, somehow, someway, you have managed to combine the two magics." Fabius looked at the ceiling as if trying to draw the right words from the air. "All magic has a signature, a—" He closed his eyes tight, searching for the word.

Jonna threw in, "A fingerprint?"

Fabius opened his eyes and looked at Jonna. "What's a fingerprint?"

"A—" Jonna shook his head. "Never mind, I know what you're saying. Please continue."

The mage nodded. "A signature which identifies its origin. Surface magic cannot, I repeat, cannot, be converted directly to demon magic because of the different rules. The intricacies are like comparing the spoken word to numbers. A one to one comparison does not exist because of the differences in complexity and scope; the relationship can only be described in concepts. On top of that, the representative symbols are innately different."

"But that is the point," Jonna countered. "You can compare the spoken word and numbers if," he raised a finger in Fabius' direction, "if you start with the correct understanding to begin with."

Fabius looked terrified and shook his head. "No, no, no! Please understand, you are not converting. You are creating!"

"And?"

The mage sighed; sweat formed in tiny beads on his forehead. "The creation of magic is held in balance. For every beneficial word created, so there must be an opposite. When an imbalance occurs, magic shifts dangerously and will attempt to balance itself in unexpected ways. If magic gets out balance enough—" Fabius' eyes stared into the Jonna's.

"But on the surface," Jonna frowned, "there are many times I created new words." His voice trailed off.

"Why do you think they brought you here?"

"They said—" Jonna caught the look in Fabius' eye.

The mage slowly nodded. "A cover story with a tad bit of truth—nothing more. Every time you create new magic, some sort of price is paid. What you did on the surface made the authorities nervous. Magic has been held in status quo for a very long time. Each area, the upper and lower, as well as certain regions, maintains control by knowing what that magic is. If a rogue mage could create magic without the proper instruction, that would give him an edge beyond the greatest masters. It could create the greatest calamities."

Jonna frowned as the truth sank in. "They intend to keep me forever."

Most of it fit, but not all. If he had put magic out of balance, what else had he awakened? Jonna heard Fabius speaking and focused on his words.

"They do intend to keep you which is why you must escape. Good luck, Jonna. Remember me when you find the surface. Do not forget. *Eimwoan Eewiouo.*"

The room began to dissolve.

"Wait," Bob pleaded. "Have Fabius repeat that last phrase. I am not sure I caught it all!"

"Bob, it's out of my control."

"Catch." Fabius threw something in Jonna's direction. "I almost forgot."

Jonna reached out and caught it. It was small. There was only enough time to drop it in his pocket.

"It will help you find my body," Fabius' voice faded away.

Jonna, Lokke, and Cassandra stood in a cavern with no light. The pixie magic kicked in and showed Jonna the sides of the cave, the walls, and the ceiling. Two beady eyes appeared in the darkness, partially washing out his pixie view of the surroundings.

"Whoa," Lokke exhaled, "what a ride! I don't know what you said to him, but we are a whole lot further up than the beginning of that map."

The map—Jonna remembered it still in his left hand. He unrolled it and focused. The subtle difference between the energy of the paper and ink revealed the details in the dark.

Cassandra's concerned voice whispered, "Jonna?"

"You didn't hear our conversation, Lokke?" Jonna looked up at the glowing eyes.

"Nothing distinct. Should I have?"

The glowing eyes moved toward him.

"Cassandra, what did you hear?"

"Nothing," she followed his voice, "but please keep talking. Seeing in the dark is not my specialty." Fabius' words echoed in Jonna's mind. 'Only a true mage or full demon...' Cassandra wasn't a true mage? This made no sense.

The sound of shuffling went quiet, except from the direction of the glowing eyes.

Jonna felt Cassandra's hand grab his arm. Those glowing eyes were still coming. "Lokke, since when did your eyes start glowing?"

The half demon's voice came from the same spot it had been before. "Wow, they glow?" He was giddy. "Hold it, my eyes have never glowed before."

"Then, whose eyes are those?" Jonna looked closely at the outline of the stranger. It was humanoid in shape, about the same height as Lokke, with two extra appendages beneath its armpits.

"Me that be," a strange, low pitched voice answered. "Faqir, I am called." Faqir reached up with the right upper appendage and touched Jonna's left side. "Sorry, I am."

Faqir sounded so pitiful, Jonna had to ask, "Sorry for what?"

"Two of your arms. Lost, of course," Faqir sounded surprised. "In shame, hide your eyes in the dark, no wonder. Hard with four, these caves are."

"But—" Jonna stopped himself. He thinks we're hiding our glowing eyes? Was it necessary to explain this? Maybe a change in thought would help. "You're not from these caves?"

"Me not," Faqir shook his head. "Harvesting, I am."

Cassandra clung tighter, while Jonna rolled the map and placed it in a belt pouch. It was not a good fit as part of it stuck out but the best he could do in the circumstance. "Harvesting?"

"Yes," Faqir nodded again. "Is soon to begin, the festival of Quei-Ug Eeuuu."

In spite of what Fabius had said, Jonna's way of translation gave him an idea of what this might be. "The Celebration of Creation," he spoke in a quiet of whisper.

Bob scratched his head, looking up from the writing. "How did you do that?" He shook his head and then thought out loud, "Oh, that's right, you're using The Sight." The writing resumed.

Jonna paused, wondering himself. Was The Sight actually helping him to translate, or was it his own normal insight? Was there a difference in this world?

"Yes," Faqir sounded excited, "come." He looked around. "All of you, the rock you must gather. To the celebration, you must come."

A possible guide? Could the 'Celebration of Creation' be in the direction of the gate, a 'rebirth' into the world of the living? Lokke had said Fabius placed them higher up in the levels. Jonna became excited himself, but what rock was Faqir talking about? He looked at what Faqir carried in his lower left appendage. It wasn't easy to see without normal light, but was that—

"You're collecting quartz?" Jonna reached out and touched the piece in Faqir's hand.

"Quartz, what is?" Faqir held up the rock. "This, we look for."

"My people call it quartz." Jonna nodded. "Of course we'll help you."

Cassandra tugged on his shirt and leaned toward him, whispering, "But I can't see."

"Just stay close." Jonna watched as Faqir moved off down the cavern. "Lokke, you coming?"

"Wouldn't miss it." Lokke made his way to Jonna's left side.

Bob stared into the darkness using his own pixie sight. "Of course, if you need a second guide—"

"Bob, I'm the only one that can hear you, remember?"

"Shoot!"

Jonna picked up the quartz and handed it to Lokke and Cassandra. It was easy to find here, and Faqir did not seem to need a whole lot. As another bend in the cave came, light struck the cavern walls, reflecting from the quartz embedded. It, brightening up the cavern, turned off the pixie sight.

Faqir stopped to see what they had. "Good, this way we go."

Chapter 8

ETHESE REMEMBERED

Their dwellings stood out on a rocky plain. They were tall cane poles leaned together and tied at the top. There was red, cotton-like material stretched over the poles.

In one side was an entrance. No entrance faced another despite the large number of huts, and each entrance was covered by leather. A gentle wind blew as it moved small sand particles from one place to another. Sand bounced off the leathery doors and red exteriors.

Jonna, slowing step, finally asked, "Where are we?"

Faqir stopped and turned toward them. "This, you do not know?"

The concern in his voice gave Jonna warning, so he thought fast and responded in the same strange way. "Far from here, our tribe is." Jonna waved to the right. "Through many caverns, we have come."

This seemed to appease Faqir; he nodded. "Sometimes others, visit we do. Come." He led them to the center of the village and took a seat on one of the rugs. "Sit. Come soon the others."

Strangely enough, the light changed at his voice. As the shadows took on greater lengths, the crackling fire in the center brightened. The culture fit descriptions Jonna remembered from the university. They were hunters and gathers living in cliff-like areas, waiting for the end of the day.

"We await the warriors," Jonna mumbled to the others, "coming in from the hunt."

"Here, all we warriors," Faqir caught his words. "Wemjemme, this is." He turned to another member of his tribe to talk.

"Wemjemme?" Cassandra looked curious. "Paradise?"

"A form of it," Jonna agreed. "For them, going out, catching prey, and having full stomachs is paradise. Apparently for this level, there is not much else in their dead existence."

"I've never seen their like." Cassandra could not help but glance toward Faqir.

Jonna nodded. "Nor, I think, have they ever seen us." Watching the fire, he found himself lost in thought. Did this Otherworld expand to other far off places, perhaps even other planets? Would he be lost from his family forever, or would he find a path that would lead him home?

Lokke looked in his direction. "What are planets?"

"Yes," Bob jumped in, "and don't you dare tell him something you haven't told me first!"

Jonna rolled his eyes. Did he say that out loud? "Hold up Bob, this isn't a contest."

Cassandra had been watching the flames in the fire. "What are you talking about, Lokke?" Her far off look changed to focus on them. "What is a planet?"

"That's what I was asking Jonna."

"A planet?" Jonna sighed, stopped, and thought. How do you explain such a thing? He started again. "Think of it as a far off town or village."

The shadows of the huts were gone, and only the firelight flickered in the darkness. One by one, others like Faqir joined around the flame. What started as a few, turned into a large horde, gathering on every side.

"Time, it is. Quei-Ug Eeuuu, here is."

A huge beast was brought through the wall of humanoids, skewered with a spit, and hung above the fire. Slowly the beast was turned, one humanoid on each side. A liquid of some sort was poured over the top, sizzling as it dripped into the flames.

Some of the humanoids began to chant.

"Welcome, welcome, here you all. Us join, us join to the call..."

They turned the beast faster and faster. More liquid spilled off and dropped into the flames. The sizzling was louder. Sparks jumped as if trying to ignite, and all at once flame shot up, tracing the liquid to the beast itself.

A roar went up from those around it as the fire consumed both beast and the bindings that held it. As the beast fell from the pole, it tumbled onto the rocks in the middle of the fire.

Another humanoid came forward, holding a knife the size of a machete. He sliced off portions of the beast, handing it to those gathered around. One by one, the slices were passed down until everyone held a piece of the beast's flesh.

"Eat we now." Faqir looked skyward, dropping his piece into his mouth. The chewing humanoids made strange grunts and growls, creating a rhythm around the fire. The noise they made was unsettling.

Lokke sniffed his. "I'm not so sure."

Cassandra took a tentative taste. "Not bad, really. A little herb flavoring wouldn't hurt."

"Eat," Faqir smiled, "our time this is; later beast is."

Jonna looked at Faqir. "Mean, what do you?"

"Our time this is. Later beast is." It was obvious Faqir expected him to understand. "Village, other?"

Jonna thought and then nodded. "Village, other, yes."

"Village, other, what do?"

A loud rattle interrupted, and all eyes went to the center by the fire. A humanoid held a staff. At the staff's top, leather-like strings connected an assortment of items: small bones, colored rocks, and quartz crystals. All these things attached to where the rattle originated. He shook the rattle again.

Faqir stood and motioned for the three strangers to join. "Beast time, now is."

Beast time? Okay. Jonna, Lokke, and Cassandra stood to their feet, following Faqir's example. Faqir went to the humanoid with the staff and handed over the quartz crystals. The others did the same.

Torches ignited as humanoids on either side created a center path. This hallway led away from the central fire. As they followed Faqir, the warriors on their sides began to thud their spears on the ground, chanting in time. "Wemjemme, Wemjemme, Wemjemme..."

Up ahead appeared to be some sort of pit; there was snarling and screaming coming from it.

As Faqir approached, a square opening was thrown open. He turned to face Jonna. "Grow back arms in creation, you may." The humanoid leaped into the opening. As he hit the bottom, there was a sounding crunch.

"Oh no." The meaning of 'creation celebration' hit Jonna. "They eat the beast, and the beast eats them."

"Then they are reborn," Cassandra added with a swallow. "They're dead Jonna. You are not."

Bob nodded. "Lokke's not either."

Jonna turned and looked at the circle of smiling humanoids. There was the white mist hovering at the edge of the darkness, immediately beyond their ranks. "That thought went through my brain, too."

"Hold it boys," Lokke turned. "This is where we take our leave."

The thudding stopped, and the visitors heard a rattle. "Down the pit, you must go." The humanoid with the rattle shook the staff in their direction, his mouth showing razor sharp teeth.

Cassandra grabbed onto Jonna's arm. "This is their idea of paradise?"

Lokke tried to hide behind Cassandra. "What are you afraid of, you're dead?"

"Speak for yourself, horn-head."

"Horn-head?" Bob burst out laughing. "That's a good one. I've got to write that down!"

109

"Bob, you're not helping."

"This is for posterity," the pixie chuckled and returned to the process of writing. "I think I'll capitalize it."

All the warrior's expressions mirrored the one with the staff; their razor sharp teeth reflected in the light. A howl went up in the distance.

Lokke yelped, "White wolves!"

The phrase echoed down the line, and chaos broke loose. Warriors ran in all directions. The humanoid with the rattle dropped the staff and ran.

Grabbing Cassandra and Lokke by the arms, Jonna tried to run, but was jerked back. Both were standing rooted in fear.

"Come on," he tugged again. Their feet started to move as he dragged them away from the howling.

Small rocks and pebbles dotted the landscape of a plain that stretched out forever, and then all at once, Jonna skidded to a halt. Both Lokke and Cassandra swung forward, sliding to a stop beside him.

Lokke's eyes were big. "What are you waiting for? Keep going! Keep going!"

"Lokke!" Cassandra pointed. Directly in front was a ravine, and it dropped down who knew how far. On the far side of the ravine, the flat plain continued. She swallowed. "Another step and—at least there is a bright side. The humanoids let us go." Her toe tapped a rock, knocking it forward. It bounced twice and tumbled over the edge. They never heard it land.

Jonna, who had been watching it fall, turned around to face the pursuing wolves. Cassandra followed his lead.

Lokke bounced between the wolves and the ravine in panic. "Only to be eaten by wolves!" He stopped to face the direction they had come. "Jonna, do something!" Howls went up across the plain.

Jonna kept quiet, thinking over the situation. With the ravine behind and the wolves in front, there weren't many options. Fabius was not here to create a gate this time, and the last thing they wanted was to go back down. They needed a place they could breathe a moment; they needed a real direction. On top of that, he was tired of running from the wolves.

Lokke shook Jonna's arm. "Jonna!"

Cassandra growled, "Let him think."

"There's no time to think." Lokke's eyes shot wider. He pointed at the wolves. "They're coming!"

Jonna thoughts settled. "Patience." They couldn't run, and they couldn't hide; it was time to show some strength. If he were to—his thoughts focused.

Cassandra heard mumbling as he went through the different possibilities. "What are you doing?"

"He's gone loopy, that's what!" Lokke waved his arms in front of Jonna and tried to get a response. "He's going to make a stand!"

Jonna pretended not to see Lokke's gyrations. "Not a stand," a peace dropped over him, "a statement."

Lokke's voice was shrill. "And what are you going to state? Please come get me?" He glanced over the edge. "I'll jump before going back!"

"No, you won't." Cassandra moved closer Jonna. "We're with you Jonna."

"Speak for yourself!" Lokke laid down on his belly, searching for something to grasp down the side of the ravine. "What if we jump to that ledge down there, stay close to the wall, and hold on tight? We do that, and we might make it!"

"Cassandra and I are not jumping. Go ahead if you like."

The howling had stopped, but the ground had begun to rumble. Three of the four white wolves showed on the horizon with the fourth appearing behind the others. They sniffed around the pit Faqir had disappeared into and then turned in the group's direction.

"They're here," Lokke panicked. He moved to jump, but Cassandra grabbed his arm. "Let me go!"

"Stop it. You're distracting Jonna!"

Stones bounced as the ground shook. One of the white

wolves took the lead. It noticed the three it hunted were not running, dropped to a walk, and turned to the right, waiting for the others. The white mist followed behind.

Jonna grinned. "And they're smart too."

Bob was jumping up and down. "I need popcorn."

"Popcorn?" That threw Jonna. "How do you know what popcorn is?"

"Isn't that what you eat at movies? Elfleda and I do talk you know."

Two of the wolves went to the right; the other two went to the left. Each took a position equal distant from the others. As one unit they closed in the semicircle, stopping about thirty feet from their prey.

"Bob, this is not a movie. This is real."

"It's a standoff," Lokke said with glee. "I can't believe it! They actually think you're up to something!" He paused, a funny look crossing his face. "And what's popcorn?"

"He is up to something," Cassandra spoke through clenched teeth.

Jonna watched; his eyes centered on the lead wolf. The wolf milled back and forth, never holding still. It was that wolf's decision when the attack should occur.

Or would he? Perhaps they were to hold them until Dagda appeared? Could be, maybe, but if they really wanted Jonna dead—the lead wolf leaped.

"Tueneup Aeneo, Qisvo, Eimwoan Eewiouo."

The wolves froze. The leader was in mid-jump, suspended in the air, though his eyes moved. A thunderclap came from somewhere above and struck the ground. The bizarre white mist spun in their direction.

The mist engulfed them, pushed them toward the ravine, jerked at their clothing, and whipped stones into the air. It caught the rolled up map, plucked it from Jonna's belt pouch, and sent it tumbling into the ravine.

Jonna gasped, trying to reach out, but it was too late. The map dropped into darkness. Ominous words hit their ears. "I will destroy you yet."

The view around all three faded as the third part of the spell kicked in. The greenish-purple grass of Bliss faded in around them.

"We're back!" Cassandra reached over and hugged Jonna. "I can't believe we got out that quick."

Bob's head dropped. "No way, I didn't get it all written down! Next time you're in danger, slow down a little."

Jonna listened to Bob's rant and sighed.

Lokke gasped, dropped to the grass, and kissed it over and over. He looked up at the sky above and inhaled. "I'm alive!"

"It's not over yet." Concern crossed Jonna's face as he felt the pocket where the map had been tucked. That white mist wanted them dead. Could Fabius' words be true? Was he really opening the door for some sort of greater evil? He swallowed. "All I did was create a delay. On top of that, the map is gone, and this place is no longer safe."

"You mean," Cassandra spoke slowly, "this can never be my home again." She sighed as her head dropped.

"Unless we figure something else out, I'm afraid not. They know you've level jumped."

Cassandra looked up, steeling herself. "It doesn't matter. It is all worth it if you get back safely."

"I tried to tell you." Lokke shook his head. "I tried to tell you she could not come, but noooo. You had to insist."

Cassandra didn't say a word. Jonna stared at him. "Shut up, Lokke. This is hard enough as it is."

Bob fell away laughing. "Oh, this is good. Can you say it again just for good measure?"

"You too, Bob."

Bob huffed. "But he deserved it."

"I—" Lokke looked from Jonna to Cassandra. "Okay," he said at last, "I'm sorry." After a moment of silence, he peeked over at Cassandra. "I am sorry."

She sighed. "Fine."

Lokke reverted to a grin. "So what's next on the agenda?"

Jonna remembered what he and Cassandra had talked about in Anaxa's hut. "We need to see the Fates."

Lokke's eyes widened. "No!"

"He's right." Cassandra looked up as if seeing something. "The only way to find the gate now is to find them."

Lokke exhaled. "Boy, did I pick 'em this time."

"How do we find the Fates?" Jonna turned to Cassandra. "In Norse mythology, they lived under the shade of Yggdrasil."

"Yggdrasil? Never heard of it." Lokke shook his head.

Could names in general be translated to demoneze? Maybe. "How about," Jonna translated the word in his brain, "Zhhesetokk? No, no," he thought again, "how about Ahhesetokk?"

Lokke grabbed both Jonna and Cassandra by the hand and attempted to drag them somewhere else. "Well, that's that. Time to go." He stopped and looked at them; despite his pulling, both remained still. "You're not moving?"

"Just a moment." Jonna studied Lokke again. "What are you hiding?"

"What is he hiding?" Bob watched intently from Jonna's shoulder; the rubbing stopped. "Oops," the rubbing started again, "sorry about that. I got caught up."

"Me?" Lokke's eyes kept watch for dead who might come too close. "What makes you say that?"

"The look on your face," Cassandra laughed. "You're a terrible liar."

Lokke spotted something in the distance and refused to take his eyes off it. "I am?"

"Is he?" Jonna questioned. "Or is he not?"

Cassandra caught on. "Or are we being manipulated by a master liar?"

"Master who?" Lokke relaxed and took his eyes off whatever he had seen. "Me? A liar? Ha!" He stuck his chest out. "I don't have to lie."

"I bet you don't." Jonna tapped his foot. "Lokke, where is Ahhesetokk?"

Lokke swallowed, noting the stern look on their faces. Perspiration formed on his brow. "I-I reeeaaallllyy don't know."

"But you've heard the word?"

"S-Soorrttta."

Jonna heard shuffling feet and sniffing behind him. It was definitely a four-footed animal.

Sir Reginald Richard The Third came from behind a clump of trees. "Good to see you found a friend." Sir Reginald wagged his tail at Cassandra.

Smiling, Jonna turned. "Sir Reginald Richard The Third, it is good to see you again."

Sir Reginald sniffed the air. "Hmm." He put his nose to the ground. "I was sure I had him this time."

"Keep trying," Jonna encouraged, "you are bound to catch him."

Sir Reginald moved off toward the lake, disappearing around a clump of bushes.

Fading in, Lokke shivered. "Do you have to encourage him?"

"Interesting," Jonna was not listening, "I would have thought Dagda had put the word out for all three of us. Why hasn't he?"

"Maybe he doesn't want to make a big deal of it?" Lokke suggested, checking their faces for any reaction. When it didn't give the desired effect, he came up with another. "He's trying to keep a low profile?"

"After what he did on the last level we were on?" Cassandra shook her head. "I don't think so."

Jonna mused, "What if that wasn't him?" He remembered the voice from the white mist.

Both looked at Jonna.

"Think about it. You're in command, and you have three fugitives running loose. Do you want to advertise this?" He moved his eyes from one face to the other. "Of course not. Advertising it would tell everyone that it can be done. So what would be the best way to solve Dagda's problem?"

Lokke gave a mischievous grin. "Quickly and silently?"

"Maybe," Jonna let them think, "but how?"

"With assassins," Cassandra's thoughts homed in.

Jonna nodded. "And now you know why they attacked. Dagda has to keep his hands clean, or questions may be asked."

Lokke stepped back. "Hold it, 'we' doesn't qualify here. She's dead," he pointed to Cassandra, "and I'm a permanent fixture, so he is really after—"

"Me," Jonna smiled. "Of course, it's only a theory based upon what we know so far."

Cassandra looked up. "Jonna, if he kills you, we don't know what will happen. He assumes you're from this land."

"And you're not?" Lokke stepped closer, studying Jonna's face. He reached up to pinch Jonna's cheek.

Bob jumped in, "Of course you're not! You would think Lokke knew better than that by now."

"How would he know, Bob?" Jonna's glared stopped Lokke. "Don't you dare."

Frowning, Bob looked confused. "Me?"

"Not you, Bob. Lokke."

"But she said," Lokke glanced at Cassandra, "you weren't from here. If you aren't from here, how can you be real? I was only checking."

"Let's get to the point." Jonna looked Lokke in the eye. "Where is Ahhesetokk?"

"Fine," Lokke's face fell. "If you want to find it—" He pointed at the dark, foreboding cave opening not far from where they were. "It is through there."

Jonna laughed.

"What's so funny?" Lokke went from watching Jonna to Cassandra; Cassandra shrugged.

"That's the one place Dagda warned me not to go." Jonna shifted direction. "Come on." Both he and Cassandra headed for the opening.

Lokke ran to catch up. "He did? Why would he—ohhh." A sparkle hit his eyes. "I see, I see, he was setting you up."

Jonna glanced back. "He was what?"

"He was setting you up." This time Lokke laughed. "But we fooled him. We went the other way. So now he thinks—no, no, no!" He ran to get ahead of both Jonna and Cassandra. "We can't go there. If he set you up, then we're walking into a trap. Don't you see, he has been driving us here all along."

Jonna nodded once. "A trap we are now prepared for."

"And there are three of us this time," Cassandra stood firmly, "and we have to get Jonna out."

Lokke jumped into the moment. "It's victory or death, let the trap close and dare it to eat our bones!"

"Yeah right." Bob shook his head. "How much longer are you going to put up with this half-demon? He's trouble."

"No more than you, Bob."

The pixie huffed. "Now wait a minute, when did I ever—" Bob stopped as a sheepish grin crept across his face. "There was that *one* time..."

Cassandra gave Lokke a look.

He cringed. "A little too much, eh?"

Jonna nodded with a sigh. "A little too much. Ready?" They reached the front of the opening.

Cassandra took his hand. "Ready!"

Lokke hesitated. "Are you sure there's not a way to talk you out—"

Jonna and Cassandra stepped into the opening.

Taking a deep breath, Lokke leaped in behind.

"What do you know?" Cassandra gazed around. "It's not dark at all."

The light shining was brighter than the place they had left. Vivid green grass grew from a soil that was white. The grass stretched out on gentle rolling hills and disappeared into the distance.

However, it wasn't this that had Jonna's attention; it was the sky. Never had he seen a tree so tall and thick. Its white bark reflected the light as if it were the sun. In awe, he voiced, "Yggdrasil, the World Tree."

Lokke looked at him sideways. "What?"

"I mean, Ahhesetokk," Jonna corrected. His eyes went to studying the tree as its branches reached beyond sight.

He had seen a lot of strange things during his stay in

117

Elfleda's world, but to see this in real life—then again, with every myth there is some element of truth.

Cassandra squeezed his hand. "Jonna."

He wondered how this connected to his own world. Surely there had to be some relation.

Cassandra tried to stay calm. "Jonna."

Lokke hit Jonna on the shoulder. "Snap out of it, man! Look!"

Jonna followed Lokke's pointing finger. There was a man clad in a tunic, shorts, belt, gloves, and an iron helmet, balancing a huge hammer on one shoulder.

"That's better," the man boomed with a smile. Raising the hammer, he swung it toward the ground.

Lightning shot in all directions; the ground shook as the hammer sank into the soil. They found themselves thrown straight up as if someone had shot them out of a cannon. Reaching the limit of their ascending height, all three started to fall.

The man below hefted the hammer and looked as if he was waiting for them to hit the ground. This was a man who took pride in his work. Couldn't he have said, 'Hello, I think you're trespassing?'

They passed through water vapor and shivered. How a single strike of an oversized hammer could shoot them straight up into the air, made no sense. Regardless, Jonna had to think fast.

"Oi Euemeoui!"

There was a noise high up in the branches of the giant tree; it sounded like a crack. The group stopped falling and drifted to the earth.

"What gods be these?" The man with the hammer stared. "One strike of my hammer should have done thee in."

"You must be Thor." Jonna stepped forward as his feet touched the ground. "Would you mind putting the hammer away?"

"Who is Thor, knave?" The man hefted the hammer a little higher, "I am Dunner, and by the gods, I will not!"

"Uh," Jonna backed up, "no reason to be hostile. How

about we lower it a little?" Perhaps sign language would be more effective? He demonstrated with one hand.

Dunner grunted and brought it down a tad but kept it within easy swing of Jonna. "Who are you?"

"I am Jonna McCambel." He bowed and tried to remember what the Vikings did at first meetings. "And this must be," Jonna thought quickly, "Ethese?"

"Aye," Dunner looked suspicious. "How is it a mortal passed over Cogsuu with the watching of the guard?"

Cogsuu, Cogsuu, what was it? There was Midgard, Asgard, the Well of Wyrd— "Ah, the bridge." Jonna looked at Dunner. "We came across no bridge. We came from the Otherworld."

"Yet no dead can cross," Dunner slowly continued, "save there be a mortal touch." His eyes narrowed. "Take them. Take them alive."

"Aw, come on," Lokke rolled his eyes. He, Jonna, and Cassandra went back to back in the form a triangle as they watched a horde of warriors approach.

"Do they have to be alive?" One of the first warriors complained. "It takes all the fun out of it." Each warrior's weapon gleamed, and the axes and swords looked sharp as they glistened in the bright light.

"For whom?" Jonna, Cassandra, and Lokke spoke all at once. They backed up further and bumped into each other. The circle of warriors closed in.

One began to strike the flat end of his sword against his shield. "Bloodshed, bloodshed, bloodshed!" The other's picked it up.

"Enough," Dunner roared with fire in his eyes. "I said alive!"

As Dunner came closer, Jonna noted the iron gloves on his hands. If he remembered right, it was the gloves that gave Thor, er, Dunner his ability to handle the hammer.

Someone tapped Jonna on the shoulder. As he turned, he looked into the face of one of the warriors.

"Nighty-night," the warrior gleamed as his fist came up. With a thud, everything went black.

Chapter 9

FATE COMES IN THREES

What was that horrible noise?

Jonna slowly opened his eyes and watched the pixie sight kick in. He closed them, opened them enough to squint, and winced at the pain. To his right was Lokke: eyes closed, and mouth open. As the half-demon breathed, the sound stayed in rhythm.

Bob exhaled, "You're awake!"

"Shh."

The pixie's voice wasn't helping. When Jonna stretched out a hand to try and stop Lokke, his hand only found air; the half-demon was too far away.

Something flickered; a light moved in the darkness. Footsteps echoed down a hall. Metal against metal shrieked as a bolt slid back. His head throbbed more.

As the door swung, a woman with long, blonde hair stepped into the room. She brought the flicker closer, moving first from Lokke to Cassandra and at last to Jonna.

"Ah, you are awake." She placed a candle and a cup on a table beside him. Pulling out a cloth, she dipped it in the cup and wiped it over his face.

Whatever it was, it stung. "Ow."

The lady spoke softly. "When faced with Dunner's hammer, most don't do this well."

Bob huffed. "Can I speak now? She is."

Jonna squinted with a grimace. "Pardon me for not rising. I seem to be misplaced." His headache pounded as he looked around.

"You are in Comtlosoos, and I am Uisye."

"Dunner's home?" Jonna tried one eye to see if the pain was better. "Uisye, are you a member of Dunner's household?" His voice was strained as he fought the pain.

"His daughter." She laughed. "You have a funny way of speaking."

Cautiously, Jonna opened his second eye. Whatever she had put on his face was helping the pain. "Thanks for the—" He motioned to the cup.

"Oh," she looked over at the liquid, "you are welcome. A mixture to help comfort."

"No," Lokke shouted, "no, no, no—" He opened his eyes, saw the candle on the table, and his voice lowered. "I told you," he looked straight at Jonna, "but no, you didn't listen!"

"Lokke—" Jonna had no patience for this. In spite of the mixture Uisye had applied, Lokke's voice tried to bring the headache back. "This is Uisye. Uisye, Lokke."

"I—er—" For the first time Lokke noticed her in the room. "Wow, I mean, er, uh, hello, I'm Lokke." He smiled, leaned toward her, and whispered, "Can you get us out of here?"

"Oh, no," she shook her head. "My father would kill me, and besides," she gave a slight smile, "you're safer in here than out there."

"That, I can believe," Jonna studied the darkness and spotted Cassandra; she was asleep. "Might I ask why we are here?"

"For court, of course." Uisye was a little surprised. "A mortal cannot come into Ethese without the permission of Ifoneemmr, the guardian of the bridge.

Bob cleared his throat. "I've never heard of Ifoneemmr. Who is he?"

"That's right." Jonna looked at Uisye. "Ifoneemmr is the one who gives everyone permission to visit Asgard, I mean

Ethese, across the rainbow bridge. So the gods think we snuck across?"

Uisye paused, a frown on her face. "What is snuck?" She shook her head. "They know from where you came. It is not a matter of trespass, but of war."

"War?" This was getting worse by the moment.

"Aye, war. They have called a court to determine how to proceed."

Lokke sat up. "Any idea on when? This musky smell is making me—" He sneezed.

Jonna looked in his direction. "Bless you. Guess you're used to the hotter parts of the Otherworld?"

Bob crossed himself. "I told you never to say that. It's dangerous to pixies!"

"Bob, what are you saying?"

"The 'bless you'. Whoops!" Bob covered his mouth, Uisye stared at Jonna, and Lokke snickered.

"Well, actually, it is sort of hot—hold it, are you trying to imply that because I'm a half-demon—"

Jonna laughed and turned to Uisye. "He is right though, when is definitely important."

"Very soon," she assured. "The council meets once a day. They assemble by Yseescsumm."

Jonna translated the name and smiled. "The Well of Urd. It is the place we want to go."

Cassandra stirred. "We're going where?" She sat up and blinked.

"Is this your slave?" Uisye watched as Cassandra looked around.

Cassandra gasped. "Slave?"

"You are dead, are you not? My father gets all his dead slaves from Noehese. How did you come to be in Jonna's service? You must be very valuable."

Cassandra looked to Jonna.

"Heroes of old would travel to the—Otherworld to retrieve those they did not want to lose."

Cassandra woke up fast and glared. "I am no one's slave."

"If I can interrupt, Cassandra is the mother of an undead child I am raising."

"So, she is your wife?"

"No." This was not coming off the way he intended. "It's a long story. Basically—"

"She is your mistress?"

Jonna's face flushed. "No, I am married."

"So is father." Uisye watched his face, curiously. "It is nothing to be embarrassed about. It is because of his mistress that I have several brothers."

"You don't understand. My wife and I adopted Elpis. I met Cassandra in the Otherworld, and she is trying to help me get out."

A tear formed in Uisye's eye. "I see. This is a brave thing you do." Her gaze went from Cassandra to Jonna. She studied him. "What is your name? Father did not say."

"Jonna." Extending his hand, he took hers lightly and released. "Jonna McCambel."

She got up. "I need to think."

"Think about what?"

"If your story is true, then my father must be informed. These are grave matters, Jonna McCambel. Undead and dead do not travel here unbidden. It is only by the Fates that such a thing can be. If indeed you came as father indicated, there is more at stake than meets the eye. I will return when it is time."

Lifting the candle, she headed toward the door. Before speaking, the others waited until her footsteps were gone.

"How about we get some light in here?" Jonna looked around. "*Mi Fsicut.*"

There was a low rumble, and the room glowed to life, revealing a few bunks around the walls with a single table of rough oak wood. Jonna moved to the door and looked through the small barred window. "It is a simple metal bar with a latch of some sort. We need a hook and string."

"A what?" Lokke squinted.

"A hook and—a fishing hook with some sort of twine?"

Cassandra and Lokke shrugged.

Of the three of them, only Jonna had surface clothes. Being dead, Cassandra created what she wanted as part of her attire, and Lokke's were made of solid pieces with no weave at all. Unfortunately, Jonna's elfin-wear did not seem to have a beginning or ending thread. Otherwise, he could have unraveled it and used it for twine.

He looked about the room. The beds were flat boards with hay thrown on top. Comfortable might not be the best word, but at least there was something. Checking his own belt pockets, he found nothing.

Temporarily out of ideas, a memory popped into his brain. Bob had used a spell on the surface to store certain items for him. If he could remember the way it was done, and translate—but that was the problem. The pixie had used no spell to store the items. He had counted to three, turned around, and stomped a foot on Jonna's shoulder.

"One, two, three," Jonna turned around and stomped the floor. Nothing formed beside him. Just in case, he did it a second time.

"Is this a dance?" Lokke walked around Jonna, watched as he performed the ritual, and imitated. "I've never done this."

"You neither?" Jonna mused. "It was worth a try."

"If this is surface magic, it won't work. What does it do?"

"What if I—" The converted words rolled through his mind. "*Uoi, uxu, uisii.*" He turned around and stomped the floor. That strange thunder occurred, a yellow glow formed, and his rolled up clothes appeared.

Bob's eyes bulged. "You did it! Wow, wait till Väinämö hears about this!" The rubbing on the parchment became furious.

Jonna unrolled his old pants, found his keys, shook out his shirt, and used the keys to scrape the shirt to start a tear. He ripped a piece of the shirttail off, fastened the key ring to the end, and tested the knot. Going to the window, he stuck his arm through the bars and swung the keys. It wasn't a fishhook, but it still might work. Lokke stayed glued to his right.

The keys hit the target but did not catch. He swung again.

Lokke's eyes were bright. "Almost there."

He swung a second time. Everyone was watching in expectation. It missed.

Lokke's tone went up notch. "Almost there."

His hand arched back, and he swung a third time. It reached the limit of its height and zoomed the other direction, barely missing the latch.

Lokke's voice was a screech. "Almost there!"

Jonna interrupted his fourth swing, pulled his arm from between the bars, and stared at Lokke. "Will you stop that? A play by play is not necessary."

"A what?"

Bob cleared his throat. "According to Elfleda, that is in reference to a commentary made when at a sporting event."

"True Bob, but now is not the time to explain that to Lokke." He looked at the half-demon. "Just please stop commenting on every swing."

"Okay, okay," the half-demon's face fell. "You can't blame me for having fun. It is like betting on runes; I can't help it."

"What?"

"Betting on runes." Lokke's face lit up. "You put runes in a wooden cup, shake them together, and dump them out. Whoever gets closest to guessing which runes will be face up wins. Of course, the general rule is, never play with a seer, but I did beat one about a year ago in—"

Jonna watched him. "Why am I listening to this?"

"You asked the question."

"Lokke, we're trying to escape, and we need to be quiet. You do understand that?"

"Sure."

Jonna motioned him to step away from the door.

Lokke took two steps back. "Of course," he bowed.

"Thank you."

Reaching through the window, he focused on the latch and swung the keys. It caught, slipped over the mechanism, and pulled.

The metal bar screeched back, and the door gave. Pulling his arm in, he rolled up the piece of cloth and placed it in his pants' pocket.

Assembling his clothes into a pile, he performed the magic again. The thunder occurred, slightly louder this time. The clothes faded from sight.

"Well done! Bravo!"

At first, Jonna thought it was Lokke, but the voice was off. In the corner of the room sat a mouse. "Wonderfully done!"

"Who are you?" He studied the newcomer. It had black eyes, gray fur, and dirty, pink feet.

"You may call me Mulo," the mouse bowed before them, "and I am, you might say, a relative of Dunner. I'm here to help you escape."

"We've already escaped." Jonna pointed toward the door and pushed it with his finger. It swung open. "If you were going to help us escape, why didn't you say something earlier?"

"And ruin all the fun?"

"Now you're sounding like two others I know." He glanced toward the half-demon and the pixie. "A relative of both of you?"

"Hey now," Bob huffed, "just because we have similar, mischievous tendencies doesn't mean—"

Lokke's eyes lit up. "He is!"

Jonna stepped forward and looked closer. "Really?"

Holding his hand up, Lokke began to count off fingers. "Let me see. On my father's, brother's, uncle's, grandfather's..." He mumbled something out of hearing, scratched his head, and then continued with a long list of names. He looked down at the mouse. "Great, great, great, great, great, great Uncle Mulo?"

The mouse bowed. "The one and only."

"It has been a long time!"

"Much too long." The mouse stepped forward and changed into something that was similar to Lokke. It grew in size and slipped forward so it would not bump into the wall. "I heard they put you in the lowest of the low." Mulo shook his head. "That was sad to hear."

"Not that they could keep me there." A twinkle appeared in Lokke's eyes. "And with this fellow here—" He put a hand on Jonna's shoulder.

Jonna gave him a look, and he removed it.

"It looks like I will make it out this time!"

Mulo's eyes were whimsical. "I am impressed, but if I know my relatives, you need to leave soon." He went to the door and checked both directions. "There are warriors about. Follow me."

He led them down the hall to the left, rather than the way Uisye had gone. When they reached a certain place on the wall, he pushed against it. "In case of siege, Dunner had passages installed."

Bob's eyes sparkled. "A secret passage?" He looked down at what was written. "Ask the details!"

"Siege? Here?" Jonna's eyes widened. "I thought the bridge was well guarded?"

"We do have our little tiffs with the giants from time to time. However, nothing like a full out war. If we do that, we go to Noehese."

"I understand. I remember many of your wars occurred in the realm of men."

Mulo stepped through the opening as the wall parted; the outside light was blinding. "Remembered from whom?"

"Oh, just—rumors, more or less." This was no time to explain his background.

"More or less," Mulo let it drop. "Ta-da, you are free." He bowed to all. "Now where?"

Cassandra was adamant, "We need to find the Fates."

Mulo's eyes widened. "That is dangerous. Do you want to go back to Dunner's jail?"

"No," Bob shook his head. "That would make a very poor ending."

Jonna studied Mulo. "Is there some complication about seeing the Fates?"

"Complication? Of course there's a complication! The Fates' hall is right next to the council hall, and the council hall is where you go for court." He glared at them all. "Need I go on?"

Jonna located the world tree. "Regardless, that is where we need to go. Which way?"

"Why," Mulo grinned off handed, "this way." He pointed away from the tree.

Lokke stepped in front of him. "Did you hear what my great, great, great—" He stopped and counted on his fingers. "Oh, forget it. Did you hear what Uncle Mulo said? We are heading toward the very place we are trying to run from."

"We need answers, and the Fates have them."

"But we just escaped!"

Cassandra stepped in, "If Jonna feels we need to go there, then it's necessary."

Jonna kept watch for Dunner's men. An uneasiness settled in the pit of his stomach the further they went from the tree. "Wait." He stopped and stared at Mulo. "Something's wrong. This is not the way."

Mulo's eyes widened as he sized up Jonna. "Let me check." His eyebrows knitted together as he studied their surroundings. "Ah, you're right," he gave a big smile, "How silly of me."

Jonna nodded without comment, and they backtracked. The man had lied, and Jonna knew it. Why had he tried to trick them?

"That's the spirit," Mulo encouraged, "nothing like a little danger to make the walk brisk. Of course, if we do get caught, they may not go so easy this time." He patted Lokke on the shoulder. "I'll put in a good word."

Lokke pleaded, "Did you hear what he said?"

Jonna nodded. It wasn't a coincidence Mulo had found them. "We're getting close."

Not far in the distance was a hall. From the back, it was hard to see clearly, but Jonna knew that was the place.

Cassandra could resist no longer. "Who lives in this land?"

"All the gods," Mulo volunteered happily. "Each have their territory."

"But here? In the Otherworld?"

Mulo started to speak, but Jonna spoke first. "We are connected to the Otherworld, and yet, we are not in it. This land is not a part of Dagda's domain."

A grin spread across Mulo's face. "He's right. You can still stop before it's too late. The Fates aren't kind to those coming from Dagda's realm."

"What do you mean?" Cassandra's frowned. "I've never heard—"

"And you won't," Mulo became sorrowful. "Punishment is swift. Perhaps Jonna should go by himself, and you stay here." His broad smile came back. "Lokke and I can watch over you."

"Now I know you're full of it," Cassandra growled. "Jonna, he's trying to delay us. Come on!" They both began to run.

At first, Lokke stood there and then swung back to his uncle. "What's going on?" Mulo was gone, so he turned and sprinted after them.

They reached the hall, arriving at the backside where ornate carvings of myths stood out upon its flank. So far, they had seen none of Dunner's warriors. Was that by coincidence or by design? How was Mulo part of this?

He remembered what Uisye had said about only entering this land by fate. The group rounded the final corner and—

A strange, female voice asked, "Why have you come, Jonna McCambel?"

Jonna halted in mid step, his foot slowly coming down to touch the grass. In front of him was one of the Fates. She was not as young as the two behind her, yet much more beautiful than the Norse stories said.

"I am Yses, oldest of the Fates, and I repeat my question. Why have you come, Jonna McCambel?"

Jonna looked around him; this was not what he had expected. Then again, what had he expected? If these women were whom they said they were, they obviously had to know who he was. "Might we talk a little less conspicuous? There are gods looking to find us."

"They cannot touch you while seeking our counsel." Answering an unspoken question of Jonna's, she added. "Mulo knew this."

Lokke stumbled forward with heavy breath, looked up, and stared.

Yses' eyes held him. "Lokke, son of Tonuo, son of Qeym, son of Qiommo, we know of what you seek." She smiled at him, and Lokke's jaw dropped. "We know of what you choose to do. Do what is right, and your path will be granted."

The second of the three fates stepped forward and bowed slightly. "I am Wisuiboeo." Her eyes bore into Lokke. "A choice that you make will not be so easy. Choose life, and die; choose death, and live."

The third of the three fates stepped forward, drawing Lokke's attention. "I am Tlyme, youngest of the three Fates. When your fate is most dread, when you see no other choice, you will find another."

Lokke eyes widened, and he closed his mouth. Jonna watched him slip behind the rest of the group, hiding out of sight.

"Cassandra," Yses nodded.

Cassandra looked at her, eyes unblinking, trapped in the Fate's stare. As one voice flowed into another, the three fates spoke with Yses starting first.

"The quest you have chosen walks the line of the gray. Beware the pit on either side."

Yses bowed toward Wisuiboeo, who continued. "Each step you take must hold to the center," and again Wisuiboeo bowed toward Tlyme who finished, "or by its motion, you will slide."

Swallowing, Cassandra did the same as Lokke and tried to hide behind Jonna. It was strange. Once the Fates spoke to either, all they wanted to do was run. Would he feel the same?

"At last," Yses looked in Jonna's direction, "it is time to answer the hidden question. What do you seek?"

Jonna closed his eyes. The immediate word was answers, and millions of things came to mind, the latest being Mulo. He had questions about his adopted daughter, Cassandra, the land above, and the land below. The Dark mages never left his thoughts. What was his place in this Elfleda's realm? Was he meant to be here at all? But most of all, he wanted to see his family; he wanted to go home. His eyes opened. "I seek to know where my home is."

Yses nodded and beckoned him toward the Well of Urd. As she reached the well, a handle turned of its own accord and raised a bucket. "Come and see."

Walking past the other Fates, he leaned forward against the well and gazed into the bucket.

"What do you see?"

"I see a sky that's deep with blue and grass that's green with clouds up in the sky."

"The way is open," Yses nodded. "Look and see."

Jonna looked a second time. "I see a sky of both night and day. The moon and stars shine reflected from a mirror in between."

Wisuiboeo came up from behind and stood beside Yses. "The bridge is there," Wisuiboeo spoke softly. "Look and see."

A leaf dropped from above and struck the surface. Waves formed outward, hitting and bouncing from the sides. She continued, "What do you see?"

"I see—" He could tell something was taking place. There were mages and movement, but because of the waves, they were only glimmers. "I cannot." A frown crossed his face. "The waves are stopping the view."

Tlyme came up from behind and moved to Jonna's right. "Wisdom passes; the wine has aged. Look and see."

As the waves stopping moving, a scene formed on the water's surface. It was far away at first, but rapidly approached. A horse with a rider? A knight with a lance? The man passed through the scene and vanished as he encountered a mountain wall, yet he did not halt or stop. For some strange reason, Jonna could hear the running horse. He could feel the man's charge.

"I see a man on horseback, charging a mountain. When he reached the mountain, he passed right through."

"Though the task you take will come to an end, your quest for knowledge will not be so. Though the gods would use you as a tool, they will find you gone before you go." Tlyme smiled, locking eyes with Jonna.

Yet, he did not run. Something about it held him, watched him, and he refused to back down. Not everyone was permitted to stare into the Well of Urd. It was a gift that few had been given.

"You would enter into our hall?" Tlyme brought him out of his thoughts.

Jonna held her gaze. The desire was there to see what other things the Fates might know, but if he did that, what would happen to everything else? Would he get so caught up that he might never leave? Jonna shook loose and looked at the Fates. "I don't think I should."

"His decisions are turning better already," Tlyme smiled though with a hint of sadness, "for a mortal. He senses a truth he does not know; he knows a truth he does not sense." She touched Jonna's face with her soft fingers. "Go to Cogsuu, and flee to Noehese. There you will find the people you seek."

"What people?" His family? Fabius? Jonna remembered the object Fabius had thrown, reached into his pocket, and pulled it out. The object was a ring with a signet set into the top. The signet matched the same initials that would be on Fabius' casket.

As Tlyme finished, all the Fates turned and headed into the hall. Jonna dropped the ring into his pocket.

Bob's eyes widened. "Can I see that one more time? I'm trying to make a drawing."

There was a yell. A small group of warriors rushed toward them.

"Later, Bob. Run!"

Jonna grabbed Cassandra's hand, and to his surprise, Cassandra grabbed Lokke's. They raced over the wavy landscape toward the one and only bridge.

The bridge glowed with colors of the rainbow, shining out in all directions. However, unlike normal rainbows, this end was attached to the green grass and white soil.

Clearing the next hilltop, they slowed. There, leaning back against the left side of the bridge, was an old man with a long white beard. His eyes were closed, hat tilted down, and none of the distant yells disturbed him. They took a tentative step toward the bridge, and the old man spoke, "I'd not be doing that today."

Jonna stepped forward. "Are you Iioneemms?"

"The same." Iioneemms did not his eyes. "Why should I let you pass?"

Lokke's eyes were getting wider by the moment. "Because we need to get away? What are you waiting for?" He started to run across, but Jonna caught him and jerked him back. Out of nowhere, a sharp edged pendulum arced past and sliced the air where Lokke would have been.

The old man looked up. "How did you know?" Iioneemms grinned. "I thought for sure I had you all."

"A guardian would never sleep on duty," Jonna shook his head, "and you were polite enough to give a warning."

"I did?" Iioneemms thought back. "Confound it. I did, didn't I?" He took a deep breath, exhaled, and pulled at his beard. "It's this old age thing. After over a millennium, you start to slow down a little."

"Jonna?" Lokke shifted to put more distance between him and the warriors. "The bridge? Remember?"

Cassandra stepped around Lokke. "Please Sir, we do need to pass."

Chapter 10

CURSED CROSSROADS

"Well," Iioneemms worked toward a decision, "since you are leaving and not coming, I guess it would be okay."

"Thank the Fates." Cassandra turned to the right as an axe flew by. It thudded off a bridge step.

"The Fates?" Iioneemms stepped in front of them. "What do they have to do with this?" He closed one eye and studied each of them. "Is something going on that I should know about?"

Jonna assured. "It is an expression, nothing more. It is time we went home."

"Home, eh?" He sniffed the air. "And not all mortals either." He looked at Cassandra. "The dead cannot pass."

"I don't want to pass. I want to walk to the other side of the bridge." The clang of weapons moved closer.

"You do, do you? How gullible do you think I am?"

Jonna sighed. "Look, we are being chased by a group of warriors set on dismembering us before our time. Well," he looked at Cassandra, "before my time."

"And mine," Lokke nodded. "Don't forget me!"

"And his," Jonna added, but he sensed the point was already made. "The Fates said, 'Go to Cogsuu and flee to Noehese.'"

Iioneemms looked skeptical, but Jonna saw he was starting to thaw. "They did? Hmm."

"Your decision, sir? Our fates are in your hands." Jonna stood there, prepared to turn and face the warriors.

Iioneemms inhaled. "Oh, alright." He reached behind one of the posts and touched something they could not see. "The Fates, you say?"

Jonna nodded. "If you don't believe us, I'll stay right here, and we can go see them together."

Iioneemms waved them on. "Go quickly, before I change my mind."

"Thank you." Cassandra touched his arm. "We shall never forget."

As they passed, Iioneemms' hand touched something again. They ducked down where the colors began and hid beside the rays which formed the railings of the bridge.

Two warriors made the crest of the hill. Out of breath, the first jumped toward the bridge. There was a metal flash as the pendulum came down.

"What are you doing?" The second stopped short. "By mandate of Dunner, we are trying to catch those trespassers!"

"What trespassers?" Iioneemms lifted his hat. "I am the master of the bridge. If someone were trespassing, I should have been told." As more began to assemble, he glared at each one. "According to Dunner, none of you can pass."

The conversation behind them left Jonna's mind. It was a strange sensation, crawling along this bridge. It felt solid enough, and yet his senses said it was not. Radiating brightness in all directions, the rails were high enough to keep them unseen, so long as they kept to their hands and knees.

"Can't pass?" The lead warrior waved the sword in his hand. "If you'd let us go, we'd catch them without crossing!"

Iioneemms raised a walking stick and pointed it in the warrior's direction. "Don't you go threatening me." He punched the warrior three times on the chest. "I am the guardian, and I say who crosses."

"You think so?" The warrior's chest grew as he inhaled. "We have Dunner's permission. What do you think of that, old man?"

"Old man?" Iioneemms stood straighter with a red face and staff raised. "Watch your words, or you might find yourself outmatched!"

"By who," the warrior shot back, "some old man with a cane?"

"That's twice," Iioneemms warned with a growl. "Three time's the charm."

"Old man, old man," one of the warriors behind shouted.

"That's it." Iioneemms jumped forward and swung his staff.

Jonna didn't even bother to whisper. "Run!"

"There they go!" The warrior pointed as the staff dropped on his head. His knees buckled. Iioneemms jabbed another to the stomach, blocked a strike from an axe, and slammed a third so hard the warrior fell backwards.

"Forget the old man," the first cleared his head. "Charge the bridge!"

Lokke kicked into overdrive and raced toward the other end. The warriors surged forward, most caught by the pendulum, but a few of the group jumped through unscathed.

"Now that's the spirit," Iioneemms grinned. "I see you're real swingers!" Iioneemms felt the point of a sword at his throat.

"Turn it off, or face my wrath!"

"Are you stupid?" Iioneemms turned to look at the warrior nearest to him. "You do know I'm an immortal?"

"We'll see what Dunner says about this."

"Fine," Iioneemms turned off the trap, "but if you step off the other side, then you're mine." He smiled a big, wide smile.

The warrior looked nervous. "Fine." He turned from Iioneemms. "Catch them!"

Lokke took off with another boost of speed. "Run!"

"You go too," Jonna looked at Cassandra. "I have to slow them down."

She faced the approaching warriors. "I'm not leaving."

"Cassandra," Jonna bordered exasperation, "I need you to—"

"Will you do something so we can all go?" She pointed toward the warriors; metal clanged against metal as their swords and shields touched. "They're coming!"

"What are you two doing?" Lokke called from the other end of the bridge.

Jonna went through all the spells he could remember, searching for one that would work the best. With a horde of approaching troops, a bridge between heaven and earth, and a god named Dunner soon to show, nothing he knew could do anything.

Besides, it wasn't an easy decision. First he had to focus, which was hard enough with the warriors bearing down upon them. Second, he had to figure out something he wanted to do. Third, he had to phrase it in surface magic. And fourth? Convert it to demoneze.

Cassandra put a hand on his shoulder. "Jonna."

"Guys," Lokke took a tentative step toward them, "come on!"

"I'm thinking." Jonna watched the warriors move closer; it was a good thing the bridge was long. What he needed was something that they would understand, and it needed to be so frightful they would stop in their tracks. He remembered one such creature from Norse lore.

Cassandra watched wide-eyed. "Jonna, now."

"*Tuoyt Jmmyeisi.*" The strange thunder sounded. The bridge they stood upon shook, and a roar, louder than the thunder, sent echoes for miles. Despite the fact that the trespassers were in sight, the warriors fled.

Jonna felt rather proud of himself but noticed Cassandra backing away.

"What is it?" she stammered out.

Jonna moved toward her, catching her hand before she ran.

"Is that a dragon?" Her eyes were wide.

"Translated to demoneze, I believe they call it the Noehese serpent. It is my idea of it anyway and scaled down, relatively speaking."

Part of the serpent's huge tail unwrapped from around the bridge, raised up, and started to descend; Cassandra screamed.

"No, no," Jonna made her focus on it as the tail came down. It landed on top but did no damage. "You don't understand," he grinned, "it's an illusion."

"But it sounds so real, and the bridge shook!"

"Sounds only and imitation." His grin broadened. There was no time to explain the excitation of air molecules, and how they created vibration, but any physics teacher should grasp the concept. "Remembering the name, I took the surface idea of illusion, converted it to demoneze, and created a creature from Norse mythology. The sounds and shakes add believability."

She shook. "Illusion or not, I want to leave."

"I do believe it's time." Jonna started to turn. The warriors were running away over the top of each other. Some gathered by the old man while others moved toward the bridge. Okay, maybe his illusion was working too good; not only were the warriors retreating, but soon every person in Ethese would be there to see it. "I bet Dunner won't be far behind."

Lokke was gazing up as they reached him. "Nice touch," he could not take his eyes off. "Almost as good as my giant frog."

"Almost?" Jonna chuckled. "How about we get off this bridge? I don't know how long they will believe the illusion."

"Good by me." Lokke dragged his eyes away. The end of the bridge touched a forest with tall conifer trees stabbing at the sky. He stepped off the bridge. When he turned to face them, he yelped in surprise. "Hey, where'd you go?"

Cassandra and Jonna followed and appeared from nowhere off to his right.

"There you are!" He stared behind them.

As Jonna followed his gaze, he saw what had happened; once off the bridge, the entrance had disappeared. Only a rainbow hung in the sky. "We don't need it anymore."

Lokke swallowed and stepped to the spot where he had come through. "But what if we have to go back?"

"Why would we?" Jonna waved his hand at the foliage around them. "We are out."

"The surface?" Lokke noticed the sun for the first time. "This is really the surface?" A smile lit his face. He took a deep breath, held it a second, and started to cough.

"Are you all right?"

He croaked, "Something in the air."

Jonna smelled the air. There was a wide variety of foliage. Grass, weeds, pine trees, and mold, all assailed his nose, but the closest thing to the group was, "Honeysuckle?"

He picked one of the flowers and held it close to Lokke. The half-demon sneezed. "So you're allergic to honeysuckle?"

"Is that what you call the blasted thing?"

Jonna laughed. "All part of the experience of life."

Lokke made a face.

"Jonna," Cassandra came closer to him, "if we really are on the surface, can I see Elpis?"

"The question is, is it our surface?"

Bob gasped. "No! You really did it?" He thumbed through something unseen; it looked as if he were holding up a book. "Uh, Jonna?" A red cover with gold markings came into focus. Though from Jonna's angle, he could not make out the title.

"Yes?"

"We may have a slight problem." Fingers reached out of nowhere and snatched Bob up. The connection popped, and the pixie was gone.

"Bob?"

Cassandra looked at him, a frown on her face. "Elpis says Väinämö is not very happy. Something about Bob giving out information he shouldn't."

"But he hadn't said anything."

Lokke cleared his throat. "Can I please have your attention?"

Both turned to look at him.

"If you don't know where on the surface we are, how do you know we're on the surface at all?"

139

"I don't know where we are," Jonna looked around at the forest, "but we will find out."

There was a quick way. But did he dare? The words Queen Freya had used on him came rolling back; the spell could take them to the elvish city. If this were the wrong place, saying the wrong type of magic should do nothing. "*Delvium Adventi.*" Thunder echoed from nowhere in a cloudless sky. All the forest noise stopped; the trees went soundless, despite the blowing of the wind. After a few moments, the sound returned. Something had tried to happen, but nothing did. Was Lokke right?

"Hmm." Jonna put a hand under his chin. "Let me try something else. *Eimwoyn Bewiouo.*"

The thunder came but not as loud. There was a brief pause of soundlessness, and the sound returned. Whatever was going on, both magics were blocked.

"Are you supposed to be doing something?" Lokke shook his head. "If you are—"

"What in the world is going on?" The image of Väinämö faded into view, though it waved in the wind. "Who is trying to—" His eyes moved to Jonna. "I should have known. Do you know how much effort it is to keep you out of trouble? What do you think you're doing?"

Jonna folded his arms. "I'm—"

"Are you trying to destroy us, or do you like shaking up the fabric of magic?"

"But I'm—" Jonna's folded arms sagged.

"But nothing," Väinämö glared. "Don't you understand there is a balance to magic? We do not mix magic. The mixing of magic is strictly taboo, not to mention most mages can't do it, but that's beside the point."

"But I didn't—"

"I want no excuses. Dagda is about to have a heart attack, the Otherworld is in chaos—"

It was the way Väinämö said it that got Jonna's attention. He grinned, "We are not in the Otherworld?"

"Of course not, and stop trying to distract me. Now, where were we?" Väinämö thought. "Ah, as I was saying—"

140

"Then where are we?"

Väinämö paused as if hearing something far away. "What are you asking?"

"I said, where are we?"

"You're—" Väinämö tried to get a better look. "You're in a forest. How should I know where you are?"

"But how did you find us?"

Väinämö smiled. "I located your magic signature."

"My what?"

"Your magic signature." Väinämö glanced at the two companions; it was obvious he did not like them listening. "The unique way a mage uses magic? And, I might add, the way in which a mage can be located while using it. The fact is, you can't go haphazardly using magic from one realm to another."

"What does it matter?" Jonna prepared for a debate. "One world's magic doesn't work in the other anyway, right?"

Väinämö waved his finger. "For normal mages, that is true, but you are different; you are not from this land. Thus, all magic spoken has some effect; with you, it is dangerous."

"But Dagda said, and Lokke indicated—"

"For them it is not an issue. For you, it could happen. The impact, even if they tried, is so minor—"

Lokke huffed. "Who's calling me a minor?"

Jonna glared at him, and Lokke closed his mouth. Jonna turned to Väinämö. "I don't understand."

"They were born in their perspective locations, limited by the laws which brought them into existence. You, on the other hand, came from a place—"

The words popped into Jonna's mind. "That has no magic. Er, does have magic but in a different form. I'm like a neutral ground on an electric circuit."

Väinämö nodded. "Precisely." A funny look crossed his face. "What's a neutral ground?"

Before he thought, Jonna answered, "It lets electricity pass through when the negative is not working."

Väinämö's frown deepened. "And what is electricity and a negative?"

141

"It's—"

Väinämö shook his head. "We need to talk about that later. Back to the point, where someone else won't have an effect, you always have an effect, even if you don't know what it is."

"Like what? How do I know the effect? Is there some sort of indication?" With so little information, the situation was frustrating!

The mage inhaled. "Hold it. If only you would have listened in class!"

"But I've only been here—"

Väinämö glared at him. "Would a few lessons have hurt? Hmm?"

It was a no win situation. "I—I suppose not, but you don't understand. I had other things on my mind."

"Daddy things," Cassandra nodded, "and he'll make a good one."

Lokke spoke slowly. "He's not from where we are from?" He stared at the mage. "Where is he from?"

Cassandra waved to Lokke. "Shh."

"Don't you 'shh' me." Lokke stood a little straighter. "I have every right—"

"Enough," Väinämö's voice roared; even the wind quieted as his gaze took them in. "Now, that's better. Jonna," the mage inhaled, "magic is held in a delicate balance. You seem to be some sort of bridge which removes the division from one magic to the next. When you do not adhere to the rules, the wrong spell done in the wrong way at the wrong time can have major consequences."

Lokke couldn't resist, "That's a lot of wrongs." He spotted the mage's eyes, closed his mouth, and swallowed. "Sorry."

"So you see the dilemma. In order for you to do your magic safely—"

"I have to go to magic school."

A cloth appeared in Väinämö's hand, and he blotted his brow. "Yes, now you understand."

Jonna gave a single nod. "Do we start now or deal with Dagda first?"

Väinämö frowned. "Forgot about that. I think it's time you learn a new spell. It's—oops."

"Oops?" Jonna waited, longer than should have been necessary. "Oops what?"

"I can't give the spell." Väinämö shook his head. "Not here, not now."

"Okay," Jonna played along, "and why not?"

"Wrong location, wrong phrase."

"What?"

"Wrong location, wrong phrase."

"I heard that the first time." He stepped back from the apparition. "What do you mean?"

"When you get there, I'll find you."

Jonna frowned. "Is this not the surface? I thought you said it was."

"Oh, it's the surface all right," Väinämö nodded, "but the spell I need to give you is good only in the land of the giants, near the Well of Nonos."

Jonna's eyebrows raised. "So I take it we are going to visit the land of the giants?"

Looking from one to another, Lokke gasped. "Are you nutty? That's out of the frying pan onto the hot coals."

"Don't you mean into the fire?" Jonna looked at him.

"No," Lokke shook his head, "I cook with hot coals."

Jonna turned to Väinämö. "So, we are going to visit the frost giants of legend?" He remembered this from his Norse mythology.

Väinämö nodded. "How else will you find Fabius' body?"

Jonna raised an eyebrow. "You know about Fabius?"

"For a very long time."

"Hold it, if you knew about Fabius, why didn't someone else come down to the Otherworld and help him out?"

Väinämö winked. "Who says they didn't try?" He began to fade away.

"No, wait."

Väinämö faded into view. "Yes?"

"What happened to Bob?"

Putting his hand on his head, Väinämö paused. "Bob?"

Jonna nodded. "He started to tell me something and disappeared?"

"Oh, that Bob."

Jonna narrowed his eyes. "Is there another?"

"An overdue elvish, library book, I suspect." Väinämö glanced over his shoulder and glared at someone out of sight. "He'll be back later."

Jonna was skeptical.

The mage began to fade.

"Wait."

The mage came back, eyes steadfast. "Yes?"

It was obvious he was not going to budge about Bob, so Jonna asked about something else. "How do we get to the frost giants?"

"Follow the tree root," Väinämö waved at the forest. "It always leads to the Well."

Jonna looked around. "Which tree root?" When he turned back, the mage was gone.

"I see all kinds of tree roots." Lokke shook his head. "Which one?"

"Well," Cassandra studied the area, "there must be something that makes it stand out. Otherwise, he would have given more details."

"You would think." Jonna nodded, knowing the truth about his mage friend all too well.

"But I don't want to see the frost giants." Lokke shivered. "There is a reason my side of the family doesn't go there, and one of those is temperature."

A thought crossed Jonna's mind. "Hold it, why do you have to go?"

"That's right." Cassandra turned to Lokke. "Now that you're out, you don't need us anymore. You can go where you want."

Lokke looked at each one. "Not exactly."

Jonna studied Lokke's face. "You're not free?"

Lokke shook his head.

"Something is keeping you from being free?"

Lokke nodded.

When no more words came, Jonna volunteered, "Now might be a good time to tell us."

"Fine," Lokke exhaled, "in order for me to be free, I've got to pass through the gates of the Otherworld."

"But we are out of the Otherworld. We bypassed all that."

Lokke shrugged. "It doesn't count for me."

"So in order to get you out, we have to go all the way back?"

"I'm tied by a curse to the Otherworld. Until I pass through the gates, I'll never be free."

"What curse?"

"It's a long story." Lokke inhaled. "One I'd rather not repeat."

"So in some undisclosed way, you did something that put a curse on you, and now you can't be free except by the gates of the Otherworld?"

"That's the basics."

"Jonna, what is this?" Cassandra pointed to a spot on the ground.

Bending down, he brushed some of the dirt away and revealed a bronze disc. On the disc was a half circle with a line drawn through it. "It appears to be a territory marker."

Two booted feet not more than a foot away caught his attention. Attached to them was a young boy dressed in green with a grin. The boy held a bow with an arrow notched and pulled.

"And I think we have found who lives here," Jonna finished.

"A bow and arrow," the boy pointed the arrow at the disc. "It is the symbol of our territory. Shall I shoot now, or will you pay the toll?"

Jonna stood to his feet. "None of those choices would be better." He looked down at the child.

The child pointed the arrow up. "Tell me why I should not shoot you?"

Lokke moved to the front. "Let me handle this." He smiled at the child. "Now, you really don't want to—"

The child pulled the arrow back further, deepening the bend of the bow. The aim was at Lokke's chest.

"Why don't you handle this?" Lokke sidestepped.

Jonna studied the bronze marker. "We haven't crossed the line. Therefore, we haven't crossed into your territory."

"What?" The child looked down and relaxed the pulled string. "You mean all this time—"

Lokke reached out and plucked the bow and arrow from the child's hands.

"Hey!"

"Now we can talk," Lokke grinned. "I'm Lokke—"

The boy ducked, spun on his heels, and took off through the brush. A loud whistle sounded as he disappeared into the foliage.

Jonna shook his head. "I don't think we should follow." Unknown territory, kids running around with weapons, and dark, unyielding brush did not make for safe travel.

"Me too." Cassandra could not see where the boy had gone, or how he had vanished so quickly.

"Oh, come on," Lokke shook his head, "it's a child, and a human child at that, not like us half-demons." He stepped over the marker and moved toward the underbrush.

"Now I've got you." The boy was back, another bow and arrow had found his hands. There was a broad smile on his face. "And this time you did step over the line." Putting two fingers in his mouth, he made a second loud whistle. The bushes came alive.

"Whoa." Jonna stepped back as the woods filled with archers all the size of children.

"The bow, please." He motioned to what was in Lokke's hand.

Wide-eyed, Lokke handed it to him.

"And now for the toll. Your money, please."

"Money?" Lokke motioned to his clothing. "Do I look like I have money?"

"You there," the boy pointed to Cassandra. "How about you?"

"Me?" Cassandra laughed. "I'm dead. How can I have money?" Cassandra changed her clothes by blinking.

All the archers stepped back, and a murmur went through the group. The boy's grip tightened. "Somebody has to have money!"

Chapter 11

DARK ELVES A HUNTING

For the first time, Jonna noticed snickering among the ranks. The boy ignored it. "You, Jonna, I think they call you, give me your money."

It was time to make a judgment call. Could these kids really be guards? "I don't have any money."

The boy's face turned red. "Somebody better give me some money, or—"

"You'll throw a temper tantrum?" Jonna looked at the arrows pointed at them. "Okay, we give. What are you going to do?"

"That's not fair," the boy lowered his bow. "You stepped over the line, and anyone who steps over the line must pay up."

"Why?"

"What do you mean, why?" The boy stepped closer to Jonna. "You just do. That's what travelers who come this way always do."

"You're sure?"

The boy nodded. "It was written down. Every traveler must pay to cross these woods." He pulled a small piece of paper from a belt pocket. It was written in a child's handwriting, almost unreadable.

Maybe they could avoid the subject? Jonna shook his head. "But we don't want to cross your woods."

"You don't?" The child stepped back. "But everyone wants to cross these woods. It is the only way to the frost giants."

"But we don't." Jonna moved back from the marker. "Come on guys."

"You can't do that," the boy huffed. "You've already stepped over the marker, so someone has got to pay."

"Not us." Jonna turned his back to the child. Risky, but then, maybe not. From all he had seen, he didn't think they were going to shoot.

The boy moved forward, out of the foliage, and closer to the three. "You can't leave."

Jonna looked in his direction. "And why not? Have it your way. Shoot."

"What?" The boy looked shocked. "You want us to shoot?"

"You said you were going to shoot if we did not give you money. We don't have money, so you have to shoot."

"That's not the way it works." The boy stomped his foot. "You pay us money, and we let you pass."

"So, you've never had a situation when you did not get money?"

"Of course not. All travelers pay."

Jonna shook his head. "But we can't."

The boy studies the three. "But we don't want to shoot you; you're our kind, and people have to stick together here. We only want money."

"Shoot or not, it's up to you."

Jonna moved back. "Let's go."

"Hold it," the boy thought it through. "I think we've started on the wrong foot."

"You think so?" Jonna turned to face him. "What do you propose?"

"Maybe we can strike a bargain." The boy looked at all the others to confirm what he was saying. They all nodded vigorously. "So I'll tell you what, give us something, anything at all, that way we don't have to shoot you, and you can pass through the forest." The boy smiled in pride. "What do you think?"

"That might work." Jonna looked around at the kids he could see. "Anything at all?"

"Anything at all."

Jonna picked up a couple of sticks that were lying on the ground. He handed them to the boy. "How about that?"

The boy looked down, frowned, and glanced at the others. "I was more thinking like something you carried."

"You did say anything at all?"

The boy reluctantly shrugged. "Yeah."

"Well, if you want us to cross your woods, you'll have to accept what we give you."

"Oh, all right." The boy inhaled. "Sticks accepted."

A wave of agreement went through the other kids. The bows and arrows disappeared, and a horde of young kids stepped out from the forest around them. Watching their numbers grow, Jonna was glad they had decided not to shoot.

"I'm Jonna," Jonna extended his hand. "My two companions are Lokke and Cassandra."

"I'm Andas." The boy who had been the spokesperson for the group stepped forward and shook Jonna's hand. "We're from the village of Ahhes."

Cassandra nodded. "A pleasure to meet you."

Lokke looked stern. "Without the arrows.

Jonna waved a hand toward the forest. "Lead the way."

Andas looked warily at the sky and turned toward the forest. As he stepped over the marker on the ground, the other children faded into the woods.

"We, Ahheses, are on constant vigilance." He found and followed a trail through the brush. "This path was designed only for those who know it is here, and should a person not know its location, they would miss it entirely. It is why we patrol the borders so carefully."

Lokke mumbled, "A patrol is as good a term as any other. More like thieves."

"I heard that," Andas glanced at Lokke, "but I will take

no offense. However, a patrol is truly what it is. It is by this method we control who and what goes through our forest."

Jonna spoke as the thought hit him. "For your and their safety?"

"How did you know?" The adults and half-demon ducked a branch that Andas walked under.

How much did they know of The Sight? Jonna decided to cover. "I've been around enough to know a watch when I see one."

"So you, too, have experienced danger?"

"We have seen our share of it."

"Good. Before this night is out, you most certainly will see more." Andas held a branch as Jonna and Cassandra passed.

Lokke slowed down a tad. "Did you say danger?"

The branch slapped him across the thighs.

"Ouch! Hey, that had thorns."

Andas gave a mischievous laugh.

"Wait a minute," Lokke hurried to catch up. "When you say danger, how much danger?"

"The woods." Andas motioned to the forest around them as they turned beside a tree. "We rule the forest by day, but the Dark Elves rule it by night."

"Dark Elves?" Jonna had heard that expression before. Someone had mentioned about elves not all being good.

Andas nodded. "Aye, Dark Elves. They come from the ground, hidden in the holes and caves of this forest. Each night we set a watch and keep fires burning on all entry points to the village."

"So why do you stay?" Cassandra stepped over a good-sized rock. "Why not leave, and go where the Dark Elves are not?"

"This is our home. We were here first."

Jonna watched the path change around them. "So the Dark Elves came at a later date?"

"Before my time, something changed, and the peace between our world and theirs ceased to exist."

"It had to be when the Dark Mages took power," Jonna thought out loud. "The Dark Mages tipped the scales between light and dark. So not only did the cycle change there, but here also." He swallowed thinking on the words Fabius had said about the creation of magic. Could he have somehow made the imbalance worse?

"What are you talking about?" Lokke's eyes darted between Andas to Jonna.

The young boy shook his head. "I know not the cause, only what happened. We had to build a protective wall against the Dark Elves."

"And you've lived that way ever since?" Cassandra frowned. "You poor child."

Andas glanced at her, a curious look on his face. "Why do you say that?"

The banks along the path became steeper. Up ahead, many trees had been dropped across the top of the path, creating a type of roof. The smaller branches and twigs had not been trimmed off. For the kids, this was not a problem; the stubs were above their heads.

Cassandra answered Andas' question, watching as she ducked under. "Well, to live in such constant fear, that must be horrifying."

"We are not afraid." The boy moved further under the roof. "It is our way of life. That is what the elders teach."

With a near miss, Jonna ducked a branch. Lokke was not doing much better. Although Cassandra had less of a problem, she kept an eye out for low hanging branches. As they reached the other side of the artificial roof, Andas stopped. "There," he pointed with pride, "Ahhes!"

The wall of the city was made of pointed wood spikes. They were decorated with runes and draped with a metal net. As the wind blew, the net gave off a soft metallic sound, catching the sunlight. Despite the shadow of the trees, bursts of light splattered off the net in all directions.

"Stay here." Andas motioned with one hand toward the wall. "I will let them know you are guests."

It took a moment, but Jonna spotted the guards on the wall, hidden in plain view. Perhaps that was why Andas and his crew had gotten so close before revealing themselves.

"You are very astute." A woman walked out from the city wall, heading toward them.

Jonna came out of his thoughts. Had she read his mind?

"The reading of minds is nothing more than knowing how a person thinks." The lady smiled. "Andas has relayed to me your meeting at the edge of the forest, and how you came out of the sky."

Lokke asked nervously, "He saw that?"

"He said you came first." She pointed at Lokke.

"Andas is very observant." Jonna thought he saw similar facial features on her as in Andas, so he made an educated guess. "You have taught him well."

"Thank you." She looked into his eyes. "There is something different about you; you are very far from home and not from these lands."

"And you, also." Cassandra caught her off guard. "This is not the place of your birth."

The woman nodded with a smiled. "Yet it has become my home and my people." She motioned toward the entrance.

Jonna looked around, but noted none of the kids which had brought them in.

She turned toward the entry in the wall and led the way. "You have quite an unusual group. Two sight-seers and a want-to-be magician."

"Now wait a minute," Lokke looked offended, "I am not a want-to-be!"

She laughed as Andas had.

As they passed into the town, Jonna noted the many access points to the walkway of the defense wall. In addition, for every one guard at the top there were two at the bottom.

"I take it you're impressed?" The woman motioned for them to enter a centralized hut, around which were five fire rings stocked with wood. Jonna pushed back the leather hanging which served as a door. A sweet fragrance drifted into the air. He held the hanging up as those behind passed through.

The woman gave him a nod. "Thank you."

"You're welcome." Jonna stepped in and dropped the hanging into place. It took a moment for his eyes to adjust; the room was dimly lit by oil pots.

She motioned toward some benches. "Please, be seated."

The woman took a seat on a large hardwood chair. Jonna and the others sat on small benches with no backs. There was a table in the shape of an oval between them.

"I am Philandia, leader of the village Ahhes. Andas' story appears to be true; you have a wit about you as well as being a sight-seer." She nodded at Jonna.

"You honor us," he nodded, "though I will say it was not easy finding our way into your forest. Your guards are most devout to their mission. They keep the trails hidden from even those with sharp eyes."

Andas with a few others stepped in through the hanging. They moved up behind the three strangers and sat.

Philandia accepted the compliment. "They are children, but as you say, most devout."

"Mother," Andas stood up, "we are more than children. We are warriors!"

"That also," she smiled, but the smile dropped quickly from her face, "through necessity, not desire."

"How did this happen?" Cassandra would have reached forward to comfort her, but the chair was too far away.

"It was not long past when a dark shadow dropped over our woods. It began with a fissure in the earth, and one by one villagers went missing."

"Dark Elves," Jonna whispered, feeling each word. It was as if he were reliving the event. "They came as the Dark Mages grew in power."

Philandia looked up, that faraway look in her eyes. "You are correct; the timing was the same. What the Dark Mages did in your realm coordinated with our own form of darkness here."

"It was Basajaun, the leader of the Dark Elves," Andas jumped in. "He and his swept through at night. When morning came, we were less."

Philandia nodded. "And so it continued, each night when the sky was darkest. They took the men first and then the women one by one. By the time we realized what was going on, it was almost too late. We built the wall you see with a metal mesh. Like us, the dark elves can hide well, but unlike us they do not like this type of metal. If they come in contact with it, they are pained."

"Allergic to metal?" Jonna thought a moment. "I've heard of other creatures which have that same reaction." His mind went to Elfleda when she had been chained; that had been metal too. Did it distress all elves this way? If so, did it disturb other creatures as well? He looked at Lokke and Cassandra. "Have you ever heard of this?"

Cassandra shook her head; Lokke stared blankly.

"Lokke?"

"A—er—maybe."

"Lokke, if you know something, you really should let us know."

"Alright, alright, stop twisting my leg!"

"Shouldn't it be twisting your arm?"

"It's my appendage, and I can say it how I want!"

Jonna sighed. "Then spill it."

"When I was down in—" Lokke glanced from Jonna to Philandia, "—a dungeon." He threw a look at Andas. "Boy, was it hot!" He turned to Philandia. "Ah—er—anyway, they had all sorts of torture techniques setup for various species. For some of us, of course, they had no real focus—"

Cassandra kicked him under the table.

"But I get off subject." Lokke grimaced at Cassandra. "I believe there must have been some Dark Elves, for when they clapped metal bands around their wrists, they hollered and screamed though they were never touched with anything else."

Jonna looked at him. "And?"

"And what?" Lokke looked from one to the other. "That's it."

"Nothing else?"

"You're the one who insisted on knowing what I knew. If you don't like the information—"

Jonna held his hand up. "I understand. Forgive me." He turned to Philandia. "How can we help?"

"What?" Lokke jumped in. "We're on a mission, and you want to stop and help someone else?"

Cassandra glared at him. "Close it, or I'll close it for you."

Philandia looked amused. "You have your own troubles. You do not need to help with ours."

"See," Lokke pointed at Cassandra, "she doesn't even want our help!"

"Lokke," Jonna called him down. He turned to Philandia. "Is there a way we can help?"

Philandia thought. "Unless you can bring the captured back or drive out the Dark Elves, I know of nothing you can do."

An idea formed in Jonna's mind. "You said captured. Those taken were not killed?"

"There was no evidence of death. They were simply taken."

Jonna turned to his group. "What would Dark Elves want with a bunch of human beings?"

Staring at Jonna, Lokke asked, "Human what?"

"Human beings, you know, people."

"Oh," Lokke got it, "as opposed to demon beings, or sidhist beings?"

Understanding hit the others at the same time, and Jonna realized he had used a phrase from his own world. Rather than address from where the phrase came from, he nodded.

Andas leaned toward Lokke. "Does he always use strange words like that?"

Lokke whispered, "Well, it depends, but every once in a while—"

Philandia cleared her throat. "Are you suggesting there might be a way to get our people back?"

Jonna nodded. "If they didn't kill them, that means they need them for something else. If they need them for something else, 'else' normally means slave labor, and slave labor means—"

"There has to be a way to find them," Andas finished, amazement in his voice.

"Precisely," Jonna nodded. "All we have to do is catch a dark elf."

Silence dropped.

"Excuse me," Lokke leaned over, "you said you wanted to catch a dark elf?"

"I did. We catch one, and he leads us to their lair."

"Just like that?" Lokke looked around. "Am I the only one who thinks that's bonkers?"

Philandia mused, "They don't like metal; they won't come in the village. It would have to take place outside the city walls."

Looking toward the boys, Jonna asked, "Do you know a good spot?"

Andas nodded. "A short distance off the trail, up on a small ridge, there is a shepherd's hut. The people were taken a long time ago. That would be the place I would do it."

"Then it sounds like a plan," Jonna turned to face the leader, "with your blessing of course."

Philandia looked at the three strangers and then changed her gaze to the boys. There was a mother's concern in her eyes, yet the children were all the city had. "You are willing to do this?"

"If we can bring the others back," Andas stood straighter, "yes Ma'am!"

"Then you have my blessing." She turned to Jonna. "I do not know why you offer to help so freely, but we accept your gift. Perhaps, when you return, we may help find what you are seeking."

Jonna caught a glint in her eye; 'The Sight' had given her

a clue. "I would like that," he smiled and turned to the boys. "Do you think we can borrow a few small items?" He whispered them to Andas.

The boy's eyes went big, but he nodded. "We will hurry."

"Thank you." As Andas and the others slipped out, Jonna turned to the Cassandra and Lokke. "Let's go." He stood up and bowed toward Philandia. "By your leave."

She nodded.

Lokke hurried to follow. "But where are we going?"

Cassandra rolled her eyes. "The shepherd's hut, of course."

"Without a guide?" Lokke looked up as they stepped outside. "Do you realize it is almost dark."

"Andas said it was not far. By his description, it should be easily seen."

"That's sort of my point." Lokke sped up and tried to place himself between them and the entrance, but he was too slow. "It's bad enough with Dagda, the Otherworld, Dunner, and others chasing us. Do we have to make enemies of the Dark Elves, too?"

Jonna stepped through the exit in the city wall and proceeded to the tunnel on the trail. "The Dark Mages somehow released the Dark Elves here."

"No," Cassandra had that faraway look. "The Dark Mages tipped the scales, but someone else stirred up the Dark Elves."

She was right. "I agree, but who?"

A pop sounded in Jonna's ear, and he knew that Bob had returned. "Jonna, I don't have much time. The—hey, I thought we were finding a trail?"

"And I thought you were returning an overdue library book?" He knew Bob's face turned red, though he could not see it.

"Just because I was a little late—" Bob shook his fist. "You would think they should be a little more understanding." Jonna sensed there was more to it but let him ramble on.

Lokke glanced over at Jonna, listening; Elpis filled Cassandra in.

Jonna watched as they walked down the trail. Though they headed toward danger, there was none at the moment. It was good to rest as they ambled. "So, how late were you?"

Bob's faced flushed again. "About a year, but that's not the point."

Jonna laughed and so did Cassandra. "A year?" Jonna exclaimed. "They should have thrown you in jail."

Lokke's eyes lit up.

Bob grinned. "Yeah, well, they sort of did, but when I told them about the chronicles I was writing and showed them the notes—"

There was some sort of noise behind Bob, and Väinämö's voice came in loud and clear. "Bob, how could you?"

"Oops, gotta go!" The pop sounded in Jonna's ear.

"What happened?" Jonna turned to Cassandra.

She grimaced. "I don't know exactly. Väinämö came in and sent Elpis out of the room. He wasn't very happy."

Jonna looked over and saw the smile on Lokke's face. "And what are you grinning about?"

"Nothing." The half-demon looked away, but he couldn't contain it any longer. "At least I'm not the only one who gets into trouble."

Jonna chuckled. "You certainly aren't, though I suspect Bob wasn't saying the whole truth." He looked at the forest around them. "We all have our vices."

The needles from the pine trees crunched under their feet, and his attention went to the landscape. The ground rose and fell in winding hills, twisting in creeks and gullies.

Andas was right. Not far from the trail, up a small ridge, there was the shepherd's hut. There was no light within. The broken items scattered around the yard were a testament to what had happened.

As he stepped in through the door, the musty odor of dust and dirt hit his nostrils. It had been a while since anyone had called this home.

Lokke sneezed.

Jonna knocked the dust off the table and checked the

fireplace. Only ashes were left of the previous tenant's fire, but a stock of wood with a layer of dust was waiting to be burned. He moved several logs into the hearth, stuck in some dry tinder, and in a faraway voice spoke, "*Fiat Lux.*"

Sparks descended onto the tinder around the logs. The wood burst into flame despite the forest dampness.

Cassandra moved closer. "Jonna, are you okay? I thought you couldn't do magic here?"

As if coming from a dream, he shook his head. "Did I?"

"Look at the fire," she pointed. "You didn't rub two sticks together."

"Did I hear the word magic?" Lokke came through the door and gazed at the yellow flames. He held his hands up, feeling the warmth. "What magic? Where?" He turned toward Cassandra. "What did he say?"

"Fiat Lux," Jonna remembered, "and sparks began to pull from the air."

Lokke looked at both, excitement in his eyes. "Is that surface magic? Is it, is it?" He jumped with glee.

"Calm down," Cassandra warned, "it is no magic I've ever heard."

Jonna turned to face them. "That's because they're Latin. It's a language from my world."

"Your Latin language is magic?" Lokke's eyes brightened. "I've got to know more!"

Jonna frowned. "But I don't know why I said it. Could it be The Sight?"

Cassandra pursed her lips. "I've never known it to give such information. For me, it is glimpses of events."

"On top of that," Jonna rubbed his forehead, "why do those words work here?"

"Let's find out." Lokke picked up a piece of tinder and dropped it on the dirt floor. "Give me something to say." He licked his lips.

Jonna thought of another Latin phrase. "Try Lux Casta."

Rubbing his hands together, Lokke stared at the tinder. "*Try Lux Casta!*"

160

Jonna grinned. "I mean try the words, Lux Casta. Try is not part of the phrase."

Lokke's eyes widened as his mouth opened. "Ah, I get it." He stared down. "*Lux Casta.*"

No sparks appeared. Nothing happened at all.

"That's not fair." Lokke stomped. "Out with a little taste of freedom, and still I can't do surface magic."

"It's not my surface magic," Cassandra shook her head, "and not yours."

As Jonna stared at Lokke, Väinämö's words sank in. All realms have their own type of magic. A mage's ability was influenced by where they were born. The Dark Mage prophecy Bob had found was written in a language from his realm. How interconnected were the realms?

The curtain door pushed back, and Andas stepped in with four others. "We've brought the metal nets and the shackles."

"Thank you." Jonna smiled. "Help me hang the net around the inside walls."

Using a type of flexible wire, they hung the net all the way around. They left enough to drop over the door, yet tied it back with a small rope.

"I get it," Andas put two and two together. "We wait, let one get lured into the hut, and drop the chain over the door. Instant trap."

Lokke looked from one to the other. "Does no one realize we will be inside with it?"

"Very good," Jonna grinned, "and what of the shackles?"

Andas looked up proudly. "If he causes trouble, we'll shackle him down."

"You can't do that." Lokke put his hands to his ears. "He'll howl. He won't be able to take the pain."

Jonna frowned. "If he won't cooperate, we'll have no choice."

"But it will bring every dark elf in the woods. We'll be a target."

"And?" Cassandra wrinkled her brow. "Do you want out? There may be time to get to the Ahhes."

Lokke wouldn't give up. "But there are hundreds!"

"He has a point," Jonna rethought the issue, "and we only want one. We'll have to knock him out and wait until morning. It should be safe with the metal net hung inside the hut."

"Knock him out? Wait until morning?" Lokke's eyes filled with terror. "You didn't see them. You didn't hear them!"

"Lokke, calm down." Cassandra touched his arm. Lokke jerked away. They had seen Lokke do many things, but absolute terror was new.

Jonna spoke with a calm, steady voice, "We'll be fine inside the hut."

Cassandra tried again to put a hand on Lokke's shoulder. "Are you okay?"

Lokke bolted, passed through the cloth door, and leaped into the evening light.

Cassandra started for the door, but Andas caught her arm.

The boy shook his head. "The dark elves begin their hunt soon. If he makes Ahhes, he'll be safe."

"He's right." Jonna turned to toward the door. "We can't risk you. I'll go after him."

Andas moved to stand in front of the flap, releasing Cassandra's arm. "I mean no one. He is on his own."

"I'll be fine."

Jonna moved toward the entrance, but Andas did not budge. His eyes filled with defiance. "No."

"Andas, I'll be fine." Jonna could see the darkness descending as the shadows grew. "But if you don't let me go now, it will be too late."

"It is too late. My father disappeared on an evening like this; I will not let you do the same. Either of you."

"How do you expect us to draw them into the hut?"

"They will come, have no fear." Andas stopped and listened. "They cannot get into the village. They do not know we have protected the hut. Our very presence draws them even as we speak."

"They sense us?"

"As only their kind can."

Jonna stepped back. "Then I suggest you step away from the door." For the first time, he could hear something moving through the brush. At first there was one, then two, then three. The numbers grew until he could have sworn there was an army surrounding the them.

Andas shifted to the right side, his muscles tense.

"They're not doing anything," one of the others whispered.

Jonna whispered back, "What would you think if an abandoned hut suddenly had a fire inside?"

Andas continued to watch the door. "Stupid humans or trap."

"Precisely," Jonna nodded. "As Andas said, they will come if only for curiosity sake."

A slight crunching sound was heard, like dried pine needles stepped upon with a very light weight. The wind whipped through the entrance, flipped up a corner of the covering, and ran its fingers through the leaping flames.

The sound stopped. In the silence, Jonna became aware of his own heartbeat and focused on other things.

Lokke had rushed out in a fit of terror. Chances were, he had been taken. Why would dark elves need slaves? Their cousins, the wood elves, did not require them. No, if dark elves captured humans, it had to be for a particular reason.

"They're here." Andas moved back further, weapon at ready.

Jonna stepped to the left, closer to the door. "Then I guess we should invite them in." He shifted the curtain.

Chapter 12

ELVES OF A KIND

A spear lunged from the darkness; the gleam of the firelight caught its darkened edge. The attack missed Jonna's left shoulder as he turned sideways and leaped back.

The spear held the curtain open as the image of a dark elf pushed out from the blackness. His face held the shape of the wood elves, but instead of a glowing countenance, a shadowy foreboding shown. The eyes were dipped in darkened rings, sharp and quick. With loathing and hatred they glared around the hut. The dark elf's gaze stopped on Jonna.

Their eyes met. The dark elf leaped forward and sliced with his spear. Andas countered from the side. Jonna avoided from the front.

Jonna reached for his sword, the Rune Blade of Knowledge, remembered it was not there, and jumped back. The Rune Blade, the sword he had recovered from the Dark Mages, the one he used to destroy their power, sat at his home in the woodland elf city completely out of reach.

He snatched up a chair and used it as a shield, but the dark elf's spear sliced through, turning it into a pile of sticks. Jonna should have anticipated the difficulty in subduing a dark elf, but during the planning, the thought had escaped his mind. "Anyone have a weapon?" Being the main draw for the attacker wasn't so much the problem—being able to defend himself was.

A dagger was tossed in his direction, blade first. Both he and the dark elf avoided the blade. It hit the top of a table and slid off toward the floor.

Jonna leaped after the dagger. The dark elf jumped after him. As he fell forward, he caught sight of other feet rushing the hut and cried out, "Door!" Both he and the dark elf crashed to the floor.

Andas turned, sliced the rope with a flick of his wrist, and let the chain drop over the entry. With the sound of the chain, those outside abruptly stopped.

As Jonna brought the dagger up, the dark elf stabbed forward. The blades collided, metal clanged, and the sound reverberated around the room. The dark elf struck and struck, each blow deflected to the right or left by the smaller dagger. Jonna kicked the edge of the table and knocked it forward. The elf's spear came down, missed its intended target, and stabbed into the wood, sticking securely.

Enraged, the dark elf heaved back. The stress of the pull snapped the spear's shaft and splinters flew. As his face became a darker shade of red, he spun, for the first time paying attention to the metal mesh that surrounded the inside walls. Jonna swallowed. What had they gotten into?

The cry of the dark elf warrior tore through the hut as he realized the metal fencing was secure even over the door. The elf noted the others staying back and with grim hatred refocused his attention on Jonna. The warrior tossed the broken shaft away and leaped, hands outstretched, going for Jonna's throat.

Jonna flung the dagger out of the way and deflected the hands as they collided. If they were going to catch this dark elf alive, he had to use caution. Of course, that was assuming they would subdue him—a hollow thud sounded as both slammed against the wall.

Jonna's muscles strained as they fought for position. Despite the dark elf's size, he was strong and agile. About the time Jonna would get him into a hold, the dark elf would slip free and attempt to do the same to Jonna. At this rate, the dark elf would win simply because Jonna would be exhausted. Shoving debris around on the floor, they shifted awkwardly, grunting and growling.

The dark elf's right leg dropped into position. Jonna shifted his own leg, grabbed his opponent's ankle, and twisted. The elf howled in pain, struggling against the hold, its strength still a boon yet unable to apply it. Beads of sweat formed as Jonna fought to maintain the twist. He glanced around the room, but no one else was moving.

"What are you waiting for?" he grunted out. "Grab those shackles!"

Cassandra rushed to the shackles and brought them near the dark elf. The creature struggled harder, his eyes riveted to the shackles in her hand.

She grabbed an arm but was thrown back. She grabbed again as another helped her. Andas and the others pinned the elf's opposite arm. The dark elf heaved, almost throwing them off. Jonna fought to keep the ankle hold.

At the first click of the first shackle, a tormented scream left the dark elf's lips. At the second click of the second shackle, the elf slumped over unconscious.

Jonna eased up the pressure, his muscles trembling from the exertion. He dropped his head back, inhaled, and rolled away from the limp body. "Done," he exhaled, wiping the sweat from his forehead.

Cassandra moved toward him. "You're hurt." She checked the cuts on his hands and arms. Neither he nor the dark elf had paid any attention to the debris they had been rolling over. "And here too," she found another spot.

Jonna jumped; something had cut him on the back. "I knew a woman that could fix these in no time," he dismissed the damage to his skin, "were she here."

"You mean, Almundena?" Cassandra continued her inspection, using a rag to clean off the wound. "Looks like you rolled over something curved."

"You know her?"

"Elpis did."

"That's right. The link between you and Elpis. You saw what your daughter saw in the city of Chernobog."

Cassandra laughed, "Ha, ha. Not exactly, but we did share a lot." She turned to the dark elf. "What do we do now?"

"We wait till morning." Jonna turned to the whole group. "When morning comes, we may need a way to secure him without the shackles. Andas, can you prepare that?"

Andas nodded.

"Good. In the meantime, we wait."

"Maybe not." One of the kids with Andas was at the door, listening to the outside. "They're doing something out there."

Jonna went to the curtain door and looked out where the wind billowed an edge of the cloth. Torches had appeared, brightening the darkness in a dull yellow. More dark eyes stared in their direction as the flicker of the torchlights cast an eerie glow around the hut.

Torches—hut—Jonna looked up. There was a straw roof. His eyes widened. "They're going to burn us out." He spun around. "We need someplace to hide and fast!"

He thought about the spell Väinämö had taught him; the one that, if used with more than one person, would transport them to that 'other' place. It would be a place of darkness, giant spiders, and who knew what else, but when faced with losing your life, it was at least an option. The spell from Väinämö's homeland was 'Unum-Clastor-Fillum', but how was he to translate that to Latin? "Suggestions?"

Cassandra pushed some of the debris out of the way, finally finding what had made the curved cut in Jonna's back. "What's this?" She cleaned around the area. "There's a ring here."

"A ring?" Jonna knelt beside her and saw it was connected to something in the ground. "A round, iron ring attached to the floor of a hut?" He stopped and helped to clear the rest of the area. There, set in the earth, was a wooden framed trapdoor.

"If it hasn't suffered damage," he speculated, grasping the ring and heaving upward. A square patch of dirt shook, breaking free as a hinged door raised. "It might be our way out."

"But the prisoner," Andas shook his head, "we must keep the shackles in place."

"Bring him shackles and all." Jonna peered down into the underground darkness. "Torch."

One of the group grabbed a broken piece of wood from the fireplace, added a wrapping of cloth, and touched it to the flame. It ignited brightly. He handed it to Jonna.

Jonna held the torch above the hole and peered down. It looked like a cellar. There was a wooden ladder which vanished into the darkness.

With no time to investigate further, he dropped into the hole, his feet finding the rungs. They creaked but held until his feet touched bottom.

The elf was passed down. Jonna supported him at the foot of the ladder. He moved toward the back of the cellar and laid the elf down beside the wall. There was no other entrance.

Something hit the roof of the hut. The smell of burning straw wafted from above. He hurried to the ladder and stared up. "What's the delay?"

All the others were looking up. Spots on the underside of the roof turned from light brown, to black, to red, and burst into flame. The burning straw plummeted from the ceiling toward the floor. Cassandra's face went pale. "Fire on the roof! Everyone in now." Her eyes caught Andas. "You too!"

Andas paused, "But—"

"No but's. I'm dead, and you're not. If something hit me, it wouldn't make any difference."

He paused, but only a second, and then gave a quick nod, following the others down the ladder. Cassandra pulled the remnants of the table and chairs closer. When the roof collapsed and burned up the hut, the additional ash would help hide their escape.

A support beam dropped and slammed into the floor. Flames shot out as it hit the ground, and the smell of burnt, smoking straw filled the room. She climbed down the ladder and pulled the cellar door closed.

The air was musky. Some sealed barrels were stacked against a wall, and a few opened crates lay in one corner. The space inside the cellar was not cramped, but there wasn't much room either.

The dark elf lay to one side, as far from the others as Jonna could place him. Despite the pain of the shackles, the coolness of the earth made him open his eyes.

He was in agony. It was in his features, but he said nothing. His eyes bore into them. Most who looked at him quickly turned away, all except Jonna.

"You really should stop that," Andas touched Jonna's arm. "It won't do any good. They have no mercy for humans."

"It's not mercy I'm looking for." Jonna turned toward the dark elf. "It's the spark of life. It is the reason why they do what they do."

A grim frown crossed Andas' face. "There is no reason. They hate to hate."

Jonna shook his head. "Very seldom is that true. There is a cause for the start of such things. Sometimes it is buried in legend. Sometimes it is no more than a misunderstanding."

Andas stared at Jonna, hope in his voice. "You think it could be a misunderstanding?"

"There is no way to tell," Jonna looked at the dark elf, "yet."

The dark elf tried to laugh, but the pain was too great. He groaned out, "You look for what you will not find, human. Our distaste for you goes beyond your comprehension."

"So he speaks," Jonna continued to watch, "and understands."

"We know your language. It is you who do not know ours, Enose caleb."

"Neboanon amitee," Jonna's voice was calm. "Liate skuldra erann liainbali."

The dark elf's face fell, and for a brief moment he forgot his pain. His eyes narrowed. "By the gods, this cannot be!"

Feeling a little self-conscious, Jonna turned to find the rest of the group staring at him. "He called me a human dog, and I told him, 'Unwise friend, it would be wise to watch your tongue.'"

"Elpis never said you knew Dark Elvish." Cassandra glanced uncertainly at the prisoner.

Jonna nodded. "Did she not mention Elfleda? How could I live in a city of the elves and not learn some Elvish?" What he did not mention was how quickly he had picked it up. He had learned that he could understand and speak with almost anyone, magically. Väinämö had showed him there was a language he could learn as well, without relying on magic.

"Elfleda?" The dark elf attempted to lunge at Jonna, despite the fact that the shackles robbed him of his strength. "You speak Woodland Elvish, not Dark Elvish." His voice hardened. "Infidel! You are worse than a human dog!"

"And you are misguided." Jonna shook his head. "We seek to find the human's you have taken."

"You may seek," his lips quivered, "but you will not find."

"We will find," Andas promised, "and when we do, your people will pay!"

There was pain behind the dark elf's eyes. "Hide behind your wall of metal while you may. It will not save you."

A loud crash sounded above. For a brief moment, light shone; the flicker of red and orange flames glowed between the cracks.

"See," the dark elf taunted, "already we burn your house and tear down your fence of metal. It is only a matter of time."

The flame on Jonna's torch dimmed. The air became harder to breath. Carbon dioxide! With the fire above and no other ventilation, the buildup was reaching toxic levels.

He looked to the ladder but dared not open the top. If they were seen, they would be caught. Then again, if they didn't get air—

A whisper came into his thoughts. Sub? Sub divo?

"Quickly, gather around," Jonna blinked and for a moment thought no one had heard him. One by one they moved toward him, all unusually sluggish. "Hold onto each other." He reached back and caught the dark elf's shackles; no one was immune.

Though the words were in his mind, it was difficult to focus. One by one the others slumped, and the phrase was trying to flee. "*Sub—Sub divo—tempus fugit.*"

A breath of fresh air poured in, and he blinked. They were still in the cellar, and yet, daylight filtered in from small cracks around the trapdoor. Rising, the group parted for him to pass.

The torch had gone out, but his eyes adjusted to the dim light. He moved up the ladder and pushed. It rose part way and stopped, but it was enough for him to look.

Debris was everywhere, but the fire had burnt off most of the heavy items. The smell of charred wood wafted downward as sparks fell.

He pushed against the trapdoor. Gray ash dropped on his head and shoulders as the door swung up. It was early morning.

How could this be? Not a moment ago, it had been night. The others followed him up.

Cassandra shook her head. "Is it me, or did night fly by?"

Andas rubbed his shoulder. "A burning building on our heads."

"It was the spell." Jonna dusted himself off. "If I remember my Latin, the last part meant 'time flies'. The first part is still a little sketchy."

"The dark elves are gone," Cassandra watched as they brought the night visitor up, "and we have our prisoner."

Jonna turned toward the dark elf. "A non-cooperative prisoner that will tell us all he knows."

The dark elf spat.

"Which isn't much." Andas looked skeptical.

"Oh, I know it's more than he thinks." Jonna watched the dark elf. Did he see fear in those elvish eyes? "What do you know?"

The dark elf tried to back up from Jonna; he gritted his teeth. "What will you do to me?"

"What do you want?"

"I want to go free."

"Done. Let him go."

Andas moved in front of Jonna. "What? You can't do that. His kind tried to kill us with fire!"

"Let him go." Jonna looked into Andas' eyes. "Trust me or not, it is up to you."

Andas shoulders dropped. "Adults! Fine. Let him go."

The others in Andas' group did not agree.

"If Jonna says let him go, we do it."

Cassandra moved around behind the dark elf, looking for the release.

The dark elf squinted at Jonna. "You are truly letting me go?"

"Yes."

"You are not going to kill me?"

Jonna watched the dark elf glance toward Cassandra. "No. Leave us in peace, and we'll let you walk away."

The first shackle clicked open, followed by the second. Cassandra stepped back, giving the dark elf a wide berth. Relief flooded the dark elf's face, and Jonna saw the same spark that wood elves hold dear: the enjoyment of being alive.

Then the spark was gone, replaced by the knowledge of where he was. A shadow dropped across the dark elf's features. "You will regret the day you let me go, Jonna, for now I know your name."

"And I yours, Hieronymus. Alsalmone."

The dark elf's mouth dropped. Closing it, he turned heel and ran.

Jonna closed his eyes. "One, two, three..." At first it was a mumble, but as he turned toward the others, the words became more coherent. "...nine, ten." He looked up at Andas. "Can you track him?"

"Yes."

"I want you to follow him at a distance. Do not get in his way."

"That's why you let him go," Cassandra cut in. "You wanted to track him to the entrance."

Jonna nodded. "And he knows I know, but he has no choice."

"Why?"

"He has to tell his queen."

Cassandra looked thoughtful. "I don't understand. If we follow, we'll be walking into a hornet's nest."

Väinämö's voice, at first distant, cut through their conversation. "Of course!" He slapped something wooden in triumph. As his voice became clearer, his wavy form appeared. He was sitting on a bench in front of a worktable. "Ah, there you are. Just who I was looking for."

Jonna half-rolled his eyes. "Checking up on your pupil, I see."

Väinämö put on a broad smile. "That does seem to have a nice ring to it. It has been a long time since I trained a good pupil."

Jonna waited for the 'but you're the exception' clause. However, it never came. Oh well, he might as well try to get some answers. "Is it time for you to give me a spell, and what happened to Bob?"

"A what?" Väinämö's attention had dropped to his books. He looked up at Jonna. "A spell that bobs?"

"Last time you were going to give me a spell, but it wasn't the right time, and someone stopped Bob in the middle of transmission."

"Oh that." Väinämö closed his eyes to think, and then snapped them open. "Nope, you're not ready." Väinämö's face darkened. "Bob is another matter."

"You said that last time."

Väinämö looked confused. "To which question?"

"The spell," Jonna clarified, "but I still want to know about—"

"And the answer remains," the mage huffed. "Why did you call me anyway?"

Jonna did a double take. "I didn't call you."

Väinämö looked surprised. "You didn't?" He picked up a book, flipped it open to a page, and read something silently.

Jonna watched at the wavy form; it was a little boring. He looked around and noticed Andas and his companions had left.

Cassandra tugged Jonna's shirt. "How did you know the dark elf's name?"

"Hmm? What was that?" Väinämo looked up from his book. "What dark elf?"

"You really haven't been keeping up, have you?" Jonna shook his head. "I thought you were watching out for us."

"I am, my boy." the mage looked surprised. "Why do you think I've been pouring over these books? Do I look like that's what I do all day?" He stopped and thought about his own statement. "Never mind. To answer your question, I've been a little bit distracted on another issue."

"Is it something I can help you with?" Jonna waved his hands around. "I mean, it's not like I'm doing anything at the moment."

"Tsk, tsk, tsk." Väinämö laughed. "I'm the only one allowed to give that kind of sarcasm. Although, I will say, you did it rather well."

"Thank you. Now, about Bob?"

Cassandra spoke louder this time. "You still didn't answer my question."

Jonna turned his head toward her. "It was a voice, a soft voice that—"

"Did I hear you say 'voice'?" Väinämö's ears perked up.

Jonna glanced toward Väinämö. "If you will let me finish." He faced Cassandra again. "I can't explain it any other way. It was the same voice that told me both spells and Hieronymus' name. I knew the moment I said his name, he would return directly to the queen. Why, I don't know."

"You met Hieronymus?" The mage frantically went through a book. "The Hieronymus?" The book slammed shut on one finger. He reached for a second with the other hand and shook the finger in the air while searching the next book. "Hieronymus, Hieronymus, ah, there it is."

"Väinämö, are you okay?"

"Yes. No. Got trouble. Gotta go." The waving image faded from view.

Cassandra blinked. "Is he always like that?"

Jonna inhaled. "Yes, though I'm never quite sure if it's an act or his real personality."

From nowhere, Andas materialized. "We've found it! He didn't even try to hide."

"Show me."

The path was short. It was curious how this entrance could be so close to the village, yet had never been discovered. However, that would explain how the dark elves moved in and out of the area so quickly.

The entrance they found passed between two boulders. Each boulder bare signs of elvish markings, a warning to those who trespassed.

Andas had a sparkle in his eye. "The troops are ready."

Jonna expected the boy to salute. "Good."

The problem was, he was not sure if he should allow the kids to come. Yes, they were doing adult responsibilities. Yes, they knew how to handle themselves. But to take them into the belly of the dark elves' lair, was that a wise thing to do?

"I see there is doubt in your eyes." Andas read the signs. "I want you to know, if you don't let us go, we will go on our own."

That settled it, and Jonna nodded. "Who is your best scout?"

"Philo."

"Philo it is."

Philo came up to stand in front of Jonna. "Sir?"

"I need you to stay in front of us, always within sight, always with a place to hide. Do you understand?"

Philo nodded.

Jonna thought back to his group's first encounter with the kids. "I take it you have a way to communicate without drawing attention?"

All in the group nodded.

175

"Good. Philo, relay what you see to Andas. We are looking for a central assembly area. From there, we should be able to find out where they are keeping the others."

Jonna was sure that upon the first steps into the lair, the dark elves would find them. Because of this, it was important not to allow the kids off on their own. At least in the group, there was a margin of protection.

Pushing away the thoughts, Jonna nodded at Philo.

Chapter 13

ALFGIEFUENID

The footing was treacherous. While the cave was smooth, its walls did allow for handholds. The moisture in the air, combined with the echos of drips, gave promise to poor traction in the dim light.

Twenty feet in, the surface light vanished. Cassandra held onto his arm as he guided her past major obstacles, though he did wonder how Andas and the others managed. A magic development? Their eyes attuned to low light? But this was not low light. This was no light at all.

"Hold," Andas whispered, holding up a hand. Philo had stopped and dropped closer to the ground. After a few moments, he gave the all-clear signal and disappeared around a corner.

Jonna looked at Andas. "What did he see?"

"A split in the tunnel. Philo is checking to see which is the most traveled."

"I don't want him out of sight." Jonna frowned. "As a group, we have a better advantage."

Andas nodded. "He will do what he must to ensure our safety."

"That's not what I said." The whole thing was turning worse by the moment. He felt a responsibility for the kid's safety. While he understood Andas and the others survived on their own in the forest, this place was entirely different.

The forest was open with many places to run. Here you were limited to whatever width and length the cave tunnel was with very few places to hide.

Reaching the corner, Jonna slipped in front of Andas and took a look for himself. Philo was nowhere to be seen, but the split in the tunnel could not be missed.

There were voices in the distance, though which tunnel they came from was a guess for anyone. The echoes distorted the sound so that neither tunnel had less or more.

Philo appeared to Jonna's right, not coming from either of the two tunnels. He came from a smaller side tunnel hidden in the darkness. The boy whispered, "This is the best way."

Cassandra dodged around an outcropping as they entered the cave. Jonna ducked; she ducked. He stood; she felt up for the absence of the ceiling and stood too. It worked out well as long as they stayed close.

Pop!

"Bet you're glad to have pixie sight," Bob grinned. "Okay, let me explain before you-know-who comes to grab me again. There's a—"

Väinämö's voice boomed, "Bob, don't you dare!"

"I'm writing for posterity!"

"Since when do you think you have the right anymore?" Väinämö glared. "Especially with the trouble you've caused!"

"I didn't do anything!"

Pop!

"There," Andas pointed. The group halted short of Philo, who knelt at the edge of an opening which slanted down into a large, lighted cavern. Buildings carved from the cavern lined streets which went off in different directions.

The roughly honed path they were on continued down the wall and toward the main floor. This side tunnel had never been finished. Perhaps Philo had found a windfall after all.

Greenish-blue fungi was everywhere, lighting the cavern as far as the eye could see. Like a full moon shining on an open field, the details were visible; the contrast was clear. Solid rock carvings, hewn stone, and stairs going to multi-storied buildings stared at them.

As Jonna stepped onto the floor of the cavern, Cassandra released his arm. Only one street appeared to move toward a large central area. Could this be the city square? He could see a dais rising from the center with a pair of short stairs moving up from one side.

They crept quietly toward the dais. Either everyone had gone somewhere else, or—it was the falling of a stone that caught his attention. It dropped from the roof of a nearby building and rolled into the square.

A shadow shown to his right with another to his left, but he could not see what cast them. Yet, there were eyes; he could feel their prickles on his skin.

"Several on the roof." Andas looked around them. "A few in the passage behind us."

Jonna gave a small chuckle. "Yeah, more in the square."

An assembly of guards moved into view, formed a line, and stood around the dais. Their weapons were drawn with all eyes on the humans.

Jonna stepped forward, "It is nice to be expected."

"You could have used the main tunnel. It is easier to follow, and the result would have been the same." Hieronymus stepped out of the shadows and moved to the front of the line.

Jonna laughed. "Now where would be the fun in that?"

Hieronymus was smug. "I knew you would follow."

"I knew you would lead." Jonna's gaze swept the group of dark elf warriors. Their weapons never wavered. "It seems you do not wish to kill us."

The elf snickered, "Why would you say that?"

"If you did, you'd already have tried."

"Perhaps, it is a matter of time," the dark elf smirked.

"Perhaps," Jonna quoted back, "but I think there is something more here than meets the eye."

Hieronymus spat at the ground. "You speak as if you

know us. Do not let your dealings with the woodland elves mislead you. We are not the same."

Jonna shook his head. "And yet, you are. Your speech, the words you use—"

"We use different words."

"The way in which you protect each other—"

"All of one kind do the same."

Jonna patted the wall of the nearest building, "The way in which you build your homes."

"Do not compare us with a common dog," Hieronymus bared his teeth. "If you do, orders or not, I will take your life."

"Enough," a female voice both new and yet familiar addressed Jonna's ears.

It was similar to the one that spoke the words of magic in his head and told him Hieronymus' name. Though the voice was familiar, the person who spoke it was not.

"Adonia," Jonna kneeled as he spoke the title of the dark elf queen.

"You are familiar with our elvish customs," the female elf looked surprised. "Hieronymus indicated this in his report, though I was confused to learn you were human."

"I have some small experience in these matters," Jonna accepted. "While I recognize your authority, how may I address you?"

She studied Jonna before making a decision. "I am Siardna, Queen of the Dark Elves, daughter of Auberon, granddaughter of Alfarr. Though you know our ways, no human may address me as 'my lady' in Elvish. In human terms, you may call me queen—" She stopped, a strange look crossing her face. "And yet, I do you dishonor." Her eyes widened. "Adonii Jonna."

Hieronymus stepped back, shaken by what the queen had said. Andas and the others turned to stare at Jonna.

"I see you have The Sight." Jonna bowed again, ignoring the questioning faces. "I am honored."

Only Cassandra had not looked at him. Her eyes were on the queen. Elpis must have relayed some of the woodland elf customs.

"Adonia Siardna," Hieronymus turned, facing the queen, "you show respect to a human? To a human who dwelled with woodland elves?"

A spark of flame burst in Queen Siardna's eyes. "Do not question me!"

Hieronymus dropped to one knee, head bowed. "Forgiveness, my liege. I meant no disrespect."

The flame in her eyes faded, and she became regal once more. She looked toward Jonna. "Why have you come to this place, Prince Jonna?"

"I ask for the release of the slaves."

The queen mused, "You mean those that still live?"

Jonna knew the question for what it was, a test to feel them out, and it brought the desired effect. Andas' face paled along with his companions. Even in the greenish-blue light, the shade was unmistakable.

"If indeed that be case," Jonna nodded, "then yes."

The queen's eyes stayed on Jonna's companions. It was not hard to guess her thoughts. They were all human children of whom the dark elves had no use.

"I see," she glanced to Jonna, paused, and then shifted to Hieronymus. "You will treat Prince Jonna and his companions with respect until I decide what to do with them." Her gaze took in the entire cavern as her eyes touched all the warriors. "They will not be harmed," she drove the point home. "Hieronymus?"

"Yes, my liege."

"Please escort Prince Jonna to my antechamber. Have the others escorted to the guest chambers."

Hieronymus issued the orders. Guards separated Jonna from the others and lead his companions away.

Cassandra was uneasy; it was in her eyes. In addition, there were his own questions. The voice he had heard in his mind reminded him of the dark elf queen. Why had she done it?

Although he had never been called 'my lord' or 'Adonii' by the woodland elves, the fact was no less true. He was married to Elfleda, therefore, by elvish law he was an elvish prince due the title of 'my lord'.

Would there be backlashes for the woodland elves? Would the human-elf couple cause hostilities in both groups? Funny how that was now crossing his mind. After going against Dagda and escaping from Cassandra's level, now he was thinking about the consequences? He caught the frown forming on his face and changed it into a non-committal smile. This was not the time to show any doubt.

His feet stopped in time to keep from colliding with the dark elf guard in front. He should have be watching where they were going, rather than thinking. Back to his right, he caught a glimmer of what he thought was the city square, but it was impossible to be sure. In front, he saw two large, wooden doors and watched as the guards opened them.

Queen Siardna was nowhere to be seen. Another entrance, perhaps? Hieronymus led him through the doors as they opened. Although Jonna specifically remembered the queen's charge concerning the visitors, not one weapon had been put away. Hieronymus was definitely loyal, but the question was, how much and to whom?

"In there," the dark elf spoke with tight lips, quickly showing Jonna where he was to go. There was an arched entrance with carvings of green living things on one side and things of the night on the other. "I've posted two guards outside to keep you safe." The elf stepped back; his gaze never left Jonna. The huge doors Jonna had come through closed like a tomb.

It was quiet. Jonna searched around the room, but he was the only one there. The glowing fungi was not only greenish-blue, but also red, orange, and yellow mixed to show elegant decor.

Ornately carved seats and benches, velvet pillows of various colors, vases, pictures, and murals sat around the room. Despite the only light source coming from the glowing fungi, the shadows were washed away.

The queen stepped in through a secondary door. "The accommodations are suitable?"

"Most assuredly. Thank you."

Queen Siardna moved toward a large chair draped in fabrics of fluorescent patterns. Turning slowly, she sat down, placing her hands on the arms of the chair. "Be seated."

Jonna bowed and chose a seat. An uncomfortable silence fell as he waited for the queen to speak. The queen stared at him thoughtfully.

When he had dealt with Queen Freya, Queen of the Woodland Elves, her very presence commanded a certain protocol. Instinctively, you felt it.

Here, it was different. The queen had lost part of her authority and power.

"You present a most unusual proposition, Jonna McCambel."

"Unusual?" He smiled. "How so?"

"Unlike our cousins, we have no use for humans." She studied Jonna's reaction.

He smiled. "Neither do your cousins."

"Even so, they do have use for you, or you would not be a prince."

Jonna had never thought about that. Why had Elfleda chosen him? Why not choose an elf instead?

"Call it curiosity." Queen Siardna sat further back. "Call it suspicion." The queen looked him in the eyes. "Call it necessity." There was a hint of threat in the last words. She snapped her fingers.

To his right, a door opened, and in walked a young elvish girl. The colors in the room danced off her jet black hair, highlighting the contours of her face and neck. The small hands and feet combined with the silk-like clothing, accentuated her shape and beauty. "This is Alfgia my daughter and next rightful heir."

Jonna remembered something Queen Freya had said about necessity when he had been asked to save Elfleda; it was before he knew she was his wife. He bowed. "Adonia Princess Alfgia."

Like a soft flutter on the wind, the princess curtseyed.

"Adonii Prince Jonna." Her eyes caught his, and she blushed. There was something behind that blush. What in the world did this queen have in mind?

Jonna turned to Queen Siardna. "While it is an honor to meet you both—"

The queen laughed, realized he had not caught on, and cut short his words. "Hear me out, Prince Jonna. You may find this trade more to your liking than you think."

"Trade?"

"You want the humans back, do you not?"

"I do."

"I want something in return."

What could this queen possibly want from him?

There was a pause. As if from far away, the words cut in loud and clear, "Give my daughter a child."

Jonna felt a nervous laugh caught somewhere between his throat and stomach. Swallowing hard, he forced the reaction away. He bowed.

"Queen Siardna and Princess Alfgia, while honored by your request, I have sworn my loyalty to Princess Elfleda. More so, I love her and cannot do as you request."

"Even at the cost of the human lives?"

He could not deny it; it was in the queen's eyes. This was not a trade; it was blackmail. "And if I refuse?"

Queen Siardna's eyes mocked him, calm and cool. "How many lives is this one request worth? A hundred? A thousand? What if I told you five thousand humans currently worked as slaves? Would any one of those be worthy of your rescue?"

"Why me?"

"Though we are not the same as our woodland cousins, we share a common heritage. Of all the elves, we are the most hated by mankind, shunned to live in the depths of the earth away from the light of day.

"We were driven here by the surface dweller's fear, hatred, and lust for power. We, unlike the woodland elves, look the least like man, though you can tell from my daughter, we are not that unalike. Do you not find her attractive? Is she not beautiful?"

"And yet," Jonna shook his head, "I am spoken for. Why me? Surely there are others who would gladly love your daughter?"

"Of course," the queen became irritated, "what elf wouldn't desire her hand?" A realization passed through the queen as she thought about to Jonna's words. "You don't know?"

"Don't know what?"

The queen smiled. "The prophecy." She nodded toward the door behind Jonna, and someone quickly left.

'Not again.' Jonna sighed, thinking to what the Fates had told him, 'Though the gods would use you as a tool, they will find you gone before you go'.

Ever since he had arrived in this world of magic, he felt as if he were being forced into things he had no desire to do. First, there was the freeing of Elfleda, which he hadn't wanted to do but had to do, in order to find his wife, who, he found out, was his wife. He shook his head.

Next, there was the whole 'go to the Otherworld world to pay for your crimes'. And now, the 'have a baby with another elf'. All prophecies? Well, this time he was drawing the line, prophecy or not.

A dark elf stepped into the room. In his hands was a scroll, decorated in what had to be the royal dark elvish seal. The elf bowed his knee beside Queen Siardna's throne and held the scroll up.

"This," Siardna raised up the tube, "is the Alfgiefuenid prophecy. It foretells of a stranger who comes to our realm from the Other-else to save it. Within its verses, it specifies that the stranger will mate with an elvish princess to provide an heir. That heir will rule all elves."

"And you think I'm the stranger?" Jonna began to laugh.

The queen ignored his disbelief. "And why not? To begin with, Elfleda chose you, against her father's and mother's wishes."

Jonna stopped and stared. "Really?" Bob had told him Elfleda hadn't wanted to be queen, not that her decision to marry him was against her parent's wishes. Could this queen be telling a lie? Was this why Queen Freya had said it was the end of all they had known?

The queen's gaze remained steady. "Second, you came from a realm outside our own."

He looked into the eyes of the queen. These facts were not guesses; she knew.

"And third, you wield the magic of this world in ways we cannot."

That appeared to be true. The more he did magic, the more everyone thought he was upsetting the whole balance of the cosmos.

"I sensed you before you came here," she continued. "Though I am not the person I once was, I knew the prophecy was to be fulfilled through you. I sent the words for the spells into your mind, thus saving your life. I had Hieronymus, my most decorated commander, go to meet you, though I knew you would prevail to his own disgrace. So I ask again, shall we trade?"

Silence dropped. The expectant queen focused on Jonna. He turned toward Alfgia who dropped her eyes.

"Then it's settled, Jonna McCambel. Deliver to me a child by my daughter, and you and the humans may go free." She turned to the guards which appeared at her side. "Take them to the Amund Frigg."

Alfgia walked to his right, her flowing black hair glimmering in the light. The lithe form, gentleness of movement, and soft voice all combined in a package that would turn the head of anyone, elf or man. Yet in spite of this, all he could think about was Elfleda.

He missed his wife; it felt like an eternity since he had seen her. He could hear her voice, see the look on her face as she smiled, and feel the touch of her hands. There was no other woman he would rather be with, and though she might understand the situation, there had to be another way.

The guards could not hide their attraction for Alfgia. Even without turning their heads, he knew they were not paying attention to him. It was the perfect time for Jonna to escape. He watched the movement of their weapons, calculated the easiest one within reach, and waited for his first opening.

A soft hand about the size of Elfleda's touched his, and he froze. A tingle went up his arm, and for the first time, he wondered if all elvish women had this effect on males. It had to be a form of magic.

The complication was not much but enough to throw him off. He had been prepared to grab the nearest weapon, use it to take out the others, and begin his journey to find his companions. Now everything changed.

The hand held his, and for such a dainty hand, the grip was secure. It was nothing rough; there was no real strength involved. Yet, he knew if he were to resist, she could slow him down to be caught.

The hall ended at two ornately carved doors with the elvish words Amund Frigg set as a mosaic into the header. The guards swung the doors open, and Alfgia lead him into the room. There was a brief pause, a flick of her wrist, the doors to Amund Frigg closed, and the two were left alone.

Like the elf palace of the woodland elves, the majesty of this room was unmistakable. Though no sunlight lit its walls, the fluorescent fungi cast a sparkling rainbow. Gems reflected and amplified the color, decorated the bed post, and sent golden rays of light all around the room.

Alfgia walked around the bed toward the left, her back to him. In one smooth motion, the ceremonial gown slipped off her shoulders and descended slowly toward the ground. The rainbow colors cast an alluring hue as they played across her body.

Jonna held his breath and finally remembered to breathe. He looked away as she turned around.

Alfgia demurely slipped into the silk sheets on the bed. "You can turn around now."

"I was going to escape." He focused on the thought to distract from her.

Alfgia smiled, wrapped in the sheets. "I know," the fluttering voice called.

"And yet, you stopped me?"

"You would have been killed, and if not you, your companions, and if not they, the humans *my mother* keeps." There was something about Alfgia's soft voice, something that said she understood far more than Jonna.

"You said *my mother* as if you did not agree with her."

"You are very perceptive," the beautiful smile increased. "Not all humans have that trait."

"You've known other humans?"

"A few," she played along with the questions, "then again—" The words hung in the air.

"Then again," Jonna swallowed, "the others did not fit the prophecy." Beads of sweat formed on his forehead.

She laughed, and her voice sounded like sparkles of light. "No, they didn't."

"Your touch, do all elvish women have that influence?" Did Elfleda do that to him on purpose?

She laughed lightly. "You mean the tingling? Only when we want them to." Her hand patted the bed. "You really should sit down."

The desire to do so was almost overwhelming. Jonna had to fight for control and tried to relax his runaway pulse. "That's the last thing I should do." Something wasn't right; his body wasn't responding.

"Let me help." Her words tried to take control. Despite his resistance, they burrowed through.

The chairs were too far away, and the room spun. He barely grabbed the bedpost in time. The jeweled stones caught the light and made it harder to focus. "What's—going—on?"

Alfgia looked at him with loving eyes. "Only what must, my dear one. Only what must."

Jonna fell half-hitting the bed. Out of nowhere, her small

hands caught him. They held him up and kept him from going all the way to the floor. Yet, it was more than that; he was floating.

Jonna remembered his first encounter with Dorothy the Pixie, and the situation above Stephanie's bed. He had managed to talk Dorothy into letting him down, but there was no talking this time; his voice failed.

The soft silk pillow bowed as his head sank back. The face of Alfgia appeared over his, stroked his cheek, and moved back his hair.

With full lips, her eyes were vivid and bright. The dark hair cascaded down one shoulder. The colors in the room played with her highlights and deepened her contours.

She spoke softly, "You will remember this night forever."

Her lips approached his as a whiff of fragrance hit his nose. His body tingled, caught in a place he could not tell where.

Darkness was all around him. Had Alfgia used magic to make him deaf, dumb, and sightless? No longer was he on a bed in the Amund Frigg. He was floating in a sea of no sensation at all. "Where am I?"

This had happened one time before, when he had faced down Lilith Magnus and was caught in a backlash of destructive magic. He stood outside of time. Why? How?

A familiar chuckle hit his ears. "My dear boy, we do meet in some of the strangest places."

"Väinämö?" Jonna reached out but felt nothing above or below.

"Glad you haven't forgotten, especially with all the philandering you are doing."

"I am not philandering!"

"If you say so," Väinämö's voice had a whimsical feel, "but something is certainly happening right now."

"It is?"

Jonna knew that Väinämö nodded, though how he knew was a mystery to him. "Why am I here?"

"There are things that happen to us beyond our control.

When they do, the mind has a way of protecting us. In your case, mind and magic have flowed together, pulling you out of the situation."

"So, I'm not there?"

"Oh, you're there." Väinämö shifted to get a better view.

"So, I'm not here?"

"Oh, you're here," Väinämö assured, "also."

Jonna shook his head. "I can't be here and there. That is not possible."

"And yet, it is." The mage laughed. "Jonna, there are more things unknown than known in magic. Your ability to control it should tell you that."

Jonna inhaled. "You wouldn't have a nifty spell to get me out of this, would you?"

"What's nifty?"

A sigh escaped Jonna's lips. "Neat, cool, really good?"

"What does really good have to do with being organized or cold?"

There was no time to explain it. "Please, ignore the first two words. So what really good spell do you have for me?"

Väinämö shook his head. "Not a thing. Remember, you are in a place that uses a different type of magic, and each type has its own boundaries."

"Latin." Jonna took that as a hint. "Okay, so I have to make it up."

"No," Väinämö was adamant, "do not make up magic!"

This was starting to grate on Jonna's nerves. "I didn't mean—"

"The consequences could be deadly. Why do you think you're in this mess to begin with?"

Remembering Fabius' reaction, Jonna decided to play dumb; maybe Väinämö would say something to shed more light. "Why do you think?"

"Don't you see? By bending the unbendable, adapting the unadaptable, you are creating something new. Normally, this type of change takes place over generations, but with you it is different. You limit traffic from neither side and allow both at the same time. The result is reforging all we know."

190

Jonna shook his head. "I don't believe it."

"You don't?" Väinämö looked at something far away. "Hmm, could be."

"Could be what?"

"Could be, could be." Väinämö waved it away. "Never mind. Only the future can tell."

"Tell what? Väinämö, you are not being clear."

"Have I ever been?" The mage gave a hearty laugh. "Some things one must find out on their own." His voice faded away. "Good luck."

"Good Luck?" Jonna panicked. The darkness was everywhere, and he had no idea how to get back.

Tiny bells sounded at a distance. Whispers came from faraway. An echo? A woman's voice? He had heard this voice before in the cellar at the shepherd's hut, but that had been Siardna, right?

"Jonna." The sound wavered in and out of hearing. A tiny sparkle formed in the darkness. "Jonna McCambel."

The voice was so close, it had to be the same. But why would Siardna want to help him now?

"I'm here," he spoke with suspicion. "Who are you?"

The tiny sparkle grew in size and moved in his direction. With each change, the color altered until a sizeable light floated before him. Within this light, a woman appeared. "Thank you for your permission."

Jonna frowned. "Permission?"

"I am Lucasta, guardian of the Kvinnea forest. It is I who helped you in the shepherd's hut. It is I who can help you now."

"But I thought—" He continued rapidly, "Siardna said she—and the voice I heard—" The guardian was right. Now that he focused, though Lucasta's and Siardna's voices were close, they were not the same. "Why would Siardna lie?"

"I think you know why as much as I. She wants the child of prophecy for her daughter."

"But how did she know?" He stopped; Siardna had The Sight. She knew what had been done and had said enough to make him think she was the cause.

He turned his attention toward Lucasta. Was Lucasta a Greek bearing gifts, too? "You offer to help me, but at what cost?"

An unknown force billowed the robes around her. "What are you willing to give?"

There was no way he was playing that game. "I seek to free the humans held by the dark elves."

Her blue eyes bore into his. "And yet, there's more."

"My companions as well."

She gave a slight nod. "And yet, there is still more."

He took a deep breath. "I want to go home."

"Of the first two I can help. Of the last, it is for you to find. A gift to you then, Jonna McCambel. Return my people, *ad multos annos*, save your companions, *liberate comes*, restore the balance, *spem reduxit*. Now, repeat after me: Fortiter."

"Fortiter."

"In re."

"In re."

"Suaviter."

"Suaviter."

"In modo."

"In modo."

Jonna paused and spoke slowly, "Fortiter in re, sauviter in modo." He stared at Lucasta. Those were the words of Jesuit Claudio Acquaviva and his book 'Curing the illnesses of the soul'. Claudio had used this phrase. "Resolutely in action, gently in manner." How did that apply?

In a direction it had never gone, his mind leaped. There were four parts to magic, not two. One, it was about the meaning as he had learned with demoneze. Two, it was about the words as Väinämö had taught him with spells. Three, it was about the intention, the desire for a specific outcome, as he had done drying his clothes. Four, it was about 'knowing' the truth in his situation; the truth took the 'hoped for' and made it real.

The last two elements he had done without realizing it,

but by understanding them, they became much more powerful. All four played their part. Lucasta was not only showing him a spell; she was giving him a message on many different levels. He looked at her with new admiration.

"Lucasta, forgive my foolish conclusions."

She smiled. "They were forgotten before you even asked. However, you must go. Speak the words of power, and return to Alfgia. Do what you must."

He gave a single nod. "I understand."

The brightness in the dark was gone, and once more Jonna saw nothing at all. *"Fortiter in re, sauviter in modo."*

Chapter 14

PRINCESS ALFGIA

Alfgia's lips approached his, a whiff of fragrance hit his nose, and they touched. It was not unpleasant, and yet, something had changed. His mind was in control of his body. The sickness and weakness were gone. He brought his hands up, moved her hair back, and stroked her face. At the end of her kiss, his voice whispered, "Alfgia."

Alfgia's hands stopped, frozen as she faced the unknown. "You—can—speak?"

Jonna chuckled. "I can."

"And move!" For the first time, she became conscious of his touch.

He laughed. "That also." Shifting her gently to the left, he came up on one elbow. She was very beautiful lying there, yet very scared and confused.

Alfgia shook her head. "This cannot be."

"And yet, it is." An amused, understanding, laugh left his lips. Of course she was confused, who wouldn't? "Are you sure you want to do this?"

A look of doubt played across her face. "I must for the prophecy to be fulfilled."

"And if you did not?"

"I—" She swallowed. "I cannot imagine what my mother would do."

"I can," he assured. "Doing this thing will only bring you grief. You do not love me, and my heart belongs to another."

"It is not a matter of love." She looked the other direction. "Love is for commoners, not those who rule."

There was a spark there and something she was trying to hide. This was her duty for her mother, not something she had chosen to do, and Alfgia was ashamed. Until this moment, she had been able to hide it, schooled well by her mother the queen. Yet, he remembered their introduction by Siardna. Alfgia had ducked her eyes at his gaze. At first, Jonna thought it was shyness, but was she indicating something else?

Jonna spoke what he thought he saw. "There is one that you do love. He is the one that you should choose."

A tear had formed in one eye. "I cannot."

"You can. You are the one who decides your fate: not your mother, not this kingdom, and not the prophecy." He reached over and touched her hand gently.

Her eyes turned to look at him. "I do not know you. How can I believe you?"

He smiled. "When you look into my eyes, what do you see?"

"I see a good man. A man that would do all to save his companions. You would willingly give your life to save theirs—" Her voice became halting. "And—give up—your own happiness—if that was what had to be done." Unbelief crossed her face. "You would destroy yourself to save these people?"

"If that was what it took to save the people above and make peace between dark elf and human, yes, but I will not be the pawn of prophecy. Do you believe me?"

The room became silent. Alfgia's eyes did not leave his. Somewhere in the distance, they could hear children. Dark elf or human, the laughing and playing sounded the same.

"I believe you." Her voice was soft. "I believe you will do what has to be done to bring peace between humans and dark elves." Her countenance changed. "You're a strange human, Jonna. Before I thought of this as a duty, forced upon me by a cast of fate, twisted, but now—" The smile on her face brightened, glowing in a way that only enhanced her beauty. "I love you Jonna McCambel."

It hit like a boulder. Had his actions pushed forward what he was trying to stop? Yet, he did sense a 'but' at the end of those spoken words.

She turned away. "Yet, my heart also belongs to another."

Jonna exhaled. "Then he is the one you must find. To do anything else would not be true to yourself."

Alfgia's voice shook, though Jonna was not sure why. She spoke in awe. "You love Elfleda that much?"

"I do."

She bit her lip. "This might cause a small problem for us."

Jonna laughed nervously and shifted from off his elbow to lie beside her. "I was hoping you might have some suggestions."

"It does seem to be a mess." She exhaled, a small quivering laugh on her lips. "We could always do as expected. It would certainly save the humans."

"Would Queen Siardna keep her word?"

She nodded. "Without a doubt."

"Would she make peace with those above?"

"That was not part of the agreement. She would simply grant their freedom and yours."

"Only to make them slaves again," he finished. "It was as I thought."

Alfgia nodded. "I'm afraid so. If not the same day, it would eventually happen."

"Then there must be another way." He rose from the bed. Although not entirely sure what to do next, something formed in the back of his mind. "We have been here a sufficient time for copulation to take place. Is it permitted for us to leave this room?"

"Of course," Alfgia wrinkled her brow, "but where would we go?"

"You could show me around the city."

A whimsical tone appeared in her voice, like a child preparing to do mischief. "I could show you all the city sights," she spoke out loud, "and explain where everything is."

Jonna gave a slight bow toward her with a warm smile. "You understand perfectly."

Alfgia rose, heedless that the silk covers slid off her body. Jonna turned away politely. While they may have reached an understanding, it was better to avoid temptation.

At his action, she laughed and slipped into the robes on the floor. A moment later, she touched his shoulder. "Shall we go?"

He extended his arm. Her hand found it and slid along the arm until their fingers touched. As the fingers intertwined, the tingle returned and ran up his arm into his body.

"Is this how you took control of me?"

Alfgia nodded. "I used a spell of touch to take control until the bonding. While I was taught an elf might resist, a human has never been known to do so. Then again," a pleased look crossed her face, "I had never met you." She gave a beautiful laugh. "I still do not know how you did it."

"I am amazed myself."

Jonna pushed the ornate doors back. Two surprised guards stepped hurriedly out of the way. Neither spoke; neither tried to stop them. He glanced toward Alfgia. "I have met the queen. Where is the king?"

"He died a long time ago, just after I was born. I do not know the reason."

"Siardna never told you?"

"There are many things my mother has never told me, one of which you have shown me today: what love for another really means."

As they reached the end of the hallway, she looked up at him and spoke in quiet whispers, "Though we did not do as instructed, there is bonding between us. I will help you free your companions and the humans. I will help bring peace between human and dark elf." Her eyes became resolute. "This, I swear."

Jonna's face could not hide the pride he had in her. "I would be honored."

The queen's voice broke their thoughts. "So, I see you two have made a pact."

They froze, though no one else could tell it. How much had she heard? How loud had they been speaking?

"I am well pleased," the queen continued, giddy in excitement. "I had feared you would refuse." She looked at Jonna. "Although, it should never have worried me. My daughter knows the ways of the Dark Elves." She smiled. "If not by beauty, then by magic."

"Your daughter is most persuasive." Jonna smiled. "Anyone would be honored."

Alfgia blushed appropriately. Siardna was content.

"Come, my love," she pulled Jonna by the hand, "let me show you the wonders of your elvish city."

Passing through the outer doors, the brightness of the cavern could pass as sunlight. Where once the silent streets had stood, the hustle of city life had returned, and the glowing of the fungi had intensified.

The voices of the children they had heard from the bedchamber were not far away. They could see them running, jumping, and playing. The dark elves were beings like any other. Yet, how could he get them to see that by harming the humans, they harmed themselves?

No elvish guards could be seen save for at the palace doors. Jonna and Alfgia drifted down a polished street. Dark elves stopped, turned to face them, and nodded as they passed; their expressions said it all.

"Not everyone agrees with our bonding," Jonna mused. It was the eyes; the disdain the dark elves felt came from their soul. "Prejudice seems to be a common trait everywhere."

"Most have heard of the prophecy, yet the old ways are hard to shake. We have always been taught that humans and elves do not mix."

"Those same ideas were in my world. Different people from different races tried to keep people apart. Even today, they still exist and try to destroy those that have peace."

"And where is your world?"

They left the area around the palace and moved into an outer sector. The light was less here; the streets appeared harsher. Up ahead, it looked like a barracks of some sort.

"Very far away," Jonna was not sure how to describe it, "but for me, a place I shall never go again."

She studied him. "Do you not miss it?"

"Yes and no," he chuckled. "It is different there. Instead of magic, we have technology. Instead of humans and elves, we vary by tradition, location, and sometimes physical attributes."

"Not unlike us then," she raised an eyebrow, "but what is technology?"

"Think of it as doing something not by magic, but as magic might accomplish the same end."

"I think—" She squinted. "I think I understand." Her hand waved toward the right. "For years the queen was responsible for calling the rivers which provided water for the city. Then one day, everything changed. The warriors were instructed to carve a series of waterways into the earth and thus direct the water to our location."

Her explanation was right, something verified it in his mind, though he wasn't quite sure what she meant. "Calling the rivers?"

She nodded. "Aqua pura vitae."

"The pure water of life."

Alfgia's eyes caught his. "You know what it means?"

"It's a pet study of mine—languages. Some of the Latin I recognize."

"I do not understand. The words I spoke are for spells not speaking."

"In my world, it was for speaking."

She looked puzzled. "If your entire world is like that, how do you know the difference between speech and magic? It would be a nightmare."

"We learn about each other. We learn each other's way of speaking."

"Like you and I." Alfgia nodded. "We had to learn each other to understand that our goals could be the same."

The barracks loomed in front of them. There were no guards posted outside, but the slits in the building were the right size for arrows and crossbows. Alfgia waved toward them. "Your companions are here."

"Can I speak with them?"

"It might be more prudent to wait until after you've been shown where the captured humans are."

Jonna nodded, following her line of thought. The queen knew of his tour of the dark elvish city. They needed to make sure it looked like what she expected.

They turned down another street and followed a worn path. The buildings here were older, some of the stones had been replaced, and the glowing fungi was not as bright. As they passed through some arches, they headed out of the city proper.

"Here is where it might get tricky." She pointed.

They approached a passageway, leading to the right and away from the city. The smallish stairs, combined with less light, cast a feeling of foreboding as they moved into the shadows.

The clang of metal against stone sounded in the distance, coming ever closer. Other sounds, the turning of wheels, the rattling of chains, and the grunting of men combined to be called slavery.

The passageway opened, revealing what Jonna already knew. The cavern before them stretched broadly out in both directions. It was filled with crude furnaces and work areas as channels were cut into the earth.

So this was how the dark elves now brought water into their cities. This was why they had captured those from above. They needed muscle.

Alfgia followed his gaze, spotting the types of ores piled up. "We keep all except pure iron. It is the one metal we do not like."

200

Jonna's mind drifted to his wife. "Will it kill you?" He remembered Elfleda in pain at the Dark Mage's arena.

Alfgia shook her head. "But the iron is painful." She grimaced. "In its pure form, we cannot stay near it."

"Which also explains the capture of the humans." He frowned. "They are needed to separate and get rid of the iron ore. I have read about this in our myths and legends, but never thought it was true."

A question formed on Alfgia's face.

Jonna changed the subject. "Why can the queen no longer call the rivers?" There was only one answer in Jonna's mind; she had lost the ability to do magic. This explained why she wanted Jonna to fulfill the prophecy with Alfgia. In this world, magic was power. Without it, entire civilizations could fall.

Alfgia's voice sounded far away. "It was after my father died that it began. The kingdom was weakened. The times of our greatness had come to an end, like the glow of the sun dropping below the horizon. Mother did all she knew to hold our people together." Alfgia looked down at the slaves, a frown on her face.

"But without magic, she was forced to find other ways."

She nodded. "How did you know?"

"It makes sense." He stared down. Wherever iron was being worked, the elves kept their distance, including the guards. As long as the elves were forced to dig in the earth, they would require non-elf slaves.

"The greatest elven magic is within those that rule, and with my mother's magic failing, she had no choice."

"She could have always asked for help." As soon as he said it, he knew why she had not. It was pride and fear; if the humans knew of the elves' weakness, they were as likely to exploit it. "I take it you have no problem with magic?"

Alfgia smiled coyly. "I do not have any difficulty. However, I will not reach my full potential until I am queen, and I am not permitted to call the waters while I am a princess. It is our way."

"And yet, you could bring the waters, no longer needing the use of slaves."

The smile on Alfgia's face dropped. "It would mean the destruction of my mother, the queen. That, I will not do."

"Doesn't it worry you that the queen's powers failed?"

A look of concern crossed her face. "I've never considered it. It was something that simply happened."

"All things have a reason," he assured, "and perhaps it's time to find out why." He listened to the approach of footsteps. "Someone's coming."

"This way." Alfgia grabbed his hand and led him back the way they had come. Reaching the mouth of the passage, the brighter light was a welcome sight—until they saw the others.

It was a group of dark elves; their faces hid behind masks of gold. In their hands were gold tipped spears with black-gold shields strapped to their backs.

"Princess Alfgia." The voice came from the one in the center. None of the others spoke; they held their spears at ready. "We would have a word with the stranger."

Alfgia's voice was sharp. "Do you not bow to a princess, or have your manners changed so much in a day?"

Silence dropped. None of the warriors moved. The one in front straightened more. They were comfortable hiding behind their masks, no longer bound by the mores of their society. With the queen unable to do magic, this culture was on the border of civil war.

Alfgia's eyes narrowed. "The stranger will be addressed as Prince Jonna. You will show him the same consideration you do me. Thus, the queen has declared."

"This is not about the queen," the voice of the leader was sharp. He pointed at Jonna with his spear. "This is about a human. Seize him."

"No," Alfgia stepped in front of Jonna, "he is my husband, and you will not touch him!"

The words dropped like a bomb. Alfgia dared any to raise their weapon. It gave Jonna the moment he needed.

"Cover your eyes," he whispered and turned to face the warriors. With a loud voice he spoke, *"Fait lux."*

Hearing the words, Alfgia threw her left arm up as Jonna grabbed her right; a bright ball of light flashed into existence. They ran down the street away from the warriors. It wasn't that Jonna couldn't have faced them, he was sure that time was coming, but at the moment, they needed to go and free his friends.

Spears hurtled by the two as the warriors staggered blindly. A second flash erupted. Those that did not drop to their knees ran into each other.

The civilian elves watched as the princess with the human hurried up the street. Reflections of the magic light bounced off the building walls.

"Did you have to tell them that?" Jonna gave a chuckle. "Somehow, I think it set me up for a lynching."

Alfgia selected the least traveled streets. "We can't let anyone know what didn't happen between us. That in itself would be your death."

"And what of your beloved if he hears the rumor of us being husband and wife?"

They rounded a corner. When she was sure no one else had followed, she turned around and stopped him in his tracks. Her eyes bore into his. "He will understand. To your companions?"

"After you." However, he did not understand her. When they had encountered the gold-clad warriors, there were a hundred other responses Alfgia could have said, yet she had spoken her words as if they were true. Why stir up the hornets?

She turned toward another corridor between the buildings. "This way."

Somehow, through the twisting and turning, they had come up behind the barracks. They pressed toward a side door. Alfgia knocked, stood back, and spoke her name.

The door opened without a word. Even the sentry was gone as they passed into the hallway. Jonna and Alfgia moved room by room, looking for his companions. They could hear voices of elvish warriors but caught no sight of them. Two doors down, around a corner, they found Jonna's friends.

There was a form of translucent material making up one wall, allowing Jonna and Alfgia to look in at the group. The room contained bunk beds, a large table, and some chairs. There was enough space for all to sit or sleep. A bowl of fruit and a bowl of nuts sat on the single table. His companions did not know they could be watched, though in several cases, they looked straight at them. It acted as a two-way mirror.

True to the queen's word, his friends had not been touched, or at least, there was no physical evidence. After the situation with the gold-clad warriors, he was sure that was about to change. "We better hurry."

Alfgia led him to a t-intersection. No guards appeared. He frowned. "Not that I'm complaining, but is this usual?"

"What do you mean?" Alfgia stayed close to the right side of the hall.

"Where is everybody?"

"What do we have to worry about down here?"

Jonna thought about it; she had a point. The dark elvish city was beneath the earth. Who would come down here except dark elves? And yet— "The door opened, and no one was about."

"I come here often," she spoke quietly. "They honor me by keeping my passage unseen."

"You do?"

She shot him a smile. "You don't think I'm just a dainty princess, do you? Though my mother does not approve, I feel that royalty should practice arms."

They reached the door. Alfgia undid the lock and swung it in. Cassandra was the first to look.

"Jonna!" She rushed forward and threw her arms around him. "You're okay!"

"Alfgia, this is Cassandra, the mother of my adopted daughter."

After a moment's thought, Alfgia extended her hand. "I see."

Cassandra stepped back. Andas and the others moved up in support.

"Hold up everyone." Jonna held out his hand and promptly stepped between them. "Alfgia is a friend."

"I bet," Cassandra wrinkled her brow. "Where's Lokke?"

Alfgia placed a hand on Jonna's shoulder. "Who is Lokke?"

"Lokke is one of our companions lost last night. We assumed he was caught."

"He is not human?" Again, her perception was uncanny. She studied something as if from a great distance.

"No, he is not."

"They will have no use for him, then. We will find where he is soon enough. Right now, we must get out of here."

"They're coming," Cassandra's eyes widened, speaking in a faraway voice. "Seven of them down the hall."

"She's right." Alfgia turned toward Jonna though she gave Cassandra a curious look. "We need a way out." Her hand closed the door, and she leaned back against it. "Unfortunately, it can't be the way we came."

Jonna remembered the translucent material allowing them to see into the room. He had been right; from the inside, it was a mirror. Picking up a chair, he moved toward the wall.

"No. Wait." Alfgia's hand caught the chair. "We can't go that way."

"She's right," Cassandra surprised herself as she agreed. "In a few moments," she squinted, "warriors in gold and black armor will take the building." Her eyes caught Jonna and Alfgia. "You had a run in with them."

His head nodded as Latin phrases flew through his mind, despite the warning from the mage. What he needed was an archway, but to where? If he could not decide, where would they end up?

Cassandra moved to the door and dropped the inside latch as something struck it. The sound echoed around the room. The bolts strained as it was struck again.

The whisper returned. It had to be Lucasta. "A..." The voice faded in and out, like bad reception on an old analog cell phone. "A capite..."

"A capite?" Jonna couldn't hear the rest. Whatever was going on had blocked the end of the message. He ran through all the phrases he knew, trying to match the words. "...ad calcem? From the head to the heel?" Then it hit him, and he remember that was the literal translation. Translated commonly in his own tongue it meant, 'all the way through'. "*A capite ad calcem.*"

The air in room quivered. An archway formed as seen in the palace of Lilith Magnus. "Quickly, move into it."

Spear points jabbed through the wooden door and split the boards, attempting to destroy the latch. The others in his group hurried into the magic arch as Jonna brought up the rear. He watched as the latch snapped and stepped backward into the archway.

A light would have been nice, but it had not come to mind. The pixie magic guided him to the beginning of the line.

Alfgia was there. Her elvish ability to see in the dark was different, but not unlike his own. Alfgia extended her right hand and caught his left. Hands clasped, the group moved forward.

The tunnel at the Magnus' Palace was nothing compared to this. You would think the arch would instantly take you to your exit, yet this one went on for a very long time. When the exit appeared, it showed nothing beyond the tunnel end. The whole group slowed to a stop.

"What is beyond?" Alfgia stood beside him. The others moved closer, converting the line to a half-circle as they stared at the glowing exit.

Jonna's mind said everything was good, they would come out where they should, but where that was, he had no idea. The spell had not been his idea, but the idea of Lucasta.

"I don't know," Jonna squared his shoulders, "but it's time to find out." He stepped through the portal's end.

A blast of wind, followed by searing heat, hit both face and hands. Throwing an arm up, he guarded his eyes and let his body adapt to the change.

It was the canal digging site next to the smelting area.

Human slaves moved back and forth, filled the buckets, stoked the fires, and hauled raw material. Most were exhausted. The air was filled with singed hair and sweat.

The slaves ignored him. They were too worn out to care. Bronze chains rattled, attached to either wrist or leg.

A faint voice called out of the heat, "Jonna."

There was Lokke suspended above the cave floor; he was held in a cage of bronze. A pulley system controlling the cage stretched over several support beams and connected to a place at Jonna's right. How long Lokke had been in that cage, Jonna could only guess, but from the sound of his voice, they didn't have much time.

The others were coming through the portal behind him. Each required a moment to adjust. As the last came through, the arch vanished.

Cassandra frowned, caught sight of the direction Jonna was looking, and followed his gaze until the cage came into view.

Jonna's voice was hard. "Andas, go free Lokke."

The boys were off the moment he spoke. Their weapons drawn, they moved through the field of slaves.

Cassandra grabbed his arm and tried to turn him. "Dark elves!"

The voice of Hieronymus boomed from somewhere above, deep and resonating. "Prince Jonna." It echoed through the chamber, stopping even the slaves. "You do not belong here."

"Am I not a prince?" Jonna mocked and took Alfgia's hand. "Has not the queen declared Alfgia my wife?"

Cassandra blinked and turned to look at the two. "Wife?"

Chapter 15

MULTUM IN PARVO

The elf sneered as his voice echoed across the cavern. "Royalty is not permitted here. They cannot be soiled by the presence of human dogs."

The warriors nearest to Hieronymus stayed close; the rest followed their led. Alfgia stepped forward arm in arm with Jonna. "Since when is royalty ever restricted?" The sound of a marching elvish army met their ears.

"When?" He slowed his pace as he approached and stopped twenty feet from them. Holding up a hand, he halted those who followed and slowly continued toward Alfgia. "Since the queen lost her power." He stabbed the butt end of his spear into the ground at Alfgia's feet. Dust shot up as the spear stuck in place. He ignored Jonna. With his free hand, he reached out and touched Alfgia's face. "What a shame you cannot take her place. You would be the perfect queen."

Alfgia released Jonna's arm. "How dare you." She slapped Hieronymus' hand away. "I am the princess, not a common laugnea!"

The dark elf growled, "You are what I say you are."

Jonna's right hand surged in an upper cut. It caught the dark elf under the chin in the only spot the mask did not cover. "Forget about me?"

The dark elf flew back as the golden mask ripped from

208

his face. He crashed to the ground colliding against those behind.

Alfgia exhaled in anger, "You will never touch me again."

Hieronymus squinted, trying to take in his surroundings. His eyes focused on Alfgia, and then turned to Jonna in hatred. "Get them!"

Jonna snatched the spear from the ground and motioned to the others as the nearest gold-clad warriors leaped forward. "Everyone help Andas. I will hold them off." He ducked a spear as it sliced high.

Cassandra hurried toward the boys; Alfgia moved closer to him. "We'll hold them off." She caught the shaft of a thrusted spear, snatched it from the dark elf who dared to attack her, and struck with the butt end between the dark elf's legs. As he bent forward in pain, she palm struck his chest. Despite the armor, it sent him back with a terrible crack. "You don't think I went to the barracks to watch."

"That I don't," he grinned, losing the grin as he dodged a jab to the side. He countered, caught the attacker's spear in the middle, sliced the shaft in half, and whipped the end of his own around. It hit the mask so hard, the dark elf was out before he hit the ground.

The warriors fanned out to encircle the two.

Jonna hollered, "Cassandra, how's that cage coming?"

She cupped her hands to her mouth. "Coming!"

Alfgia jumped, brought down her spear to support her in the air, caught the shaft of another with her free hand, jerked the attacker forward, and struck another elf's body with her feet. Jonna parried, took out the feet of another, and dropped a third with a blow to the midsection.

The number of warriors escalated. Jonna could not turn to see Cassandra's progress. "Come on, guys!"

Alfgia fanned more to the right as he went to the left. The gap between them increased as they tried to keep back larger numbers. So far it had worked, but—

Cassandra cried a warning, "Jump!"

Both Alfgia and Jonna leaped away from each other,

209

neither sure where the cage would come down. The rope that held the cage smoked against the pulleys. A screech assaulted their ears. In agony, those closest to the sound dropped to their knees.

The bronze cage struck, landed on some of the warriors, and crushed them beneath the cage's great weight. Jonna rose to his feet as the remnants of the sound faded. Identifying the lock, he used the end of the bronze spear to break it. The lock fell off, and Alfgia jerked the cage door open before leaping back into the fray.

Kneeling down, Jonna looked over the half-demon. "Lokke?"

Tortured eyes squinted. "Thanks." As his eyes closed, his head hit the cage floor.

"Get him up," he stepped quickly out of the cage, his voice hard, "and keep him by the iron." He joined Alfgia in keeping back the elves.

Cassandra lifted one side of Lokke as Andas held the other. They hauled him safely out. When they stopped, Cassandra felt Lokke's forehead. "We need water."

Philo found a drinking bucket, jabbed the dipper into it, and handed the result to Cassandra. She held the dipper to Lokke's lips.

The half-demon stirred. "Where am I?"

Jonna caught the words as he parried a blow. There was no time for niceties. "Can he walk?"

Lokke struggled to rise, but the water was not enough.

Cassandra's voice filled with concern. "No, he shouldn't move at all right now."

Jonna glanced back. "We'll have to carry him." His spear parried and sliced.

"There's no time." Alfgia pointed at the base of the walkway. They had been drawing the focus of the attack, but they could handle no more. Warriors blotted out the ground, so many had reached the cavern floor.

Hieronymus gave a maniacal laugh. He had risen to his feet and retrieved another spear. As he pushed toward Alfgia, the warriors beside him gave way. The attack lulled. With back straight and chest out, he called, "What will you do now, Princess Alfgia? What will you do against a whole elf army?" The warriors listened.

"It is the Crown's army, not yours," her voice echoed around the cavern. At her words, the warriors at the back took notice. "There is only one who commands the elvish army, and that is the queen. You are not fighting humans here. You are fighting against the Crown."

Hieronymus' laugh echoed away in the quiet that followed. "Our loyalty has never changed." He turned, encouraging the warriors with a smile. "We protect the people. We protect from the filth of humanity. You have sided with the humans and have broken the law. Obey me, and I might be persuaded to go easy on you. After all—" He bowed slightly, keeping his eyes locked with hers. "We would not hurt royalty, only the traitors. Lay down your weapons."

Jonna's eyes swept toward his companions and finally stopped on Alfgia. The look of disgust on her face said all he needed to know. "Speaking for all," he smiled toward Hieronymus, "I think we're good."

Hieronymus gritted his teeth. "I was talking to the princess, human scum."

"Let's put this another way," Jonna stepped forward casually, "you lay down your weapons and leave. All will be forgiven."

Hieronymus began to laugh. "You are in the middle of a huge cavern, surrounded by slaves and dark elf warriors, and you are telling me to back off? Maybe I'll make you the court jester."

The light reflected from their spears and masks. The warriors took position. Yet, despite this, they did not resume the attack. For the first time, Jonna was sure, they realized the true conflict was not between them and the humans; it was between Hieronymus and their royalty. If it could be done without further bloodshed, why should they kill their own?

The slaves stopped. All work ceased. For the first time

since entering the cavern, silence descended, like the calm before a storm.

The queen's voice echoed, "Stop, I command it!" On the topmost walkway, Queen Siardna appeared. She was dressed in robes of velvet and sapphire; she wore a crown that glistened with light. "Hieronymus, what are you doing? Answer me!"

His voice was sour. "Only what we agreed upon, ensuring the construction of the canals."

"At the cost of my daughter?" The queen scorned him. "No Hieronymus, this is not the way."

"And yours is?" he growled. "Where is your promise I would have your daughter's hand? Where is the promise I would be king?"

"Mother," Alfgia's eyes widened, "what have you done?"

The queen's face was grim. "Only what I had to, child. With my magic gone, I had to protect you."

Alfgia waved a hand. "And what of the humans?"

It was strange hearing a dark elf concerned for the people her race had enslaved; Jonna could read that thought on the faces of those around them. There was surprise, shock, and hope. The dark elf warriors listened to the words spoken by their queen.

The queen shrugged. "They were of no consequence. That is," she looked at Jonna, "until Prince Jonna came. It was then I knew the prophecy could be fulfilled here. It was then I knew there was another way."

"No," Hieronymus roared in anger, "I will not give the throne to this human!" He glared up at the queen. "He will not have Alfgia as his wife!"

"It is too late," the queen smiled sadly, knowing that her words would seal her own fate. "Jonna and Alfgia have been to Amund Frigg. The prophecy will be fulfilled. A child will be born to Alfgia."

Hieronymus' face turned red, eyes widening in disbelief. "I will not permit this!" Blind rage filled him as his gaze turned toward Jonna. He rushed forward, but to Jonna's surprise, it was at Alfgia.

Jonna leaped, caught Hieronymus in the midriff, and knocked the spear from of his hands. They hit the ground, flipped over several times, and tumbled into the unfinished canal.

Rolling and striking the rough ground, they hit against the far side. Dust and dirt flew in all directions. The impact broke them apart. Both opponents looked dazed.

Hieronymus shook his head, the blind rage abating only slightly. By the time he was on his feet, Jonna matched his movements. Each made a circle opposite the other, like two expectant panthers.

A glint of yellow hit the light as Hieronymus' hand revealed a bronze dagger. He slashed at Jonna; Jonna leaped back. He drove Jonna toward one end of the canal as loose stones crumbled underfoot. Large rocks littered their way in the midst of wheelbarrows and buckets.

Hieronymus lunged; Jonna blocked. Curves of light cut across the air as the dagger sliced this way and that. Jonna caught the wrist, shifted forward into Hieronymus, elbowed to the abdominal nerve, and back-knuckled to the face. He grabbed Hieronymus, hooked the head with his right hand, and slammed it down into a waiting knee. The knife grip broke as he stepped behind Hieronymus leg, and tossed him over with a throat directed sword-hand. As the blade dropped to the ground, Jonna kicked it. It bounced deeper into the canal.

"It's over," Jonna stood over dark elf, staring down at his unmoving body. "Surrender now, and you will be spared."

Hieronymus' eyes were closed. His chest barely moved. Slaves and dark elves side by side stared down into the canal.

The lips began to move. "It is not over, Jonna McCambel. The war has only begun."

A wispy, white form rose from Hieronymus' body, mirroring the one Jonna had spotted watching. It formed a face in a show of rage and spoke. "You have come as I predicted, Xun Ove. I was kept from harming you in the Otherworld, but once you came to this domain, there was nothing to protect you."

Jonna knew the voice. It was the voice of Cassus, the leader of the Dark Mages. He defeated this mage before the destruction of the Eye of Aldrick. Jonna's head shook. "You could not have known I would come here."

"And why not? You defy authority, and you forge your own way. You play with powers you do not understand. Manipulating you was child's play."

Things clicked into place. Dagda's warning of never to enter the cave. The white wolves forcing them back to Bliss. Lokke's misdirection? No, Lokke was the unknown factor, and so were Fabius and Cassandra. Mulo, though, could have been a part of it. Jonna's face hardened; he hated to be manipulated. "So now that you have me here, what are you waiting for?"

The image smiled. "Indeed. Shall I tell you?" The form hovered, gazed over those gathered, and stopped on Queen Siardna. "You have betrayed me."

Her voice was laced with venom. "You stole my powers. You sought to steal my kingdom."

"I protected your daughter." Cassus gave a sneering smile. "A protection I now take back."

"No!"

Alfgia reached for her throat. Her chest struggled to take in air, but none would enter.

Jonna found a large rock, used it to jump, and caught the top edge of the canal wall. Pulling himself up, he watched as Alfgia crumpled toward the ground.

There was no time. A hatred came from the depth of his heart, buried when he first fought the Dark Mages, and shot to the surface of his mind. He remembered when Elfleda was to be sacrificed; in the arena of the Dark Mages, she had been dying too.

He rolled to his feet and leaped to grab hold of Alfgia's hand. There was only one spell that could help; it was the second one Väinämö had taught him. It could create a false body for a person by shifting their essence into the ethereal, leaving an image that would fade away.

214

The warnings of using the wrong magic in another realm beat into his brain, but he had to do something, and there was no time to waste. Throwing a last glare at the hovering form, he focused his heart and mind. "Go to the deepest pits of the Otherworld, Cassus!" His hand touched Alfgia's as his body hit the ground beside her. "*Unum-Clastor-Pratima!*"

Cassus' wispy form laughed. "Wrong spell, mage. Your form of magic will not work here." He pointed a finger at Queen Siardna. "And now, for you." His hand moved in a horizontal arc; he took in the whole cavern. "Today, all of you will die."

The cavern shook. The distant rumbling Jonna heard when he used the wrong magic thundered all around them. From out of nowhere, lightning streaked. In panic, humans and elves fled. Cassus threw a surprised glance and narrowed his eyes. "What have you done?"

A sharp ping sounded above them, like a shard of glass breaking in a window pane. Terror filled Cassus' eyes. He saw a horror they could not see; he felt a horror they could not feel. His hands shot up to guard himself but to no avail. The invisible terror tumbled down and crashed upon him. The image of the mage quivered as if caught in maelstrom it could not fight.

He screamed as a torrent of air ripped through the cavern, building in volume and mass. "What have you done?" A vortex, black and foreboding, twisted into view above Cassus' head. He fought against it, but piece by piece, molecule by molecule, his essence was shredded as it sucked him inside.

"You fool," Cassus screamed as he faded. "You don't know what you've done!" He screamed again, struggling against whatever was happening in the plane of his existence, and then he was gone.

The rumblings stopped. The room went silent. The panic which filled humans and elves abated, and a wonder crossed their features. Everyone spoke at once.

Alfgia gasped in a choked voice, "Where am I?" She stood

up slowly. "How did I get here?" Her eyes were wide as she pointed down at her crumpled body. "And who is that?"

"Alfgia!" Queen Siardna pushed through the warriors, heedless of the weapons they carried, not waiting for any to give way. Reaching the floor of the cavern, she rushed toward her daughter.

"Mother," Alfgia extended her hands, "I'm well." Her eyes were wide. "I'm not hurt." Yet, as she watched the queen hurry toward them, her face fell.

The queen's wail echoed through the cavern. She dropped to her knees and knelt beside the crumpled figure. "My daughter, my daughter, what have I done?"

Jonna attempted to stand. The world around had a slight spin. A groan came out as a sharp pain hit him. Through the pain, he cringed, "You're safe."

Accepting this, Alfgia turned toward her mother. "Everything's fine. That's not me." Trying to touch the queen's shoulder, her hand passed right through. Her eyes snapped to Jonna, and then gazed in horror at her ghostly body. "What is this?" She touched them together, and they appeared solid.

"The magic will last," he inhaled, "for a little while." His pain started to subside, although the ache was still there. "It was all I could do to keep you from dying."

As others approached, Alfgia watched. "Do they know that?" Everyone looked down. The solemn faces stared at the prone bodies.

Jonna frowned. "That shouldn't have happened." His brow wrinkled. "The spell was only meant for you, not me, and they can't seem to hear us." He reached over and took her hand. His touch reassured her. "It will be okay."

Something had modified the original spell, but it was more than that. The vortex, which formed above Cassus' head, was directly from his thoughts and did exactly what he told it. He had sent him to the depths of the Otherworld.

"He's not moving." Cassandra hurried to Jonna's motionless body. She put an ear to his chest and listened. "There is no breath."

The queen looked up at the gold-clad warriors and dared them to contradict. "Bring them to the palace, carefully." The warriors hurried forward and gathered the two. No one barred the way.

Alfgia watched as their bodies were lifted. "They don't know, do they? They don't know we're alive."

Jonna shook his head. The dizziness was coming back. "No one here has seen this spell. In fact," the words of Cassus tumbled into his mind, "it shouldn't have worked at all." A puzzled look crossed his face. "Väinämö, where are you?"

A buzz caught the air around them. It grew louder, faded out, and grew in volume.

"Jo—" the voice faded in and out. "Jonn—" Like a radio losing signal, the connection was very poor. "Jonna," the voice hit, "what have you done?"

"Me?" The world around had changed to a wavy form, and he could not see Alfgia. It felt as if he were fighting a current of water.

"Yes you! What have you done?"

"I—"

"Don't give me that," Väinämö scolded. "We can't fix what we don't know happened!"

"But, I don't—"

"Come on, spill it!"

"Will you stop that!" Jonna inhaled. "I'm trying to tell you. Hieronymus—"

"Ah ha!" The mage flipped pages in a book, the sound of which came from all directions. For a moment, Jonna thought they were being attacked by a flock of birds. The mage continued, "There it is."

"There is what?"

"Hieronymus is Cassus."

Jonna's mouth dropped, "Really? I would never have known."

The sarcasm was lost on Väinämö. "I told you, my boy, I can see the future. Don't you remember our first meeting at the hut?"

Taking a deep breath, Jonna growled, "If you knew this, why didn't you tell me?"

The mage chuckled. "You had to learn it in your own time." He shook his head. "But, that's not the point. The problem is you've created a partisomium."

"A partisomium?" Jonna repeated skeptically. "What in the world is a partisomium?"

"How do I know? You're the one who did it."

Jonna growled; enough was enough. "How do you know if I did it if you don't know what I did?"

"Tsk, tsk, tsk, there's no reason to get upset. What was the last thing you did?"

"Touched Alfgia's hand and said a spell." Jonna imagined Väinämö adjusting his spectacles and looking over the top, even though he did not have any.

The mage looked startled. "And who is Alfgia?"

"The—"

Väinämö raised up a hand. "No, don't tell me." He flipped pages in his book. "Ah, I see, the woman you were philandering with. Princess of the Dark Elves," he winked, "and attracted to you, I must add."

"I was not philandering!" His eyebrows narrowed. "She is in love with another."

The mage picked up a different book, opened it to a certain place, and read silently. "Hmm, nothing about that here." He looked up at Jonna. "Is it possible I left something out?"

"What?"

"Never mind." Väinämö shook his head. "Tell me about this spell, hmm?"

"It was Unum-Clastor-Pratima." A rumble shook the air around him, even though he had not intended it to work.

"That won't work there," the mage dismissed. "Tell me the real spell."

"That was the real spell." Jonna's frustration turned to anger. "You're not listening!"

"Oh contraire, my boy." Väinämö looked straight at him. "I am. Did you not hear that?"

218

"Hear what?"

"The rumble, the rumble when you spoke the spell."

"But you said it couldn't work."

Väinämö shook his finger at Jonna. "What I said was, *that won't work there.* There is a difference."

"A difference of what?" Jonna inhaled. Sometimes, talking with Väinämö was like trying to swim exhausted.

The mage chuckled again. "It seems, my boy, you have fractured magic."

"The magic continuum?" Jonna's voice dropped to a whisper as the realization sank in. "Is that possible?"

"Till now," the mage shook his head, "no, but you're not from this place. No one here could have done this. Remember when I told you the danger of creating your own magic spells?"

Jonna nodded.

"Well, you've stepped beyond that now. You've reached from one magic section into another, and quite successfully fractured the partition between the two."

"The crack," Jonna thought. "The ping of fractured glass?"

Väinämö's curiosity was piqued. "You heard it happen?"

Jonna nodded. "And so did Cassus. I sent him to Otherworld."

The mage's interest was beyond curiosity now. "This, I must investigate." He flipped through several books, sounding giddy.

"Väinämö?"

The sound of pages flipped back and forth.

"Väinämö."

Books shifted, but no one answered.

"Dang it Väinämö, answer me!"

"Eh?" The mage looked up. "Did I miss something?"

"What am I supposed to do?"

A grin crossed the wavy form's face. "I'm working on that, my boy. Working on that right now." His voice faded away.

"Jonna?" Alfgia shook him out of his thoughts. Väinämö

was gone. The cavern was gone. They had reached the palace, though, Jonna scratched his head, he didn't remember walking there.

The dizziness had left, but there was something uneasy in the pit of his stomach. He tried to think back. What had happened right before the spell had executed? It was the feeling; it was the hatred he had felt when Elfleda's life was threatened. It came from some place hidden inside, and somehow, someway, it shattered the magic continuum. Did that mean he could do Väinämö's magic here now? If so, what would happen? Did he dare take the chance?

The great palace doors opened. An entourage of gold-clad warriors followed behind and in front of the queen. How could the queen trust the soldiers? He certainly didn't. Yet with Hieronymus gone and the evil, wispy creature vanquished, confusion was in the ranks.

The knowledge that the queen had lost her magic had not been common. As the news spread through the palace, dark elves whispered to one another.

The warriors that carried their bodies ignored the whispers. They formed a barrier to protect the queen. The two prone figures were taken to a chamber and laid regally on a bed. Dark elf physicians rushed in.

Jonna's group stayed close as well as Queen Siardna. There was a faraway look in Cassandra's eyes.

"Something's not right." She turned to the queen, stopped, and realized she had broken protocol; she had not been given permission to speak. "I—I mean—"

"It's alright, child," Siardna frowned. "Tonight, I am not queen or elf. Today, I have lost a daughter."

"No," Cassandra blurted out, "she is not lost."

Siardna turned, despair in her eyes. "Do you dare give me hope when there is none? The evidence is clear. My daughter is gone. The void is in her eyes, and there is no breath in Jonna. How are they are not lost?"

Cassandra bit her lip. "I—I only know—"

Siardna's turned to her daughter's prone body. "Do you know what sight-seers are?"

Though Cassandra knew, she shook her head.

"Sight-seers can see things about the future and the past. It is a talent I have always possessed, but with the loss my magic, its strength diminished." The queen dropped her head. "Had my magic still worked, I might have prevented this circumstance."

"You cannot stop the webs of fate." Cassandra placed a hand on the queen's arm. "It is how we respond to those webs that chooses our destiny."

Siardna laughed bitterly. "Do you know why I lost my powers?" Her head remained down. "It was a foolish thing, one done in my youth, and one I sought to hide for a very long time. When I met my husband to be, I thought the agreement had been broken, but it could not. Cassus continued to draw upon me until I had nothing left to give."

Tears began to flow down Siardna's face, and Cassandra felt her own cheeks become wet. Queen Siardna attempted to wipe her own tears away, only to find more replaced them.

"It cost my husband's life, and now it's cost my daughter's."

Cassandra could not bear to see the queen's grief. "That is not true."

Queen Siardna turned and stared at Cassandra. "Prove it then. Prove to me my daughter is not dead."

The voice of Jonna came from the air. "Perhaps, I can help."

The queen eyes darted toward the bed, but the two bodies were gone. "How can this be?"

Cassandra pointed. There on the bed's left side, two forms faded into view.

"By the gods, this cannot be!"

"No gods," Jonna assured. "Only magic."

Alfgia released her grip on Jonna's hand and hurried toward her mother. Siardna met her with open arms. "My dear, little girl!"

"Not so little anymore." Alfgia laughed. Tears of joy showed on her cheeks.

"But how," Siardna looked at Jonna. "How have you done this?"

"Is he not a great mage?" Alfgia intercepted. "The how does not matter—only that he did."

"I am in your debt," Siardna turned from mother to queen. "Ask what you will, and it shall be done."

Jonna did not hesitate. "I've only two requests: free us and the slaves, and make peace with the humans forever."

The queen shook her head. "You don't know what you ask. You don't know what will happen if I grant your request."

"I think I do, great Queen Siardna. If you will do this, I, too, will give you a desire of your heart."

The queen stared at Jonna.

Alfgia turned to look at him, already reading his mind. "You can do this?"

Cassandra mouthed words without making a sound at Jonna. "What are you doing?"

"Do what?" Andas had tried to follow, but had missed something in the conversation.

Jonna grinned. "I believe I can. Although, how I know, I am not sure."

"If you can do this," queen swore solemnly, "the kingdom is yours. Do with it what you will."

The dark elves in the room inhaled and waited to see Jonna's response. Alfgia stared at him with no expression at all.

"I do not want your kingdom. Only your word."

The room exhaled; relief flooded through those of the dark elf kingdom, all except for Siardna and Alfgia. Alfgia's expression remained the same. Any other answer, Jonna knew, and the result could have been a civil war.

"Done." The queen straightened. The tears from her cheeks were gone. She resumed her queenly presence with all hint of her emotions washed away.

He closed his eyes. "That is all I needed to know." However the dark mage had taken her powers, it surely could be reversed.

But how? He had experienced a recharging from Elfleda, but it had to be by this world's magic. The effects of forcing the wrong magic to execute in the wrong realm continued to linger in his body.

Väinämö and Lucasta might know, but neither was here at the moment; it was either put up or shut up. The image of the slaves held by brass chains clung to his mind. Think, Jonna, think...Okay, let's try this.

He stilled himself as spoke out loud, "*Ex malo bonum*, from bad comes good. *Ex scientia vera*, from knowledge, truth. *Fluctuat nec mergitur*, it is tossed by the waves but will not sink."

Beads of sweat formed on Jonna's forehead. His palms trembled. It was a beginning but only a beginning. He knew what he wanted to say, but with only Latin phrases, it was hard to sort through it all. Something was happening, but inside he knew it was not enough.

What else could he do? Despite his delay, all eyes were upon him. He had to let go. Listening was what needed to be done, but listen to what? The Sight? He relaxed. From very far away, he heard words flow into his mind. Stamus...stamus contra malum...

It was Lucasta; she was watching! Her words flowed out through him. "*Stamus contra malum fortes et liber. Fortitudine vincimus in infinitum.*" His eyelids opened, and he caught Siardna's eyes. "We stand against evil, strong and free. By endurance, we conquer."

A glowing haze formed; it pulled from the air. A vortex of color swirled around the room and matched sparkle for sparkle against the rainbow of the glowing fungi. The sparkles shifted softly toward the queen. They surrounded her in gleams of light.

As the sparkles became more solid, the shadows in the room were pushed away. The light became brighter and sharper. As it touched her skin, tiny pinpricks of lightning flashed.

Queen Siardna opened her mouth. The sparkles moved

into her body, down her throat, and into her lungs. Her chest heaved, shock crossed her face, and then all at once, peace. It changed the contours of her frown into a smile. She bowed to Jonna. "Adonii Prince Jonna, this is a great gift indeed. You have saved my people from certain death."

"Not I," Jonna shook his head, "but another." As he stepped over, the image of Lucasta came into view.

The queen's eyes softened. "Lucasta."

"You have not spoken my name in a very long time, Queen Siardna. It is pleasant to hear you say it."

"I have not been myself in a very long time." Siardna inhaled with a smile on her lips. "The waiting is over."

Lucasta nodded. "Indeed. Keep your word to those above, and all will be well. If you do not—"

"I understand forest spirit." Siardna bowed. "It will be done."

Lucasta moved toward Jonna; she looked into his face. "Your heart is good, despite the difficulties you have brought. As Siardna has found her way, so will you."

"To where?" Alfgia was at his side, taking hold of his hand.

"My dear Alfgia," Lucasta's smile brightened, "you cannot keep this stranger. He is not yours to love."

Tears began on Alfgia's cheeks.

Queen Siardna stepped forward. "Have comfort, my daughter. You have been to Amund Frigg. A child will be yours."

"No, mother." The sobs from Alfgia increased. "A child will not be mine, and now I lose the one I love." She turned her head away and released Jonna's hand.

Siardna gasped, "No."

Compassion crossed Lucasta's face. "It is not your daughter's destiny to have this child, but another shall bear the gift." She stared into Siardna's eyes. "You know the truth of this."

Though the queen fought against the words, it could not last. The defiance faded, the light of truth shone through, and her heart melted. She whispered, "Yes, I know."

"Return the humans as your pledge. Let hostilities between you and those cease. Do this, and prosper."

The queen nodded. "It will be done." She put an arm around her daughter. "This is the way it must be."

Alfgia turned toward Jonna; her eyes locked with his. She wanted that which she could not have.

The realization hit him. "There was no other love in your life? You were pretending?"

"No," Alfgia swallowed, "there was not. You were the only one from the moment I saw your soul."

The moment came to Jonna. It was when he returned from the darkness, and she realized he was not under her control. There had been surprise, shock, and something else.

His heart ached in sympathy. What could he say that would soothe the hurt? There was nothing. Only time could heal what she felt inside if she would let it.

Shifting toward Lokke, Cassandra caught their attention. "Will he be alright?"

The half-demon's eyes were closed. He had not stirred since the boys had brought him.

Lucasta touched his brow. "*Multum in parvo.*"

The eyes fluttered, and he coughed several times, but he did not get up. The meaning of that Latin phrase was clear to Jonna, 'From little comes much'. He wondered how that applied to Lokke.

"Your friend will be fine," she called to them all. "It is time for your journey, *A capite ad calcem.*"

An archway of light formed to the left of Lucasta, and she motioned them to step inside. "Follow this tunnel to the village of Ahhes. From there, you will take the path to the sea."

Jonna nodded. "Thank you, Lucasta." He turned to Lokke who still had not risen. Were they to leave him? If so, how was he to get through the gates?

Lucasta caught Jonna's eye with a grin, "Do not forget." She raised a hand and smiled. "Alsalmone. Go in peace."

Cassandra moved close. He knew there were questions she wanted to ask.

Behind them, Lokke, having opened his eyes, abruptly stood up and followed. "Don't forget what?"

The three burst into laughter.

"What?" Lokke looked at them. "Did I say something funny?"

As they calmed down, Jonna chuckled, "It's good to have you back, Lokke."

"It's good to be back." He patted his body. "It seems I am as good as new." As he noticed the dark elves in the room, his eyes became wary. He started to open his mouth when Cassandra's voice cut in.

"Good, because the next time you go running off, I will kill you." They started into the tunnel.

A mischievous look dropped into Lokke's eyes. "Is that a challenge?" He, Andas, and the others brought up the rear.

Cassandra hit him and drove him back. Andas and the others snickered.

Lokke rubbed the place she struck. "I get it, I get it," he assured. "No more running off."

"Good."

The walk was short. As Jonna stepped through the end of the tunnel, he could smell the fragrance of flowers combined with the odor of trees and green plants. The village of Ahhes was to the left; the path through the forest continued to the right.

Andas came up beside them. "This is where we must part." He fondly took in Jonna, Cassandra, and Lokke. "We must tell the village what has happened. We need to prepare for the return of the others."

"That you should," Jonna smiled. "I wish you all the best."

Andas hesitated. "Will you not come in and say goodbye?"

"Your mother will know." Jonna winked at him. "Our journey has been delayed long enough."

"So be it." Andas paused one last moment, his eyes taking in the three. "Thank you." Stepping back into the green, he vanished. One by one, the other children vanished too.

Chapter 16

WHERE THERE'S SMOKE, THERE'S HOT COALS

A million questions plagued Jonna's mind. They started with the prophecy, Queen Siardna and Alfgia, Cassus coming from Hieronymus, and not least of all, the breaking sound that he had heard when trying to save the princess. The pain he felt was gone, but a dull ache stayed with him. When that spell was performed, he knew the result went further than what they saw.

The ground changed to a mixture of small stones and dirt, as if at one time the path were made of cobblestones. The trees around them blew in the wind with the fragrance of a salt sea in the distance.

"We're getting close." His words were the first spoken since Andas had left.

The words acted like a catalyst, and Cassandra could no longer be quiet. "Were you faithful?" She blurted it out and put a hand to her mouth. Her voice became quiet. "I'm sorry. I know it was improper, but you have a daughter to raise and—"

Jonna laughed, catching her off guard. "No," he smiled, "I was not unfaithful."

She caught the humor in his voice. "Then how?"

"It was Lucasta who gave me the answer."

Her eyes widened. "The woman in the light?"

He nodded. "Had it not been for her—" How would it have turned out? "—we might still be guests."

"Then nothing went on between you and Alfgia?"

"Nothing," he assured but frowned. "For my part, anyway, but I am concerned what will happen next."

"For the Dark Elves?" Lokke slipped between them, exasperated. "After what they did to me?"

"They thought you were the enemy. It was Cassus who drove them to it."

"They tortured me!" Lokke's eyes were full of anger. "They tortured me and didn't even ask questions!"

Cassandra narrowed her eyes at his irrational expression. "Lokke, calm down."

"I will not calm down!"

"Lokke," Jonna's voice rose above normal, "calm down." Even Cassandra jumped, eyes wary at his voice.

"How could you?" Lokke squeaked, refusing to be silent, though the anger was somewhat subdued. "You helped them. You saved them."

"We saved you, too." Jonna reminded sternly. "We saved the humans and restored peace to the forest."

"But they hurt me," the half-demon whined. "They should be punished!"

"They have." Jonna remembered the look on Queen Siardna's face when she thought her daughter was dead. He remembered the gold-clad warriors coming to take them, and how the queen had suffered all these years trapped in Cassus' plan to catch Xun Ove. From the beginning, the white, misty form that followed him from the surface was Cassus. Somehow, the mage had worked a deal with the Sidhist. Was that the real reason for his arrest? Fabius believed there were others involved.

"Jonna's right," Cassandra touched Lokke's shoulder, "they've suffered enough."

Lokke shook his head. "That's easy for you to say, but I will remember."

Jonna knew what the half-demon meant. It was hard to

228

forgive such blatant, hostile actions. His mind recalled what Azazel Sampo Elam had done to him and to Almundena when he was trying to rescue his wife. Could he rise above those emotions? Did he want to?

Tiny drops of water pelted Jonna's face. The path ended. It changed into a white, sandy beach. The beach stretched out toward a wide, open sea. Large, rock islands stood out of the water. Blasted by waves, the action created white, sparkling foam.

Cassandra stared in awe. "I've never seen this much water before."

As the aqua water stretched away, it changed into a deeper blue beyond the rocks. Gull calls fell from the sky. The birds glided, dropped toward the water, and snatched up food as the waves flipped fish onto the air.

"If this were a vacation," Jonna chuckled, "it would be close to paradise."

Lokke could not help but ask, "Vacation?"

"A place to get away from everyday life."

"Why would you do that?"

Jonna laughed. "You would have to have an ordinary life to appreciate it."

Lokke huffed. "Are you saying I'm not ordinary?"

"Not at all." Jonna followed the shore with his eyes. His gaze changed to the treeline. "We need to find a way across the water."

Cassandra's eyes remained on the sea. "We could build a boat."

He nodded. "Perhaps a raft." The trees were tall enough, but without the proper tools, it was going to take a while.

"We could always go back to the village and ask for help," Lokke volunteered.

Jonna frowned, feeling very tired. "Maybe we should." He sat down and realized it had been a while since they had slept. All the fatigue hit at once. His shoulders slumped, and that ache remained in the pit of his stomach.

"You're tired." Cassandra sat beside him. "While we were waiting at the barracks, you were trying to save the slaves."

"I could do with some rest," he yawned, "but the longer we wait, the longer it will take to get across, find Fabius' body—"

"And get you home." Cassandra followed his thoughts. "I know. I'm dead and don't need sleep. Lokke, here, is entirely different—"

"Hey."

"And," Cassandra kept her eyes on Jonna, "you're the only one who is truly alive."

The half-demon narrowed his eyes. "I'm alive. What do you mean? Just because I'm—"

"Hush, Lokke." She pointed at Jonna. With his eyes closed, he had begun to snore, despite the fact he was sitting up.

Where am I?

Jonna found himself in a square cell with three of the stone walls made of different colored blocks. There was no window and only one wooden door. The wall with the door was made up of thick, strong, bronze bars. In his cell and on the outside, swirling sparkles spun about.

"You're dreaming, Jonna." Alfgia appeared radiantly pregnant, standing on the outside of the bars. "It's only a dream."

He shook his head. "A dream with a cage?" He could hear a psychologist now, 'This is a classic illustration of a person trying to escape their destiny.'

"Not a cage." She pointed to the wall behind him. "A fracture."

"A what?" He studied the wall. Lines of stress reached out from a central point.

Moving toward it, he ran a hand over the lines. They were so smooth, they could have been drawn with a pencil.

He dropped his hand and turned to look at Alfgia. Alfgia was gone, and a pregnant Almundena took her place. "It has happened. If not stopped, a new reality will be born."

Almundena vanished, and Elfleda appeared pregnant as well. "There is a balance to all worlds of magic. It maintains our existence."

Was this a free-for-all, or could anyone enter his dream?

"My boy, my boy," Väinämö slipped in as Elfleda faded away, "should the magic partition shatter, all worlds will cease as we know them. New worlds will be born."

At least the mage wasn't pregnant. Väinämö was gone, and no one came to replace him. The swirls of color dropped away, leaving only darkness beyond the bars.

He was tired, weary, and wanted to go home. He missed Elfleda, Elpis, and Bob. Speaking of Bob, when was he coming back?

A ping came from the wall, the cracks grew, and the wall shifted. The tiny center cracked again. A plug fell out, and the cell began to vibrate.

Jonna touched the area around the hole. It was warm and felt alive. What if they were wrong? What if the partitions separating magic should be removed? He bent down to look through the hole.

Jonna's eyes opened. In front was a crackling fire contained in a hand-dug fire pit. A stack of wood sat to one side where Lokke and Cassandra lay asleep.

The ocean breeze was cool, not cold. The water appeared black. Only the sound of the lapping waves betrayed its location in the distance.

Above him were the stars of an alien sky. Where was this place that Elfleda had brought him? Could he be on another world, or was this another reality?

His eyes closed. He needed sleep. His body was exhausted.

A stick snapped in the distance. As he listened to the sound, there were more sticks. Something was coming toward them.

Without thinking, he spoke, "*Hov*—" and stopped. The dream was still vivid in his mind. If he had fractured the magic partition, the smallest spell in the wrong language might have a major influence. Running through Latin phrases, he found one. "*Absit omen.* Let there not be danger here."

231

In his mind, he pictured what 'hove' did in the other magical realm, praying he was not straying too far from this world's magic. The blue dome appeared. It formed above the center of their camp and dropped to encircle them, driving the darkness away. There was no thunder.

He waited. Either nothing was there, or the dome had done its job. Relaxing, he could feel the domes presence as he closed his eyes; its magic was apart of him. How long could he maintain such magic? Would it stay around if he fell asleep? His thoughts drifted off.

"Jonna?"

He jumped. The sun was back, not much above the horizon. The blue dome was gone.

Cassandra's frown changed to a smile as he opened his eyes. "You feel better?"

He yawned. Despite the dream, the sleep had been restful, and the ache in the pit of his stomach was gone. Stretching his muscles, he sat up and realized a straw mat was under his body. Somebody had moved him. "How long have I been out?"

"All night and most of the day."

"I've wasted time." He jumped to his feet and dusted off his clothes. Despite the mat, sand from the wind had built up while he slept. What he wouldn't give for a nice shower and some clean clothes!

Cassandra shook her head. "No, we haven't wasted time. Take a look for yourself."

As they rounded a large group of boulders, they were met by a grin on Lokke's face. "See, I can be useful." He stepped out of the way and revealed a raft equipped with a sail and rudder.

"How?" Jonna looked from the raft to the half-demon. "All by yourself?"

Cassandra cleared her throat. "He did have a little help." They stepped to the right and were joined by Andas and his companions.

"I take it you're Jonna." A broad shouldered man

approached with a smile on his face. "I'm Alkae, Andas' father." Philandia came up beside Alkae. He put his arm around her.

Philandia hugged back. "You don't know what your help has meant, Jonna."

"I take it Queen Siardna kept her word?"

Alkae nodded. "And more." From a small bag secured at his waist, he pulled out a parchment and handed it to Jonna.

The parchment rolled out smoothly with the faint hint of a fragrance Alfgia wore. To Jonna's surprise, he could understand the writing. Silently, he read:

'Be it known, henceforth and on pain of death to those that break this writ, that a truce is declared between Dark Elf and Human, an edict by Queen Siardna, witnessed by her heir apparent, Princess Alfgia. Be it known, that this truce shall in no wise stop, but as the moon rises in the night and the sun rises by day, so shall peace be established between these two races, forever. Sworn to and signed by Queen Siardna and Princess Alfgia, this day, Aquatus Unum Qo Sum.'

At the bottom was the royal seal.

"Congratulations! I am happy for you and your people." He handed the scroll back.

"And for you, Jonna, and your companions." Alkae waved behind him. With supplies hefted onto shoulders, others came and loaded the raft.

When they were finished, a group on either side of the raft lifted it from its support base and carried it into the water. As the water came waist high, the raft floated, and a plank was dropped from shore to boat.

Philandia squeezed Alkae again and smiled at Jonna. "It is ready when you are."

"Thank you, all of you." A gentle wind caught the bright, white sail, filled it up, and pulled. All that waited was to let it go.

Alkae nodded toward the raft. "You should start while the wind is with you."

"We seek the land of the giants."

Philandia nodded. "Go due north. The winds will guide."

He shook their hands and roughed Andas' hair. "I can't thank you enough."

Philandia reached over and gave Jonna a kiss on the cheek. "You already have."

Alkae smiled. "You will always have a place here if you wish it."

Cassandra and Lokke moved to the raft. Jonna came after, noting the many other footprints left by those who had helped.

Stepping onto the plank, he could feel it bow. As soon as he reached the other end, those holding the raft released. The plank splashed into the water as the boat leaped out. With full sail, the wind drove them toward the deep while those on board grabbed hold of the rails.

"It is a good sign," Alkae laughed from the shore. "You will develop your sea-legs in no time."

Jonna watched as those on the shore shrank into the distance. He waved farewell, used the tiller to turn the raft, passed through the rock islands, and slipped into the open sea.

He had never been much of an ocean traveler, so he didn't know what to expect. The deep water was calm as the sun glinted off the waves like diamonds shining on a beach. When his gaze went toward the raft, Lokke was going through the supplies.

"Raisins," the half-demon smiled with glee. "I love raisins."

Curious himself, Jonna opened one of the bags beside him. It was filled with apples. "Here." He tossed it to Lokke.

"An apple. I love apples."

Jonna found an orange and did the same. "And here."

"Oranges. I love oranges."

He laughed. "Is there anything you don't love?"

"When you've been in the Otherworld as long as I have," Lokke licked his lips, "you'd love everything, too."

"You might be right." Jonna noticed a rumbling in his own stomach. "I seem to be hungry myself."

"See?" Lokke tossed the orange back, and Jonna caught it with his right hand. "Go ahead."

The peeling came off easily. The smell of the orange struck Jonna's nose. Upon the first taste, his stomach went into overdrive. Had he not separated it into pieces, he would have tried to swallow it in one gulp.

One apple, two oranges, and a bunch of raisins later, Jonna sat back satisfied, at least for the moment. It was amazing how good he felt. Eating needed to be done more often. In the Otherworld, it did not seem as important.

Cassandra was going through the other storage containers. "Bread, meat—"

"Meat?" Lokke's ears perked up. "I love meat."

"I bet you do, but finish what you have first." She sealed up one and opened another. "They even gave us some packs to carry it in." She turned to Jonna. "This is amazing."

"What's amazing is the two of you," Jonna glowed in appreciation. "If it hadn't been for you two working together, we wouldn't have this raft now."

"It was nothing," Cassandra blushed. "We did what we must. We're all in this together."

He watched her put all the food back. "Cassandra, you're not eating?"

She shook her head. "I'm dead, remember? I don't need to, so why not save it for the two that do?"

"I'm sorry, I should have remembered."

"I think it's sweet." She moved closer and kissed him on the cheek. "It proves how good a dad you'll be."

"I hope Elpis is all right." Jonna frowned. "She did not like that snake, and Dagda took me away suddenly."

Cassandra's eyes twinkled. "She's fine. Like any child, she's been up to no good, sneaking around the palace and trying to learn what's going on."

Jonna's ears perked up. "And has she heard anything? Has she talked to Elfleda? Did she find out why Väinämö cut Bob off?"

"Väinämö won't say, and Bob is red-faced quiet. From the small snatches Elpis overheard, your situation has become a court issue." She frowned. "The laws are not in our favor, and there's no provision for this unique situation. The only way to have you released is to prove you are innocent."

Innocent? He was anything but innocent, and he knew that would not be the way. Though the laws he had broken were beyond his knowledge, ignorance was never a defense, especially if they wanted you convicted. "I'm not innocent. I was accused to hide a bigger crime." Jonna stood to his feet. "We have to show that Dagda had other motives than the breaking of the law to bring me to the Otherworld. We have to show the true intentions of Dagda and Cassus."

"But how do we prove—"

"Dagda doesn't know we have a way to communicate with the others." Could that be why communication with Bob had stopped? Someone had caught on? "Tell Elpis. Have her to relay the information to Elfleda and Väinämö. They will know what to do."

Cassandra nodded, and in some unexplainable way, she started to talk with Elpis.

The horizon stretched forever. If the land were there, it had to be a long way off. The sun beat down. It dried out the vines on top of the raft, causing them to shrink and tighten. While at the same time, those in the water loosened to compensate.

With a full stomach, Lokke crashed, pulled into a ball, and laid across a bunch of bags. With no sleeping quarters, they'd all be doing the same as darkness approached. Cassandra sneezed.

"Bless you."

"Thank you." She gave an appreciative smile to Jonna. "I've not heard that in a very long time."

"You don't get sick in the Otherworld?"

"Not on our level, ours is Bliss, but on others?" She shrugged.

"Sickness is bad enough during one's lifetime. To be

236

constantly sick when you are dead? That, I don't want to imagine."

She nodded. "It would be bad."

The sun beat down, and it began to get hot in spite of the wind that stayed with the raft. The weather around them had not changed. The sparkling ocean was a beacon of light, stretching out as far as the eye could see.

By sundown, the view was no less beautiful. Jonna looked up at the stars in the sky and tried to spot patterns in the constellations. Yet, no matter how much he tried, nothing would match his world. "Still that same alien sky."

Cassandra had fallen asleep, and Lokke had yet to awaken. Strange, Cassandra said sleep was not necessary in the Otherworld, yet here she was sleeping for a second time; it started with the night on the beach.

The sneeze, he thought back, that bothered him, too. If nothing on the surface could influence those brought up, why did she sneeze?

Looking at the half-demon, Jonna chuckled. It must have taken Lokke a lot of time to find Andas' village, convince them he was telling the truth, and get the whole process of building the raft going.

A meteor lit the sky, moving from south to north, with the brief image of a child sitting on top. As it arced overhead, fireworks sparkled and dropped, falling into the sea. As the sparkles neared, Jonna heard a child's voice crying out as it plunged into the water. At first, he thought he was hearing things, but it bobbed back to the surface. "Help!"

Lokke jumped awake. "What was that?" He felt the bags shift under him. "Did you hear something?"

"I think we did."

Cassandra had not stirred, and from the look on her face, she was in a wonderful dream. Jonna turned the boat, heading toward the voice in the water. It was near but in the blackness not very easy to see.

"Help me!"

"Keep calling out." Jonna did his best to guide the raft, though it was in conflict with the wind. "Can you see us?"

"Help!"

"We're coming." The idea that this was a little bit strange crossed his mind. Then again, everything in this world was strange.

He picked up a mooring vine and tied a wide loop in the end. "Grab the vine." It flew in the direction of the voice. Something heaved, almost pulling him into the water.

Lokke stretched and watched Jonna. "Mind if I help?"

"Please."

Both of them heaved hard. Slowly, the vine came back, hauling whoever-it-was closer to the boat. A hand reached up and grabbed hold of the wooden side. The wood strained and bent dangerously close to the water.

"Oops," the voice apologized. The child-like quality was gone. "Sorry about that. Let me make an adjustment."

The vine relaxed. Instead of a heavy weight, it seemed to weigh nothing at all.

"Give me a hand, will you?"

Jonna reached down and hauled the young man up; he practically lifted him from the water with no more than a touch.

The stranger coughed out seawater and took a deep breath. "I see you're headed to the land of frost giants." He stood up straight. "Terrible stuff, saltwater. I can barely stand to drink it."

"And you are?" Jonna looked at the man's soaked clothes. The tunic top, stitched pants, and rope belt did not match.

"Altair, of course. Surely you've heard of me?" He stared at Jonna, refusing to believe he had not.

Jonna imitated. "Surely."

"Nobody?" Altair turned to Lokke. "Not you either?"

Lokke just stared.

Altair motioned to Cassandra. "Well, perhaps this charming lady—"

"Don't—wake—her," Jonna warned him off. "She's had a hard day."

Altair frowned. "I see. Well," he turned to Jonna, "let's talk about you."

"Me?"

Altair nodded. "There are a few things you should know about the giants, especially since you will be there soon."

Jonna looked skeptical. "This sea is that small?"

Altair chuckled. "Not at all. From the moment you brought me aboard, we skipped many hundreds of miles. Surely you know about magic? No one less than a great warrior or mage would dare to enter these borders."

Jonna couldn't decide if he liked him or not. "How about we take one step back. First, why and how were you riding a meteor?"

"Doesn't everyone?" Altair's eyebrows raised. "It is the fastest form of travel."

"Skipping that issue," Jonna plodded forward. "Why the interest in me?"

The moon rose. Its bright, yellow glow lit their sail like a lighthouse on the shore. Despite the difference in constellations, the shape of the moon's face was familiar.

"Ah, Rigantona," Altair sighed in wonderment. "How beautiful is your face tonight!"

A female voice answered, "A beauty reflected in your eyes." The body of a woman faded into view as the words finished. "I see you've found some friends."

"Indeed." Altair nodded toward the others. "Meet Lokke and Jonna." His hand swept around the raft. "Cassandra is the one sleeping." Jonna didn't remember telling him Cassandra's name.

Rigantona extended her hand to Jonna. "It is a pleasure."

Not quite sure how to proceed, Jonna touched the hand and nodded toward the woman.

"You're so quaint," she teased. "It's been a long time since a man was quaint with me."

Altair placed a hand under his chin. "He seems to have unusual characteristics. Human, no doubt. Male."

"Definitely male," Rigantona concurred, "with a touch of uniqueness."

Jonna turned to Lokke. "They talk as if we aren't here."

The half-demon nodded.

"Touché," Altair admired. "I am certain we have found the right man."

Rigantona walked around Jonna; her eyes bore into him. "You have done well, Altair." She touched Jonna's shoulder, running a finger down his arm. "What do they call you?"

Jonna frowned. "Altair told you—"

"No, stop." Rigantona turned away and then twirled to face him. "Jonna McCambel, a.k.a. Xun Ove." Her eyes brightened with excitement. "Altair, you didn't tell me you had found Xun Ove himself."

Wonderment filled Altair's voice. "I didn't know." His eyes widened. "Could he truly be?"

Lokke stared at Jonna. "*The* Xun Ove?"

Jonna sighed. "It's no big deal. It was a name given to me by a friend named Gernot."

"Oh, contraire," Altair shook a finger at him, a wild gleam in his eye. "It is the name of the one who will change all worlds. It is the name of the one who will shake the foundations of magic!"

Enough was enough. Jonna stepped back so he could see both newcomers at the same time. "What do you want from us?"

Rigantona smiled. "Nothing you aren't already going to do." Patting Altair's shoulder, she sighed. "Please love, settle down. You're scaring them." A hand reached forward and touched Jonna's cheek. "And the rewards may be greater than you know."

The whole 'shaking foundations' talk made Jonna nervous. He steadied himself, and his voice deepened in warning. "My reward is getting to go home."

"Perhaps." Rigantona waved a finger in the air, pulling sparkles from the space around them. They looked like those in the dream. "You seek to free Fabius from the curse of half-death. We would like to help you."

A wary look crossed Jonna's face. "Why?"

"Why not?" She looked at his pocket. "He gave you the ring, did he not?"

Jonna touched his pocket. He reached in, pulled it out, and held it up. "You know this ring?"

"Of course, may I see it?"

Jonna hesitated.

"I don't bite," she smiled, "at least not yet."

Altair laughed. "You are such a tease."

Jonna started to hand her the ring but stopped again. "Who exactly are you?"

"I am Rigantona, High Priestess and goddess of fertility and the Moon." She moved closer to him, whispering into his ear, "Let me help, Jonna McCambel. It will aid you in your quest. And the rewards? Let's just say you want me on your side." She slowly touched the side of his cheek. "How else will you fulfill your prophecy?"

This didn't make sense, and he had no desire to fulfill prophecy, but despite how he felt, he placed the ring in her hand.

"Thank you," she accepted, smoothly stepping back. She held it up and spoke without hesitation, *Flamma fumo est proxima.*"

The sparkles floating in the air changed direction, pulled into a vortex, and then centered on the ring; the ring absorbed them all. When the vortex was gone, she handed the ring to Jonna. "Use this as a guide. It will tell you the direction of Fabius' tomb."

He slipped it on his finger. The ring glowed to life.

"Where there is smoke, there is fire?" Jonna translated the Latin phrase and shrugged. He would never have thought of using those words to do that, but it did make sense. The ring led to the tomb, like smoke shows the source of fire. "Thank you."

Rigantona shook her head. "No, we thank you, Jonna. Find Fabius' body and release him. That is all we ask." She turned to Altair. "Come, my love, it is time to leave."

"Farewell, my friends," Altair waved. "Perhaps we'll meet

again." Both of them leaped, their bodies changing into light as they streaked up into the sky.

"And Jonna," Altair called as the streak began to fade, "watch the colors." The only evidence of their visit was the ring on his finger, glowing in the dark.

Chapter 17

WISH UPON A FALLING STAR

A meteor appeared in the northern sky and moved toward the south. Was that Altair going back where he came? And Rigantona, if she had come with the rising of the moon, was she now watching over them?

"The gods," Lokke shook his head in warning, "never mess with 'em."

"You knew who they were?"

"Of course."

"You lied about knowing Altair. Why didn't you say something?"

Lokke's eyes went round. "I did not lie. I just didn't say anything."

Jonna stared at him.

"I-I think I'll go to sleep now." The half-demon found a spot and covered his eyes. Jonna leaned back against the mast. Water lapped against the sides of the raft. The wind blew in the sail.

Cassandra was still fast asleep. If the dead did not need to sleep, wouldn't that make her a very light sleeper? However, from a human point of view it was expected. They had been gone from the Otherworld for a while. If being here had any influence, she should be exhausted. Did that mean she needed to eat?

Looking at the ring, he remembered Altair's words. They would reach the land of the frost giants soon. Come to think of it, how far had they come? When would he see his family again?

With fire in her eyes, he remembered Elfleda standing in front of Väinämö's hut. If she only knew what was going on, he was sure an elvish army would battle down Dagda's gates! Of course, Bob was there when Fabius had brought the truth to light. The pixie should have let her know.

The raft bumped into something that floated in the sea. Jonna got up, checked the edges, and looked for any damage. He reached over the side and pulled the object closer to the boat. It was a tree trunk, old and rotten. How close were they to land?

In the distance through a rising fog, he could make out something. In his world, warm currents moving around islands with cooler air could create that result.

Tiny lights winked into view, creating small clusters here and there. More than likely, these were dwellings on a mountainside.

The glow of the ring lit up the raft, brighter than the moon. Turning the ring upside down, he closed his fist. The light diminished, but the reflection of the moon on their white sail glowed brightly. If they were approaching land, a shining beacon was the last thing he wanted.

Too late. From the larger clumps of lights at the bottom, smaller lights were separating. They moved out along the horizon and grew in size. "Lokke, help me grab the sail."

Without skipping a beat, Lokke looked up. "I'm asleep, remember?"

"Now." Jonna moved to the other side of the raft as Lokke took position. On cue, they released both vines, lowering the sail to the deck.

The half-demon moved beside him and whispered, "Now what? What did you see?"

Jonna checked the current by using the end of a vine with a light weight. It pulled toward the land, away from their pursuers. However, the current was not very fast. "You see those lights?" He pointed at the horizon.

Lokke nodded.

"Steer us away from them." Jonna placed a hand on the tiller. "Hold this here."

"Gotcha." Lokke grabbed hold. The raft weaved back and forth. Jonna reached out and stopped the motion.

"Here," he iterated and placed both Lokke's hands on it.

Lokke released the tiller and saluted. "Yes sir." He jumped and grabbed it back again as the raft tried to change course.

Shaking his head, Jonna moved next to Cassandra. He hated to do it, but he had to wake her up. "Cassandra?"

Her eyes fluttered as she turned and peered up. "Miksim?"

A frown crossed Jonna's face. "No. Jonna. We're still on the raft, remember?"

As her eyes gained focus, she looked down along her body. "That's right," she frowned, "I'm dead." She pushed on quickly. "What's going on?"

"We have reached land. I assume it is the land of the frost giants."

Lokke tried to peer into the darkness. "It doesn't seem very frosty to me."

"Their cities may be closer in, further to the north." Jonna motioned toward the distant blackness. "For that matter, it could simply be their name."

Cassandra sat up, catching the lights to their right. "We've been spotted?"

"They saw us before we got the sail down. I don't know who they are."

"Better to hide first. We don't know how our visit might be welcomed."

Jonna nodded. He searched for a paddle but found none nor was anything else on the raft a help. Depending on the depth, he might be able to drop in, reach the bottom, and pull them along.

While Lokke kept hold on the tiller, and Cassandra kept a watch on Lokke, Jonna slipped off his elvish shoes, tied a vine around his waist, and dropped over the edge. The warm water soaked his clothes, weighed him down, and made it hard to swim—harder than it should. It felt as if great weights were attached to his ankles. With the vine connected to the front of the raft as a safety, he ignored the feeling and dove down.

The water was colder the further down he went. After about twenty seconds, he touched bottom and moved toward the surface. To his surprise, the raft had moved faster than he thought. He caught its back edge and pulled himself toward the front.

"Too deep to walk it in," he called up to Cassandra as he bobbed in the water. "I'll see if I can help pull it along."

She looked nervously at the dark water. "Be careful. It feels—odd."

Shifting forward, he tested to see if his speed was more than the current and swam toward the shore. It wasn't much, but at least it was something, and without oars or a pole, it was better than nothing at all.

It had been a while since Jonna swam. Despite his rather active life, his muscles were not used to it. He was glad he had eaten the fruit, that in itself would help with fatigue, but he could not keep this up forever. And what of the ships that were coming their way? Despite the lowering of the sail, would they be able to spot this raft?

From above, Cassandra whispered, "Jonna, the lights, they're going the other direction. You must come out now."

He nodded absently and dove down into the sea to test the depth, reached the bottom, and shot back up. It took less time to reach the seabed. On top of that, their ploy had worked; the pursuers had lost them in the dark.

Despite this change in events and Cassandra's urges, something in him would not let go. They had to push on; they had to keep going. Something drew him toward the shore. Despite the weariness in his body, it seemed he had no choice. But these dang weights on his ankles...

As his feet touched the bottom without diving, he walked the raft in. The raft moved forward with better speed. It was a relief not to constantly swim, but the effort left him exhausted.

The boat pulled along and finally beached. As soon as the raft touched the sand, he fell to his knees. Water, he needed water. His throat was so parched.

It was an effort to untie the rope; his fingers didn't work right. Someone ran toward him, but from what direction he could not tell.

Cassandra pressed a cup to his lips, tilting it for him to drink. As the water poured down his throat, his body collapsed.

"Lokke, grab his other arm."

They lifted him and brought him back to the raft. Cassandra laid him on the floor and looked into his eyes. "Warding spells," she frowned. "The water around the land is protected. The spells tried to kill him by driving him to exhaustion." She gazed at the beach. "We must be careful."

Jonna began to shake. Between the temperature of the water and wind blowing off the sea, he was chilled.

"Pull off his clothes. We've got to keep him warm." While Lokke slid off Jonna's pants and shirt, Cassandra looked for blankets. Inside some leather bags, she found them. They wrapped Jonna up.

The frequency of the shakes decreased but not the severity. They needed to get him out of the elements.

The waves of the ocean grew in size. In the sky, she could make out rain clouds blotting out the stars. The spells hadn't given up, and they needed shelter. Where could they go?

"There!" At the edge of some trees, hidden on a bluff, Lokke spotted a small cottage.

They hauled him over crudely cut, rock steps and reached the door as the first flash of lightning hit the beach. Small wisps of wind spun off in different directions.

Jonna opened his eyes enough to see Cassandra push

the door open. In the single room cottage, she and Lokke hauled him to the only bed. There was a fireplace, a table, and two chairs. It was too dark to see anything else; the flashes of lightning kept interfering with his pixie sight.

Laying him down, they both headed out of the cottage. Small puffs of dust hung in the air and floated gradually down.

He coughed. There was a flash of light. Above the door, carved into the header, the letters 'Tyrche' appeared as thunder shook the building.

The room went dark. Only a faint glow of light came through the partially opened door. Lightning flashed from one cloud to another, but nothing was as close as that first lightning flash.

The ring on his finger, still upside down, glowed against the coverings. Taking a deep breath, he forced himself to relax. The shaking was better, but he still felt cold. When he moved his arms, the coverings shifted. Where were his clothes?

Wrapping a cover around him, he slid his feet over the side of the bed though his legs were weak. The door burst in; it was Lokke with wood and Cassandra hauling bags.

"What are you doing?" She dropped her bags by the door. Putting his legs back on the bed, she covered him up. As Lokke closed the door to seal out the majority of the wind, Cassandra opened one bag and pulled out another blanket. The wind whistled through the cracks in the cottage.

"You stay here," she pointedly tucked the blanket around him, "until you warm up. You will not move. Do you understand?"

Jonna laughed. "Yes ma'am." She was right, and it was warmer in the blankets.

Turning her attention to the fireplace, Cassandra's voice was firm. "Lokke, the fireplace, please."

Tossing the wood in, Lokke stared at it. "How? I've never started a fire without the help of magic."

Cassandra huffed. "The old fashioned way, of course.

Rub two sticks together, and create a coal. It turns into a spark which turns into a flame." Going to the side of the fireplace, she found a tinder box. It opened to show both tinder and flint. "Better yet," she handed Lokke two pieces of flint, "strike these together while holding them close to the dried grass."

A spark jumped out and smoldered. Cassandra blew. The spark changed to an ember, and the ember burst into a flame. The rest of the dried wood caught.

The wind struck the side of the cottage, shaking the eaves. Thunder, lightning, and the beating of rain announced the storm had arrived.

Jonna watched the other two as they shifted away from the fireplace. The flames in the hearth caught his eye. Orange, red, and yellow flickered in dances within its embrace. Wind whistled from the chimney. Thunder crashed outside. Whatever storm stirred, he was glad they were off the raft.

A warm glow lit the cabin in comfortable browns. The single table had carvings of leaves on its edges, and the chair legs stood with flowers carved at their joints. No pictures hung on the walls, though there was a pantry in one corner. As he thought he was going to sleep, his body shook.

Cassandra held him down and stopped him from shifting off the bed. When the shaking stopped, she wiped the sweat from her forehead. "That was close."

In exhaustion, his body slumped. It reminded him of hyperthermia.

"Eat this," Cassandra forced him to sit up. There were raisins, orange slices, apple slices, and...

"Please, stop," he begged. "I can't eat anything else!"

"You need your strength," she warned but did back off. Pulling a chair up beside him, she set a vigil.

Three more times the shaking came, and each time she kept him steady, making sure the covers were tight. After a while, he no longer needed the covers, but it wasn't until she fell asleep that he dared shift them.

The longer Cassandra was on the surface, the more she was changing; he could feel it. It was in her mannerism and opinions; even her skin was developing a vibrant glow. Was there a way to reverse the process of being dead?

In his world, that was impossible, but here? Was this why the dead were kept locked up? Going through these ideas, he fell asleep.

*   *   *

Daylight peeked under the door, and he spotted his clothes. They dried in front of the fireplace. Lokke was asleep, curled up in a corner with blankets. Cassandra had leaned back, eyes closed, and stayed upright in the chair.

He slipped on his clothes and moved Cassandra to the bed. She did not stir. After tucking her in, he made his way to the door, opened it quietly, and stepped out.

The sun rose to the left; its rays skated across the top of the sea. They were on a bluff high enough to see in both directions down the shore. It was a good place to keep watch.

The raft was gone. Either Cassandra and Lokke hid it, or the storm washed it away.

Between the disrepair and the dust, the cabin had not been visited for some time. Maybe it was a get-a-way from the city? Whatever it was, it would make a good returning point when they decided to head back.

The ring on his hand was still upside down. Twisting it over, the top glowed brighter, but instead of a steady light, it began to pulse.

Holding it up, he moved it from east to west with no change in the pulse. However, when shifted further north, the rhythm changed and became faster.

Bingo. He moved around the outside of the cottage to follow the pulse. The woods were thick. A single path led off in the direction he wanted to go. Part of him wanted to go back and get the others, but the other part wanted to follow the ring.

A barely perceptible whisper met his ear. "Come Jonna, follow the ring. Come Jonna, the time is now."

From nowhere, Cassandra was beside him. "Don't believe them Jonna." She walked around him, drove off the whispering voices, and threw a glance at the ring on his hand. "They want to trick you. They tried to take your life last night."

"They?"

Carrying a backpack, the half-demon appeared. "Lots of goodies in here," he pointed with his thumb. "Good to see you up."

"Thank you, Lokke." Jonna inhaled. It was good to be walking around again. He turned back toward Cassandra. "You said 'they'?"

"The Tjaard. They are warding spirits that protect this land. You stirred them up when you walked through the sea." Her eyebrows crossed. "We are strongest as a group, and you have been targeted. Do not wander off without us." Although firm, her eyes pleaded.

Jonna's smile was genuine. "Thank you, Cassandra. I will endeavor to do as you ask."

She inhaled. "Good. We may get through this in one piece." Her eyes went to the forest around them. "I think the voices are gone—" They resumed the walk, heading north down the path. "—for the moment." She glanced at his finger again. "They didn't give that to you, did they?"

That's right, Cassandra had not been awake when Altair and Rigantona had come to visit.

Lokke jumped in. "You should have seen it," his voice went off at high speed. "A burning rock appeared across the sky, Altair fell off and splashed in the water, and then Rigantona appeared." He leaned toward her. "She's not a bad looker if I say so myself. Then, she takes Jonna's ring, says a spell, and wham," the half-demon slapped one fist into another, "he's told it will lead him to Fabius' tomb."

Jonna whistled. "All that in one breath?"

"Certainly," he beamed, "I was always told I had good lungs."

Cassandra spoke with a straight face, "Lots of hot air."

"That's right. Hey," he closed one eye to stare at her, "that's something I would say."

Jonna nodded. "Lokke covered the facts. That's how the ring began to glow. Fabius gave me the ring."

Cassandra breathed a sigh of relief. "As long as the Tjaard aren't responsible, it should be safe. If we stick together, they won't come around. Their strongest influence is on those who travel alone."

She was right; the voices had left, but he could still hear them, though indistinct. They hovered on the fringes, waiting to come back.

In a way, the Tjaard's presence comforted Jonna. It meant what they were doing was of importance, and yet at the same time, he wondered why it was significant.

The path branched off in three directions, none of which had a sign. However, it didn't matter; they had the ring. The group headed toward the right.

With the sun above and behind, the forest shown in bright light. It sprinkled through the trees and struck the ground with a warm, yellow glow. Instead of a search, it was starting to feel like a stroll. It was the kind of stroll he liked to take with Stephanie before he had come to this magical land. Loneliness hit, despite the company around him.

Lokke pursed his lips. "What voices?"

"The Tjaard voices," Cassandra returned. "The ones that Jonna heard."

Scratching his head, Lokke wrinkled his nose. "I didn't hear any voices."

"Maybe only mages can," Jonna threw in. "I'd rather I didn't."

"Or those with The Sight," Cassandra added.

Lokke wrinkled his brow. "How can I watch for something that I can't hear?"

Cassandra laughed. "Stick close. We'll let you know."

"Thanks." He spotted a group of flowers catching the rays of the sun. "What's that?"

"Flowers?"

"Not those. That." He pointed at a blue-grey stone. It had a flat angular side with carvings. Had the wind not blown the flowers at the moment he looked, he would never have seen it.

Jonna bent down and ran his fingers over the engraving. "Runes. It's a marker of some sort, but I don't understand the language." That puzzled him. Normally he knew; it was a sixth sense he linked to magic.

"Nor I," Cassandra agreed.

Additional markers appeared with the same letters expressed on each one. As they reached a small archway, the reason for the stones was apparent.

"Property markers," Jonna studied the arch. "Interestingly enough, the archway is made of the same material as the markers along the path." But what really caught his attention was what they saw past it. The entrance to a city.

It was huge, all decked out in blue-grey stone with the walls as tall as skyscrapers. The entrance they stared through was the smallest of two. In front of the larger archway were two, huge, oaken doors, tall enough for a being four times the height of Jonna.

"Ice giants." Lokke stared up at the doorway in awe and shook himself. "But we know how to deal with them." That mischievous smile crossed his face. "An extremely big frog."

"Let's hope it's that easy."

They followed a smaller path. It led away from the front to a door in the city wall. The door contained a smaller window. There was no handle to let them in.

Jonna knocked on the door. A large man with a stained front shirt opened the window and stared out. The voice was deep. "Name."

"Jonna."

The man swore. "Not your name, your patron's name."

"Patron?"

"You know, who do you belong to?"

Jonna paused but only for a second. "Tyrch." The name had been carved above the door at the cottage. He remembered seeing it from the bed.

"Tyrch? Tyrche, you mean?" The man squinted at Jonna.

Jonna nodded. "Tyrche. It's a new name for me."

The man grumped. "A fresh slave, then. Better remember three things: one, never walk down a giant's path; two, if the ground shakes, stand near the wall; and three, don't be caught out after dark. Got it?"

"Yes sir."

"Good, you'll live longer." The man opened the door and allowed Jonna to pass through. Cassandra came up behind, but when Lokke tried to pass—

"Hold it right there." The man pointed his club at Lokke's horn. "I've never seen the likes of you. Where are you from?"

The half-demon halted. "Down in the—south."

"Down south, huh?" They could almost hear the wheels turning. "You mean from the island? Strange things come up from the island. Tyrche?"

Lokke nodded vigorously.

He waved Lokke on. "Go on then."

Lokke hurried to match step with the other two. They stopped beside a stack of barrels and kept out of the main line of traffic. The ring was still pulsing, but at the speed that it pulsed, the pulsing was getting harder to see. The closer they got, the more all the directions showed the same thing. It was almost as if—

"Catacombs." The word left Jonna's mouth before he could catch it. "He could be in a mausoleum somewhere underground."

Cassandra frowned. "Mausoleum?"

"A burial chamber where they put bodies in holes in the walls."

Lokke kept his eyes on the street.

"Fabius said he was in some sort of box."

The half-demon tapped the ground with one toe, looking around, unable to concentrate on what Jonna said. "When do you think they come out?" He tried to peer unobtrusively around a corner.

Cassandra smirked. "The bodies? They don't. Only Fabius will when we let him out."

"No," Lokke's eyes widened, "the giants. I haven't felt a rumble yet."

"Maybe they're all asleep," Cassandra grinned. "They might have too many slaves to do their bidding. I thought you had a way to deal with giants?"

Barrels beside them jumped, and the people around them grabbed for something solid. When the thundering stopped, the line of traffic resumed.

A skeptical look crossed Lokke's face. "And we're going underground?"

Jonna nodded. "We have to find that mausoleum, and to do it, we need information." His eyes stopped on a large, three-story building across the way. The words on the top said 'Brighid'. Slaves carried bundles, wrapped in cloth, both in and out of the place. As one of the doors closed, he caught a glimpse of shelves. "And I think I know where to get it."

They merged with traffic and turned by a signpost. Signs pointed in different directions, but nothing said how to get across the street. Ordinarily, this would not have bothered him, but with the warning to never walk on a giant's path and the rumblings, the least amount of attention the better.

In the street, a pair of white lines cut across a longer pair of yellow, perpendicularly. The lines were made of stones placed side by side, matching their appropriate color. Slaves would stop, look both ways, and hurry across to the other side. Were the paths of giants marked by yellow?

They slipped up beside a group of slaves and waited. As the group went forward, they did too. Heading up Brighid's steps, they passed through the columns in front of the doors.

"Where do you think you're going?" A man in a white toga with a blue sash stepped from behind a pillar. He held a spear in one hand; there was a sword on his belt.

Jonna thought fast. "Slave entrance, please."

"To the left, around the side." The man waited, making sure they went in the right direction.

That was close, and it had been Jonna's fault. He would have to watch more closely.

As they worked their way around the building, an entrance came into view. They pushed through the smaller door and stepped into Brighid.

It was a library. Slaves moved in every direction; some had ladders and some did not. Though they removed items from the shelves, they always replaced them with others.

The three slipped into an empty aisle. Jonna studied the symbols stamped on the item's edges, reached over, and pulled one out. It wasn't a book; it was a large, clay tablet. Light weight, he held it up, trying to see what language they used. It was as unknown as the property markers, containing the same type of carvings.

Cassandra's face was caught between disappointment and encouragement. "It was a good idea."

Jonna sighed. "We've got to find another way." He placed the tablet back on the shelf.

Kneeling down, he studied the bottom row. Why could he read the word at the cottage, actually know the letters to pronounce it, and not be able to read what was in the library? Was there a magic spell he could use to read this?

"Trying to learn the giant's language?" An older man in a white robe stepped around them into the aisle. "No human has ever done it." He reached up, pulled a clay tablet from a particular row-column, and tucked it under his arm.

Jonna guessed, "But they allow us to try?"

"Most certainly," he smiled. "As long as it doesn't interfere with our jobs, they encourage us."

"A progressive culture."

"Yes," the man's eyes lit up. "I see you're a man of education." He extended his hand. "Maxima Apeldorn, at your service. I serve as a guide for the new recruits. You are all new recruits?"

Jonna shook the outstretched hand. "You could tell that quick?"

The man laughed. "Once you know the pattern, it's easy to spot. If you have any questions, let me know." He headed around the corner.

Jonna stood to his feet. "Uh, Maxima?"

Maxima turned. "Questions already?" He wasn't a bit surprised.

"Where might we find a map of the city? It would certainly help in learning directions."

"But of course," Maxima pointed to one of the main aisles. "Follow that to the center of the library. You are free to look around." He shook his finger at them, "But mind your manners. If a giant approaches you, be sure to show respect." He hurried to his duties.

"Great idea," Cassandra's eyes were shining, "a map."

Lokke shook his head. "I don't like him."

"Don't like Maxima?" Jonna questioned. This was strange behavior for Lokke. "What makes you say that?" Jonna spotted Maxima helping another slave, and then watched as he hurried to another part of the library.

"Too nice," Lokke was adamant. "Nobody acts that nice to a new person doing their job."

Jonna considered. "Without any further questions." Now that Lokke said it, it did seem a little too easy. "You would think he would have asked more about us. Who we belonged to, or how long we had been here." He nodded in agreement. "We need to watch our backs."

Cassandra pointed to the center of the library. "And fronts. What was the patron's name you used, Jonna?"

"Tyrche."

"So what happens if we run into Tyrche?"

None of them knew Tyrche. Then again, Maxima had not asked who their patron was. They stepped from the aisle into the center of the library.

The floor was made of smooth marble with changes of colors forming the shape of a W with a line struck through; it was one of the symbols on the property markers. In the library's center were large desks and chairs along with reading couches, all designed for the giants. For a slave to use them, they would need a ladder to get on top.

Where was the map? To the right of the sitting area, up against one wall, a tall desk stood. Above it, shown in a mosaic on the wall, part of a city diagram was embedded.

"Had we come in the front door, we would have seen it." Lokke gazed up.

"Shh." Jonna tried to find a good spot to see the entire wall. He bumped into something behind him.

A giant's voice called from somewhere above, "Who is your patron, slave?"

They all froze. Turning around, Jonna looked up into the face of a towering giant. "Tyrche, sir."

The giant huffed. "Tyrche, eh? Didn't know he had resumed taking slaves." Eyeing all three, he shook his head. "Watch where you're going, or next time I'll tell Tyrche myself. Do you understand?"

Jonna bowed as best he could while still looking up. "Yes sir. Thank you sir." The three hurried away from the area, ducked under a large desk, and moved around a chair. Without either going to the front door, which was not the way to stay unnoticed, or climbing up on a giant chair, which would not be wise, he could see no way to view the whole map.

"There." Lokke pointed toward the left; Maxima was watching, his smile unchanged. "Told you he was trouble."

Maxima, spotting Lokke, slipped down an aisle.

"You're right." Jonna frowned. "We don't know who to trust."

"Trust no one," a voice whispered to their right. Turning, a slave with a broom was sweeping in an aisle.

"You said something?"

"The tablet you want is here," the slave looked directly at Jonna, speaking in a normal voice. Stepping back, he indicated a spot, second row on the left.

"Thank you." Moving into the aisle, Jonna reached for it but stayed his hand. His voice dropped to a whisper. "Who are you?"

"Someone like yourself. Someone who doesn't belong."

"I don't understand."

"Do you think you're the first to sneak into Wspadden?"

Curious, Jonna took the bait. "How many are there?"

"More than they know." The slave with the broom gave a slight smile before it completely de-materialized. "If you're interested, meet in the Fisher's Block right before sunset." The man began to sweep again, moving to another aisle.

"Fisher's Block?" Lokke shook his head. "We still need to know where the cryp—"

Cassandra put a hand over his mouth, and Lokke's eyes widened. He mumbled, "You can let go now."

Daring him to speak, Cassandra released her hold.

"Your hands are really soft."

She flipped him on the horn.

"Ouch!"

"Will you two cut it out?" Jonna took Lokke by the arm and pulled him into the inner aisles. "You're starting to draw attention."

"I'm starting?" Lokke rubbed his horn. "That hurt!"

Cassandra glared at him. "Not like it's going to."

"Hold," Jonna caught her hand, right before she tried to deck him. "Where's the two I knew back at the beach? The two I remember helping each other?"

"He woke up and brought me to my senses." She folded her arms and glared at Lokke. "We should have left him in the cage."

Lokke put a hand to his chest. "That hurts." He fell back against one of the shelves in a pretend faint. The shelf shook, and a tablet bounced. As it teetered on edge, Jonna grabbed for it. He missed.

In the silence of the library, the crash was unmistakable. Jonna cringed, "Move!"

They headed deeper into the maze of aisles, putting as much distance between themselves and the broken tablet as possible. The giant's entrance loomed to their left with the map on the wall to the right.

259

"There," Jonna pointed toward the wall. Thank God it was not written in the giant's language. "We're next to the south wall. Fisher's Block is a few streets in front of us."

Lokke tried to push up closer. "Let me see—"

"No," Cassandra and Jonna whispered at the same time.

A hurt expression hit Lokke's face. "That's not very nice."

"Maybe you should of thought of that 'before' breaking the clay tablet," she growled.

"I didn't break the clay tablet," Lokke pointed to Jonna. "He's the one that missed!"

A commotion rose where the clay tablet broke, catching the attention of others. The rumble of voices grew, moving from one aisle to the next. Several white togas with blue sashes passed by the huge city map and came to investigate.

"Enough." Jonna moved toward a marble stairway which went down. It appeared to go under the entryway for the giants. At the bottom of the stairs, the hall continued straight. There was a door in the right wall with a sign saying 'Keep Out'.

Up ahead, the stairs rose, coming out on the opposite side of the library; it was closer to the entrance used by the slaves. Should they follow the stairs? If they went fast enough, they might avoid being caught.

But the ring on his finger had other ideas. At this level, one floor below, the color of the ring changed to blue as the pulsing slowed.

Lokke's eyes widened. "What does that mean?"

"It means—" Jonna tested the door; it was unlocked. "—we go this way."

"But what if it's a dead end?"

"Then we'll come out."

As the door swung open, the light from the hall filtered down into the darkness. There were torches on the walls, but they were unlit. Jonna let his eyes adjust and took hold of Cassandra's hand. Reluctantly, she took Lokke's, squeezing it hard.

"Ouch!"

"Big baby."

Jonna couldn't help but chuckle. It was either that or leave them both behind.

Angling down, wooden stairs, past the doorway, stopped at a long hallway. The hallway stretched off with a rock-dirt floor. Support beams were placed evenly, adding strength to the continuing ceiling.

Cassandra watched the blue light of the ring reflect off the walls and reluctantly conceded. "That ring is a big help." She noticed additional details around them. "There are pictures on the walls."

Jonna gave them a glance. "Murals and drawings by others who have come down here. It is like graffiti from my time."

"So I take it graffiti means pictures?"

"Sort of," Jonna considered, "though sometimes they could get rather rude." He took a closer look at the wall. "Most of this looks like people leaving their mark."

"Under a city? Why?"

Jonna shrugged. "Who knows how long ago these tunnels were made. The city above could have been built on another. It might even have been before the giants ruled."

A deep voice echoed behind them, "Is someone down there?"

Chapter 18

THE WELL OF NONOS

Jonna barely whispered, "Move," praying the sound was camouflaged by the noise of their pursuers. He hurried down the tunnel with the light from the ring hidden. Cassandra clung to his sleeve. Lokke's feet sounded overly loud.

"Can we slow down a little?" the half-demon complained, trying to whisper but not doing a very good job.

Cassandra threw him a glare. "Shh!"

"I'm having trouble with the whole 'not level' floor thing," he huffed.

She answered through clenched teeth without turning around. "Like we're not."

The half-demon's voice rose. "But that's my point!"

"Lokke, be quiet." The hushed voice of Cassandra sounded louder than if she shouted.

He rolled his eyes. "And they call me moody."

Jonna felt Cassandra release his sleeve, and a startled Lokke exclaimed, "Ouch!"

Jonna turned. Neither Lokke nor Cassandra was moving. He could see them, at first a blur of two heat signatures, gradually separating into two people. Cassandra had one hand over Lokke's mouth and another holding the back of his neck.

Taking hold of her arm, Jonna tugged her to follow. They

changed directions at the crossroads. The hard packed, dried dirt would help to hide their footprints, depending on how observant those that followed were. Cassandra dragged Lokke behind her, refusing to let go. At the next crossroad, Jonna chanced a look at the ring. The ring indicated left.

Following the ring's route, small patches of green, glowing fungi appeared. It casted eerie light and distorted the view ahead. He took a closer look. It was similar to the fungi in the dark elvish city. "We're moving deeper."

Satisfied their pursuers were far behind, Cassandra released her hold on Lokke.

"It's about time." Lokke coughed. "It was getting hard to breathe!" He listened to the echoes of those behind. "Besides, how do they expect to track us in this? You can't tell anything because of the echoes. And I know; I did the same in the Otherworld."

"Our echoes say we're here." Jonna checked the walls; empty burial cutouts dominated the landscape. "They are watching the floor, seeing where we've disturbed the dust. They will track us eventually, no matter how far ahead we are."

Lokke bent down and ran a finger across the floor. "I see."

At the next crossroad, Jonna held up a hand.

"We're stopping?"

"Give me a moment." He released Cassandra and disappeared in front of them. Despite of the fungi, a person could not see very far with normal sight.

He moved down each of the corridors, checked with the ring, and doubled back. It was the one to their right, yet another yellow light shone to the left. Was it an exit to the catacombs? Turning around, he hurried back and ran into Cassandra.

"You're back!" She threw her arms around him as if he had left for days. "Remember your promise; no wandering off by yourself."

"I haven't sensed the Tjaard since we entered the city."

A cackled old voice came from nowhere. "There's a reason for that young man."

He rotated the ring on his finger to hide it, closed his fist, and turned around. Out of the darkness came an elderly woman bent over as if crippled. She used a tree branch as a staff, decorated in tiny symbols, with the twigs trimmed raggedly off.

A hood hid the woman's face, and the pale, yellow light on top of the staff flickered like a flame in a gentle wind.

"What brings surface dwellers into these depths?"

Jonna noted her worn clothing and patches. "Surface dwellers? You're not one of them?"

"I have no love for the giants. The catacombs give me all I need."

Cassandra looked a little confused. "That doesn't make sense. There's nothing down here."

The old woman threw Cassandra a look. "Nor does one walking around that's dead."

Jonna sought those hidden eyes. Would she know if he lied? The man upstairs had said to trust no one. Steeling himself, he made a decision. "We broke a tablet in the Brighid. It required a quick escape."

"Brighid, eh? Maybe I'll help you get out then. The catacombs are no place for the timid." She laughed in a crackling voice, "Getting lost down here can drive you insane."

Jonna had the ring as a guide, but wouldn't a person that knew their way be better? There was this nagging feeling in the back of his mind that she was part of this. He made a decision. "So you know the catacombs?" Did the old woman catch the hope in his voice?

She peered at him, and Jonna could feel the scrutiny. "There is no corner I do not know." Her voice was whimsical, "Are you looking for something—in particular?"

Jonna remembered Maxima and the man who had told them about Fisher's Block. He had no idea who was friend or foe.

"A tomb," he spoke at last. "A tomb with the letters R.K.H."

"That's not much to go on," she chuckled. "There are many initials and many tombs."

He made a decision. Despite the fact that the ring could lead them to the tomb, who would guide them out? "The casket in the tomb is gold covered. It is possibly made of gold."

"Gold?" The old woman's head jerked, and for a moment Jonna thought she was going to straighten up.

Jonna confirmed it with a nod. "Gold."

A single finger rose on her right hand, disappearing into the darkness of the hood. Jonna imagined she had pressed it to her lips in thought. What could be going through her head?

"If I take you to this casket of gold, what will you do then?" Her voice held laughter as she spoke the words. "Would you rob the dead?"

"No!" Cassandra looked stunned. "We are—" She stopped and looked toward Jonna.

They had come this far; they might as well go the rest of the way. Jonna gave a reassuring nod to Cassandra and finished, "We are here to free a mage named Fabius."

"Fabius who?"

"You don't know Fabius?" Lokke looked shocked. "Group talk." He grabbed Cassandra and Jonna by the arm and pulled them a few feet away. "I don't know about you," his attempt at whispering was terrible at best, "but I don't trust her. If she doesn't know about Fabius—"

Jonna sighed and looked into Lokke's face. "What are you doing?"

Lokke looked back. "Why, I'm, er—"

"Exactly." Jonna broke out of the group and turned to the expectant old woman. "We don't know much more. We only know that he is trapped in a sort of half-life, held here and there at the same time. We have promised to free him."

"You promised," Lokke corrected. "I just want out of the Otherworld."

Cassandra elbowed him. "You are out of the Otherworld."

"Am not."

"Are so."

Jonna pulled the old woman's attention back. "Please, don't mind them." He hoped the scene would not run her off. "We really could use your help."

The finger removed from the hood, and for the first time, he realized the staff was floating. Once her right hand encircled it, it drifted down to touch the floor.

"I can guide you to the golden casket," the old woman assured, "but first you need to do a favor for me. Retrieve three petals from the House of Reina. Do this, and the casket is yours."

"Uh," Jonna hated to show his ignorance, but he saw no other way, "you wouldn't happen to know where the House of Reina is, would you?"

"The paths of surface dwellers do not concern me." She pointed the staff in Jonna's direction. "You will find the House. I will find the casket."

"I take it that's a no?"

"I didn't say that," the old woman cackled again, "but this is something you must do on your own. I cannot help you."

Why did that sound like Väinämö? Probably, because it was something he'd say. Maybe she would at least answer a different question. "The way out, perhaps?"

She pointed with her staff. "Follow the yellow light." At her words, the pale, yellow light on top of her staff leaped out and headed around a corner down the hall. "When you have found the petals, come to this place. I will be here."

Jonna turned the corner, looked to the left, and spotted the yellow glow he had seen before. If it was the way out, why had he not seen the old woman standing there? And if it was the old woman that produced the glow, how was the exit there now? The staff that floated came to mind. Magic, of course. He turned back. "What's—" Except for Cassandra and Lokke, the hall was empty. "She's gone."

The half-demon nodded vigorously. "She faded away."

"Jonna," Cassandra shifted toward him, "are you sure we should do this? We don't even know what these petals are for." She motioned to the ring on his hand. "We have the ring. Why not find him ourselves?"

"I thought of that," he agreed, "but there is something—" How did he put it in words? "—about this woman which makes me think we need her. I don't understand it and don't know how to explain it, but meeting her can't be a coincidence."

The footsteps were back. Jonna waved them toward the hall to the left. "This way."

They hurried down the hall, bypassing the other turns and twists as they moved closer to the yellow light. His curiosity about the old woman piqued. She knew which casket they sought.

His concerns were many. In what way was this woman connected with their quest? Would they have to carry Fabius out to revive him? If not, would Fabius know the way out, or would he be lost like them?

The yellow light grew and showed stairs that lead up. They followed the stairs, turned ninety degrees, and ended in a room. The room was empty save for narrow windows beneath the ceiling. The yellow glow they saw was a result of the daylight bouncing off the walls. Up a few more stairs, they turned to the right and passed into the outside world.

"So there's more than one entrance to the catacombs," Jonna got his bearings. "I thought so. Now, all we have to do is find the House of Reina." He looked around. "That seems to be a tough one."

Having been unusually silent until now, Lokke decided to speak. "We could always head to the Brighid."

"I don't think so," Cassandra growled, "since somebody wore out our welcome."

"They don't know it was us," Lokke encouraged, that mischievous smile coming to his face. "And while we're there—"

Jonna shook his head. "Whatever you're thinking, the answer is no. We need a guide." He gazed across the road at the buildings in front of them. He could not help but note the large number of slaves. It seemed strange that in the midst of this city, they had only seen one giant.

"Excuse me." Jonna reached into the crowd, grabbed a man's arm, and pulled him to a stop.

The startled the newcomer frowned. "Uh, I'm sorry, what was that?"

"Might I ask directions to the House of Reina?"

As the slave's eyes focused, a strange look crossed his face. "You don't know the way to Reina?"

Jonna looked surprised. "Should we?"

The slave noticed the others and lingered a little longer than Jonna liked with narrowed eyes. "Everyone knows the way to Reina. It is how they brought you in."

Jonna coughed, pulling his attention back. "We didn't know. Sorry to bother you."

"No bother," the man's brow wrinkled. The moment they let him go, the man disappeared into the fast moving crowd.

Lokke huffed. "That didn't go good. How many times can we hit a dead end?"

Jonna spoke absentmindedly, "No it didn't, but it took Edison over a thousand tries to make a light bulb."

"Who's Edison, and what's a light bulb?"

Jonna realized what he had said and caught them staring at him. "That's not important right now, but the concept is. Any other bright ideas?"

Cassandra stepped forward, moving closer to the crowd. As a group of male slaves approached, she tripped, pretending to try and catch herself.

The crowd spread as she fell forward. A dozen slaves reached out to help. One caught her, lifted her up, and placed her out of the line of traffic.

"You should be more careful."

"Cassandra," she extended her hand. "Call me by my first name."

"Cassandra," the slave nodded, "it's accidents like that which can get you trampled."

"I'm so sorry," she apologized. "I was on my way to the House of Reina, hit my head, and somehow got turned around."

The man frowned. "Maybe we should have a look at it?"

Cassandra tilted her head, letting her long hair flow off her shoulder. "Do you see anything?"

There was a sparkle in the man's eyes. The man continued, "No outward damage, but you should take it easy." He pointed to their right, against the flow of traffic. "Reina is back that direction, straight down the street. Do you need some help getting there?"

Cassandra gave him a warm smile. "May I have a name to thank you by?"

He bowed, a slight color coming to his cheeks. "Emre, ma'am."

"Thank you Emre. You're a gentleman of the highest caliber."

Emre's face turned red as he smiled. "If all is well, as reluctant as I am, then I must be going." He shifted into the crowd, though he glanced back. Cassandra waved and smiled.

"That was great," Lokke could hardly keep the excitement in. "You played him like a flute."

A little pink crept onto Cassandra's cheeks.

"Not exactly my words," Jonna joined, "but an excellent job."

Feeling a little too conscious of the praise, Cassandra pointed toward the direction of Reina. "Don't you think we should be going?"

"Of course." Jonna lead the way through the traffic, checked both directions, and cut a path to the other side of the street. The sun, no longer high, looked to be around three-thirtyish.

He wondered what his family was doing? Even though he was technically not in the Otherworld, Väinämö had given no news. Unfortunately, every time the mage showed up, all he did was read through books.

A bluish stone building with white steps and floors loomed as if from nowhere. Carved beneath the roof into the exterior wall were the words 'House of Reina', written in both human and giant languages. He wondered if anyone had used this as a comparison for translating the giant's script? It was obvious this was the one place the giants wanted everyone to know about. No wonder the first slave they had asked acted so surprised.

Of all the buildings they had seen, this was the one place which had both a giant entrance and a human entrance in the front. They were side by side with slaves going and coming almost as fast as the traffic on the street. Unobtrusively, they stepped up to the end of the line where slaves entered the building. In less than a moment, they were whisked inside.

Jonna's eyes widened as he looked at the multistoried configuration. Angling a brightness which washed away all shadows, light bounced through open apertures in both the ceiling and the roof. Stairs with railing sides appeared open and light. The white steps were set with a surrounding edge of blue.

Mosaic designs decorated the floors. There was red, yellow, and green in one part with purple, orange, and blue in another. No matter where they went, a bright white stone outlined each mosaic. It was like going to a grand ballroom with all the decorations set in array. Yet, a big question remained in Jonna's mind. Why was everyone here?

No one carried anything out. No one carried anything in. The group knew this was the receiving center for the slaves. They knew that the slaves came and left in a constant flow. Why?

Lokke echoed what was on everyone's lips. "Now what?" With a sudden gasp, his eyes bulged. A giant passed by them going in; within the door were ten to twenty more. "So that's where they're hiding."

As the large entrance swung shut, they glimpsed an indoor pool with steam rising from it. Giants walked with robes draped around themselves or lounged by the side of the pool. A few swam in the clear blue water. The slaves were doing the same, but through another, smaller door. It opened and closed more quickly than that of the giant's.

"An indoor swimming pool." The idea had not occurred to Jonna before. "Reina was a—"

"Bathhouse." Cassandra translated, peering toward the giant's entrance.

Jonna nodded. "A good description."

"Well," Lokke took a deep breath, "there doesn't appear to be anything ominous about this place. Smiling slaves go in. Smiling slaves come out. Let's go find those petals."

Jonna threw him a glance. "What happened to the warning we were told? Trust no one?"

Lokke stood straight with his chin raised. "This is a place, not a person."

The answer was too easy. Maybe it was the expectancy on the faces of all the slaves that entered. Maybe it was the complete euphoria on the faces of the slaves that left. The bathhouse couldn't be that great, could it? With a city this big, ruled by giants and worked by slaves, something had to keep them in line.

They shifted forward, moving closer to the slave entrance. With each opening a waft of fragrance floated in the air; it was a combination of smells that tickled the nose, pleasantly drawing them on.

Cassandra smiled. "This may not be all bad. It's been a while since I had a bath."

Sniffing his shirt, Jonna wrinkled his nose. "We do seem a little rank after that seawater."

"Speak for yourself." Lokke watched the door open and shut. "I don't smell."

Cassandra's laugh was unusually light. "We all think that. In the Otherworld, I never had to worry about it. But on the surface—" She stopped and tried to catch Jonna's eyes.

Jonna watched those around him as they spoke. Curious glances were coming their way. "A conversation for later," he smiled, but there was something about this place. It was something that was relaxing them all.

As their turn came, the door swung in, and the full smell of what awaited inside struck them like a wall. They swam through a sea of fragrance. It consumed the air, devouring them whole.

A nagging memory popped into Jonna's mind. The giant's entrance had been wide open, yet no smell came to them from that direction. It was only the slave's entrance that had the smell. The reason for the segregation? Maybe.

Every muscle in his body relaxed. He could see the same response in the others. They were lead to an area of holes in one wall where the smell came through more strongly. For those who had no robes, one was readily available.

Cassandra stretched in slow motion. "This is Paradise."

In a blink of an eye, her clothes disappeared. Jonna spun around, bopping Lokke to make him do the same. She gave a small laugh as she reached for one of the robes.

"Uh, Cassandra," Jonna whispered, "couldn't you have created the robe?" Lokke turned around and admired how well the robe fit her. The half-demon's tongue was practically hanging out.

She lightly laughed again. "Where would be the fun in that? Besides, it would look a little strange when we have to take them off." She pointed to the archway at their right. From where they were, they could see the start of the pool; two unclothed bodies relaxed around the edge.

"Sounds good to me," Lokke grabbed a robe, dropped his own leather clothes, and threw the robe around him.

"Have you two gone insane?" Jonna looked from one to the other. "We have to get the petals." Despite of the fuzziness in his brain, he refused to lose focus on their mission. "We have to get them to the old woman."

"I don't see the hurry," Cassandra feigned offense and at the same time put a lure in her voice. Lokke took it: hook, line, and sinker. "The quest can wait till after the bath."

Lokke beat her into the pool room and disappeared around the corner. Cassandra paused at the archway. "Coming?" A twinkle was in her eye.

It was the fragrance, it had to be; even Jonna's determinism tried to melt away. Could that be how the giant's kept control? Something in the smell?

"Coming," he smiled though his mind fought against it. He would not give in. He would not.

Cassandra disappeared around the corner, but her final words hung in the air. "You promised."

Jonna inhaled, gasped, and wished he had held it. The fragrance was too much, and his normal logic was losing control. He had to get out of here before—

Another person entered the changing room wearing a robe and a look of concern on his face. "Are you okay?"

"I don't feel well."

"It'll pass," the man assured. "It was the same with all of us for the first time. Although," he winked at Jonna, "it appears the women are less afflicted. A good thing for us." The man smiled, but the look of concern returned. "There is no reason to fight it."

"Fight what?"

The man paused, studying Jonna. Little by little, the frown dropped away. "Why don't you wait over there," he nodded toward the left side of the room beside another archway. A bench was pushed against the wall. Outside light shown on it.

Nodding, Jonna made his way toward the light. As he took a seat, he squeezed his eyes closed and tried to force out the influence of the fragrance. It was no good. Despite of his best effort, he could feel the fragrance winning.

The spinning in his head was less. His mind relaxed. What did it matter if they took a break? It was a privilege to be here, and it had been so long since—

In the back of his mind, a tiny image appeared. Too small to see at first, it became larger and then smaller, back and forth. Like a fish trying to swim upstream, it struggled against an unseen current, fighting desperately to reach—

The image of Väinämö appeared. He mouthed words in Jonna's direction and pointed toward the archway. Despite the movement of Väinämö's mouth, no sounds came out.

Was it the promised spell? Was Jonna close to the Well of Nonos? No matter how hard he tried, the syllables Väinämö spoke did not make sense. Perhaps it was the fragrance stealing his mind, confusing his thoughts, and taking his soul.

Elfleda appeared. She replaced the image of Väinämö and stood hovering before his closed eyes. The lips moved, but the words would not come. She slowly faded away.

A second image, Elpis, appeared. Her arms held forward, she reached out to hug him. The face of Bob replaced it. Bob, whose link to him had been cut.

His family. The word 'family' echoed as it reminded him of his responsibilities. He fought for them. If he did not fight, he would not return. Fight, dang you! Drive the fragrance from your mind! Opening his eyes, he saw what was through the lighted archway.

It was a garden. An open roof allowed sunlight in. Small trees and shrubs grew, and in the middle of the room was a stone well. Was this the Well of Nonos?

A plant of white flowers floated on its watery surface. As a petal dropped off, it fluttered down and struck the top of the water. Like a bomb, the fragrance increased. It was then he knew. Those were the petals he had to attain.

Jonna stood, turned to the garden, and walked toward the well. Väinämö's mouthed words floated in the back of his mind. What would happen if he went on not knowing them? They still did not make sense.

His legs were heavy. His feet like lead. The closer he went, the stronger the smell, and the stronger the smell, the harder it was to focus.

There were carvings in the stone floor, written in the slave language, placed in ever closer circles around the well. The outside ring of words said 'pleasure' repeated around the outer concentric circle. The next inner circle of words said 'beware' repeated in the same way. The third said 'come no further', and last, most inner circle, said 'death'.

Death, those words were only three feet from the petals themselves. As he passed the second ring, 'beware', a pain built in his head. The fragrance was too strong. It was overloading his sense of smell and clogging his lungs.

Regardless, he took the next few steps. His lungs burned. The edge of 'come no further' floated before his eyes. Feet sliding forward, he could feel a thousand needles prick him inside his chest, stabbing at his heart. A bead of sweat ran down his face as the engraved words of 'Death' stared up at him. Did he dare make the next step? Already he could feel his heart pounding. His body could not take much more. Yet, he had to try.

His eyes rose from the words on the ground and stared at the Well of Nonos. They had to have those petals, but he knew he would never make the journey.

His brain could not think straight. His thoughts came in and tried to fly away. The longer he stood there, the less chance he had of getting back. He knew his body was dying. Its strength was ebbing away.

A spell, he must use a spell. "*Stamato Zamon*, stop time."

A rumbling cracked the sky. It was the wrong magical language, but his mind could not focus on anything else. There was a ping of glass.

The look on Cassus' face came to mind. The terror in the man's eyes had been real. The falling of something like glittering glass had plummeted Cassus from an unseen source.

But there was nothing like that here, only the rumbling followed by the ping. The burning had not left his chest, yet it did not get worse; he was weak but not getting weaker. Jonna could make it to the petals.

It was only three feet, but he held his breath. Heart beating rapidly, he moved forward to stand next to the well. Reaching out, he touched the stone around the top. The water waves of the last falling petals were frozen in place, held still by the spell he had cast. He reached down, plucked out three petals, and then for luck took some more. There was no way he wanted to repeat this experience.

Placing them in a pouch, he made his way toward the bathhouse with great relief. The burning sensation ebbed as he took in the view. Hundreds of people stood frozen, held as if made of stone. He spotted Cassandra and Lokke swimming in a game of touch-tag. With their robes on the bank, they acted like everyone else. Only Lokke's unusual form and color helped to pick them out of the crowd.

Jonna cringed. A half-demon chasing a dead woman? Under the influence of the flowers fragrance, he might have been doing that too. He stepped onto the water.

His feet sank, the water coming up to his waist, but his clothes did not get wet. The clothes displaced the water without any absorption. Since time had stopped, only he was influencing the elements.

Catching his friends around the waist, he hauled them toward the side. He had to be careful; he did not want to hurt them. With robes draped around them and secured with ties, it was time to get everyone outside. When these two realized what they had done...

Neither one was heavy, but to carry them out of the building, around the corner, and to a private location took effort. He brought along Lokke's clothes.

As he finished, he stepped back. The spell was still in effect. He had expected it to be localized, but somehow it had influenced a larger area than that. How did he turn it off? Did he chance using the wrong language, or could he find another form of localized magic?

He shifted to Latin. It was one of the phrases Lucastra gave him. If his intent was correct, the words were only a medium, right? "*Tempus fugit.*"

Chapter 19

TWO SIDES OF A COIN

It should have been immediate, that was the picture in Jonna's mind, but the wind began whirling like a tornado. His hair blew, his clothes tugged, and the wind struck him like a wave. It picked him up and slammed him against one of the blue building's support pillars, right before it dropped him to the ground.

"Jonna," Cassandra helped him to his feet, "you're bleeding!"

He reached back and felt his head. "I am?"

"You are." She used the robe to wipe the blood from his neck. "I told you to stay with us."

He gave her a funny smile. "I never left."

"Where are we?" Lokke gazed around. "I remember—" Wonder crossed his face. "—us in the pool?"

Cassandra frowned. "That's right," she looked horrified, "we were. What did I do?"

Lokke grinned. "You mean, what did we do?"

"Oh my word!" Cassandra turned and slapped Lokke.

Lokke jumped back. "What was that for?"

"You know what!"

"But—"

"I know when I've been taken advantage of," she growled. "You knew better!"

"But—"

As she raised her hand again, Lokke cowered.

"That's better," she growled and pointed at a spot three feet away. "I want you there, now!"

Lokke took one giant step back, eyes wide, to the place she pointed. "Yes ma'am."

She turned to Jonna and huffed. "You were the only gentleman. What happened?"

"I got the petals." He inhaled, gasped, and grimaced from the pain. "We need to get to the catacombs."

"Not until you stop bleeding." She pulled off the robe, her clothes having returned. Lokke looked disappointed. She wrapped part of the robe around Jonna's neck and held pressure on the wound. "You'll be fine." Her frown deepened. "What did you do?"

"I'm not exactly sure."

Lokke spotted his clothes and stepped beside a pillar to dress. "No peeking." Cassandra glared at him, and Lokke ducked out of sight. Out of the front of the building, slaves began to run.

Jonna glanced toward the street. "Something's going on."

Cassandra released the pressure and checked the wound. "The bleeding has stopped. It wasn't as bad as it looked." She tossed the robe into the nearby foliage. "Be careful. We don't want it to start again."

He stopped from putting a hand to the hurt. It might irritate it. Lokke stepped out from behind the pillar and tossed the robe. With everyone ready, the trio moved toward the street.

At the edge of the building, they heard roars from inside. Additional screams followed a crash. Jonna reached out and caught one of the runners. "What's going on?"

The man blabbered out before wrenching free of his grip, "Someone's desecrated the Flower of Reina, and the giants blame the slaves!" As he ran away from the building, he glanced back. "Run!"

It no longer mattered which side of the street they were

on, or if they stayed on the sides. Slaves ran by them. Shops shut their doors. Everyone fled in terror.

The trio fought their way down the street, forced to run like everyone else. They avoided collisions and dodged obstacles. Never had Jonna seen something like this, not even during the panic of Chernobog when Azazel had chased him.

The ground shook. Thuds struck the ground and thundered in waves, knocking them off their feet. The trio tumbled into the turmoil and fought to regain their balance. Horrified slaves froze in fear and stared the way they had come.

A horde of giants clad in gleaming silver armor marched toward them. They bore down upon the slaves, blood and fire in their eyes. They were merciless to the slave stragglers and callous to the carnage they caused.

In the lead was one giant clad in gold with a red ruby gleaming from the top of his helmet. His sword longer than Jonna, he held it with an ease that did not belie his strength.

"Kyrillos," a slave beside them wailed, dropping to his knees and pointing up at the gold clad giant. "Kyrillos comes to kill us all!"

"Get up." Jonna pulled the man to his feet and pushed him away from the giant horde. "Run!" The man took off.

The throb in Jonna's head had not abated, and he felt woozy from the wind slamming him back, but something had to be done to save these people; it was his fault they were attacked. He turned to the others. "Both of you, head to the catacombs." In spite of the screaming around them, his friends heard the words.

"Not without you," Cassandra's eyes showed fright. "We are sticking together." She glared at Lokke. "Right?"

"Uh," Lokke swallowed nervously, "right." He watched the giants heading in their direction. "Can we at least hide?"

Jonna worked his way toward the center of the road. "Do what you will." He stood his ground right in the path of the giants.

Lokke dashed for the side, but Cassandra caught him

and dragged him toward the middle. "Where do you think you're going?"

Lokke screamed to be heard above the noise. Or was he just screaming in fear? He jabbed the air toward the giants. "What can you do against them? They are too many!"

Jonna stared at the approaching warriors. "I don't know, but I caused this."

The half-demon turned toward Cassandra and begged to be let go. "He doesn't know!"

"Lokke, look at me." She stilled herself for what she had to say next.

The half-demon looked straight at her.

"Did you like what happened in the pool?"

The terror lessened in Lokke's eyes. "Yeah."

"Do you want to do it again?"

His eyes brightened.

"Hold your ground, stand with us, and I'll think about it."

He swallowed and turned to face the giants. "You promise?"

Cassandra's eyes glanced at Jonna. "I promise."

Jonna gave a slight smile. "Thank you."

His eyes focused on the giants. As they ripped apart slaves within arm's reach, his anger built. The death and destruction they caused was unforgivable. How could he respond with anything less than what they did to the slaves?

There was time to think of a spell, yet nothing came in Latin. Though he dared not use Väinämö's magic, he could at least get closer by using demoneze. "*Qisvo!*"

His shout rose above the screams and stomping feet. Glass pinged and rumbles struck their ears.

The giants stopped. The running slaves stopped. Both stared up at the sky. In the silence, dark storm clouds swirled together. They came from nowhere and formed from nothing.

Kyrillos' voice boomed, "Who dares call magic in the land of the giants?"

Jonna had never known magic to take so long to

respond. The dark clouds changed and became black as night. Small bits of lightning whipped between the clouds. The lightning grew in strength with each strike larger than the last.

Lokke's voice was a squeak, yet in the silence it thundered, "What's going on?"

Cassandra could not take her eyes off the giants. "They've stopped and are waiting."

The half-demon's gaze went to Jonna. "Waiting for what?" A light drizzle began to fall.

Could he be wrong, Jonna thought. In the Otherworld, there was an instant flash. The spell cast to resume the flow of time had acted strangely, as well.

Though he looked up at the sky, Kyrillos laughed. "Who dares to think a little rain will scare the king of the frost giants? Shall I teach you as I taught Fabius the mage? We giants are protected by a greater power than mere human magic."

Lokke jumped up and down. "Fabius! Did you hear that? He knows Fabius!"

Cassandra put a hand on Jonna's shoulder, a faraway look in her eyes. "Have faith Jonna."

The last of the slaves were clearing the street, but they still needed time. Whatever was happening, it was overcoming another form of magic.

"It is I," he called at the top of his lungs and stepped forward. "Jonna McCambel, husband to Elfleda, and prince of the Woodland Elves, conqueror of the Dark Mage Cassus."

The sky was so black, it was a night without stars. Lightning burst from cloud to cloud. It gave brief glimpses of illumination.

"An elf," roared Kyrillos with laughter. His voice boomed across the city. "You have no power here, elf, be ye woodland or dark."

"But I am not an elf," Jonna shouted. "I am a man." And with a voice that felt not like his own, he said the spell again, demanding action. "*Qisvo!*"

The ping came easier; the rumble was deep. Lightning pulled from all four directions and created a swirl of fire in the sky, but it did not descend.

"You cannot harm us, mage," Kyrillos boomed. "A ancient dome of protection guards this city. Your time is up." The giant pointed to the trio in the road, his eyes settling on Jonna. "You cannot harm us, but we can harm you. Get them, now!"

The giants leaped forward. Their huge feet beat upon the ground. The ground shook, and despite the tough blue stone, cracks formed. It was a matter of seconds, and the horde would be upon them.

Keeping her voice level, Cassandra called with urgency, "Jonna, you must say the spell one more time." She grabbed hold of Lokke and fought to hold him still.

"Let me go!" The half-demon broke her grip and ran toward the side of a building.

Kyrillos gloated. "Hiding will not save you."

"Who says we're hiding." Jonna stared at the impending collision, and a calm dropped over his heart. Whatever happened next, he would not move. "Kyrillos, *Qisvo*."

The torrent of flame dropped from the sky and ripped through the darkness. It struck an invisible barrier, above the city, and set the entire city aglow. Flames leaped, a screech sent shivers down their spines, and the barrier collapsed.

The giants gazed up as magical fire burned through. On the buildings of the city, it cast a yellow-red light.

Kyrillos dropped his eyes to take in Jonna. "What have you done?" Streaks of flame penetrated the air and shot down in the direction of the giants.

The giant warriors scattered. Kyrillos watched as the fire descended. With a roar of anger, he raised the sword at Jonna. "You will die!"

Lightning hit; it was a mere tap at the end of the upheld sword. It lit the sword in sparkling blue, reached the giant's hands, and zapped through his body. The ground burst. Kyrillos convulsed. Like a mountain toppled, he fell in the trio's direction.

"Come on!" Cassandra grabbed Jonna's shoulder. They rushed to the side, jumped for the nearest wall, and prayed the hit of the giant's body would not shake the supports of the street apart.

The hit was devastating, the buildings around them jumped, but it was not the fall of the giant which caused the chaos. Multiple lightning strikes hit the street, scorched the stones, and caught those giants who failed to hide. Stones burst apart as fire poured upon the giant horde.

"Crawl," Jonna tugged at Cassandra, "we have to get to the catacombs." When she did not move, he turned back; part of a wall had fallen across her body. "Cassandra," he shook her. "Cassandra!"

Moving the debris out of the way, he lifted her up. They bounced as he made his way to the entrance.

The steps shook. With the sun blotted out, there was no light to see by, but his pixie sight did not fail him. As he reached the bottom of the stairs, he could hear a terrified whimper. "Lokke?"

The whimper stopped. "Jo-Jonna?" Lokke tried to follow the sound of his voice. "You-you're alive?"

"Never better," but he frowned at the body he carried in his arms, "though I think Cassandra might be hurt."

"Hurt?" Lokke hurried toward him and bumped into a wall before heading in the right direction. Jonna felt something touch his head.

"Lokke?"

"Yes?"

"Your hand."

"Oops."

As Lokke backed off, Jonna gently lowered her to the ground. A rock was used to support Cassandra's head. With the pixie sight, he saw no broken bones.

The old woman's voice cackled down the tunnel. "There is a reason why the dead stay in the Otherworld." In the distance, a lighted staff appeared, moved slowly forward, and approached the trio.

283

Jonna's eyes remained on Cassandra. "What's wrong with her?"

"She is becoming human again. She is becoming undead."

"You mean alive?"

"No," the old woman shook her head. "She can never be alive as she was, that part of her journey is over, but she can be hurt, cry out in agony, feel, and love in a way she never could below. When the change becomes final, she will lose herself forever, forget who she was, and be a new person. The longer she is here, the harder it will be when she returns."

Jonna looked up at the old woman. "I don't understand."

"Of course you don't. You've never experienced death. When a person dies, they pass to the Otherworld. It is the natural course of events. With her, life is making natural what is unnatural. The spirit cannot handle this, so it simply goes into nothingness, and the person is reborn. Their past is lost forever."

Jonna swallowed. This was Elpis' mother. She gave up her life in Bliss to help him escape. She did not deserve this. "What do I have to do?"

"Return her to where she belongs before it is too late."

The words 'too late' held an ominous ring as if there were no chance at all. There had to be a way. "How much time do we have?" All he could think about was Cassandra losing her daughter forever.

"You will see for yourself." The old lady waved a hand at her. "The process has begun."

He looked down at her face. Her eyes fluttered. He bent close. "Cassandra?"

"Jonna?" As her eyes focused, she threw her arms around him. "Jonna, you're safe!"

"Of course we are," he smiled back. "Are you okay?"

"I'm fine." She moved to sit up and groaned. Her gaze and hand went to her side. There was an ugly yellow and purple spot showing where once the skin had been pale. "But I'm dead," she looked up in wonder, "how can I be hurt?"

Jonna, startled, realized Cassandra was naked. "Cassandra, your clothes."

She concentrated, but no clothes appeared. Looking at Jonna surprised, she caught sight of the old lady. "What's going on?"

"You are changing, my dear. You are being reborn."

"Reborn?" Cassandra's eyes widened. "There were stories about those from the Otherworld being reborn." Her voice sounded far away. "They lost their memories." Fear crossed her face. "They become someone else."

The old lady nodded. "So it is. You will forget all you knew. The feelings you had, and the things that occurred in your previous life. You will only know now. You will be reborn."

"I will forget my family." She looked up at Jonna as tears slid down her cheeks. "I will forget Elpis." Her hand shook as she reached up and grabbed Jonna's shirt. "Help me, please!"

Jonna turned to the old woman. "We have the petals. What do we lack?"

The old woman stiffened and slowly extended her hand. "Show me."

He reached into his pocket, pulled out three petals, and dropped them toward her shaking hand. The old woman took a deep breath and exhaled softly as the three floated down toward her palm. In slow motion, they touched the surface of her skin. Remembering she had an audience, her voice came back, fist closing on the petals. "You've done well. I will take you to the casket."

Cassandra's voice quivered. "It is so cold in here."

"It is the catacombs," the old woman sneered, "not a place for a woman undressed."

Jonna's eyes narrowed. "She needs clothes."

The old woman cackled, "I only agreed to take you to the casket, not become a tailor." But her voice softened, "Perhaps there is something I can do." She reached into a bag hidden under her cloak and pulled out some rolled up material. "Try this on."

It turned into a long cape. The cape covered Cassandra from her head to her ankles and was wide enough to wrap all the way around her body. It was adequate to keep her from freezing.

Lokke had a mischievous grin. "I can wrap my arm around you to help keep you warm."

Cassandra glared. "You lost that chance when you ducked and ran."

"Oh, come on," the half-demon begged. "I stayed with the group most of the time!"

"Though I hate to say it," Jonna sighed, "Lokke has a point. You're going to have to stay warm, and without additional clothes, it's not going to be easy. You could wait up top—"

"No, we came this far together. We're going to finish together."

"You, at least, need shoes," the old woman admitted curtly. Searching the bag, she pulled out two items. They looked like small leather sacks. "Place them on your feet."

As Cassandra did, both conformed with a perfect fit and finished out with thickened soles. A smile lit Cassandra's lips as she looked up at the old woman. "Thank you, that's much better."

"Humph," the old woman turned, "we need to be going."

Making sure Cassandra was set, Jonna turned to follow the old woman. "We're ready."

Lokke's arm went around Cassandra. His hand played with the end of her garment. Her eyebrows knit together. "The cape stays closed."

His fingers stopped. "Yes ma'am."

"That's better."

Jonna almost laughed but caught it before it came out. Looking over, he studied the old woman as they followed. She was not unkind, yet she pretended to be uncaring. She had agreed to help them, and yet she never warned them of the danger involved. He cleared his throat. "What is your name? Why did you want the petals?"

Her old voice cackled. "The young ask questions they do not want the answers to."

"I'm not as young as you think."

The old woman burst out in laughter. Throwing him a glance, a slight smile was on her lips. "Oh, you are young, have no doubt."

He pressed. "How about the name then?"

The old woman looked up, seeing that which she could only see. "If I give you my name, Jonna McCambel, there may come a time when you wished you did not know it."

He had given up a long time ago asking how they knew his name. "Why are there never any straight answers?"

She ignored him and continued. "I felt the earth quake when the giant Kyrillos fell. You think that you've defeated him?"

"I don't know. In our hurry to get away, I could not check."

"He is not dead, though you have delivered a blow to his world that will bring about its demise. When he goes, this land will change forever."

Jonna frowned. "For the good, I hope."

"What is good or bad?" Levity was in her voice. "Are they not two sides of the same coin, flipping to land where they may?"

"A person can know the difference if they want to, no matter how hidden."

"For such a young one," she chuckled, "you do show some wisdom. Howbeit, such is not what you have asked." A slight smile curved on her lips. "You will know my name soon enough."

Warning signs shot up inside of Jonna, and a prickly sensation spread across his skin. Until now, he knew that the old woman was some sort of mage, but nothing had pointed to something evil. Now, he felt the potential. Then again, as she had pointed out, maybe he wasn't perceiving correctly. He checked the ring. By its indication, they went in the right direction; the color was gradually fading from blue to green.

Several turns down, along a hallway, the old woman brought them to a darkened room. The glowing moss, which sprung up everywhere else, did not show here. The light that flickered on her staff was the only source as he kept the ring hidden. Something about this did not feel right to Jonna. Out of reflex, he spoke, "*Fait lux.*"

The old woman threw him a sideways glance as light sprang up from inside the room. When they stepped in, tall bronze lamp stands stood in each corner, sending out light and heat. Names and initials showed around the walls on large square plates.

Jonna addressed them all. "You know the initials, R.K.H. Now we have to find him."

Curiously enough, the old woman joined in the search, taking the wall the others did not. She was anxious. For what?

"I found it, I found it!" Lokke jumped up and down. "It's here!" He pointed to a location ten rows over and three rows up. "It's decorated in gold!"

"As Fabius said." Jonna walked over to Lokke's find and ran his fingers across the letters. He held up the ring. It was a solid green with no variation. This had to be the place. "But how do we open it?"

The old woman held up her staff. "Why not try this?"

The warning was back in Jonna's head, yet what choice did they have? Fabius had not said how to open his casket. He had only asked to be released.

Jonna accepted the staff, once more noting a slight smile on the old woman's lips. "But it's only wood." He frowned.

"It will be enough." She backed toward the far wall.

He nodded at Cassandra and Lokke. "Both of you do the same. We don't know what will happen."

The old woman added, almost mocking, "A wise choice."

That didn't help the feeling Jonna had. If anything, it made it worse. He couldn't trust her, he knew that, and yet something told him this was the only way. Raising the staff, Jonna aimed the butt end of the staff at the lettered plate, pulled back, and struck.

The plate imploded; the pieces sucked into the void around the casket. The action pulverized the shattered remains into dust and then shot them out in a whirlwind.

The onslaught caught Jonna and hurled him against the wall. As he dropped to the floor, he felt warm liquid on his neck. He groaned; not twice in one day!

He grunted but shrugged off help to get up. "We need to get that casket out."

The old woman watched amused and picked up her staff. It, too, was tossed across the room. "So young." There was a knowing look in her eyes, and he could hear the unspoken words, 'and unlearned.'

He turned from her. "You knew that was going to happen. You could have done it in a different way."

She shrugged. "It's not my quest. Mine's another."

The statement made him pause, but they had come too far to stop now. Between the three of them, Jonna, Lokke, and Cassandra, they lowered the casket to the ground and dusted it off. The old woman did not twitch a finger to help. Jonna studied the seals on the casket. "Suggestions on how to open this?"

The old woman knew he was addressing her. "Try the latch."

The latch, ornately molded with multiple runes, held the top down and was placed in the center. He lightly touched the latch. Before flipping it up, he bent down for a closer inspection.

Three sharp pieces of the metal protruded beneath the catch, exactly where the latch would be grasped. Had Jonna grabbed it with his fingers, the sharp pieces would have slashed his fingertips. Why trap the latch? You would think Fabius was some sort of villain.

He remembered the request by Fabius to free him, and the summary-like explanation about him showing up in the Otherworld. Cassandra had stated misgivings, and now, there was this old woman leading them to the prize but keeping the details to herself.

Motioning the others back, he turned pointedly to the old woman. "How about you open the casket?"

The old woman smiled sadly. "I cannot. It is not my destiny to do this thing, or, most assuredly, I would have done it a long time ago." She threw back the hood, motioning to her long gray hair. "His curse is my curse. He was banned to the Otherworld; I was banned to walk these catacombs."

Starting to fold his arms, Jonna thought better about it. He needed to keep an open mind. "Why was this done?"

Levity was back in her voice. "So many questions from the young, but I will answer this. Fabius and I were caught in a war with the giants. When the Flower of Reina was brought, the humans of this land were enslaved to do the giant's bidding. It was then we were placed here, both of us, separate and yet always together."

"You fought the giants?"

Her smile mocked him. "We did."

"I don't believe her," Cassandra stepped up. "There is something about it that is not right."

"She's telling the truth," Lokke assured. "I remember the stories Fabius told. Both were enslaved when the giants came."

Jonna turned to stare at Lokke. "You knew this old woman and didn't tell us?"

Lokke swallowed. "N—not really. I only knew there was another."

Jonna rubbed the back of his neck. Was this some sort of trap? The old woman admitted she could not free Fabius; someone else had to. If they did not, both Fabius and the old woman would be stuck here. On top of that, Väinämö had also agreed that this was his task. So why the consternation?

The old woman's voice held urgency. "It is important that you free Fabius. If you do not, all you have attained will be undone."

His action of facing down the giants rolled back through his mind. He could see the running of the slaves, along with the killing and death that the giants wrecked upon them. He

290

could feel the magic as it crackled down and struck the street in all directions. This could not be allowed to happen again; the giants could not be allowed to rule the slaves.

Jonna looked into the old woman's eyes. What she said was true, and yet, some part of him said by doing this, she would gain in unexpected ways.

"The latch," she said firmly. For the first time, Jonna noticed how tight she was clutching her left hand. It was the hand he had dropped the petals into. "Open it."

Jonna reached down, worked his way under the catch, and carefully avoided the sharp spikes. The latch lifted slowly until it snapped up. The room around them went still as the noise of the pop echoed away.

The old woman saw nothing but the casket. "Now," she licked her lips, "open the top."

Cassandra stepped forward to help, Lokke somewhat more reluctant, but Jonna waved them away. If something bad happened, he did not want them too close.

He heaved, barely managing to lift the lid. When the air hissed, he released it. The casket rumbled, stopped, lifted slightly, and rumbled again. Warily, Jonna stepped back. The lid shot off with the third rumble and headed for the old woman. Her staff lashed out, struck the top, and shattered it into a million pieces.

Fabius stood at the head of the casket. "Witch, I knew you'd be here," but he did not step from within. "Did you think to entrap me as I woke from the Otherworld?"

"It was never about entrapment," the old woman cackled. "I simply wanted these." She showed him the petals which lay in her hand. "Find them if you dare, Fabius! *Cantaksah!*"

Chapter 20

PINK IS HER COLOR

Blinding light leaped from the petals and encircled the old woman's body. Wrinkled flesh became unlined. Gray hair turned a blondish-brown. The yellow light on the staff sparkled brighter.

The cackling voice was gone. A high, taunting, seductive voice took its place. "I've waited a long time for this Fabius. We'll see who lives to win this war." She turned toward Jonna. "And you, we most certainly will meet again. Once Fabius is defeated, you will be mine. Thus says Lezevel, queen in the land of the giants." With a strike of her staff, she faded away.

Jonna stared at the spot where she had been. "What have I done?"

Fabius laughed. With a wave of his hand, he dismissed the exit. "She over dramatizes; never mind her. However, I would appreciate it if you could help me out of this casket. Please?"

Cassandra hurried to his side. "Of course."

Fabius admired her cape. "A pleasure to see you again, young lady, but you do seem to be different." He touched his chin, "Becoming undead, are we?"

Eyes wide, Cassandra nodded. "I'm changing."

"And you will," he frowned, "for as long as you remain

out of the Otherworld. There's a reason for gates, you know." He said it as a joke, but when no laughed, he dropped it.

Jonna's voice got Fabius' attention. "But we didn't go through the gates."

"Didn't go through the gates?" Fabius looked stunned. "Really?" The brightness in his eyes increased.

Jonna nodded. "Really. We found a way through Asgard." When Fabius didn't know what he was talking about, he translated the word. "I mean, Ethese."

"Ethese? I'm impressed. However, you know what that means?" He took in the face of all three. "You have to go back."

"We have to go back for Cassandra. She has to be returned."

"That too," Fabius nodded, "but there's more. Since you did not leave by the gates, you must go back to go out the gates."

"But I didn't go through the gates to begin with," Jonna countered. "Dagda brought me."

"Exactly." He waved it away and looked at the devastation. "She has quite a temper." The mage chuckled.

Jonna paused, not making the connection. "Are we talking about the same thing, or have you changed subjects?"

"Talking?" Fabius made a funny smile. "Sorry about that. My mind drifted for the moment. What were we talking about?"

"Dagda? The gates? He did not bring me through them."

"Entering the Otherworld with Dagda is the same as entering through the gates." The mage shrugged. "If you leave with him to the surface, it also counts the same."

"So either I go back with Dagda—"

Lokke grinned sarcastically. "I'd try that first."

Jonna threw him a glance. "—or we have to attempt the gates. In any case, Cassandra and Lokke must go back."

"Well—yes," Fabius thought for a moment, "he definitely does. She does too, unless of course—"

"I want stay who I am," Cassandra spoke doggedly. "I don't want to lose my memories!"

Fabius sighed. "Then you'll have to make the journey."

"Is there no other way?" Jonna's mind rolled with this turn of events.

"Not that I know of," Fabius winked, "but then, I can't do cross-magic." A faint humor stayed in the air.

"Are you telling me—"

"I'm not saying anything," Fabius said firmly. "Do you want me to get my mage license revoked?"

Jonna wrinkled his brow. Väinämö had never said anything about a mage license. "You have a mage license?"

Fabius pulled out a small piece of metal. On its surface were some numbers and letters. After showing it to all, he stuffed it back where it came from.

Jonna was bewildered. Why had Väinämö never mentioned a mage license? "But who issues a license for mages?"

"The Mage Consortium, of course." Fabius looked flabbergasted. "Surely you've heard of them?"

Jonna shook his head. "If there's a Mage Consortium who issues licenses, why didn't they stop the Dark Mages?" He could feel his face heating up. "And why don't they police their own?"

"Calm down," Fabius laughed it away. "They never get involved in minor disputes."

"Minor disputes?" A funny thought crossed Jonna's mind. "You're not related to Väinämö, are you?"

Fabius looked perplexed. "Väinämö who?"

"Väinämö—" Jonna shook his head. "Well, he certainly knows of you." He shrugged. "Never mind."

The ground shook. Dust fell from the ceiling.

"There they are." Fabius chuckled. "Ready to go finish this once and for all?"

Jonna paused. "Isn't this your battle now?"

"What kind of mage would I be if I didn't share?" Fabius feigned offense but gave a small grin. "Besides, I want to see the look on Lezevel's face when we both show up together." A wicked grin interrupted the smaller one. "This is going to be fun. See you in a minute."

Jonna took a step toward him. "Where are you going?"

"To bring in reinforcements, of course." Fabius shook his head, staring at the ceiling. "Wisdom is lost on the young."

As if to block the door, Jonna stepped over though he knew it would do no good. "But how do we get out?"

Fabius waved and vanished, leaving all three standing in a room with four oil lamps, a destroyed gold coffin lid, and one empty casket. The ground above them shook. Supports shifted. He waved toward the door. "Come on!"

They reached the first corner with Lokke huffing behind them. "Can you slow down a minute?"

Jonna glanced at them. Cassandra did a good job keeping up, but why Lokke was so out of shape made no sense. His eyes switched to the front. In the dim light, Jonna was not sure which way they had come.

"Go right," Cassandra answered the unspoken question, "while Lezevel kept you distracted, I was counting paces. We turn right here, go up thirty-five steps, and take a left. I'll continue from there, so we don't get confused." A rumble shook the tunnel.

He breathed a sigh of relief. Cassandra was right. Lezevel had purposefully kept the conversation going, stretching it out so Jonna would not pay attention to the path they took.

The thundering overhead threatened to bring the ceiling down. Dust and rocks rained. Supports split and cracked. Was it the curse of Lezevel and Fabius which had kept it together all these years? As they raced down the corridors, the ground shook.

Cassandra noticed the pensive look on Jonna's face. "You are troubled."

With Cassandra being such an adept guide, he had not realized they dropped into silence. Despite this, he laughed. "Sorry about that." He forced a smile on his face. "I was thinking."

"Thinking of what to do when we get to the surface. Thinking of how we are to make it to the Otherworld. Thinking of your family, and if you'll ever get back."

She had mirrored his thoughts almost exactly, almost. "That's the gist of it." He felt tired. "Since I arrived in Elfleda's world, I have done nothing but battle one creature after another. A constant progression of evil tyrants and their minions, these beings do nothing but try to hurt others."

Cassandra seemed surprised. "Was it not so in your world too?"

"Not like this. Not in this way."

"Do you miss it?"

It was only a second before he answered, but that second took forever. His own world was mundane. It was limited to ordinary happenings, not magic, mages, and killer giants. And yet, in their own way these creatures existed there as well, only as human creations.

"Yes. No." Jonna half-shrugged. "Maybe. We called some of them government, technology, corporations, and taxes," he gave a small laugh, "among other names, but it's all different here. Who would have guessed I would be a mage? Väinämö said there is magic in all realities—" he noted the word realities went over her comprehension, "—lands. There is magic in all lands."

Cassandra nodded. "So we have seen. Yet, you cross those boundaries in ways no mage ever did."

"By luck."

She shook her head. "By The Sight, that you have not accepted. In all of us, magic exists. For some, it is obvious; it drives us to do things when others cower in fear. For others, it is hidden; it allows us to live a life from beginning to end never having to face danger. In both cases, it is there, ready to do what we will allow."

"You'd make a good cheerleader." Jonna could not help but chuckle. "I can see why you made such a great mother."

Cassandra blushed, though Jonna saw the word 'cheerleader' did not register. She moved the conversation away from herself. "How did you meet Väinämö?"

"Väinämö was the first mage I encountered. He helped me when I was trying to save my wife. Why?"

"You compared him to Fabius."

Jonna laughed. From the look on Cassandra's face, this was the reaction she was trying to get. "They do act like each other. Lots of jump-in-here, jump-in-there, usually help, but forget what they are doing."

"I'm glad Fabius turned out to be good." She sighed. "From the way we met and his associations," she glanced at Lokke, "I was starting to doubt it."

"Hey." Lokke had not been listening. He was focused on staying near the wall when a rumble hit, but he caught that. "I should take offense."

"You probably should," Jonna chuckled at him, "but you won't. Instead, you'll take it as a compliment."

The half-demon grinned. "Of course, what half-demon wouldn't?"

"We're here." Jonna moved up stairs and traveled around a bend. He stayed close to the side, peered out, and checked to see if the coast was clear. He felt Cassandra's touch on his shoulder, looked in her direction, and followed her pointing finger as it spotted a billow of dark smoke.

The black clouds were gone, but the day moved toward night. The stars shone in a sky clear as twilight descended, and a full moon lit the streets. The dark smoke rose as its edges reflected the light of the moon.

Fabius had not said where to go when they reached ground level. He had not indicated when he would return.

As they stepped out into the street, there were distant murmurings with the flicker of torches casting eerie glows. The trio followed the sounds. They had found the meeting on Fisher's Block.

"Here, here!" A loud, boisterous man called. He struck a mallet on a wooden box. "We need order!"

Another part of the city shook. Those gathered ignored the rumblings and the man's words, but gradually the sound of the mallet pierced the voices. One by one, the area quieted.

"That's better," the man glared. "Does anyone know what made the giants attack?"

A single man stood and looked around at the large assembly. He spoke in quiet tones. "I was there. Somebody stole petals."

Silence dropped. Rumblings were heard in the distance.

The man with the mallet nodded and pursed his lips. "So the time has come. We must fight."

An uproar sounded as everyone voiced opinions.

"Order!" The mallet man struck. "We must do this with order! For those of you who are new, this assembly has long had a plan for this contingency."

"But the sky," someone called to the right. "The sky burned. This is the omen." Murmurs echoed agreement. The mallet struck until silence resumed.

"As I was saying, we laid out a plan a long time ago. There is no need to panic. If anything, what happened will speed us along—"

"To where?" another older voice called standing to his feet. "With the city gone and giants trying to kill us, all we have known will change. Do you expect us to toil in the fields like common men of burden? We are men of culture. We do not have callouses on our hands."

The man with mallet glared. His voice rose. "You would stay slaves of the giants, even as they try to kill us?"

"We did no wrong and did not steal the petals. The real questions should be, who did, and how can we turn them over."

Cassandra's hand hooked Jonna's arm and pulled him into the shadows. Lokke dropped back and tucked into a corner.

The man with the mallet gazed around the room. "Do not be deceived. They would take the person you offered and make an example of all the rest. Who they don't kill, they will hurt. Those that survive will be tortured. Do you remember the legends of old, how this city came to be? Built on the bones of us, our ancestors—"

"And yet, the omen says," the older voice had not sat down, "the offering of the offender will right the wrong."

The man with the mallet growled. "You are mad. Everyone knows those words can be translated a million different ways."

"No," the older man pointed, "we are all mad to fight the giants!"

Lezevel's voice called from in front of the man with the mallet, "The omen is two-fold." A brightness formed, and she stepped out of thin air dressed in queenly apparel. "You translate incorrectly, oh foolish one." She waved a finger at the older voice.

The man's eyes widened as he took his seat. "Lezevel."

"Yes," she took pleasure in hearing her name, "it is I. It is time to fight the giants, but greater than that is at stake. Fabius is here as well."

"Fabius," the murmur moved throughout the crowd. The old man narrowed his eyes. "But Fabius is dead."

"No more than I am banished," her voice echoed off the walls. "The spell is broken, removed by the most unlikely of heroes."

"Hey," Lokke started forward, but Jonna threw him a warning look.

She continued, "Which presents us a way to rid the land of Fabius for good. Who will be my faithful servants?" She struck the end of her staff on the platform, and tiny points of a pinkish light rippled across the floor. Whoever they touched, a look of wonder crossed their face. The whisperings stopped. In their place, a low chant built. "Lezevel, Lezevel, Lezevel... !"

Jonna backed to the entrance, snagged Lokke, and felt Cassandra's hand grab his arm. "Time to leave," he whispered. The pinkish ripples went out in a radius, stopping short of the shadows along the walls.

"Queen in the land of the giants," Cassandra huffed. "If she has to use magic to get a man—"

Jonna laughed.

"It's true," she stated firmly. "I don't know what Fabius sees in her!"

"Fabius?"

"You saw his reaction in the catacombs. Despite his battles with her, he holds her in high affection."

Now that Jonna thought about it, Fabius did give a hint of affection. "Hmm, come to think of it, she also acted—you don't think they were—?"

Cassandra nodded. "I do think. I think something happened that drove them apart. While they bickered with each other, the giants came."

"So we're in the middle of a lover's quarrel?" Lokke howled with glee. "This is going to be fun!"

Cassandra's eyes widened. "Fun? Don't you know what happens in this sort of thing?"

"What?" Lokke begged. "Come on, tell me!"

Jonna chuckled. "You mean, in all the years you've been around, you've never been caught in the crossfire of two people in love?"

"Now, that really hurts," the half-demon put his right hand on his heart. "What's love got to do with it?" He looked from one to the other. "For a demon, it's just plain s—"

Holding up his hand, Jonna stopped him. "Too much information."

"Surreal." He frowned at Jonna. "What did you think I was going to say?"

Cassandra shook her head. "It's bad enough between a woman and a man, but a female mage and male mage? That's dangerous."

The half-demon rubbed his hands together. "This is going to be good."

Jonna groaned. "It might be better if we left."

"Leave?" Lokke stared at them. "We can't leave. We promised Fabius we would help."

"We didn't promise," Jonna corrected. "He assumed, and you know what that makes of you and me?"

The last part threw Lokke. "No, what?"

Jonna stared at him. Since he really couldn't tell which language he spoke, due to the magic, maybe the letters didn't look the same. In English, he knew it was a play on words. Assume: ass-u-me.

The half-demon squinted at him. "You're trying to confuse me. He needs our help with the giants." He begged, "We can't let him down."

Cassandra scolded him. "You don't care anything about the giants. You want to see what will happen between Lezevel and Fabius. If you had cared," she glowered at him, "you would never have left Jonna and I when we faced them down."

The half-demon huffed. "Do you always have to bring that up?" With a sniffle, tears formed on his cheeks. "I was only—"

Had they in truth hurt his feelings? Jonna wasn't sure, but the presence of tears made him wonder. Even Cassandra was starting to soften.

"—I'm not as brave as—" he sniffled again and pointed at both. "—as—as you two." A tear finished running down his cheek, dropped off, and dashed against the road.

Cassandra raised her hand and slapped him on back of the head.

Lokke shifted toward her and showed bewilderment. "What was that for?"

She growled. "For trying to play us."

Despite the sting, he grinned, rubbing the back of his head. "But you've got to admit, I was pretty good." His face beamed, looking for agreement. "Better than last time?"

Jonna stuck an arm out, stopping her from going further. "Shh!" They had moved a few streets over, and a block or two up, but here the streets were not quiet.

Giants carrying torches came up the road. They marched to the step of one, two, three, thump, and each time they thumped, the ground rumbled.

"What are they trying to do?" Cassandra watched them repeat it.

"They're trying to intimidate. It lets everyone know they are in control of the city."

"So what do we do?"

"We meet on the Field of Hel." Fabius appeared, stood beside the three, and gazed at the approaching giants.

Lokke grinned. "Fabius, how have you been? Great to have you back. Have you seen Lezevel lately?" He winked.

The mage was caught off guard. "Have you?"

"Unfortunately, yes," Jonna said solemnly. "She turned a bunch of slaves into zombies."

"A trademark of hers," he waved it away. "What color was the spell? Pink?"

"How did you know?"

"Pink's her favorite color."

Jonna thought about that one. "How did you know that?"

"Pink's her favorite color."

"You already said that, and that's not what I asked. How did you know pink was her favorite color?"

Fabius stopped; his gaze moved from one to the other. He caught the gleam in the half-demon's eyes. "Is there a point to this?" He glanced toward the advancing giants. "If not, we should be going."

Lokke squared his shoulders, stepped forward, and grinned widely. "We think you are either in love with Lezevel or were in love. We think this is a lover's quarrel."

Fabius stepped back and stared. "Well, I've never—you're serious?" His face turned red. "I'll have you know, I am not in love with Lezevel and not likely to be doing that tomorrow. Whether you three realize it or not, this situation is serious. We have giants to battle, and it won't be easy. I expect each of you, each of you," he pointed a finger, especially at Lokke, "to be ready to win tomorrow. Humph!" He turned around and looked up at the starry sky. "In love indeed!" The mage vanished.

"Well, that takes care of that." Lokke looked up the street; the giants moved closer. "So what about them?" he pointed a thumb. "Are you going to blast them with lightning again?" His eyes lit up.

Frowning, Jonna looked at Lokke. "If you hadn't jumped

in feet first, it wouldn't be necessary. As it is, it still isn't, at least not yet." He looked up and spoke to the air. "We might be a lot more help tomorrow if we knew where the Field of Hel was."

"Who are you talking to?" Lokke looked around. "Fabius is gone."

"No, he's not. Give him a moment to calm down."

Cassandra drew their attention. "A moment may be all we have."

The giant in front stopped the march and turned his head to find their voices. When his eyes spotted them, he motioned to a few of his warriors. "You four, get them!" The road bounced, stones jumped, and walls shook.

As the trio bounced, they tried to steady themselves. Jonna pointed his right hand at the warriors bearing down upon them. "*Qisvo!*"

A rumble followed the ping of glass, and Jonna cringed. He kept forgetting that was demoneze. A burst of lightning shot down. It struck four times around the approaching giants. A roar of pain went up as the giants crashed to the ground.

The leader of the giants was unimpressed. "It takes more than lightning to kill us! Ready? Launch!"

More than a hundred, hungry, bladed shafts, sliced the nighttime air. In sparkles, the bronze-colored points reflected the light of the moon. There were too many to dodge. The trio dived for cover.

Spears bounced off walls and buildings; some zipped over their heads. Fabius' disembodied voice came from nothing. "Here!"

A strange oval appeared behind the three as two hands reached out, grabbed Jonna, and yanked. Jonna flew backwards, dragging Cassandra and Lokke. As they passed through the oval, they skidded to a stop and bumped across a thick carpet of green and red. The giants were gone.

"Where are we?" Jonna gazed up at the decor of the room. It was decorated with silver candle holders and oil lamps. The walls looked like murals, woven together on thick carpet as one continuous piece. The ceiling and the floor was of the same material but with patterns of red, blue, and green.

"A tent?" Cassandra asked. Wooden poles held up the roof and sides, not completely hidden by the decorations.

"The campsite for the battle," Jonna was sure. Off to one side, wings of the tent went to individual sleeping quarters. The door hangings were rolled back and tied.

"At least the floor's soft." Lokke bounced up and down on the carpet. "That street would have been hard."

Fabius glared down at them. "Is that all you can say? A little *thank you* might be in order."

"Thank you," Jonna chimed. "It was taking a moment to get our bearings."

"Well, you better be ready for tomorrow." The mage's eyes narrowed. "There are no second chances when it comes to death."

"Except for you," the half-demon grinned, "and Lezevel."

"Half-death," the mage countered and refused to catch the joke, "and Lezevel had nothing to do with it. We joined to fight the giants, but not before they prepared a trap. While we bickered over our next move, the giants netted us. Because of the bickering, they decided to curse us together. That's why I was in the Otherworld and Lezevel was in the catacombs. They thought we were a," he cleared his throat, "badly married couple."

Jonna asked solemnly, "So, you aren't lovers?"

"Of course not," Fabius' anger leaped out. "She is evil, bad for this land, can't make up her mind, always has to have her own way, no tolerance for the unexpected—" Exasperated, he waved his hand. "I could go on and on. Why do you think I would ever be interested in her?"

Cassandra, who waited quietly, answered, "She acts like a woman who has been spurned."

"She—" Fabius pointed a finger. "And that's enough from you, young lady. I may be a good mage, but I do have my limits!"

"Oh really?"

Fabius' shoulders dropped. "No, I am a good mage. Maybe that's why I could not bring myself to hurt her."

The three said at once, "What?"

"Why do you think I wanted the three of you to join me?" He nodded toward the front door. "Of course the giants, but as soon as they're done, Lezevel will be right here, young and vibrant, battling me, a worn out, old mage."

Extra petals were still in Jonna's pocket. "Fabius—"

"I know," the mage shook his head, "it should not matter. Magic is magic, but I can't help but feel the years I've lost. Trapped in the Otherworld, I aged away in that casket."

"Fabius, I—"

"Sorry to act this way," the mage looked at the trio. "Can you forgive for me for the tongue-lashing?"

Jonna reached in his pocket, pulled out three petals, and extended them. "Fabius!"

The mage's head snapped toward him. His gaze fell upon the three petals lying upon Jonna's palm. Astonishment brightened his eyes. "For me?"

"Hold out your hand."

As Fabius reached forward, the petals fluttered into his palm. Using a finger to position them into a triangle, he took three steps back. "*Cantaksah!*"

A circle of light engulfed him, changing the old, wrinkled face to chiseled, angular features. The gray hair altered to jet black. His eyes shown with the fire of youth.

"Thank you," a clear, concise voice responded. "We shall see who is surprised on the battlefield tomorrow. In the meantime, all of you should rest."

Chapter 21

OLD MAJIK COMES IN TWOS

The covers around Jonna were silky soft. The mattress, whatever it was made of, was firm and comfortable. Despite these most superb accommodations, he could not sleep.

At Fabius' invitation, all three had moved off to their separate quarters. Cassandra's growl had been heard as she ordered Lokke out of hers.

Jonna could not help but smile. First, the two fought like crazy, and now Lokke acted like a lovesick pup. On top of this, there was something between Fabius and Lezevel.

No matter how much Fabius denied it, it was obvious to all but him. Maybe it was obvious to all but her as well? What would that mean when they met the giants tomorrow? Love was a driving force very few people could control. He couldn't. Look at what happened to him when dark mages took his wife.

The thought of Elfleda made Jonna wonder what time it was in the city of the woodland elves. Was she up and about or trying to sleep like he was? Had anything else befallen her or Elpis? Thinking of Elpis brought him back to Cassandra. With Cassandra becoming undead, could she still sense her daughter?

He was worrying. It was not like him to worry. Fret a little, maybe, but... Focus on the happy times. Elfleda rescued, Elpis coming to their home, Elpis calling him daddy—

Jonna's heart relaxed. Despite his initial panic at the great responsibility, he loved the fact he was the little girl's dad. After all, he had survived the rigors of the Otherworld and come out again—well, almost. He sighed. They still had to go back to save Cassandra and rid Lokke of the curse.

The idea to let Cassandra see Elpis seemed foolish now. Cassandra was dead and could not survive outside the Otherworld. On top of that, could Cassandra go back to Bliss after breaking the Otherworld's rules?

His heart beat faster. No wonder he could not sleep. The only hope was to push them away and let things take their natural course. Well, as natural as magic could make it.

That word 'natural' stayed in his mind. He still was not sure he belonged here. The idea of magic banged against the left side of his brain. In a way, it made sense, yet it violated every law of nature he knew. There was no such thing as magic, yet time and again it had worked. He had even seen the source of the magic with the dragon Dagurunn.

Jonna closed his eyes. Morning was coming, and he needed the rest. He turned this way and that.

There was the prophecy of the child, mentioned by Siardna. What had she called it? The Alfgiefuenid? If the prophecy were real, why hadn't Elfleda said something?

Enough. He brought the cover over his head, cut off most of the light, and mumbled quietly, "Ninety-nine, ninety-eight, ninety-seven, ninety-six..."

His mind twitched. Images fluttered into view. They disappeared and reappeared, hanging on the fringes of his conscious mind. Good, he was beginning to dream, and once dreaming began, sleep would follow—if only that were true.

A huge gate stood before his eyes, secured, yet held shut by nothing. He could hear the voice of Fabius, telling him again of the three trials he must conquer to pass out of the gate: what you don't know, what you do know, what you will know. Fabius' older form fluttered away changing into a host of butterflies.

'Choose,' he heard in the voice of the fates. 'What do you see?' They fluttered away as well.

'Nothing,' he heard his own voice answer. 'I see nothing in the surface of the water.'

Jonna lurched upward, fighting to become awake. In front of his bleary eyes, odd shapes, stretching and changing, danced around him.

"You are an intruder," a wispy finger pointed at him. "You do not belong."

"It is time to leave," another called out using a sensual, female voice. "Your loved one awaits impatiently."

"You cannot fight that which you don't know," a third had formed, floating to his right. "Leave while you can or lose all you hold dear."

Jonna rubbed his eyes and attempted to see what was not defined. Looking from the solid objects in the room to the shadowy images, he realized it was not his eyes, but the beings themselves. "The Tjaard. Thank you for meeting me." This explained the uneasy thoughts and dreams. They tried to manipulate him.

There was a pause in the voices.

Jonna nodded. "So you are not only protection spells, but beings that can think. I am pleased that we could have this conversation."

"This one is intelligent," the female voice shifted closer to Jonna. "He sees us for what we are."

The deeper male voice was stubborn. "Our position is clear, and our mission is certain. There can be no exceptions. He did not succumb to the petals. He cannot be allowed to stay."

"I sense no threat," the female voice reached out a wispy hand, touching Jonna's face. "He survived where others had not."

"He had help," the male voice boomed. "Had he not, he would be claimed."

Jonna studied the female's shadowy face. The faint light in the room showed long hair with a narrow face and darkened eyes. The Sight hit him. "You want to be free."

308

"Our desire is not ours to command," the male voice pushed his way forward. "We are what we are. There can be no change. Do not try to distract us from your own end."

The female figure spun on the male, a whirlwind of light and shadow. "Perhaps that is your desire. You want to keep us here."

"I am the elder," the male voice boomed. "I have been here the longest, and know the truth."

Up until now, Jonna had been fishing, trying to find out what these beings were about. He had confirmed they were individuals, he had confirmed they could think beyond their mission, and now he knew they had trouble in the ranks. That feeling of The Sight burst into Jonna's mind. "But the truth of what? A truth of loneliness? A truth of giving up?"

The male shadowy voice blared at Jonna. "It is not our plight under discussion. It is yours."

"You are right." The female pointed her shadowy finger at the male voice. "We are the youngest. We know the desire of what was lost. But you," her ghostly finger floated in front of the others' face, "have given up, seeing no way of going back."

"The human male plays you," the male voice formed shadowy hands and used them to indicate the other. "He turns us against each other, defeating our cause." It glared. "Are you this gullible after all the times we have faced intruders? You call me old and you young, but time is a relative thing. Tell him how long it has been."

The female looked down, emotion draining from her voice. "Hundreds of years."

"And for me thousands," the male voice echoed, "but what of it? We are who we are. We can never go back." As the male voice dropped away, cold stillness seeped into the room.

Jonna dared to break the silence. "What happened?"

The female spoke first. "It—it happened—"

The male voice boomed, "No, do not do it!"

The female's features became harsher. "—a long time ago."

"I said no!"

309

"Be gone," and with a heaving of her shadowy chest, she blew a ghostly wind. The other Tjaard swirled in a whirlpool of light and dark, fading away.

Jonna watched the whirlpool vanish. Whatever had taken place, he was sure the other two would not be back as long as she was here. "Has it really been hundreds of years?" As she turned toward him, he saw a tear fall down her cheek.

"It has." The female voice sighed. "I shouldn't have done that." Squinting her eyes at nothing, he knew she bordered on leaving. It was important that she stay for both their sakes.

"It seems the others do not listen."

"No." She looked up at him and searched for his sincerity. "They do not listen. Their minds are closed."

"Tell me your story. There may be some way I can help."

Hope was in her eyes. "You would help one that would kill you?"

"I would."

Watching him intently, her voice was wary. "It is not a ploy to save yourself?"

Jonna laughed. "No, I do care."

The female Tjaard turned away. "This land was unprotected before the giants came to rule. The giants lived in the cold north. The humans lived near the coast. In order to protect the land, our queen sought the ability to create sentinels. These beings were to function as the ultimate guardians and keep the coast safe."

Jonna could hear an implied 'but' coming. "Something went wrong?"

The female figure nodded as the words came slowly. "The deal the queen struck to create these sentinels was made with the leader of the giants." Her eyes narrowed as she turned back. "He was anxious, too anxious."

Jonna prodded her gently. "And?"

"And, although warned," her eyes stared at the memories, "gave no heed to those warnings. The price was paid. The coast secured—"

He inhaled. "And the queen got more than she bargained for."

The female voice looked away. "How do you know these things?"

"It seems to be a running theme."

With narrowed eyebrows, she looked at him.

"The story is not unusual." He reached out a hand to reassure her, but the hand passed through.

A shadowy smile hit her face. "I appreciate the effort."

"Do you know how the arrangement can be reversed?"

A look of fear crossed her face. "You cannot. If this is done, the coast will not be protected."

"I think protection from the outside world is not the problem. The giants used this to enslave the humans. For them alone, you were tricked into protecting the borders."

Disbelief, possibility, and horror sank in. Gazing at her shadowy hands, she moved them with palms held up. "We have done this?"

His voice was solemn. "I'm afraid so." He started to raise her shadowy chin and caught himself. "But there is hope." His eyes dared hers to meet his gaze. She did.

"Hope," her voice echoed. The ghostly eyes brightened. "In the morn, I will help you fight the giants. No more will they enslave our people."

"Thank you—" Jonna paused. "I don't know what to call you."

Her voice was sad. "The Tjaard have no individual names—" A look of wonderment crossed her face. "—but, I remember—remember—"

"You remember who you are."

"Yes," her eyes held the wonder, "but the name is so far away. Ar—armi—" An incredulous look crossed her face. "Armida?" Excitement flooded through her. "They called me Armida! My mother—" Her face fell and tears flowed. "—she was so proud when I was chosen."

He frowned. "Armida, what's wrong?"

"She's dead," the female voice sobbed. "She died long ago, and I couldn't even remember."

"A lot of things may come back," he sympathized. "As you become who you were meant to be, I'm sure the memories will return."

There was hope in her voice. "But you will help me through this? I cannot turn to the others."

"I will help," he promised and prayed he could keep that oath. There was too much about the Tjaard he did not know.

Armida straightened. "And I will help, too," she promised. "Thank you. You have reminded me of who I am. I will be forever grateful." She blew a shadowy kiss in his direction. As it reached his face, his eyelids drooped. "Have no more disturbing dreams this night."

He found himself in his and Elfleda's bedroom. She was beside him. The warmth of her body touched his as they shifted. His fingers caressed her cheek. Their bodies intertwined, holding close, and somewhere in the back of his mind, he could hear her voice. 'Jonna, Jonna,—'

Cassandra's eyebrows rose. "Jonna, wake up!"

His eyes came slowly open.

With a frown, she caught the smile on his face. "And what have you been doing?"

"Visiting home," he mumbled while trying to figure out where he was. The tent walls and carpet drew him back. As his dream faded, reality returned like a slap. "Wow."

"You went home?"

"I was home." His eyes darted around the tent. "It must have been a dream."

"And some dream," Cassandra noted the disheveled mess of the bed.

He sat up on one elbow as the cover slid down his chest. "It's a little more complicated than that. I met the Tjaard last night."

"Here?" Fear spread across her face. "I knew we should have stayed together."

"It's not like that," he tried to calm her down, "but I think I know why you could not tell." He spotted his pants and nodded toward them. "If you don't mind?"

"Sure," Cassandra twisted around and waited.

"This." After slipping on his pants, he reached inside a belt pocket, pulled something out, and handed it to her. "The petals are used by the giants to enslave people and ward away the Tjaard. Unless a slave is processed with these, the Tjaard will hunt them down."

"So I—"

"Have been processed. I have not."

She noted when he pulled on his shirt. "And this matters how?"

"That's why you didn't know they were here. Otherwise, you would have been under their cold stare."

From the look on her face, she did not see the connection. "But what does this have to do with going home?"

"Armida—"

Cassandra's voice shook with anger. "Who is Armida?"

It came out with such venom, Jonna could have sworn she was jealous. "Cassandra, are you okay?" He followed her gaze; it ended at a second pillow. In the pillow, there was an indentation as if someone had been lying beside him. No other clues appeared. "It was a dream, right?"

Cassandra moved to a chair, took a seat, and faced the bed. Her face wore a scowl. "I don't know the dream. Tell me."

"It was after I met one of the Tjaard named Armida. The Tjaard were tricked into serving the giants. Armida promised to help us."

"That was part of the dream?"

"No, that was before the dream." He squinted, trying to remember the details, but the dream slipped away.

Her voice was icy. "And the dream was?"

This was making no sense to Jonna. "I can't remember." He looked at Cassandra. "All I know is, I was home."

Fabius strolled into the room with a carved wooden staff adorned with golden ends. Over his shoulder was a gold-threaded sash, lying against his flowing, blue robe. "It's time to get ready." He caught the looks on their faces. "Am I interrupting something?"

313

"We don't seem to know." Cassandra was curt. "We suspect we've had a visitor."

"No one came through my charms last night," Fabius assured. "This tent is well protected."

It was interesting to Jonna how confident Fabius was. Perhaps it was the reviving of his youth, but the issue at hand was something else entirely. How Cassandra was acting did not make sense to Jonna. If anything had happened, he was the one that should be upset. "Are there others beside ourselves?"

Fabius frowned. "If you'd like to be more clear—"

A female maid walked into the room. Her long black hair and flowing robes sparkled in the light. Cassandra stared as the maid placed a pitcher on a stand. The maid curtsied and made her way out.

"Obviously, we're not the only ones." Cassandra threw the mage a look, but Fabius was on the wrong page of thought.

"You think I own slaves?" He shook his head. "They are not servants. They are paid laborers. Do you think I would have slaves after what the giants have done to the us?"

Cassandra huffed. "You said there was no one else."

"I was talking of important people." Fabius stopped. "That didn't come out right." His face flushed. "I mean guests. Of course I have hired laborers. How else could I maintain everything and still have time to do my job?"

"This is not about you." Her eyes switched to Jonna. "It's about him."

Fabius didn't believe his own words, even as he spoke them; Jonna could see it on his face. "Did you bring someone else in here?"

Jonna shook his head. "No."

"Well then," Fabius pulled up one of the chairs, "what's this all about?"

The reaction Cassandra had taken, the unspoken accusation, the burning jealousy... "Come to think of it," Jonna turned to her, "what is this all about?"

Her cheeks turned a soft pink and stood out on the not-so-white skin of her face. The less dead she became, the more her natural color was returning. "I—I don't know." She leaned back in the chair, feeling faint.

"Cassandra, do you know who you are?"

"Of course I do." She took several deep breaths and closed her eyes.

Rising, Jonna knelt beside her chair. Perspiration formed on her forehead. When he touched her, she was clammy and cold.

"She's changing," Fabius watched him quietly, "and it may already be too late."

Jonna glanced at Fabius before his eyes returned to Cassandra. "No." He picked her up, noting Fabius had provided her a change of clothes, and laid her down on the unmade bed.

Her eyes blinked open; there was a sparkle within. "Miksim?" She smiled. "Miksim, you've come home!" She threw her arms around him, held on for dear life, and then pushed him away. "But Miksim, there's something wrong with me. The things I knew so clearly, they're fading. I don't know what to do. Our daughter," she looked around as if trying to make sense of her surroundings. "Where's Elpis?"

What would make more sense to Cassandra now? Should he play along with what she thought she knew or try to tell her the truth?

"Elpis—is staying with a friend, Cassandra." He hoped the speaking of her name would give her some orientation.

She closed her eyes. "That's nice." They popped open again. "What am I doing?" Throwing her legs over the side, she sat up. "We have giants to fight." The look on her face dared anyone to contradict.

"We have plenty of time," Fabius pretended. "In the meantime, you should rest."

Cassandra laid back. "That's right, we're going to have a baby together. I want to name her Elpis."

"I think you should sleep." Jonna helped her by placing her legs back onto the bed. He kissed her on the forehead.

"Nu-uh," she tapped a finger to her lips, "we're married now, remember?"

"Uh, sure," Jonna hesitated, but a moment later saw it was not necessary. She had fallen asleep. He turned to Fabius and whispered, "What's going on?"

"The process of becoming undead is mixing up her mind. Gradually, all her past will be forgotten. She won't even remember why she came here in the first place."

"What can we do?" Jonna knew the battle was about to begin, yet he hated to leave her here alone. What would happen if she woke up and walked away?

"I'll stay and watch her," Lokke volunteered enthusiastically.

Jonna shook his head. "I don't think so. Who knows what you would tell her."

"Oh, come on," he begged. "I promise, nothing bad."

Jonna shook his head.

"You don't trust me?" The emotion Lokke put into the words proved it was an act.

"Not this time. She needs some sort of stability, not someone playing mind tricks."

"Or treats?" The mischievous smile appeared on Lokke's face.

Fabius reached out and gently guided Lokke away from the room. "I think you and I should find something to do during the battle. A job of importance."

Lokke's eyes widened. "An important job?"

As the pair left, there was only Jonna in the room. Cassandra had been too long from the Otherworld; leaving her until after the battle would be the equivalent to killing her. But what could be done?

There was little time. When the battle began, she must be safe. He remembered the casket they found Fabius in. Could something like that work for Cassandra?

Maybe, but he did not know the magic involved. Could he take a chance using 'guess' magic, the magic he did so often, when a person's memories were on the line?

He closed his eyes and listened to the wind as it blew outside the tent. He didn't understand the depression on the pillow any more than Cassandra did. What had happened had been a dream, though what that dream was he could not tell.

Opening his eyes, he looked down at Cassandra lying upon the bed. Raising one hand, he imagined a dome-like energy field protecting her body and keeping it within a single moment. "*Circulus—*" An orange glow pulled from the air and surrounded Cassandra where she lay. "—*ab aeterno.*"

The Latin phrases were simple: 'Circulus', circle, and 'ab aeterno', from eternity. If it worked, the circle should protect her from the effects of time, halting the process of her changing until they could return her home. There were no footsteps, but Jonna knew Fabius was there.

"Ab aeterno," Fabius scratched his chin, "from the eternal?" He looked at Jonna. "I've never heard it put that way before." Studying the glowing bubble, the mage surmised the rest.

"I'm trying to hold her in a status field." He wondered if Fabius would understand the phrase 'status field'. "Remember when you were in the Otherworld?"

"Ah," the mage's face lit up, "like my casket in the catacombs, only she won't feel the changes of time."

Jonna nodded.

A horn, long and forlorn, blared. Jonna took one last look at Cassandra resting peacefully.

Fabius made a symbol with his hand, and a blue portal glowed into being.

Jonna noted the difference. "You used no words?"

The mage chuckled. "There is more to magic than words. As you learn, you will understand." He waved a hand toward the opening.

As Jonna stepped through, one moment he stood in the tent, and the next he stood on a high outcropping as the wind pulled at his hair. Below him, the battle tents spread out in both directions. Beyond that was an open field, and beyond that, the giants had formed a line. With the giant's armor reflecting sunlight, Fabius' army stared into a series of bright suns.

"They will expect us to send an emissary." Fabius laughed. "That's what they are waiting for and the purpose of the horn. Traditionally, the person sent out will state our intentions, and then will be forced to flee if the choice is war. When that happens, they will attempt to kill him."

"I will go. There is no sense in anyone else risking their life."

The mage mused over this. "You cannot take them all, and you will not be able to stop this war."

"Kill or be killed?" Jonna nodded. "That's not a foreign philosophy where I come from. Maybe we can find another way."

Fabius shook his head. "Not this time. You don't know them as I do. Conflict is part of the human experience, Jonna. It makes us who we are and brings out the strengths we never knew we had." He smiled. "I believe myself to be better because of my trip to the Otherworld. It opened my eyes to the giant's true intent."

The sensual voice of Lezevel faded in around them. "You let the young one go first, Fabius?"

"Lezevel, a pleasure," Fabius gave a bow. "I was wondering when you would show up."

"This is a boy's affair," she brushed it off, "not mine. I am queen, remember?"

Fabius gave a humorous smile. "But queen of what?" The mage could not help himself. "I see no ownership here."

"The land will be mine again," Lezevel assured. "It is only a matter of time."

Fabius scoffed. "You could not hold it before the giants. You will not hold it after."

She raised her staff to strike, but stopped. "No, our battle will be after the war. It makes no sense to duel before." Her look softened as if seeing Fabius for the first time. "You've changed." She turned toward Jonna. "What have you done?"

"We only gave him the gift we gave to you."

"What?"

Jonna saw conflict on her face. Part of her rose in anger, and yet the other part—

Calming down, she lowered her voice. "It seems the young mage may not be so naive after all." Her eyes bore into Jonna. "Could I have misjudged you?"

Jonna grinned. "Before I return, I take it you two won't be at each other's throats?"

"She won't try anything, yet." The mage threw a glance at Lezevel. "She still needs us."

"I do not!" Lezevel raised her staff again. "I should strike you both down just for the thought."

Fabius' eyes glowed with humor. "Please, do."

"I will," she warned but hesitated. "Fabius, you are still so infuriating!" Striking her staff on the ground, she vanished.

Again, the words popped out of Jonna's mouth, "And you're sure there's nothing between you?"

Fabius looked stern. His eyes left the field in front and moved toward Jonna. "I told you, she is evil."

"Have you considered she might be acting out to get your attention?"

"Like a petulant child?" He shook his head. "Why would she do that?"

"I take it you've known her for a very long time?"

"For a while." He rubbed his mustache in thought. "Could she truly be?"

"Infuriating is not normally a word you use with an enemy. It implies a desire to be understood."

The mage grinned. "No, I don't believe it."

The horn blew and echoed across the field.

"As amusing as this conversation has become," Fabius could not help a chuckle, "it's time to let them know our answer. Emissary, go tell them we are prepared for war."

Jonna's gaze took in the Field of Hel. Spotting a trail that led to the valley, he started down the side.

"What are you doing?" The mage moved his hand, and a blue portal appeared. "There are faster ways."

Jonna waved it away. "Thank you, but I need time to think."

"Godspeed."

The wind whipped the words away, blowing his hair and tugging at his clothes. His clothes. He sniffed his shoulder. Had Fabius cleaned them in the night?

The trail went behind the camp tents, moved up the middle, and headed toward the valley floor. At the base of the trail, he heard a noise.

Lokke backed up from a tent. "I will not," he glared. "I'd rather be thrown in the middle of battle than to help do that again!" Not watching where he was going, the half-demon backed into Jonna. "And you," the half-demon whirled around. Embarrassment crossed his face. "You aren't who I thought you were." His cheeks turned a deeper red.

"Obviously not." Jonna laughed. "What are they having you do?"

"Cleaning out chamber pots, because they say I'm so full of—" Lokke stopped and looked at Jonna. "I get it now." He hit himself on the forehead. "It was a joke."

Jonna burst out laughing and resumed his walk. "Well then, if you're through with the chamber pots, do you want to do something fun?"

"Fun?" Lokke's eyes sparkled. "Sure. What's up?" He picked up speed.

"I'm about to tell the giants we are going to war."

Lokke's pace slowed; his eyes watched as Jonna moved ahead. "That's fun?"

"Sure, didn't you say you'd rather be on the field of battle?"

Lokke mumbled, "Those chamber pots are looking better already." He hurried to catch up. "You're really going?"

"I'm really going," Jonna assured. "Are you sure you want to come?"

"You mean, I have a choice?"

"Of course you do. You're a friend."

"I—I am?" Something in Lokke's words made Jonna turn to look. A tear formed on his cheek, but the half-demon quickly wiped it away. "I am," he spoke proudly.

"Yes, you are, and I don't want you to get hurt."

Determination arrived in Lokke's voice. "I am coming." He moved forward, widened his stride, and matched Jonna.

They reached the center of the valley and crossed a narrow stream. The reflection of their faces in the water bounced up at them as they moved from stone to stone. Silt gave evidence of flooding.

Jonna mused out loud. "How many brothers does the giant king have?"

"What?"

"I was thinking of a story I learned long ago. It was about a small boy named David who slew a giant."

"With a stone?"

Jonna looked at him. "You've heard of it?"

"Only as a legend from far off in the east."

"You lived in the east?"

Lokke's eyes took on that mischievous smile again. "Despite my appearance, I have done some traveling. I am older than I look you know."

Jonna teased, "Even if you don't act it?"

"Of course," Lokke chuckled, "it's a part of my nature." His face shifted from carefree to serious. "But I'm not going to leave you this time, Jonna. I'll be there to guard your back."

"That's good to know," Jonna gave a fond smile. "The three of us have been through a lot together."

"We have." Lokke's eyes took on a faraway look, and for a moment Jonna thought he had The Sight. It was possible. Lokke could do magic in the Otherworld.

Jonna nodded at the bank of the stream. "Pick up three stones, will you?"

Lokke grinned. "Like the boy who slew the giant?"

"The story I heard was five. One for the giant and the others for his brothers."

The half-demon chose three, nicely rounded stones. "I don't know how many brothers this giant has. Will these do?" He admired how the light glistened off the rocks.

"Perfect."

As they approached, the line of giants loomed ahead. The reflecting armor was blinding. Each held a spear, a sword belted to their waist, and a shield held stationary by a human slave in front. It was interesting to note, despite their attack upon the humans, certain slaves were loyal. Loyal to the giants, or afraid of losing their way of life? Did the reason make a difference?

The horn blew the third time, and Jonna halted, waiting to see what would happen next. As the line of giants parted, a human slave was pushed forward. Even from this distance, they could see terror in his eyes.

"He doesn't want to meet us." Jonna spoke the words before realizing it. If what Fabius said was true, and he declared their choice for war, any in the field would forfeit their life.

Stopping within twenty feet of Jonna, the slave cleared his throat, and yelled, "Kyrillos, king of the frost giants, demands to know the reason you have gathered." His eyes went to Jonna but then noticed Lokke. He whispered, "Why are there two of you?"

Jonna returned with a question. "Is it against the rules?"

"Well, no," the slave paused, "but you have to admit, it is a little unusual." He leaned toward Jonna, "It's not the safest job."

A smile crept across Jonna's face. "Of that, I'm sure."

The man smiled, glad to see a rapport established. "And since we're having such a congenial time, how about it? Can I announce you agree to withdraw? We can all go back to the city. Of course, I'm sure there'll be some sort of punishment involved, but—"

Jonna shook his head. "I afraid not. We're going to war."

The slave's eyes widened.

"Nothing against you personally, though."

"Uh," the slave grimaced, "thanks. Are you certain?"

"You heard him," Lokke took a step forward, realized what he had done, and hurriedly stepped back. "Do it." His eyes went to Jonna, verifying he had done the right thing. Jonna nodded.

The slave glanced back. Jonna thought he could make out Kyrillos through the warriors' line by the largest tent. The slave cleared his throat to speak when Jonna held up a hand.

Hope shone in the slaves eyes. "You want to surrender now?"

Jonna shook his head. "No, let me make the announcement."

"But that's not procedure."

"What do you have to lose?"

The slave hesitated. "I—I see your point."

"Good. Then we are agreed?"

"Oh, why not?" The slave turned around to face the line of giants and motioned with one hand in Jonna's direction. "It's all yours."

Jonna bowed slightly. "Thank you." He fixed his eyes and raised his voice. "Why does the great Kyrillos send a slave to do a king's job?"

The line of giants murmured, but the king did not stir.

"Kyrillos, are you a giant or a coward?"

The slave made the universal sign for cut it out. When he saw neither Lokke nor Jonna was listening, he closed his eyes and shook his head.

It was not Kyrillos' voice. "Who dares call the king a coward?"

"It is I, Jonna, stranger to these lands. We know the giants will fight for their king, but will the king fight for the giants?" He had yet to identify the voice. It came from somewhere in the middle.

"Will Kahrlos not do?" Two giants pushed apart the line. Another stepped forward. "I am advisor and brother to Kyrillos the king."

"It's a start." Jonna nodded. "I take it you have advised your brother not to come forward?"

"Royalty does not bow to wishes of paupers," Kahrlos spat at the ground, "and you are no more than a nuisance."

"Would you like my answer, or shall I call another?"

"It is not your place to announce to the king. That honor was given to the slave who met you." Kahrlos' eyes bore down on the slave. "Speak!"

"Perhaps the slave would rather not die, since you value his life so little."

A rolling laugh came from behind the line of giants. Kahrlos frowned. Kyrillos stepped up, his head and neck shown at the side of his brother.

"You again?" Kyrillos moved to pass, but Kahrlos stopped him.

"Brother, no—"

"Am I not the king?"

Kahrlos nodded and allowed Kyrillos to pass. Kyrillos' armor gleamed. The ruby gem in helmet flashed as the king moved his head.

"I am here, mage," Kyrillos spoke the last word as a slur. "What would you say that I do not know?"

Jonna met his gaze. "There is no reason for this war."

A strange murmur went through the line of giants, but Kyrillos hushed them with an upheld hand. "I agree," the giant smiled. "Lay down your weapons, and I will see your punishment less severe."

Jonna looked up into the giant's eyes, his own eyes glinting with mirth. "May I speak?"

Kyrillos nodded. "You are entertaining me. How could I refuse?"

"I came to your land to free a man. One known to me as Fabius."

"That was his human name," the king concurred. "We called him by another." A quiet chuckle went down the line of warriors. "Please, proceed."

Jonna nodded. "What I found was a city, not unlike the great civilizations of my own world. Though I've only been here a short time, there is some merit to what you've created."

"Praise from a human?" A funny look crossed the giant's face. "What subtle deceit is brewing now?" Kyrillos nodded. "Continue."

The slave beside Jonna glanced toward the king. Lokke's brow furrowed.

"If the giants will agree to work with the slaves as equals and release the Tjaard from their curse, we will agree to lay down arms."

Fabius' exasperated voice appeared inside of Jonna's brain. "What are you doing?"

"I'm trying to stop a war," Jonna answered in the same way. "If peace is possible—"

"It is not! Jonna, there are some things, some natures that cannot be changed. The giants placed me in a half-dead state. They turned the human's against Lezevel and me by using the Flower of Reina."

"And yet, they did not kill."

"They knew better than to make us martyrs."

"So you think whatever they say, they will lie."

"Absolutely."

Jonna looked up at Kyrillos. Was it better to let it go or try to work out peace? When it came to the Dark Mages, there had been no choice, but here and now?

"I know what you're thinking," Fabius' voice spoke Jonna's thoughts, "but you weren't there! You've only experienced a little of what the giants did."

Jonna remembered something from his own land. "The sins of the fathers shall not be given to the sons."

Fabius' elevated voice abruptly dropped. "Jonna, these are the fathers."

Jonna looked to the line of giants. His stopped on Kyrillos. "What?"

"The giants that caught Lezevel and me—these are those."

"But—"

"That's impossible?" Fabius chuckled. "The giants of this land have a longer life span than humans. It is why there has never been any successful uprising. They agree to terms favoring the opposing side, wait for the perpetrators to die or entrap them, and do it again. It is a game they've played many times."

Jonna's eyes met Kyrillos'. What he had translated as a look of interest, now took on that of mockery. Before he could say another word, Kyrillos called to his brother. "What do you think, Kahrlos?"

Jonna knew Fabius was right. He had stepped into a spider's trap.

There was a slight smirk on Kahrlos' face. "Perhaps a diplomatic meeting..."

"The word is war," the voice of Fabius spoke quietly in his head. "If you will not say it, I will do it for you."

"I understand."

Kahrlos' words faded into focus. "...but it is ultimately your decision." Kahrlos nodded toward Kyrillos. Their voices drifted away again.

Jonna had to get Kyrillos to betray his plans, and they had to be heard by all the slaves everywhere. "Fabius, do you know a spell that will reveal the contents of Kyrillos' true thoughts?"

Fabius gave a small laugh. "Possibly, as long as he is not expecting it. What do you have in mind?"

Though it had not ended, Kahrlos' speech was coming to a close. If they were going to do something, it had to be quick. "What do you mean by 'not expecting it'?"

"Magic is somewhat dependent upon the individual's will. Kyrillos has been around for a long time. Therefore, he has built up a strong resistance to those types of spells. His resistance was the only thing that saved him when you struck him with lightning, destroying the city defenses. Also, certain things can be resisted by simply knowing they are done."

"He thinks I'm about to surrender the opposing force."

"Use the words, 'Ex abundanica cordis, os loquitor', which means 'from the abundance of the heart, the mouth speaks'. Focus upon your intent. If your will is strong enough—"

"It will work." Jonna was sure. "Ex abundanica cordis—"

Fabius finished at Jonna's hesitation, "Os loquitor."

Jonna focused on Kyrillos. "*Ex abundanica cordis, os loquitor.*" In addition, he added, "*Audio.*" 'Audio' was the Latin word for 'hearing'. If it worked as he intended, everyone in the Field of Hel should get a big surprise.

"Thank you, Kahrlos." Kyrillos' voice was clearer. "Your support in these times is of great importance." Kyrillos focused on Jonna. "And your offer to find a peaceful solution is admirable."

Jonna's smile was humble as he nodded.

"We will accept your terms..." Kyrillos smiled down toward Jonna.

Fabius voice began to rise. "Jonna."

"Give it time," he barely mumbled.

Lokke leaned near. "Give what time?"

"I'm talking to Fabius."

The half-demon grinned. "How?"

Placing his hands behind his back, Jonna continued to smile.

"Oh," Lokke's eyes darted around, "I get it. Mum's the word!"

The slave caught notice. "Who's Mum?"

Kyrillos switched to all the warriors. "...and welcome back our people." The glow of the sun struck his armor. "You don't know how easy you have made this." He waved his hands around and took in the whole field. "In less than a year, we will have full control, the House of Reina will be rebuilt, and we will depose Fabius and Lezevel—"

A frown crossed Kahrlos' face, and he leaned toward him. "Brother, what are you doing?"

Kyrillos ignored him. The idea of the human's laying down their arms was intoxicating. "—and I will murder the mages who thought to kill me, including the one named Jonna."

"Brother!" Silence dropped over the whole field as Kahrlos' rebuke echoed.

Kyrillos froze, red coming to his face. His eyes caught Jonna's. "You tricked me." It was spoken in a whisper, but the hearing spell was still in working.

Jonna gave a slight bow. "You only said what was in your heart."

The red color turned to a deeper magenta. Kyrillos whole body shook.

"Lokke, run."

The half-demon grabbed the slave's hand and jerked him into motion. "Come on!"

The slave stammered, "B-but—"

Lokke dragged him along. "Run or die!"

The slave's legs fought to keep up, but barely touched the ground. Twenty feet away, the half-demon stopped. The slave's arm nearly came out of its socket as Lokke jerked to a halt. Lokke turned back to Jonna. "You're not coming?"

"No, run."

The half-demon hesitated. "Why aren't you coming?"

"The longer I stay, the more time you have to get away." His eyes stayed locked with Kyrillos'.

Kahrlos jumped forward. "Do not do this brother! It is not worth it!" He tried to distract Kyrillos, but the king would not take his eyes from Jonna. In a last, desperate attempt, Kahrlos shook Kyrillos. "We await your orders." Kahrlos turned to glare at Jonna. "We can deal with this mage ourselves."

Kyrillos' face turned blood red, and grunts came as if against a great opposing force, "*Post-hoc-obitum!*" Lightning flashed. With a glare, he gave the slave translation, "After this, death!" With the audio spell working, the words made Jonna's head ring; in pain he dropped to his knees.

Fabius voice boomed. "Jonna, get up."

Grass entangled Jonna's legs. It worked its way up his body, growing in width and strength. He tried to focus on something other than the noise. "I didn't know Kyrillos could do magic."

"Yes, he can, though somewhat different from our own.

When they use magic, it comes from a part of their soul. They sacrifice a bit of themselves every time they do it."

"Then, for a giant to do any magic—"

The voice of Fabius was solemn. "—brings them closer to death. For that reason alone, they must be desperate. I've never seen Kyrillos do magic before."

Jonna swallowed. "I don't think he's ever hated anyone this much." The ringing was gone, but he could not move. His last free arm battled to hold off the embrace of the grass.

Lokke and the slave ran up and jerked at the growing plants but could not break their hold.

"Go," Jonna demanded.

"You need our help!"

"Go!"

"You're sure?" Lokke's eyes pleaded.

Kyrillos jabbed his spear into the ground. It stuck firm as the giant drew his sword.

Kahrlos took hold of Kyrillos' shoulder. "Brother, do we attack?"

Kyrillos threw off Kahrlos' hand. The force knocked Kahrlos off his feet. The sword raised above Kyrillos head. "Thus shall I do to all my enemies!" His eyes danced in fury as his teeth clenched. "Goodbye, mage." He stepped close to Jonna.

Jonna threw up his only free hand. "*Hove!*"

The sound of breaking glass streaked across the sky. The rumbling boomed like thunder. The blue dome rose and moved over the top of Lokke, the slave, and Jonna. It glowed in the brightness of the sun. The giant's sword hit the dome. In all directions, sparks flew.

"Brother," Kahrlos called from the ground, his own anger building, "this is insane. He is but one slave!"

Kyrillos spit out words in rage. "He is mine! He has destroyed the shield of our father, the one he gave his life to create, the one that protected our city, Waspadden. He shall not live!"

The sword of Kyrillos came down, struck the dome,

bounced up, and struck again. Over and over the giant pounded, and over and over the blue shield held. The sword dulled and flattened; pits and cracks showed.

However, the dome was weakening too. Jonna could feel the drain. It stunned him. The two magics were cancelling each other out.

The words Kyrillos spoke were the key. The giant was giving his life to kill Jonna. It was the magic of centuries against one man.

"Fabius, now might be a good time to attack."

He knew Fabius crossed his arms. "You're sure you've had enough?"

"Positive."

Fabius chuckled. "Maybe next time you'll believe me."

Jonna managed a grin. "About not being able to take on the whole giant army?" Each pound by Kyrillos echoed in his ears. "Yeah."

Fabius' voice boomed in Jonna's head. "Attack!" A dark haze filled the horizon as the army of the slaves rose.

The Kyrillos' sword struck the blue shield, now more of a club than a sword. It bounced, rose up above Kyrillos' head, and the shield winked out. Weakness swept through Jonna. His knees buckled, and he fell.

Lokke threw his hands up as if by sheer will power he could keep the sword from coming down. A soft wind began to blow.

The king bellowed; the bloodlust glowed in his eyes. He saw nothing else: not the warriors behind him, not his brother, and not the opposing forces that rushed upon him.

The sword flew down, its damaged edge more of a hammer than a cutting weapon. Despite its shape, the air whizzed by. In slow motion, Jonna watched it descend.

The weakness was easing, but he could not move. He closed his eyes and waited to feel the impact. The soft wind become a swirl, played with his hair, and touched him gently on the cheek.

"Jonna," Armida called, a soft laugh on her lips.

He opened his eyes. "Armida?" The sword hung above him, dropping in minute steps. That could not be right. It should have hit.

"I told you I'd be back."

"Now might not be the best time." He glanced up at the sword. "I'm not in a position to help."

"Ah, but you have." Armida whirled around him. "You woke up my soul. You've made me remember. I have convinced the others to fight on your side." She waved toward the horizon.

A dark mist rose over the slaves; it was the Tjaard. A smile lit his face. Let Kyrillos stop that!

Armida, pleasantly, read his thoughts. "And I have come to return the favor."

"You can stop the sword?"

She shook her head slowly. Her hair waved back and forth in a soft, smooth motion. "But I can do this."

Armida became a mist. She enveloped them, spread out, and rested over every part.

The sword struck. The plants shredded and ripped. Great heaps of dirt shot in the air. Buried stones were crushed.

Jonna's whole body was tingling. A strange euphoria filled his mind. The three of them were exactly where they had been, despite the fact that there was no ground to hold them up.

He could no longer see Armida, but he could feel her presence very close. "Armida, are you okay?"

"I'm better than that," she smiled, but he could not see her face, "and you have helped to free us."

"How?"

"The night you helped me find who I was. The night I stayed to make sure your dreams were protected."

"I don't understand."

"Of course not," her voice was jovial. "I watched over you the rest of the night, so the others would not return, and in doing so, I gave you a part of myself."

None of this was making sense. "And this did?"

"By giving you part of myself, I was able to do this now."

"Keep us from being destroyed by the king?"

She nodded, though how he knew she nodded, did not make sense.

It hit him. "Old magic counters old magic. The giants used their own magic to create you. You have used it to protect us from him."

"Yes."

The shadowy mist shifted them to the side. In confusion, King Kyrillos stared at the ground. They watched as the king dropped to one knee and brushed at the debris with his free hand.

Kahrlos got to his feet, drew his sword, and looked down at Kyrillos with disdain. "Call the attack!" His sword touched the side of Kyrillos' neck. "If you cannot, I will!"

The words of Kyrillos' pierced the air. "You would threaten your king?"

Kahrlos glared. "I would save our people, and so should you!"

Kyrillos dropped his head and adjusted the sword to his left hand. "You are right, Kahrlos. I have been neglectful." He lunged back with the sword, not even bothering to look. Kahrlos gasped. Turning, Kyrillos saw the sword plunged under his brother's ribs and stood to his feet. "Thank you for reminding me of our duty. Our father would be proud."

Taking Kahrlos' sword, Kyrillos turned to the line of warriors. As Kahrlos' body fell backwards, he raised the sword. "Attack!"

The line hesitated. Kahrlos' body bounced before becoming still.

"I said, attack!" Lightning flashed across the sky. A roar went out across the line of giants as they started their march.

Jonna nodded toward the king. "So what happens now?" Neither Lokke nor the slave responded to what was going on. They were held frozen as if time had stopped.

"We part." The shadowy mist shifted. A section pulled

itself together and formed the smiling face of Armida. She continued to swirl around them, brushing Jonna's cheek. "Until you're ready."

"Ready for—"

Armida winked, fading away.

"—what?" He stared at the place she had been. The noise of the world came back in living color.

Lokke slowly lowered his hands. "What—what happened?" He glanced down. "We're still in one piece?"

"Jump." Jonna leaped for the hole that Kyrillos had made; Lokke was only a second behind. Spurred into a run by Kahrlos' body, the slave was gone.

The giants bypassed Kahrlos' body and thus the hole. Kyrillos, rather than leading his army forward had turned around and walked toward his camp. As the line of warriors passed them, a giant throne came into view. Kyrillos sat down heavily, his eyes falling upon the body of his brother.

Lokke grabbed at Jonna's foot as Jonna climbed out of the hole. "Where are you going?"

"I'm going to talk to Kyrillos."

The half-demon's eyes widened, speaking slightly above a whisper. "We did that, and look where that got us."

Metal struck metal as both sides engaged. Kyrillos' bitter eyes adjusted to Jonna and watched him approach. "You should have died." There was a pale look in his eyes, and his face was drawn. "Not Kahrlos."

Jonna held the king's stare. "I didn't kill Kahrlos. He did not have to die."

"A stranger you are not to understand the ways of power." As if for the first time, Kyrillos studied him. "Why have you come to my land?"

His voice was level. "I came free Fabius."

The king laughed bitterly and waved a hand. "So the rest was an afterthought?"

Jonna considered. All he had done was react to his situation, not try to start a war. "It wasn't a thought at all."

"Luck then?" Kyrillos bellowed, "The king of the frost

giants done in by a stranger." He sat back in the throne waiting, but waiting for what? "Why do you not gloat?"

"Why do you hate the slaves so much?"

His brow wrinkled as his face grew paler. "They are cattle."

Jonna's temper rose. "Because they live on your shores and stay away from your cities? Because they have intelligence that rivals your own? One race does not own another."

"Because," Kyrillos gritted his teeth, "it's the natural order of things. Slaves were created to serve the giants. You are smaller, you multiply like rodents, and you destroy your resources. The size alone proves your inferiority."

Jonna motioned to the battlefield, steeling himself. "And yet, your army falls. Is this the legacy you want to leave?"

Kyrillos looked upon the field of battle, his countenance unconcerned. "It matters not who wins or loses today. What is one life of a few hundred years compared to a name that will last eons?" It is only a matter of time, and of that, I have plenty. A smug look crossed his face.

Kyrillos' one effort to kill him could not have taken all of his magic. Something else was happening, and Jonna needed to know what.

"We all have a finite time." Jonna shook his head. "I pity you."

Kyrillos glared at him. "Do not pity me, slave. Where two are strong, there will always be battle."

Jonna gave him a sad smile. "And who will lead when you are gone?"

The king laughed. "Whether I am here or not, my memory shall live on. The giants will win, regardless of this battles outcome. Look," he pointed at the heavens, "even now the end is near."

The lightning, that had earlier ripped across the cloudless sky, had not gone away. Held by an invisible force, it bounded and rebounded growing in volume.

"I did not give myself merely to kill you, Jonna. This is something my brother did not understand. I will not leave one opposing slave alive today. The land of the giants will be free from them forever!"

A wave of thunder sounded across the valley. Dark clouds formed in the same way Jonna had called down lightning.

"They will praise my name, Jonna. They will call me the Great King of the Highest. I will be placed in the sepulcher of my father with pride and dignity. I will be elevated as my father was." His eyes looked straight into Jonna's. "Who will remember you?"

As the dark clouds continued to build, the girth of the lightning strikes grew. They rebounded, grew in strength, and flashed in power.

In his mind, Jonna called, "Fabius, we have a problem. Kyrillos is going to kill everyone in the valley. I don't know how."

"Everyone heard," Fabius chuckled. "Your hearing spell is still working."

That's it, Jonna smiled. He knew exactly how to save the humans. All he had to do was keep Kyrillos talking.

Turning to Kyrillos, he goaded him. "And you would sacrifice your own people, the very warriors you have sworn to protect, their friends, their families, all in the name of killing the slaves?"

A maniacal look crossed Kyrillos' face. The clang of weapon on weapon, the howls pain, all slightly subsided. "No sacrifice is too little. My army will gladly give themselves for my glory."

The noise dropped again, though the lightning had accelerated.

"Then your own people are worthless to you," Jonna prodded, "just like the slaves. They are a piece of disposable property. That is all your kind mean to you?"

Kyrillos laughed, blinded by the victory he could taste. "What is the life of one single giant when it comes to the glory I shall have for all eternity? You may have eluded my sword, but you will not elude my water of wrath! You will all die altogether in the deluge that comes!"

The buildup of lightning reached a peak and shot off toward the east side of the valley. A huge, glowing ball hurtled toward the earth and struck. The ground rumbled and went quiet. In the silence, the battle stopped.

Kyrillos frowned and sat forward on his throne. "What have you done?"

"It is not a matter of me, but you." Jonna walked closer. "You, who killed your brother, you, who would kill the slaves, and you, who would kill your own people." He stopped not ten feet from the king. "Those are not the actions of a glorified king. Those are the actions of a traitor."

"Traitor!" Kyrillos stood straight up. The suddenness of the move caught Jonna off-guard. "You are the traitor!"

From nowhere Kyrillos swung a spear, arcing it toward Jonna's legs. Jonna jumped and ducked as the spear came back, swinging the other direction. The king was weakening. If he could push Kyrillos a little further, get him to use a little more magic, the effort would kill him. He taunted him. "No weapon for the slave? Surely you can do better than that?"

Kyrillos raged, "If you had one, it would do you no good!"

Jonna leaped further away and fell backwards. The ground vibrated. Like a stampede of animals, the rumbling grew.

Some on the field of battle stared off toward the east. Others fled toward the far side. The smell of water was in the air as the wind blew in. The rumbling turned into a roar as frolicking white foam glistened atop a huge wall of blue water.

"Cowards!" Kyrillos jerked the spear from the ground and stared at both armies. Slaves and giants fled for their lives. "Traitors! You are all traitors! Stand and fight!"

Jonna rose to his feet and came up behind the king. He spoke with a mocking smile, "I don't think they're listening."

Kyrillos swung around, the rage in his face blood red. "This is your fault. You will die today!" The spear glowed and launched with a speed Jonna had never seen. There was no time to move.

Out of nowhere, he heard Lokke's voice. "No!"

Chapter 22

HEL HATH NO FURY

The edge of the spear sliced Jonna's shirt as his body spun sideways. He crashed into something hard. Warm liquid flowed into his hair. The thud of the spear had a softer sound as it slammed to a stop.

His eyes blurred. They closed tightly, and he rubbed them with the back of his hands. Where was the pain? As his eyes focused, he found no spear and turned to gaze at the tent beside him. The spear had flown into the tent and ripped a hole in the thick cloth wall.

Jonna struggled to his feet and caught sight of Kyrillos. The mad king ran down into the valley, waved his hands insanely, and screamed out threats. With the huge wave of water coming toward them, there was little doubt what would be the king's end. Yet, he had to be sure. The giant could not be allowed to live. As he turned to follow, there was a whimper inside the tent. It was small, slight, and easily overlooked.

Lokke, where was Lokke? He had heard the half-demon's shout right before—Jonna turned and stepped through the rip. The slight glow of the dark light refused to illuminate the tent's interior. The pixie sight kicked in and showed the spear. It stood in the midst of a group of large pillows. One of the pillows stirred. Moving closer, a head with a horn raised slowly. "Lokke?"

A grin crossed Lokke's quivering lips. "I've still got them." The half-demon's right arm rolled to the side as his fist opened. It revealed the three stones.

A lump formed in Jonna's throat, but he forced his voice to be cheerful. "You did great." He took a deep breath. "You think you can keep them a little while longer?"

The half-demon's head dropped back, his voice growing weaker. "Sure thing." The right fist closed on the stones.

Jonna cleared his throat. "I mean it, Lokke, no sleeping on the job."

Two eyes snapped open. "Yes sir."

"Good." Jonna studied where the spear had penetrated Lokke's body, and cautiously shifted the pillows. The half-demon groaned. The point was sticking out his back, but so far, there was no blood.

The eyes began to close.

"Lokke."

The half-demon's eyes snapped open.

"Are you keeping watch?"

The eyes started to close as he nodded.

"Lokke, can you move your legs?"

A cough escaped his lips. "Haven't tried." His breath rasped. "It feels better—to lie here."

"Lokke, I'm not a doctor, but—" He remembered the connection he had with Fabius. "Fabius!"

"Jonna? Jonna!" Fabius voice was frantic. "You're not still down in the valley are you?"

"Sorta, slightly up the opposite side."

"Leave now. We're helping out stragglers on this side: giants and slaves."

"Fabius, Lokke—"

"Get out, there's no time for prattle."

Jonna growled, "Lokke's hurt, and I can't move him." Turning around, he hurried through the tent door and stepped to a spot where he could see the valley.

The ground started to shake. Pieces of tent material wagged back and forth, tent poles wobbled, and the throne jumped. Off to his right, the huge wave grew larger, towering into the sky. Lokke groaned inside the tent.

Nothing in here could resist that flood, and he could not move Lokke in his present state. Worse than moving him, the spear was at an awkward angle, and the shaking might make it dislodge. If the spear came out—

"Armida, I need you."

A soft breeze moved into the tent. It floated, mist-like, and looked around the room. "I am here."

There was no time for long explanations. "Lokke took the spear meant for me, the valley is about to flood, and—"

"You can't move him." Armida nodded. "What would you have me do?"

"Can you take him to the others?"

"And you?" Her shadowy figure moved around the room and paused over Lokke.

Jonna shook his head. "I have to find Kyrillos."

"Kyrillos is gone. When the flood comes, he will not return."

His eyes hardened. "I have to make sure."

"You will kill him, then?" Armida voice was without judgment. "You are not that person, Jonna. You cannot kill without provocation."

"And yet, I have." He frowned. "I fought to save my wife. I've fought to save my friends."

"Fighting in defense is different from hunting." Armida's voice had a cold edge. "What you do now, you do out of hate. Kyrillos killed slaves, he hurt your friends, and you've chosen to hunt him down, even if it means your death."

She spoke his mind, and he did not like it. "How do you know this?"

"I told you. A piece of me is part of you." Compassion showed on her face. "I will do as you ask. I will help your friend." Armida made a swirl of shadow and lifted Lokke into an ethereal state. The shaft of the spear passed through and dropped to the pillows.

With a last swirl, she went around Jonna and touched

his face again. "If you need me, call. I will be there." Both Lokke and Armida vanished.

The feeling of loneliness dropped like a bomb. It was the second time he felt this; the first was when Dagda had dumped him in Bliss. Shaking his head, he centered his thoughts. He had to quickly find Kyrillos.

Stepping out the door, he searched the valley, but the valley kept its secret well. The wave of water was advancing. The closer it came, the more debris it carried. The once dark blue water took on a murky brown, tainted in a way that was unnatural.

He thought about Armida's words. She said that hate was his driving force, but he did not see it that way. It was necessary to insure Kyrillos never hurt anyone again. He had to make sure the king was dead.

Jogging toward the valley, it was hard to stay on his feet. The advancing wave was the only sound. The hearing spell continued to work, yet Kyrillos was silent. When had he stopped raving?

Armor and weapons littered the area. The dead had been left, and the wounded carried away, yet in none of this was Kyrillos.

Then Jonna saw him. Lying on his back, the king was using a rock as a pillow. The chest of the giant moved up and down. The giant's face stared skyward.

Reaching for a spear, Jonna wrenched it from its place in the earth and walked toward the king. He could hear the deluge distinctly now. There would not be much time. Within three feet of the giant's head, he raised up the spear and held it.

Kyrillos did not open his eyes. "What are you waiting for, mage? Strike."

Jonna's brow wrinkled. "You want to die?"

"I am going to die," the king corrected. "What does it matter if it is by spear, water, or the magic ripped from my soul?"

"You could always leave."

Kyrillos laughed. "And what would you do then? Wait till I could fight, and soothe your conscience with a kill? I killed your friend. It should have been you. Strike before the water comes." The giant smiled. "I would."

Despite the feelings in Jonna's heart, his arms would not move. "Can there be no peace with you? The warriors under your control have sought refuge with the slaves."

The king spoke harshly, "They are no longer my warriors." His voice despised even the words. "I do not know what 'can be' anymore."

"Then, there is hope?"

The king's maniacal laugh was back. "If I were to live," he chuckled, "to my dying breath, I would strip hope from every one. I would hunt them down. I would kill them, their loved ones, and all they have known. Betrayal is not an option, and they have betrayed their king!"

"No!"

The spear came down, sliced the air, and stabbed. The rock cracked loudly as its point penetrated.

Kyrillos' body jumped, but when he opened his eyes, he saw the spear next to his ear.

Jonna shook his head. Armida was right; he could not kill in cold blood.

"You've had your chance, mage." Kyrillos rolled over and rose to one knee. He plucked the spear from the ground like a toothpick and turned the end toward Jonna. The spear point sparkled as a shadow blotted the remaining light. "I won't be so nice."

The wave was there, and there was no time to run. "Kyrillos, suit yourself and stay in Hel. *Absit omen!*"

A blue dome encircled Jonna as the water struck Kyrillos from behind. It snapped Kyrillos forward. The spear flew into the air. The water dragged the king into its murky depths.

The dome's fluorescent blue shone brightly as the water dashed upon it. Armor, weapons, rocks, and soil twisted about. The water pushed, but the shield held. The land that formed its base stayed dry.

Jonna exhaled. The magic had worked, and there was no ping of glass. Fish swam by. Kyrillos must have busted a dam or opened a river to create the flood. No, the king had said deluge. That sounded a whole lot bigger.

The fish he saw appeared more salt water than fresh, but all his knowledge was based upon his own world. Things here could be totally different.

"Cassandra!" He had left her in a tent protected by the magic container above the valley floor. "Fabius?"

There was no answer. Surely they had gotten away, and even if the water did cover the container, it was designed to protect her from time itself. She would be safe.

Minutes ticked by. The hand of the watch became his focus. How long would it take the water to drain? It would spread across the valley, ideally becoming lower as it filled it up. Of course, that depended upon its source.

He was cut off, Lokke wounded, and Cassandra frozen in time. All of them waited for the water level to drop, and none of them knew when it would.

A glance at his watch showed thirty minutes had gone by. His eyes began to tire. He might as well rest.

Oxygen, the thought hit him. He was in an enclosed space with a limited volume of air. His brain could be suffering from increased carbon dioxide.

There was a spell. He remembered it from the shepherd's hut. It was—from Lucasta—but he was so tired. Jonna closed his eyes.

Behind his eyelids, two words came from very far away. They waved back and forth until they stabilized. 'Sub' stood there and stared, followed by the word 'divo'. "*Sub divo*?"

The blue dome wrenched from its place under the water. As the dome broke the surface, a gust of air whooshed in. It filled his lungs, heaved out the smell of death, and allowed his brain to wake. He tapped the ground. It was solid beneath him. The dome was more than a bubble; its protective field formed a sphere. It bobbed in the midst of a wide sea.

"Fabius?" Fabius did not answer. "Armida?"

The gentle breeze returned at once, and before she said anything, he could feel her reassuring presence. "I am here."

"Are the others safe?"

Her shadowy head gave a single nod as a smile lit her lips. "They have Lokke. They are doing all they can."

"Will he make it?"

"The spirit of a creature is their own. If he is strong, they may find a way."

"Did they save Cassandra?"

"She is also with them."

"Thank you."

Armida circled around him. "I knew you could not kill him." She moved closer, the wind blowing her smooth, shadowy hair.

Jonna looked away. "No, I couldn't."

"And that disappoints you?"

His face tried to hide the anger he felt, but it did no good. "He killed without cause and endeavored to destroy his own, yet, I could not take his life."

Armida shook her head. "Had you done that act, it would have tainted who you are. He has received his punishment."

"So he is dead?"

"Possibly."

Jonna's eyes widened. "You don't know?"

"I am not all knowing," she laughed. Her arms reached out, stretching against the wind, and she took a deep breath. "The only person I know is you."

"About that," Jonna frowned. "There was an incident that happened after I fell asleep—" His eyes looked into hers. "You don't know what happened, do you?"

A smile lit her face. "I do. Shall I show you?"

"I'm not sure—"

Armida merged with him. A feeling of pleasure passed through his body, and he found himself back in the city of the woodland elves, standing in his and Elfleda's bedroom. The sun shone through the high, elvish windows, glittered off the water pitcher, bounced off the bed and tables, and sparkled off the chairs.

"Jonna!" Elfleda's eyes sparkled. She threw her arms around him. As if in slow motion, their lips met.

He sighed as they released. "I've missed you."

"And I, you," she spoke in wonder, "but how can this be?"

"I—I don't know." Searching his mind, he sought for an explanation. "A friend is helping me." His brow wrinkled. "She knew the desire of my heart."

"And last night, it was the same." She looked into his eyes. "When I awoke, I thought it was a dream, and yet," she touched the lower part of her stomach. "I know it was not."

"We—" The memories all came swirling back. "You were real?"

Her face glowed as she spoke. "We're going to have a child."

"But," his eyes widened, "it's not even a day."

Elfleda's laugh was intoxicating. "I do have The Sight, silly. We elvish women know these things."

"Daddy!" Elpis came from nowhere and threw her arms around them. The pair loosened their grip on each other, and Jonna lifted Elpis into his arms.

"How's my girl doing?"

She hugged him tighter. "I've missed you!"

"I've missed you, too." His thoughts fell back to Cassandra. "Elpis, your mother—" The words stuck in his throat.

"I know, daddy," she reassured, "and it's okay. I know she'll be fine."

Jonna smiled though a part of him was not sure. "Of course."

Elfleda brought him back from his thoughts. "But how long can you stay?"

Jonna looked around the room. Even now, the walls were not quite as bright. There was a tug from far away gaining in strength, and his own flesh was not as solid. "I need to go, but know that I love you very much." He handed Elpis to Elfleda, kissing them.

They both said together. "We love you, too."

He held Elfleda's hand and watched it fade away. The scene was replaced by the sound of waves striking against the dome. Armida floated back and took a deep breath. The pleasure he felt was gone as he wiped a tear from his eye. "I don't know how you did that, but thank you. Words are not enough."

Armida smiled. Her eyes glowed despite the shadowy darkness. "It is my privilege. The love you have runs very deep. It is the only way I could do it. Cherish the love you have. It is priceless."

Sadness crossed her face, and Jonna's heart went out to her. "Is there no way I can help you?"

"You did that by awakening me," she smiled and whirled around the dome. "Of that, I am most grateful."

"And there's no other way?"

"Love is something only two can share. Be content, Jonna, there will come a time when you can do more."

"I don't understand."

"As you should not," she smiled and stroked his cheek again. "We have arrived at the shore. It is time to meet your friends."

Fabius called from outside of the bubble, "Jonna!"

"Fabius! Is everyone safe?"

The mage nodded. "Give me a second to get you out. *Sublimis ab unda.* Rise from the waves."

The blue dome rose from the surface of the water to hover over the land. The top was only part of the protection. The dome completed a perfect sphere.

Fabius' hold was a little too high to discontinue the spell. Jonna pointed toward the ground. "Have it barely touch."

As Fabius did the request, Jonna's mind whirled. Normally, he just turned off the dome, but this was a little more complicated.

"Non Absit omen."

He was sure he had butchered the language, but the blue fluorescent dome dissipated, and there was no ping.

Without the bubble to keep it up, soil dropped in all directions. He fell with it, hit the ground, and scrambled away from the avalanche. Making it to his feet, other hands helped dust him off.

"Thank you." There was too much help. "Thank you, I'm fine."

"We feared you had been killed." Fabius frowned and studied Jonna's face. "You should not have gone after Kyrillos."

"I know. He was dragged down by the wave of water. If he makes it through that—"

"We'll deal with that another day," the mage assured. "Right now, it's time to celebrate our victory!"

"We won?"

"It seems," Fabius chuckled, "I misjudged. The giants themselves are not unkind. It was their leaders who had made them appear so. When they heard Kyrillos' true intentions, they laid down arms and joined us."

"Then the land is free?"

"It is. Both free men and giants can rebuild. No longer will slaves be tolerated." He grinned at Jonna. "You got what you wanted in spite of me."

"Not quite," Lezevel's voice came from nowhere as her youthful body stepped into view. "We still have a score to settle!"

"Can I not have one night of peace?" Fabius huffed and turned to face her. "Woman, you have been a pain in my backside for years! What will it take for you go away?"

Her expression turned hard as she aimed her staff. Lightning leaped out while at the same time Fabius shot a blast of his own. The colors, red and blue, met at the center, sending fire and sparks in all directions. A light, brighter than the sun, made those who watched cover their eyes.

She yelled, "Your pain has only begun!" Yet despite the anger in her voice, Jonna caught another underlying tone. He glanced at the center where the two magic's struck, hid his eyes, and spoke, *"Non Fiat Lux!"*

346

The light winked out. Lezevel and Fabius shot backwards. Fabius landed in tall grass; Lezevel struck the pile of dirt left over by the blue dome.

"You meddling mage," Lezevel screamed, "how dare you interfere!" She waved her staff in Jonna's direction.

Without hesitation, Jonna pointed a finger at her. "Hush!"

She stopped, stunned. Instead of Jonna casting magic, he had simply told her to hold her tongue.

Fabius scrambled to his feet. "Where is she? Why did you do that?" He turned to glare at Jonna.

"You too!" He pointed, and Fabius closed his mouth. "I think it's time you both listen."

Fabius deepened his voice, "This is none of your concern!"

"None of my concern?" Jonna glanced at the sky. "I didn't come all this way to see you killed now!"

Lezevel's lips curled into a smile. "At least he knows the better magic."

"And you," he turned on her. Her smile dropped away. "I want to know what this is all about!"

"What do you care?" her voice mocked.

"Because I do. Because I think there is more here than a fight between good and evil."

"He called me evil?" Lezevel whipped her staff in Fabius direction. "I am not evil!"

"Then prove it," Jonna dared her. "Show me the truth."

"I—" She bite her lip, keenly aware of the audience around her. "Not here." Waving her staff, she struck the ground.

The world around them faded, and new surroundings came into view. Fabius, Lezevel, and Jonna stood on top of a high plateau, overlooking mountains in all directions.

Lezevel's voice was harsh. "Now we talk." She spun on Fabius, but instead of pointing her staff, she pointed with her left hand. "Evil?" Her voice rose, echoing across the mountains. "Evil!"

Fabius threw the words back. "What would you call it? Taking control of people who do not want to be lead? Trying to establish a kingdom when peace was already there?" Fabius stepped toward her, his fury unveiled. "How could you have done this—" His voice dropped in supplication as he looked into her face. "Varra?"

Silence dropped. The wind blew over the plateau with no other sound.

Lezevel's answer was but a whisper. "It has been a long time since you called me that." She looked into his eyes.

"Varra—" Something in Fabius' face changed, and a pain, long unspoken, bubbled to the surface. The anger in the mage's eyes melted way. "—I'm sorry." The words caught in the wind and spun out into the mountains.

She turned away and refused to look at Fabius. "It's not enough."

"Don't you two see?" Jonna stepped forward, drawing their attention. "Whatever happened between you two, whatever bad things tore you apart, there is something stronger still. It pulls you both together." Though he did not know the details, he could make a good guess on the rest. "You have fought, yet not killed each other. You have battled, yet both you stand. I believe you two are in love."

Lezevel glared. "Impossible!" Fabius shook his head. "It cannot be!"

"How else do you explain it? Even the giants saw the connection, and as a condition of your punishment, set you apart eternally."

Lezevel's voice, still seductive, shook in anger. "I can kill him!" She directed her staff at Fabius. "*Dies Irae!*"

A blue blaze burst toward Fabius. He stood there, frozen, staring into Lezevel's face. With a strange look in his eyes, he did not raise his staff.

It barely touched him, but the force spun him around. His staff flew from his hand, and his body was thrown like a rag doll. The mage landed to the side and did not move.

Lezevel stared; her face contorted in pain. She raised her

staff again, determination in her eyes. Jonna readied his own spell.

She cast the staff from her as tears fell down her cheeks. In seconds, she was at Fabius' side and rolled him over. "You old fool." The tears that fell hit his chest. "You were supposed to fight back!"

Fabius did not open his eyes. "Varra," he whispered, and then cleared his throat. "He's right."

Her voice was hard. "I know." Yet it softened, though she still growled out the words, "and you know how much I hate to be wrong. Can it ever change between us?"

"It already has." A slight grin lit Fabius' face. "I didn't attack."

Something about that struck both as funny. Jonna found himself shaking his head, a smile on his face. In the midst of so much fighting, it was nice to see this turn of events. He picked up Lezevel's staff and hunted until he found the one for Fabius. Though in whispers, he could not help but hear their words.

"I love you, Varra."

"I love you, Fabius."

He could only imagine what went on from there.

Stepping to the edge of the plateau, he saw what he thought was the Field of Hel, off to the south. It reflected sunlight like a huge swimming pool.

Fabius was saved, in more ways than one, and the land of the frost giants was free. There were two others that needed him now: Cassandra, held in the magic container, and Lokke, damaged by a spear meant for him.

It was time to head to the Otherworld. Not that he wanted to reenter Dagda's domain, but he had to pass through those gates if he wanted to be with his family. A laugh left his lips. "And one of them isn't even born."

Laying the staffs beside a large rock, he locked his eyes upon the Field of Hel. He toyed with the idea of flying, but the dizzying height was somewhat daunting. The comic book characters of his youth conjured up images his brain could see. Was such a thing even possible? Why not?

"Jonna?" The mage was on his feet, his arm around Lezevel. Both glowed with smiles on their faces. "Ready to go?"

"I was debating about how."

Retrieving their staffs, Fabius bowed to Lezevel. "Would you do the honors, my dear?"

Her laughter floated on the wind. "Most certainly." She waved her staff. The plateau around them vanished. Once more the shoreline along the Field of Hel came into view.

Giants and men rested in groups. What could be salvaged from the previous camp was setup on this shore. Jonna gave a nod toward Fabius. "Where is Lokke and Cassandra?"

He was taken to a tent. The flap was secured so no one would enter. As the ties were removed and the cloth door opened, his two friends were obvious.

Fabius stepped in behind him. "Like Cassandra, Lokke is in suspended time."

A lead weight hit Jonna's stomach. "You could not save him?"

"The best we could do was keep him in the moment."

He studied Fabius' face. "Who can save him?"

Shaking his head, the mage raised his hands. "I do not know. None of our healing spells would work."

"It was Kyrillos' magic." Jonna swallowed. "Lokke took the spear meant for me."

Fabius closed his eyes, and his head dropped. "I had no idea Lokke could do such a thing."

"I know," he placed a hand on Fabius' shoulder, "and you've known him longer than any of us."

"But I've never known him to sacrifice for anyone, even those he joined in the Otherworld. It was always about him, and his ultimate escape."

Those facts only made Jonna feel worse. Lokke was a selfish, little half-demon who gave his life to save Jonna. Who would have thought? And yet— "What happens to half-demons when they die?"

Fabius shook his head. "I don't know how Lokke came to the Otherworld, but I'm sure he was not dead. Why?"

"If returning to the Otherworld will restore Cassandra, will it also heal Lokke?"

Lezevel ducked into the tent. "Yes. If you can get him back, there is a good possibility."

"Possibility?"

"It is only a legend," she shrugged her shoulders, "but at least there is a chance."

Fabius saw the problem. "How will you get them back?" There was something in his voice, and Lezevel picked up on it.

"No," she looked from one to the other and stopped on Fabius. "You are not going back there."

"It's not like I'm dead."

"If they catch you, you will be!"

Fabius laughed. "Jonna's not dead."

"That's different," she growled, "and you know it. Dagda would like nothing better than to find a reason to keep you there."

"He won't," the mage took her hands. "We freed ourselves from one curse. We will not get caught by another."

The look in Lezevel's eye told Jonna what he had to do. "Fabius," he squeezed the mage's shoulder, "thank you, but I believe I can make it on my own."

"How are you going to carry both? Take one back, and then return for the other?"

A sparkle shown in Jonna's eye. "I won't have to. All I need is a place to return to. A place I know very well."

The mage nodded slowly. "Cassandra's level."

"Yes."

"A barrier exist between here and there, and only the dying can cross it. Others must find a special doorway, such as the Otherworld's gates, Iioneemms, or Dagda himself."

Jonna nodded, the sparkle still there. "You're sure there is no other way?"

"For us?" Fabius rubbed his chin. "No. For you, I don't know. Officially, you were never let out."

"And because I'm from another place?"

The mage shrugged. "I can't say. You remember the Mage Consortium? They would ban me if I encouraged such conduct." The mischievous grin he gave Jonna reminded Jonna of Lokke. "But if I don't encourage anything—"

Since Jonna was not part of any mage group, how could he be under their rules? And if he wasn't under their rules, none of their rules applied. Of course, not knowing the rules was what got him sent to the Otherworld —he dismissed it. "I understand."

"But Jonna," Fabius' eyes narrowed, "if you do this, if you manage a breach to the Otherworld, it will not go unnoticed, and there will be consequences. It would be better if you followed a normal route."

"I am tired of these games." Jonna's gaze fell upon his two comrades. "It is time to take them back."

He thought to how Lucasta created a passageway from the dark elf city to the surface. Could the same spell work now?

"*A capite ad calcem.* All the way through."

Chapter 23

THE GNOMES KNOW

There was no ping, but there was something else. Like a great metal drum struck by a hammer, waves of magic shook him to his core. A gut wrenching twist dropped him to his knees as nausea swept through him. Fabius kept him from falling.

"I'm fine." Jonna inhaled, waiting for the nausea to pass. It did, but he knew the spell had used up all magical reserves he might have gained through rest.

The opening formed. It was a dark, long tunnel dropping into the earth. It would take little effort to carry Cassandra and Lokke now. The angle of the descent was steep enough to slide.

The winds of the Otherworld wafted up and chilled the hearts of those around him. Taking firm hold on the two magical containers, he caught sight of Fabius and Lezevel. "Together, may you find happiness all your lives."

"And you as well." Lezevel hugged him. "May you find your way home."

With a warm smile, Fabius extended his hand. "Goodbye Jonna. If you're ever this way again, you better come by."

Jonna released his hold on Cassandra's container long enough to shake the mages' hand.

Cassandra's container tilted and started down the incline. Jonna's hand shot out, but his fingers missed. It plummeted into the darkness.

He leaped forward and dragged Lokke's along. His pixie sight saw nothing, but this did not surprise him. Pixie sight relied upon a comparison of energy signatures to reveal the outlines of objects. This tunnel delved into the depths of death itself. The only thing he could hope to see was— Cassandra's container glowed ahead.

He gained on it. While the tunnel was invisible, the container was not. Shifting his feet forward, he glided to the side and grabbed her with his free hand.

They slid, though for how long it was hard to say. There was no friction, but he knew they moved. There was nothing solid beneath them, yet something held them up. The slant never varied, and the speed became constant.

A tiny dot appeared beneath them. It was the end of the tunnel, and the end of their ride. The speed changed, the angle of the tunnel became less steep, and he slowed to a stop.

The glow of the two magic containers shown as beacons on the grass. The swans in the lake swam toward him. One cob in the lead reached the bank, changed into a man, and ran up the hill. It was none other than Brutus Augustus.

"What have you done?" He reached forward but was afraid to touch the magic that held Cassandra. "What have you done to her?"

The hound sniffed up to Lokke, and Sir Reginald Richard howled. "I found him!" Murmurs came from all directions. The dead moved closer. Sir Reginald bayed, "The trickster is here. The nose knows!"

Jonna had no time for these games. "Back off!"

Brutus and Reginald took a step back, but it did not stop the others from coming. Jonna calmed himself. He had not anticipated being the center of attention.

"Reginald?"

The dog stared up at him.

"Lokke gave his life to help me. I've had to bring him back to help him."

Reginald scratched behind his ears. "Then he's no longer a trickster?"

That struck Jonna as funny. "I don't know about that, but I do know one thing. Lokke is a hero." A breath of wind whipped around the three.

"And Brutus," he caught the man's eye, "Cassandra has been too long in the surface world. She gave herself to help us accomplish our quest." His thoughts went back to many things, including when Lokke and Cassandra had carried him to the hut from the sea. "She is a hero, too."

The wind, no longer gentle, pulled at the tops of the trees and bent them deeply as they swayed. Winds like these did not happen in Bliss. Those around scattered. Some ran to the water. Others hid in the grass. Reginald sat on his haunches, never leaving Lokke's body.

"Reginald," Jonna shouted over the wind, "what are you doing?"

The hound barked back, "If he's a hero, he must have an honor guard."

A deep voice came out of the wind. "Jonna McCambel, come."

The wind swirled, creating a vortex. While hurricane forces stirred outside, the inside was calm. The eye of the storm laid on its side, providing him a path to walk into. It was a portal to who knew where.

Jonna looked to Reginald. "Guard them both until I return."

Reginald moved between them as the wind whipped his ears.

Jonna stepped into the vortex. The sounds of the wind cut off. In an instant, Bliss was gone, and he stood before two large gates. A chain with a lock held them together.

A female voice from nowhere asked, "Jonna McCambel, what do you seek?"

Jonna paused. He remembered Yses, the first fate, asking him the same question. This time, he had an answer. "Knowledge."

"Jonna McCambel, what do you seek?"

Again, this question had been asked by the fates, and he

remembered their words: the way is open. He gave his own. "A path."

The voice asking the questions changed. It was baritone, with a warning if he failed. "Jonna McCambel, what is more important than knowledge or path?"

Scenes from the surface passed through his mind: Andas' effort to rescue his father, Alfgia's protection from her kind, Cassandra and Lokke giving their lives, Fabius with Lezevel, and holding Elfleda and Elpis in his arms. It all came back to one thing. All were forms of— "Love."

The chain that held the middle of the gate shook. The lock fell off. He watched the chain rattle across the bars and drop to the ground. Of their own accord, the two sides swung back. The way was open; he could go home.

He stared at the open gate. The knowledge was there, the way was open, but the last of the elements was not in play.

"Love," he spoke to no one. "I have two friends, Lokke and Cassandra. I can't pass without them."

"You must pass," the baritone voice returned, "you must step through the gate."

The answers to the gates questions made sense. The hints: what you don't know, what you do know, what you will know, made perfect sense. All these things being true, to step through that gate without his friends would be answering the questions wrong, no matter how much he wanted to go home. He steeled himself. "I will not go without my friends."

The protected body of Lokke appeared held in the moment that Fabius had placed him. As Jonna watched, the spell released.

The half-demon blinked. "Am I alive?"

A grin burst from Jonna's face. "Yes, you are." He helped him to his feet.

Eyes wide, Lokke touched where the spear struck. "Did Fabius heal me?"

Jonna shook his head. "It's the gate. You are free to go."

Lokke's eyes showed wonderment. "But I never answered the questions."

The chuckle from Jonna was involuntary. "You didn't have to speak them. You showed them with your heart."

The half-demon's face glowed with excitement. He took a tentative step forward but looked back toward Jonna. "Aren't you coming?"

Jonna nodded. "I will come when it is finished."

Lokke's brow wrinkled. "You promise? Don't you dare not get out now!"

Laughing, Jonna held up a hand. "I promise."

Lokke nervously gazed through the open gates. One last time, he glanced back, looking Jonna in the eyes. "Thank you. You are a true friend." With a final step, the half-demon vanished.

"You must pass," the baritone voice echoed without emotion. "You must step through the gate."

"We lack one other," Jonna stood firmly. "Cassandra. She gave her life for her friends. She deserves to see her daughter."

"She is dead. She cannot pass."

"She must," Jonna determined, "or I will not leave."

The ground he stood on rumbled. The gates shook. The Cassandra's container appeared and then faded away, leaving only the bed and her upon it.

Jonna moved to the sleeping form and took her by the hand. "Cassandra?"

The opening eyes fluttered and stared. He guided her to sit as her eyes stayed locked on him. "Where am I?"

"The Otherworld. At the gate to see your daughter."

"Who?"

Panic gripped Jonna. Had the magic not been successful? Had he failed to save her memories? "Fix her," he cried. "You thought I was bad before, wait till you see me now!"

"She is dead," the baritone voice began and all at once stopped. To one side, a black door slid open, and a gnome grumbled out. "Fine," he answered in a squinty, small voice. "Let me see her!"

The gnome probed her arms and then worked his way to her eyes. The pupils dilated as a flickering candle appeared in his hand.

"You can fix her?"

"Shh." The gnome watched her eyes. He gave a huff and turned to face Jonna. "I don't know. It could be permanent."

It was unacceptable. "But you can fix her?"

"Maybe," the gnome scowled at Jonna, "but regardless of what happens next, it is off through the gate with you, got it? We've never given concessions!"

"Both of us."

The gnome huffed. "Does she have a petal?"

Jonna thought back. "Petal?"

"Do you think we are blind to what takes place in the surface world? We are not deaf and dumb. Yes, a petal from the Well of Nonos."

Jonna blinked. He had forgotten about that. It was given to her for an explanation. His head nodded toward her. "Open your hand."

Cassandra opened her fist, and upon her palm lay a single petal.

"It is enough," the gnome nodded. "Three are required to regenerate the body, two for the spirit, and one for the mind." Despite his irritation, the gnome's eyes brightened. "We have not done this is very long time."

The last request Jonna had asked rolled back into his mind. "Both of us go through the gate, right?"

The gnome waved him away. "Yes, yes, both you, but she comes back in one day. One day!"

Jonna watched as the gnome picked up Cassandra's left hand, placed it on her forehead, and slapped it.

Her head bobbed, her eyes narrowed, and she slapped him back.

Rubbing his cheek, the gnome asked, "Cassandra, are you ready to see your daughter?"

At first, the expression was empty, but then a smile crept over her face. "When?"

"Right now." Jonna took her by the hand. As they stepped toward the gate, he turned toward the gnome.

The gnome waved irritably toward the bed. "I'll have it moved. Please, leave!"

Two additional gnomes appeared. They put their shoulders to one end of the bed, took deep breaths, and heaved. The bed went sliding away.

Jonna shook his head. "It's not that. How does she get back?"

"Three taps," the gnome's voice became distant. "Tap her shoes together three times."

The area around the gates vanished. They stood within the woodland elf palace hall.

"Mom!" Elpis leaped into her arms. Cassandra barely caught her in time.

"Elpis!" Cassandra looked in her smiling face. She wrapped her arms about her and refused to let go.

Jonna saw he had not been wrong. Elpis did look like her mother, and now both of them glowed with delight.

"It has been so long!" Cassandra's eyes closed as she hugged Elpis tighter.

"But I'm never far away." Elpis hugged her as tight as possible. "I am glad you came to see me!"

Tears formed in Cassandra's eyes. She did not try to stop them. Elpis wiped the tears away.

Väinämö walked around the corner. "Welcome back, my boy. The council is waiting."

"You knew we were coming?" A look of disbelief crossed Jonna's face. Then again, this was Väinämö who had a knack for knowing future events that he only told you about when they happened.

"Of course we did." Väinämö made a funny face. "What kind of mage would I be not knowing?"

"A normal mage?"

The mage dismissed it with a wave of his hand. "If you want your stay to be permanent, we have to address the council."

"But the Otherworld let me go. They don't want me back."

"Interesting," Väinämö chuckled. "Never heard of that before." There was something he was not saying and for the first time, Jonna didn't care. His attention switched to Cassandra and Elpis.

"Don't worry about us," Cassandra assured him. "We'll be fine." She squeezed her daughter.

Väinämö tapped his shoulder, and Jonna turned, but listened to Cassandra's words as they disappeared behind him.

"Let's go see your room!"

In a race, mother and daughter took off. Their feet echoed in the other direction. Jonna beamed though it dropped as he entered the council chamber.

There, on one side of a long table, was Dagda. He sat with three of his own kind, scrolls in front. On the opposite side was Queen Freya, Elfleda, Bob, and two chairs.

Neither side appeared to be happy, but when Elfleda saw Jonna, the smile returned to her beautiful face. She rose, barely containing her excitement. As his arms went around her, he held her close, ignoring the others in the room.

"You made it!"

Jonna remembered the last time they had talked, when he had found out Elfleda was pregnant. He met her with a long kiss.

Dagda cleared his throat. "If you two would be so kind." With a frown on his face, he motioned to the seats across the table. With a final peck, their arms released, and they sank into the appropriate chairs. Bob threw him a grin.

"As I was saying," Dagda growled, "damage to the different levels, upsetting the balance of untold souls, contamination of one level to another—" He shook his head. "It is unbearable! Add to that the kidnapping—"

"Kidnapping?" Jonna jumped in.

"If I may finish," Dagda bore his eyes into Jonna. Jonna bore them back. When at last Dagda became aware of the uncomfortable silence, he turned his face to the others.

"As I was saying, kidnapping of a dead person against their will—"

"You mean me?" Cassandra strolled in with Elpis at her side. Her face was bright with a smile no one could miss.

Dagda stuttered, "W—what are you doing here?"

"The gates of course," her smile was infectious. "I have been allowed to see my daughter."

The color drained from Dagda's face. He uttered a sound no one could make out, and his eyes swept to Jonna. "It is completely irrelevant."

In perfect calm, Jonna rose to his feet. He was ready to do what he should have done at the very beginning. Dagda face twitched, his knuckles going white.

Väinämö tapped the desk where Jonna was sitting. It caught Jonna's attention, and he waved him toward his chair. The older mage spoke evenly. "Patience."

Though his eyes never left Dagda, he sat.

The mage smiled amiably. "It seems certain rules have been broken."

"Yes, it does!" Dagda pointed an accusing finger at Jonna. "You have broken our laws, again. We demand you pay the price!"

Väinämö looked down at the table. A light flashed, and a small parchment appeared. He handed it Dagda.

"What is this?" The sidhist king frowned. Reading the page, he inhaled, eyes growing wide until they thought he would explode.

"Summarizing the contents of that scroll," Väinämö smiled. "The gate of the Otherworld granted Jonna passage; in truth, they don't want him back. It also appears, someone subverted the rules in order to have Jonna placed there to begin with. I would suggest you start cleaning house. We wouldn't want the mage consortium involved, now would we?"

The Dagda's group mumbled among themselves. Jonna was tempted to cast a hearing spell but restrained. There would be no more pings if he could help it. Of course, once he learned the spell in this realm...

361

"This is preposterous," Dagda slapped the table, "absolutely ludicrous!" His eyes darted to Väinämö, and his face turned red. He struck the table again and stood to his feet. "All charges against Jonna have been dropped, and his record wiped clean." His lower lip quivered as he ripped the parchment, tossed it on the table, and stomped out of the room. His minions scurried behind him.

Väinämö leaned back satisfied.

Elfleda reached for the pieces of the parchment, but as her fingers touched them, they fell to dust. "What did you do?"

"While Jonna worked to free Fabius, I did some research."

Jonna remembered the times Väinämö had appeared. "In the books we saw you going through?"

"Precisely! It seems our good friend Dagda struck a bargain with an old friend of yours, one called Cassus."

Elfleda looked surprised. "The leader of the dark mages?"

"I saw him," Jonna agreed. "He used another to trigger an uprising in the dark elf city. I sent him to the Otherworld in a rather unorthodox way."

Väinämö's voice was grave. "You've breached the Partitions of Majik, Jonna, yet by doing so, you did something completely unexpected. It drove Cassus back, perhaps the only thing that could, and allowed you to complete your quest. However, this does not change the gravity—"

This talk was way too serious for such a happy reunion, so Jonna changed the subject. "You know, Väinämö," he cleared his throat, "you never did give me that spell."

A funny look crossed Väinämö's face. "Spell? What spell? Did I forget a spell?" A book appeared in front of him, and he began to search.

Jonna caught Elfleda's eye and winked. In a low voice, he said, "If that doesn't keep him busy, nothing will. There is so much I have to tell you."

Elfleda smiled. "Bob let us know what was going on, at least during the first part. It was he who told Väinämö how to turn the tables on Dagda."

362

The pixie blushed. "It was nothing." His eyes glowed with the praise. "Elpis helped too, but you can say it again if you like."

Jonna grinned, thankful that Bob and Elpis had gotten the idea to Väinämö. Giving Bob a sideways glance, he asked, "So why did you disappear?"

Bob ducked his head before Väinämö's gaze caught him. The mage's eyes narrowed. "When a certain little pixie thinks they have a bigger head than they should," his voice growled, "certain restrictions have to be set!"

Elfleda coughed. "Bob grew cocky, and the council became suspicious. He was using too many supplies from the royal stores. Dagda had him followed, and when he couldn't catch him, placed an assistant here to keep watch for anything unusual."

Grinning sheepishly, Bob swallowed. "But the story I got!" He looked toward Jonna. "Maybe later you might fill me in on the rest? Please?"

"I know," Elpis teased Bob, "and I'm not gonna tell."

Cassandra gave a stern eye to her daughter, but her voice was soft. "You shouldn't tease Bob. He's a hero like you."

Laughing, Jonna stood to his feet. "You're all heroes in my book."

Elfleda followed suit, her voice sounding like beautiful bells. "And I think it's time we had our own talk." Her eyes were bright with promise. Elfleda turned to Cassandra. "Would you mind entertaining for a little while longer?"

Cassandra's face was nothing but smiles. "I would love to."

Moving arm in arm, Jonna and Elfleda left the council chamber, and headed to a place that only they would know. Through the windows of the hall, the warm sun glowed in sparkling colors. Birds flitted and sang as the couple strolled along.

"Something disturbs you?" Elfleda's soft voice put on a frown. "Dagda's plans have been defeated. Cassus has returned to his place. What else bothers you, my husband?"

He shied away from the question. "Is everyone okay?"

"We are all fine. However, that is not what weighs you down."

He sighed. "I cracked the Partitions of Majik, and the barrier which holds their separation."

Elfleda pushed it way. "But by it stopped an evil plan. Why should this cause you worry?"

"You saw the look on Väinämö's face. I know that it's not over."

Squeezing his hand, she pulled him along. "It is for now."

As they found their room, she put her arms around him. "I have you back. It is all that matters."

Their lips touched. The troubling thoughts rushed away. They focused on each other, and left their cares behind.

Bob appeared on Jonna's shoulder and grinned. "Come on, enough of this. What about the rest of the story?" He reached over and pinched Jonna's ear.

Elfleda and Jonna shouted together, "Bob!"

ABOUT THE AUTHOR

J.W. Peercy spent his early years in California, (fifteen minutes from Disneyland!). As to the effect of this experience, we can only guess, but imagination makes the top of the list. His later years in Texas, he holds a BA in Computer Science with a minor in Math. Although analytical, the creative side has to find a way out. To ease the pain, he designs websites, programs code, and writes. If you like the book, drop him a line. If you don't like the book, drop him a line anyway. He will appreciate the feedback. As in the words of J.R.R. Tolkien, 'May the hair on your toes never fall out!'